# ESTORIL

Born in Yugoslavia in 1965,
Dejan Tiago-Stanković is an author
and translator. He graduated in
architecture in Belgrade before moving to
London. Since 1996 he has lived in
Lisbon, translating between his native
Serbo-Croatian and Portuguese.

# ESTORIL

# A WAR NOVEL

## DEJAN TIAGO-STANKOVIĆ

Translated by Christina Pribichevich-Zoric

*An Apollo Book*

First published in Serbian in 2015 by Geopoetika

This is an Apollo book. This English translation first
published in the UK in 2018 by Head of Zeus Ltd

Drawing of a cow on page 290: André Tiago-Stanković

9 7 5 3 1 2 4 6 8

A CIP catalogue record for this book is available from
the British Library.

ISBN (HB): 9781786698155
ISBN (E): 9781786698148

Typeset by Adrian McLaughlin

Printed and bound in Great Britain by
CPI Group (UK) Ltd, Croydon CR0 4YY

Head of Zeus Ltd
First Floor East
5–8 Hardwick Street
London EC1R 4RG

WWW.HEADOFZEUS.COM

*To André, Filipe and Lúcia*

# THE GOLDEN DAYS
# OF THE RIVIERA

The story of mysterious wires first surfaced in the mid-eighties of the last century, when the Hotel Palácio Estoril underwent complete renovation and two more floors were added to the building. They found so much cabling under the carpets, behind the skirting boards and wallpaper, that, according to the press, 'there was enough to circle the planet and still have some left over'. No one could say who had installed it, when or for what purpose, but it was widely suspected that it had to do with redundant listening devices from the Second World War, left behind and long forgotten.

The news came as no surprise to Mr Black. He confirmed that various clandestine intelligence services had operated in these parts throughout the war, especially during the first two or three years, and that his hotel had been considered a spies' nest, though of that there was no proof because, as he put it, 'we shall never know the whole truth since the very nature of such work precludes it'.

Sidestepping a request to relate a favourite story from his wartime days as the manager of the Palácio, he joked:

'Please, don't ask something like that of me. I'm so old that all I remember is what I've invented myself.'

He was not prepared to say more. It was useless to try to persuade him otherwise. Mr Black was a hotelier of the old school, whose ethics did not allow for indiscretion, even in retirement. But it did get him thinking. If he had to pick a story from his already-fading, half-gone memory of the war, he would probably tell them about that sunny afternoon when he met Gaby.

# THINGS I INVENTED MYSELF

The war had broken out in Europe the preceding autumn but nothing much had changed in the country until late spring, when refugees started inundating Lisbon and the coast.

We were caught by surprise. There were no reports in the press about anything unusual happening but even the sliver of truth that did reach us was worrying. And not without reason. The refugee crisis, as we were later to learn, was getting worse and more complicated by the day. A state of emergency was declared, and it was not just because of the Portuguese leadership's stubborn belief that the truth was harmful, especially if it was disclosed. Mr Black tried to perform his duties as if nothing out of the ordinary was going on. When the need arose, he would spend days calming people down, always repeating the official line:

'Ladies, gentlemen, there's no cause for alarm. Just enjoy your stay here, everything will be just fine.'

It wasn't difficult to believe him. Everything did indeed look just fine. In fact, Estoril was more like Biarritz or Monte Carlo than ever. With hindsight, it is interesting that no one at the time realized what was more than palpable all around us: that these were the first days of the brief but glamorous period that was to become known as the golden age of the Riviera.

The hotel manager was so busy that day that he didn't even have time to smoke a cigarette. It was not until the late afternoon that he managed to extricate himself from his duties. He announced that he did not wish to be disturbed. Once alone in his office, he stretched out in his chair and put his feet up on the desk, like a cowboy. Even if he had been seen in that position, nobody would have blamed him: his feet were so sore that he could feel them tingle in bed at night. Also, he was an American and Americans did not consider such behaviour particularly rude.

Noteworthy items on the desk included, apart from the Palácio manager's feet, the daily newspaper and a folder containing the hotel guests' registration forms. The front page of the paper *República* declared: *The Longest Day of the Year!* It was true; it was already past six o'clock on the wall clock but outside the sun was still shining bright. However, there was not a word in the paper about the refugees or the widely rumoured German invasion of Portugal. He had intended to look through the hotel registration forms before handing them in to the police but simply didn't have the energy.

He closed his eyes. In the darkness behind his eyelids he heard sounds he otherwise seldom noticed: the hubbub on the other side of the walls of his office, footsteps on the floor above, the distant whistle of a train.

★

A knock at the door startled him awake. He looked at his watch. It must be something urgent; it was only six-thirty. He sat up in his chair, straightened his cuffs and collar, brushed the dandruff off his shoulders and waited for the second knock.

'Come in!' he called out.

It was Lino, the concierge. He walked in and briefly stated the problem.

'Excuse me, Sir, but the matter appears to be delicate. I'm afraid it requires your attention ...'

Lino was an experienced member of staff and if he had had the choice he most certainly would not have disturbed Mr Black. But situations that only the manager could resolve, once rare, had become increasingly frequent of late. It was always the same story: guests wanted to pay their bill in valuables instead of cash. And Mr Black always had the same dilemma: whether to buy their jewellery, art and antiques at a price that suited him, or turn them away because they had no other way of paying.

He did not need to ask any questions. He told the concierge to bring in the guest and since Lino was already acquainted with the problem he could stay and help out if there was a snag.

The guest squinted, as if he had emerged from a dark dungeon. He shook hands with Mr Black and sat down on the proffered chair. He was clasping a glass of lemonade.

For the first few seconds they stared at each other across

the desk. The manager kicked off the conversation with the conventional:

'How can I help you, young man?'

The guest, speaking fluent English with what sounded like an Afrikaans accent, briefly explained that he needed full room and board at the hotel for an indefinite period of time.

'Are you travelling on your own?' the manager inquired.

'Yes, on my own,' the guest replied. He did not seem bothered by the indiscreet question.

The manager thought it might be a good idea to check the guest's papers, and asked him for his travel document. He gleaned from the Belgian passport the following basic information:

Name: Gavriel Franklin
Sex: Male
Marital Status: Single
Date and Place of Birth: 23 July 1930, Antwerp
Permanent address: Pelikaanstraat 612b, Antwerp.

The proper Portuguese visa, issued in Bordeaux a few days earlier, was signed *Mendes*. The room had been booked in time. The only problem was that Master Franklin would be turning ten in less than a month. Master Franklin was a child; a lost child.

From afar, the boy's unusual clothes made him look older, but upon closer inspection you could see that he was a kid with freckles and a pug nose who looked even younger than ten. His hair was as ragged as a haystack; in the afternoon sun it looked as if a hairy animal was nesting in it. Golden side-locks framed his face. His clothing consisted of a white shirt and sombre black suit, long rekel and black, broad-brimmed hat. His outfit looked entirely inappropriate for a boy his age to be wearing on a hot day in the twentieth century. Had somebody dressed him *à la mode* and cut his hair, young Master Franklin would have looked like a perfectly nice little boy. This way, all he needed was a false beard to look like a child dressing up for carnival as a Ukrainian rabbi.

The next question was painful but necessary:

'Do you have parents, young man?'

'Everybody has parents,' the boy replied.

'Not everybody,' said the manager. 'Where are your parents?'

'They're coming,' the boy said.

'When do you expect them?'

'Very soon.'

The boy was wan, the expression on his face wistful. Somebody later described him as looking lonelier than an asteroid in space.

'Do you know approximately when? In how many days?' the manager pressed, not being a man who knew how to deal with children.

'I don't know, but I know that my mother and father always keep their word. If they said they will come, then they will come,' the homeless boy replied.

'Where will they come?'

'Here.'

'When you say "here", what do you mean exactly?' the manager asked.

'Here. The Palácio Hotel,' the boy answered.

No one will ever know why the manager did not simply conclude the conversation right there and then, because he already knew what he had to do. He had enough information to make a decision without thinking twice about it. Instead, however, whether out of curiosity or courtesy, or perhaps even pity or lack of heart, he continued questioning the boy.

'Forgive me for sounding inquisitive, but I'd like to know why your parents didn't come with you.'

Gavriel Franklin replied one minute in French, the next in English, always calmly and more rationally than one might expect of someone his age. His tale matched the story of the recent exodus that the manager and concierge had already heard about from other refugees.

Mr Black did not ask him his religion. Gavriel was obviously Jewish, belonging to one of those Hassidic sects that believe civilization reached its height some one hundred and fifty years ago and, ever since, its members have changed neither their costumes nor their customs.

He said he was an only child, though not for long because his mother was pregnant. He said that his father and his uncles owned a gem-cutting workshop. That's to say they had owned it until a month ago. And until a month ago he had gone every day, except for the Sabbath, to the school attached to the synagogue. He was good at interpreting the holy books and Gaby's uncles teased his father that the boy would become a rabbi not a jeweller. Then, early one morning in mid-May, they picked Gaby up out of his bed and carried the bleary-eyed boy to a car. The rumble of warplanes flying over the stream of refugees on the road jolted him awake.

They crossed into France and headed for Bordeaux. They had heard that evacuation ships were setting sail from there. But when they reached the port, the last ships had already left. War was approaching and the only safe passage led southwards, towards Spain. But for Spain they needed entry visas, and at the consulate they were rejected without explanation. A Polish rabbi there advised them to get Portuguese visas, which would automatically give them transit rights through Spain.

They found the Portuguese consulate general in Bordeaux closed, and a crowd of people aimlessly standing around in front of the building. For several nights, they slept in the car. But the consulate, following orders from above, had stopped issuing visas. The consul general in Bordeaux, Dr Aristides de Sousa Mendes, sought instructions from Lisbon as to what to do in this situation of humanitarian catastrophe. The Ministry did not respond to his daily cables. The dense crowd of desperate people swelled, waiting for a miracle. And in the end, there was a miracle. For no apparent reason, the consul general assumed the responsibility himself and ordered that visas be issued to everybody, without restriction. Anybody presenting a passport at the Portuguese consulate was granted a visa, signed and stamped. They were not even charged any consular tax. This went on for several days until the consul general was declared to be of unsound mind and recalled.

With visas now in their passports the family proceeded with their journey. But not for long. At the Spanish border they once again found themselves amid a crowd of refugees. The border crossing was closed. At Lisbon's request the Spanish authorities had stopped accepting visas issued by Mendes. Gaby could not really explain how he wound up on Spanish soil without his parents. From what the boy said, Mr Black had the impression that, without telling the child, his parents had paid a Swiss man, who was on his way to Brazil, to take the boy across the border in his limousine, pretending he was his child. As soon as the boy realized that his parents were not following him, he tried to go back, but as he had no entry visa for France he was not allowed into the country.

The last glimpse he had of his parents was from a distance. They were shouting to him across the checkpoint barrier, saying he should wait for them, but not there; he was to stay with Mr Rikli who knew where to take him. The Swiss gentleman wired the Palácio from Spain, booked a room in the name of Monsieur Franklin, drove the boy to Lisbon, helped him buy a ticket for Estoril and put him on the train. The boy walked from the Estoril station to the hotel.

When he had run out of questions, the manager again had to face the same unpleasant decision. Sensing his discomfort, the boy spoke unprompted for the first time.

'Don't worry, Sir. My parents will come. They always keep their promises.'

'Of course they do,' the manager agreed, nodding his head. He did not have the heart to tell the boy that the only possible decision he could take was to turn him away. The hotel was neither equipped nor qualified to take care of unaccompanied children. This was a commercial enterprise and there was no place for sentimentality.

But the strange boy pressed on.

'Don't worry. I have enough money to pay. I have around twenty-five thousand dollars. I have pounds too. And Swiss francs. And I also have cut diamonds. See, here they are, in the lining,' he said touching the hem of his rekel as if wanting to make sure that they were still there. 'The money is in my suitcase.'

'What suitcase? Where is it?' asked the manager.

'I left it by the door. Shall I go and fetch it?'

But before he had finished his sentence, the manager was on his feet; he opened the door, picked up the abandoned little suitcase and placed it next to the boy's chair. The boy thought the manager was angry at him for having left the suitcase outside.

'I'm sorry. It's the first time I've done that. I'll never leave it like that again.'

Suddenly, the manager was not sure what he should do. He was not angry; he simply had a feeling of trepidation and a guilty conscience. How had the boy even survived? What was he to do with him? The room that had been reserved was waiting for him, but what if his parents got held up on the way? What if they never arrived? Given the value of the money the boy was carrying with him, all problems were soluble. Or were they? No, they certainly would not send him to an orphanage. He had enough money to go to a good boarding school in Switzerland or America.

Lino, who had said nothing until then, jumped to the aid of his boss. He spoke to him in Portuguese so that the boy would not understand:

'Sir, it is already late. May I suggest that we end this conversation for today. We are too busy and the young man needs to eat and get some sleep now. We'll deal with everything better tomorrow, God willing.'

The manager was level-headed and quite aware of the delicacy of the moment. Reason told him to warn the boy that this would probably be only a temporary solution. But he did not know exactly how to formulate this advice. He was afraid it would sound as if he was saying 'if your parents don't show up soon you'll have to go to an orphanage'. Instead, he held out his hand to the boy:

'Welcome to the Palácio! I assume you haven't had anything to eat yet? My driver Bruno will take care of you. But first, you and I will put your money and jewels in the safe; then we can have dinner.'

# WILLKOMMEN, BIENVENUE,
# WELCOME

When you approach Lisbon from the sea, just before the boat turns into the river, to the left, in the background, you will see a bluish mountain. That is Sintra. It blocks the path of the rain clouds and as a result Estoril offers visitors more hours of sunshine than any other resort in Europe. At least so says the tourist brochure for the 'Sunshine Coast', that being what our little Riviera is officially called. But it is still popularly known as the Estoril coast, or even just the Coast.

The gently undulating slope that dips down to the bay looks south, to the ocean. It is dotted with the villas and summer homes of Lisbon's more prominent families, whose privacy is assured by dense greenery and high walls. It is always windy at the foot of the mountain, where the waves wash over the sand. The beach is studded with phalanxes of sunshades, changing cabins and canvas deck chairs. Just above it, a recently opened railway track follows the sickle-shaped line of the coast, and next to it is the motorway: to the right, not even half an hour by car, is Lisbon; to the left, so close you can see it, is Cascais.

13

If you come by train, you need to get off at Estoril station, then cross the tracks and the road to the big rectangular French-style park. Perched among its palm trees, cypress trees and its variegated bushes, is the famous resort's biggest attraction: the Grand Casino Estoril. Right next to it is a white, three-storey building, its windows offering stunning views of the park and the ocean. And on top of its dark roof is a big sign saying: 'HOTEL PALÁCIO'. Estoril has any number of hotels, but we will leave them aside, not because they are smaller or cheaper but because, while each would deserve to play the leading role, our story already stars the Palácio.

One summer morning in 1940, the phone rang in Mr Black's office. It was Reception.

'Senhor Cardoso would like to see you.'

Mr Black wished he could say he was busy, but he didn't dare. If there was one person he could not refuse to see it was Cardoso, superintendent and head of the Estoril Unit of the PVDE, the Surveillance and State Defence Police that dealt with extremists of all kinds: anarchists, communists, liberals. The PVDE also monitored the activities of foreign nationals in the country. Although Mr Black himself was apolitical, being both a foreign national and the manager of a hotel popular among foreigners he was of interest to the police. Whatever Cardoso was actually working on, judging by the amount of time he had been spending at the hotel recently, the Palácio was high on his list of priorities.

*

A small man in a cheap suit and smelling of cologne water walked into Mr Black's office. His balding grey hair made him look older than he was. In fact, Superintendent Cardoso resembled a lowly clerk more than a high-powered police officer. He accepted the cup of coffee offered him and came to the point unusually quickly.

'I don't want to bore you with the technical details, but it's important for you to know that you may soon receive an unusual request ...'

Here the inspector stopped, expecting the foreigner to show some curiosity. As there was none forthcoming, he continued:

'You might be asked to provide accommodation for the Duke and Duchess of Windsor,' he said, looking at the manager meaningfully.

Mr Black merely nodded his head.

'In the event of such an occurrence, I would kindly ask you for, so to speak, a personal favour. If possible.'

Mr Black again nodded.

'I would ask you not to let them into the hotel for the next forty-eight hours. Is that feasible, do you think?'

The manager sounded as if he had not properly understood the inspector:

'Not let the Windsors in?'

'That's right. Not let them in.'

'All right. The hotel has no vacancies anyway,' the American said.

'That's resolved, then!' the policeman said, pleased, crossing out the relevant entry he had made in his notebook. He then went on:

'There are a few other little matters. You have another two reservations for today that we need to discuss. One is for seven beds in the name of Baron von Amschel, and the other is a table for lunch for eight in the name of Gaetan.' It was not clear from the policeman's tone whether he was asking or informing the manager. 'They are false names. You know who they really are?'

The manager once again nodded.

'Excellent. Just a few more minutes and we're done,' said the balding little man, taking a bunch of photographs from his inside pocket. He carefully laid them out on the table and asked: 'Do you recognize any of these people?'

The manager glanced at the headshots and shook his head. The inspector was forced to try another method: he pointed to each photo.

'Maurice Maeterlinck? The name doesn't mean anything to you? Alma Mahler? No? Franz Werfel? Golo Mann? Heinrich Mann? No? Nothing? None of them?'

Mr Black shook his head.

'I'm terribly sorry that I can't help you. I see too many new faces every day to remember them.'

'They are all well-known foreign nationals staying with you on full room and board or frequenting the restaurant. They are mostly writers. Mr Maeterlinck is a Belgian Nobel Prize winner. And this young German here, Golo Mann, is the son of a famous writer. He likes men.'

'So?'

'So nothing. I'm just saying, it's an eccentric crowd. That's why I'm warning you to keep an eye on them.'

'All guests are equally important to us here at the Palácio,' the manager said.

'These particular gentlemen are designated as politically sensitive cases,' the inspector said in a low voice, as if in confidence. 'There may even be leftists among them.'

'You think so?'

'I don't think so, I *know* so, just as I *know* where the danger to our society lies. That is my job. Yours is to do your job to the best of your ability, to ensure that your guests have as nice a time as possible here and leave as friends of Portugal. We are here to keep an eye on things and, if necessary, to thwart anybody who even thinks of abusing our hospitality. You just need to notify us if you notice anything unusual. Right?'

It was not really a question; nor could the manager's smile be taken as an answer. The meeting was unusually brief, lasting barely a quarter of an hour.

That same morning, a call from the household of the Duke of Windsor was transferred to the hotel manager. Mr Black listened to the request, thanked the caller for his interest and said that, to his immense regret, he was unable to be of any help. Thinking that the manager did not realize whom he was talking to, the gentleman from the Duke's staff explained that he was speaking on behalf of the former king of the United Kingdom, Edward VIII, who required accommodation that very day. The information changed nothing. Mr Black declared himself deeply honoured by the Duke and Duchess's interest in his hotel, repeating that unfortunately there were no vacancies for the couple. If they could wait a day or two he might be able to secure them appropriate accommodation, Mr Black said politely. His offer was just as politely refused.

At around one in the afternoon, the hotel manager stepped into the courtyard to await the Gaetan family. He knew that the name was a front for the Habsburgs. With a 'Herzlich willkommen!' he bowed to the Empress Zita and kissed her hand. He had met them before, in Madeira in 1922 where they had found refuge after the collapse of the Austro-Hungarian Empire. At the time, Mr Black was the manager of a hotel they often stayed at, but that was a long time ago and he did not think that she would recognize him. The last time he saw her was at the funeral of her husband, the last emperor of Austria, Charles I. She was heavily pregnant, her face hidden behind a thick black veil, surrounded by her young, weeping children. He did not want to remind the unhappy empress of those tragic times, so he shook hands with the heir to the throne and other crown princes and personally led them to a carefully chosen table in the corner of the restaurant, aware how worried they were that Hitler's powerful hand could reach them even here and carry out the death sentence pronounced on them as enemies of his regime.

They had not yet finished their starters when seven people arrived with rooms booked in the name of Baron von Amschel – the pseudonym used by the Rothschild family. They were the wealthiest banking dynasty in the world but the Nazis could not forgive them for being Jewish. They too lived in fear and insisted on absolute discretion. They were taken quietly to their suites, where they said they did not intend to stay long because they would be continuing their journey as soon as it became possible. Mr Black thought, at first glance at least, that they looked more like royalty than the actual royals.

Mr Black knew from experience that billionaires and royals were not the most difficult guests. When so many people who have lived such pampered lives swoop down on one place there are bound to be all sorts of strange characters. Often, the same people who were begging for accommodation only a minute ago would start making demands as soon as they got their rooms. They wanted an astrologist for the wife, a piano teacher for the child, and, to make them feel more at home, someone to hang the paintings they had brought with them into exile. Several days earlier, for instance, the majordomo of a Dutch merchant, who was staying at the hotel with his family en route to the Far East, asked the hotel manager where his employer could find some entertainment. It had to be a discreet place, and the girls had to be black. That's how far things could sometimes go.

For all that, come early evening, when the hectic pace had eased a little, Mr Black retreated to his office, as was his wont at this time of day. He switched on the radio. The red arrow pointed to London. The evening news was just starting.

*'British troops have withdrawn from the continent. General de Gaulle has established the Legion of French Volunteers in England...'*

The hotel manager did not have the energy to listen to any

more. He turned the dial. On station after station, sombre voices were broadcasting the latest world news. He kept turning the dial until he finally found a station playing some melancholic piano music. It was the *Adagio sostenuto* of Rachmaninoff's Piano Concerto No. 2.

Sitting in the dark, his eyes open, he thought about the laments of the men and women he had been listening to all day. In all his many years of experience he had never had such a packed hotel or such unusual guests. He knew that, in spite of everything, he was lucky. A very select group of exiles, a couple of thousand out of the two million estimated to be roaming through Europe, had come to Estoril. A few hundred of the most resourceful among them had found accommodation at the Palácio: those with the best connections, the most money and the greatest luck. And now these most privileged of the privileged were complaining and despairing. His position was such that he had to listen to their complaints and only occasionally remind them that those of us who found ourselves not in Paris, Vienna or London but in Estoril on this 26th of June 1940 were the lucky ones. We had more than enough to eat and drink, we had electricity and water. We sunbathed on beaches that were not encircled by barbed wire, and when we strolled under the palm trees there we encountered no armed patrols. We slept well at night; there were no air attacks or policemen banging at the door to wake us up. If only we could remember how many people were living under occupation, how many were lying in roadside ditches with their mouths full of ants, we would stop complaining. But if it was a person's lot to spend their time aimlessly waiting, then where better a place to do it than here? All one needed was enough money to pay for one's stay and this damned war would be over as quickly as a summer holiday. There would be nothing to bother us. Only the mosquitos.

# SUCH A PITY

The boy was lying on the grass, his eyes closed, his mind blank. Basking in the warmth of the sun, he suddenly forgot where the warmth was coming from.

He thought he heard somebody calling him, 'Gaby', and opened his eyes, but the sunlight blocked all feelings and thoughts from his mind. That was why he did not notice how blue the sky was, how green the treetops above. The only thing he saw was a single ladybird. It alighted right next to his head, scuttled on its little black legs across the mossy grass and made for the pupil of his eye, as if it wanted to get inside. The boy was startled by a nearby voice:

'Gaby? Gaby, where've you been?' Papagaio was leaning over him, his hands on his knees, trying to catch his breath.

'Get yourself to Reception right away! Hurry! You've got a phone call. Hurry! What are you waiting for?'

Gaby jumped to his feet and ran as fast as he could, but it was too late.

'*Tate! Vater!*' he cried into the phone but the connection was dead.

Gaby had been waiting for this phone call since the day he arrived. His eyes welled up with tears.

Renato at Reception had first tried to transfer the call to Gaby's room, but there was no answer. Then the staff ran out to find him.

While waiting on the phone, Gaby's father told Renato that he and his wife were still in France, doing their best to obtain the necessary papers and continue their journey. He said that he had been trying to phone every day, but had been unable to get a connection. He promised to come by train as soon as possible.

'Tell Gavriel to wait for us there, at the hotel. Tell him not to budge. We will come for him,' Gavriel's father kept repeating. At least that is what Renato said.

Mr Black stroked the boy's head.

'Don't worry. Everything will be all right… We're here until they come for you… Papagaio, please take the young gentleman off somewhere… Go on…'

Mr Black had neither an affinity nor the patience for children. He left that to Papagaio, who could tell when his friend was sad, how sad he was, why he was sad, what he should say and do to cheer him up. And he also knew how to console you, more with gestures than with words, by hugging you, ruffling your hair, giving you a rap on the head. He was good at that.

'Let's go to the kitchen… My mum is the cook. We'll say that it's the manager's orders, and they'll give us anything we want – ice cream, anything! Let's go…' said Papagaio, giving Gaby a nudge. But the boy didn't feel like it. Instead of going with his friend, he went upstairs to his room. If he was good, listened to his father and waited here, then nothing bad would happen to him.

Later, over dinner, while the staff were talking about what had happened, Lourdes sighed.

'Poor thing, it's not his fault. The boy just went out to play for a bit… I suppose they'll come if they promised they would,' she said, wiping away her tears with her apron. 'The boy can't be left all alone like this, without his family. And he's so well behaved. There's nobody to kiss him good night when he goes to bed. Poor thing.'

# DROP BY FOR A CHAT
# SOME TIME

Gaby's house in Antwerp was by no means small, but it was much, much smaller than this hotel. In fact, all the houses Gaby had ever been in before – his uncles', aunts', grandparents', even the school and synagogue – were smaller than this building.

Three flights down, Gaby ran into the head of Reception in the hallway. He liked the man very much. He looked like an opera singer, the rotund kind that plays kings:

'Good afternoon, Senhor Renato.'

'Good afternoon, young man. How can I help you?' the head of Reception said with his nicest smile.

'I'm a little bored all by myself in my room,' Gaby confessed.

'Why don't you go out and take a walk? Fresh air always does one good. Go out, play and don't worry. If somebody phones I'll call you, just stay in the courtyard so I can see you,' the professionally reliable Renato said with a smile.

In the courtyard, some boys were playing hide-and-seek. All but one of them ran off and hid. The one left, covering his eyes with his hands and sticking his head in a bush, counted aloud:

'*Eyns, tsvey, dray… nayntsn, tsvantsik…*' At the count of twenty he turned around and started looking for them. He searched high and low, as if looking for a lost cat, and then suddenly, as if on command, the children came running and shrieking out of their hiding places. The slowest was next to cover his eyes and count.

'*Eins, zwei, drei… achtzehn, neunzehn, zwanzig.*'

Another round and then the third boy would start counting:

'*Jeden, dwa, trzy… osiemnaście, dziewiętnaście, dwadzieścia…*'

Gaby watched them from nearby. They didn't notice him. There were enough of them and they didn't need reinforcements. Anyway, Gaby was not particularly good with children. He knew he wasn't like them. Even when they spoke the same language, he didn't get along with them. He liked to ask questions and children didn't like being questioned because they didn't know how to give clever answers.

Gaby went back inside, and on his way to the reception desk he noticed an elderly lady dressed in black sitting in an armchair in the corner. Wearing a pearl necklace around her shrivelled neck, she was gazing out of the window, knitting slowly. Tears were trickling down her face even more slowly. The boy pitied the woman and stopped. She noticed him. He smiled. She smiled back.

Senhor Renato was busy at Reception registering new guests. He spotted Gaby out of the corner of his eye and winked. He didn't say anything, meaning there was no news, so Gaby didn't ask, he just slipped past.

He did not get far. The door behind Reception was ajar. Gaby slowly walked over to the door and peered into the narrow corridor. It was empty except for a thin gleam of light from the depth of the darkness. The boy crept down the corridor and peeked through the crack in the door. He saw the same office he had been in the day he arrived. The same big desk, which had been neat then, was now piled with papers. The same Mr Black, who had been so nice and friendly then, was now so preoccupied and busy that he did not even raise his head when Gaby walked in. That is how the boy noticed that the hair on top of Mr Black's head was thinning. On the desk was an ashtray full of cigarette butts, and a cigarette that had died out.

'Good afternoon, Mr Black,' Gaby said.

Mr Black's left index finger stopped where he had been adding up figures on a piece of paper, and he looked up.

'Hello, Gaby. What are you doing here? Is everything all right?' he asked, smiling.

'Fine. Your cigarette has gone out.'

'I know, but I don't have time to relight it. Just wait a minute until I finish what I started…' He returned to his figures, writing on the piece of paper. Finally, he read out the total sum, more to himself than anybody else:

'So, six hundred and twenty-two thousand.'

'Thousand what?' Gaby asked.

'Uh? You still here?' Mr Black looked surprised for some reason.

'Thousand what?' Gaby repeated.

From the outset, Mr Black had kept his distance from the

boy, like a Victorian parent. However, on his regular rounds of the restaurant he never failed to exchange a few words with him about the meal. That was enough for him to see that Gaby was an unusually inquisitive child, that if something caught his interest and he asked a question about it he would not let it go. And so, every couple of days he would set aside a few minutes to sit down with the boy at his table and answer as many of his questions as his patience would allow. But this time he was not in the mood to talk.

'I'm sorry, young man, but I have no time for amusements right now. Can't you see that I'm busy?'

'Yes, I can see that,' the boy replied.

'But you're still here?' It was a rhetorical question and without waiting for the boy to respond the manager waved him away. 'You can go, young man!'

'Tell me, please, what are you counting?

The manager realized that the boy would not leave him alone until he answered the question.

'Marbles,' he said.

'Marbles?! Where?'

'Nowhere, I was joking,' Mr Black admitted. 'You don't seriously think anybody would be counting thousands of marbles do you?'

'Well, what are you counting, then?' the boy persisted.

'It's really irritating when somebody keeps asking the same thing… You are old enough to know, young man, that if somebody doesn't answer you the first time it may be that they didn't hear you, but if they don't answer the second time it means that they don't feel like talking.'

28

'Money?' the boy hazarded a guess.

The American shrugged his shoulders, which the boy took as a 'Yes.'

'That's a lot of money?' The boy was honestly interested.

'Yes, it is.'

'And what are you going to do with it?'

'If you give me a good reason why I should share that information with you, I will,' said the manager.

'Because I've got money but I never count it. Do you think I should start counting my money too, like you?'

It was a logical question, so the manager answered it:

'Counting as such is unnecessary. A bank will gladly do it for you for free.'

The boy continued with his perfectly logical questions:

'And what will you do with your money?'

'First I will cover my costs, and the rest I will put in the bank with interest. Or else I'll invest it.'

'How do you do that exactly, that thing with interest and investing?' asked the boy.

'How would it be, young man, if you let me finish my work and in return I promise to dine with you today or tomorrow and answer all your questions, assuming I have the answers? Okay?'

'Okay! See you!' said Gaby, turning on his heel and walking out.

Having nothing better to do, he decided to go out again, only this time he went to the main, front door. Standing there was the doorman. As he was young and single, they didn't call him Senhor, they simply called him by his name, Manuel.

He was wearing an officer-like cap and a long burgundy over-coat with gold trimming and epaulettes. He was clearly proud of his uniform; he looked like a colonel from a South American military junta. A handkerchief decorated with red squares peeked out of his pocket. He was always there, standing at the front door, but they hadn't had a chance to chat until now, except for saying 'Good afternoon' whenever Gaby passed by, and that was rare enough.

The boy walked towards the door and Manuel opened it for him with a smile. As expected, they wished each other a 'Good afternoon', Gaby stepped out and Manuel closed the door after him. When Gaby headed back in, Manuel again opened the door with a smile and then closed it behind him. Manuel was the busiest person in the hotel.

'Back so soon, Monsieur Gaby?' the doorman asked. Something in his tone indicated that he had more he wanted to say.

The boy found the man interesting. He thought he looked like the conductor of a circus orchestra.

'You know my name?'

'Of course. I know everybody in the hotel.'

'And I know your name,' the boy informed him. 'You're Manuel.'

'That's right,' said the doorman. 'I am Manuel.'

'I want to ask you something, Manuel. Why did you open the door for me and then close it after me?'

'Because that is my job. I'm a doorman and doormen officially work the doors.'

'But why don't people open the door for themselves? Anybody can open the door for himself. I can.'

'Of course you can, you are a strong young man, but the rule here is that the door is opened by the doorman, in other words by me,' Manuel explained. He was stopped from elaborating by the arrival of three fat Germans. He opened the door for them and wished them '*Guten Tag!*'

Manuel had barely closed the door when he had to open it again.

'*Bonjour!*' smiled the doorman, greeting a new group of arrivals who were chattering away in some strange tongue. None of them replied.

'There! You did it again. I don't understand.'

'There's nothing to understand. Those are my orders,' the doorman explained, before opening and closing the door again. He then took his funny hanky out of his pocket and wiped his brow.

'You know, young man, this is not easy,' he said. 'I'm like a host. I work the doors one shift, my colleague works the other. So there's always somebody here to welcome the guests. It comes with the service and is especially appreciated by people who are lonely.'

'Now that I think about it, your job is actually meaningful. Maybe because it makes you think about others and not just yourself,' Gaby nodded.

'Of course it's meaningful. It used to be easier too. We didn't have so many guests and I didn't have to keep opening and closing the door all the time.'

'And?'

'And nothing,' said Manuel. 'That's the problem! My duties are the same but the number of hotel guests is growing by the day.' All this talking had distracted Manuel, who had forgotten to close the door.

'And?'

'And now I don't have a second to myself anymore. About thirty people have passed through here since we started talking. Good afternoon, Madam.'

Gaby stopped to think for a moment. He had an idea.

'Why don't you stand at the door and just hold it open all the time? You could even do it with your back. Then people could come in and out at will. You would just have to smile and wish everybody "Good afternoon", and when you got bored with that you could talk to some of them. The way you are talking to me now. Plus, the hotel would get some fresh air. Instead of being the doorman you could just be the welcomer. What do you say?'

'That's some idea you've got there, but it's not how it works. And even if it did, it wouldn't really help,' said Manuel. 'What good is it if I can't sit down and give my feet a rest?'

'Pity.'

'Pity.'

'I wish I could be a doorman. Doormen are never lonely.'

'You speak several languages, you could easily find work in any hotel. Just give yourself some time until you're a little older.'

'I'm off,' the boy said to the doorman.

'Off you go then… Drop by for a chat again some time,' the doorman said.

As he was leaving, Gaby spotted the old lady in black again. She was sitting where he had left her, with the same tears. He smiled at her but this time she did not notice him.

32

# CHICKEN STEW

I t was late in the afternoon and there wasn't a soul in the hotel dining room, just neatly set tables and empty chairs from one end of the room to the other. The embroidered napkins, crystal glasses, porcelain, silverware, and especially the fresh flowers, looked as if they were waiting for the guests to arrive at the wedding of, say, a king in exile. But it was simply an ordinary evening at the Palácio.

The swinging doors at the back were there to separate rather than to connect the two rooms; they opened only long enough to let someone slip through. Made of the same reddish wood as the surrounding wall panels, they blended in perfectly. You knew they were kitchen doors because they were rimmed at the bottom with copper so that the waiters could kick them open if their hands were full, and at the top they each had a round window so that the staff could see if somebody was coming and avoid a collision. Inside the kitchen, dinner was being prepared for the restaurant.

It was not just any kind of dinner, it was a feast, *à la carte*, for hundreds of people. The kitchen was bustling like a beehive: the cooks and apprentices were hard at work; dinner

# Menu, 23 July 1940

| | |
|---|---|
| Soupe de Langouste avec Armagnac | Crayfish Soup with Armagnac |
| Salade de Crevettes | Shrimp Salad |
| Aspic de Viande | Venison Aspic |

≈

| | |
|---|---|
| Steak de Thon aux Fines Herbes | Tuna Steak in Fine Herbs |
| Dorade en Croûte de Sel | Sea Bream Baked in Salt |
| Moules Marinières | Mussels in White Wine |

≈

| | |
|---|---|
| Rôti de Porc Fermier aux Marrons | Village Roast Pork with Chestnuts |
| Filet de Boeuf au Poivre Vert | Beefsteak in Green Pepper Sauce |
| Côtelettes d'Agneau à la Menthe | Lamb Chops with Mint Sauce |

≈

| | |
|---|---|
| Crêpe Suzette | Crêpe Suzette |
| Gâteau au Chocolat | Chocolate Cake |
| Guava Pâté de Fruit et | Guava Pâté and Cottage |
| Fromage Blanc | Cheese |
| Crème Glacée | Ice Cream |

was to be served in two and a half hours, which left little time for everything that had to be done. Soups were simmering on the stoves different kinds of meat were sitting in various marinades, cakes were being kept on ice, the dough was rising and the ovens were baking. Kitchens like this had been rare enough before the war, but even then it would have been hard to believe that any would survive the catastrophe on this side of the ocean.

Customers who frequent restaurants like this are of a special breed: they do not ask the price, but they expect the best because that is all they know. The menus in such establishments must cater to every taste, accommodating both religious taboos and health requirements. And the daily menu did just that.

The real action was not expected to start until around six-thirty. Then the pace picked up in the kitchen and the various delicacies were glazed, garnished and gratinated. The *Maître d'* would await the guests at the door and usher them to their table. The waiters would come bearing plates full of mouth-watering food, seeing to it that everyone was content and serving good wine with their meals.

The hotel manager was of the view that if you want good service you have to have a dedicated, happy staff, and if they are to be happy, they have to be fed properly. You did not have to worry about the cooks, they always managed. And so did the waiters. The rest of the staff did not eat *à la carte*, but fared just as well, because they had somebody to look after their stomachs: Maria de Lourdes.

Lourdes, the head cook for staff who lived in-house, had a separate 'little kitchen' behind the main cooking area, at the end of the hallway, near the servants' entrance. There, in her own little realm, using tried and tested recipes, she cooked on a wood-burning stove, in big pots, the way her mother had taught her: simple but tasty food, the kind prepared for people who burn up what they eat while working. There was only one dish on her daily menu. Today it was chicken stew, and Lourdes' was very good.

Until not so long ago, before this deluge of guests started, Lourdes could do everything herself, but now she had so much work she could not handle it all. So Mr Black found her a young assistant. Her name was Isaura, she was only fifteen and not yet of much help, but she was a quick learner. And Lourdes was patient. Looking at the clock on the wall, she said:

'The staff sit down to eat an hour before the restaurant opens, and chicken stew takes no more than an hour to make. In other words, it's time to start. So, go on now and dice this onion as finely as you can while I cut up the chicken. Like this: the quartered white meat, then the neck and the tail; it may not be much but it's tasty… Like this, with the bones, you can make a good sauce with the bones. Then the drumsticks and thighs separately…'

Maria de Lourdes was round and her face was lovely and full. She had a Cape Verde complexion and white teeth: there was African blood in her. She'd braided her hair and covered it neatly with a hairnet, as a cook should. And she was always smiling; even when she complained, she looked as if she was in a good mood. Her son Rodolfo, better known as Papagaio, took after her in that respect.

'Tonight we are sixteen for the first service, and another eight for the second. Now, take this big pot, it's just the right size, and cover the bottom with some oil, like this... Don't use too much, these things are expensive. Then add the onions and keep stirring, we don't want it to burn...' All the while she was talking, Lourdes demonstrated each step along the way, adding and stirring with her wooden spoon. 'When the onions look shiny like this, add the chicken and turn each piece over like this, until it turns white on each side. If you don't do that the meat will simply fall apart into pieces. Then pour in the wine, just enough to cover it... Pass me that bottle, if you don't mind...' The girl gave her teacher a half-full bottle of red wine. 'The waiters bring me the bottles the customers don't finish,' she said, pouring the wine over the chicken, but only after having taken a sip herself. 'This wine is excellent. Then you add the tomatoes, a bay leaf, some salt, not too much, it's not good for your health, but it has to have at least some. Never put the salt straight into the pot; first put it into the palm of your hand like this, and then into the pot. That way you can see how much you're putting in.'

The girl thought that she would never be able to learn such a complicated process, but there was more.

'Then you add the pepper, again not too much, and let the pot simmer on a low flame.' Lourdes shook the pot on the stove. 'And you just cover it with the lid and leave it next to the stove for half an hour, forty-five minutes, until the chicken is done. Like this. Can you hear it whispering? That's how it should simmer.' Lourdes put the lid back on the pot. 'Now let's go and peel some potatoes.'

Isaura was glad it was time for the potatoes; she knew how to peel. As they worked side by side, Lourdes explained the house rules regarding staff meals.

'Tomorrow we'll have beans. We can't have meat every day and beans are the best substitute. I'll add the bone of ham that I got from the restaurant to give it some flavour. The day after tomorrow it will be sardines. We've got to be frugal. These are hard times… Here, thank God,' she quickly crossed herself, 'nobody goes hungry, but there are people who have nothing to eat… and their number isn't small… some wretched folk would be happy to scrape a few grains of rice off the floor just to have something to eat, people who once had everything… that's fate for you,' said Lourdes. The girl kept quiet. She would have had plenty to say; she knew what it meant to go hungry and to live off half a sardine and a crust of bread for lunch.

Three-quarters of an hour later, the most wonderful smell rose up from the pot of reddish, thick stew. The cook pricked a drumstick with a fork to see if it was ready.

'Just a bit longer and it will be as soft as butter,' she said as she left to put on a clean apron to serve dinner. She gave an identical white ironed apron to the girl. 'The two of us should spruce ourselves up; when people come to dinner all nicely shaven and dressed, in ties, it would be a shame to welcome them looking like servants.'

As they washed their hands and fixed their hair in front of the mirror, Lourdes groaned:

'When I think of what I used to look like, and look at me now… Beauty fades with youth…' They had touched upon a new subject but Lourdes dropped it in favour of giving the girl a psychological portrait of the hotel manager. 'I forgot to tell you about Mr Black. He's an old bachelor and a loner. He hasn't got a living soul, not even a dog or a cat, just this job. He prefers eating alone in his office. He sits in company only when he has to, when he's got a meeting or a visitor; otherwise, Bruno the driver brings him a plate of whatever we eat here. He's not fussy. Sometimes he comes to the kitchen to compliment my cooking, but I think to myself what good are your words when you leave half of it uneaten? The only plate of food he licks clean is cod…'

After pausing to lift the lid and cast a glance at the pot, she returned to practical matters.

'But the two of us have nothing to worry about because I always make enough for him as well, just in case. If he doesn't want it, somebody else will eat it, nothing is thrown away here…' said the cook cheerfully, pricking the chicken with her fork again.

'It's done. Look, as soft as butter,' she showed Isaura. 'See that tray over there? It's the manager's. Pass me a plate… Now, you choose a nice piece of chicken like this, not too big, and add a potato or two, not too many, he eats like a bird. There. Then you pour the sauce over it, put the plate on the tray and cover it. That's it. Now go and ring that bell.'

Not a minute after the bell sounded, there was Bruno at the door. He looked good in his chauffeur's uniform. The man shaved and changed his shirt twice a day. Waiting for him was a tray bearing a silver dome that looked so impressive you would have thought it was covering a lobster, not a stew.

'My, that smells good,' said Bruno, taking the tray and rushing off to give it to the manager, because he wanted to return as quickly as possible and join his colleagues for dinner.

Lourdes' kitchen was known as the 'little kitchen' even though it was not that small. It had a stove and china cupboards, and in the middle, a big marble-topped table that, at a push, could seat some twenty people. There was no need for her to announce dinner, because everybody on shift was already converging on the table. Lourdes grasped the handles of the piping hot pot with a teatowel, brought it over to the table and placed it in front of them. She took off the lid and her job was done, at least for the time being. She could relax while they ate. She never ate with the others; having spent all day in the kitchen cooking she had had her fill of smells and tastes. She stood to the side, her hands on her hips, watching them eat.

'Serve yourself some more, child, that's not enough,' she said to Isaura, but the girl was too embarrassed to do anything so Lourdes turned to Rodolfo: 'Rudi, my love, give the poor girl some more potatoes, look how thin she is, she's so skinny it's a wonder the wind hasn't blown her away... And she works like a horse. Give her some more, and a bit more of that sauce.'

All these people lived in the hotel. Ever since the rooms in the attic had been converted to accommodate more guests, the staff had been squeezed into the basement. The day and night shift receptionists and doormen, for instance, took turns sleeping in the bunk beds. That's how crowded it was. And although they kept bumping into each other they had so much work that they seldom had time to talk. Except at mealtime.

Bruno would spend much of his working day sitting at the reception desk, or, if it was very busy there, then at the bar, waiting for the hotel manager or whoever else he was supposed to drive. There were various local and foreign newspapers in the hotel and by evening he would have read all the news. As a result, his colleagues were always asking him what was going on in the world.

'Abroad, the war is heating up. At home, nothing new...' he would say.

It wasn't that he didn't like to talk. Quite the contrary, he discussed events at home and abroad with the hotel manager every day, but he did not like to express any opinions in front of his colleagues, especially not about politics. It never did anybody any good. If it had been the football season, he would have told them the latest scores, because at least that was something one could always talk about. But for now, all he could add was:

'And the papers say that the *Nea Helas* will set sail for America in seven days. Which means we'll have a big new rotation of hotel guests.'

\* \* \*

Gaby arrived for dinner early, ahead of everybody else. Instead of going to his place, by the pillar, he walked through the empty restaurant to the main kitchen and down the side corridor to the rear exit. He stopped in front of the door to the little kitchen, hesitated for a moment, and then quietly opening it, he peered in.

Nobody noticed him slip inside. 'Bonjour!' He surprised everybody and they all immediately jumped to their feet, following what they thought was proper etiquette when a hotel guest entered their quarters. Manuel was the first to find his tongue.

'How can I help you, young man?' said the doorman politely in French, putting himself at the service of the new arrival.

The young man may have looked shy but, as we have already had occasion to observe, he always spoke his mind.

'May I eat with you here this evening?'

'What did he say?' asked the others who didn't speak French.

'He says that he wants to eat with us,' Manuel translated.

The situation was so strange that nobody knew what to say or do. They just looked at each other.

'It's my birthday,' the boy explained.

'Well, why didn't you say so?!' Manuel said with a broad smile, and then translating for the others: 'It's his birthday.'

'How old?'

'Ten,' the boy said proudly, holding up all ten fingers.

Suddenly everybody relaxed. Papagaio, with whom the boy had already made friends, was the first to rush over and hug him. Then the boy shook hands, one by one, with the other men around the dining table, some of whom patted him on the back. 'May you live a hundred years!' they said. Lourdes kissed him on the brow. Nodding her head, Isaura congratulated him from the back of the room. And everybody squeezed together to make room for him on the bench.

'It smells good,' said the boy politely.

Lourdes had already brought him a plate.

'If I'd known it was his birthday I would have baked him a cake,' she muttered to herself.

The Honourable Mr Cardoso
Superintendent
Monte Estoril
Lisbon
5 October 1940

## LETTER

(added by hand)
POSSIBLY POLITICALLY SENSITIVE!

In the late hours of 4 October 1940, a group of 6 (six) Polish citizens came to stay at the 'Palácio Estoril' Hotel, within the territorial jurisdiction of your Unit. The group consists of His Excellency former Prime Minister Mr Ignacy Jan Paderewski (79), his sister Antonina Wilkonska (82), his personal secretary, his driver, as well as His Excellency Dr Selwyn Strakacz (42), the Polish ambassador to the League of Nations, with his wife and young daughter. His Excellency Paderewski is the former Foreign Minister and Prime Minister of the Republic of Poland, and a world-famous musician. Since the occupation of Poland last September, he has become politically active again as head of the parliament in exile.

At 13:00 hours local Portuguese time of that same day, the Prime Minister showed his diplomatic passport at the Badajoz-Elvas border crossing, along with a letter of guarantee from the US ambassador in Madrid stating that the group was in transit en route to the United States. They entered Portugal legally and were given rooms that same evening at the 'Palácio': (rooms 37–41).

### ORDER

Ensure the privacy and safety of the group. <u>Prevent, at all costs, any politicizing of their presence in the country.</u>

WARNING: The Prime Minister has a bad heart and may also show signs of dementia. His sister has for years suffered from diabetes. Should the need arise, ensure that all members of the group receive medical treatment and care.

For the Good of the Nation!
Chief

(signature illegible)

# POSSIBLY POLITICALLY
# SENSITIVE

On the second day of his stay in Estoril, the former Prime Minister of Poland already had two important meetings in the hotel. In the morning, he met with a reporter from the Lisbon daily *Diário de Notícias* and explained the humanitarian and political aspects of his trip to the United States. In the afternoon, the J. Carneiro & Brother concert agency offered to arrange a piano recital during his stay in Portugal.

'My answer is yes, as long as the proceeds go to saving Poland, and, of course, as long as you do not expect me to play for too long,' he replied.

His entourage tried to persuade him that the concert would put too much of a strain on his health and they begged him to change his mind, but it was no use. He wouldn't hear of it. He saw the concert as a chance to embark immediately on his patriotic mission.

'I dreamed of this, but I never dared hope, at least not before America. I've already decided on the programme. I shall open with "The Funeral March", the symbol of enslaved Poland.

Then a few mazurkas. I'll play two polonaises: the "Military" and the "Heroic". If there's an encore and if I've got the energy, I'll play the "Revolutionary Etude". It's short and emotive. What do you think?'

The Poles were disapprovingly silent, everybody except for his sister who was thrilled by the idea.

The hotel management had a baby grand piano brought to the former Prime Minister's room. Paderewski practised with long-forgotten ardour and announced that he did not want to be disturbed. For the next ten days, the strains of romantic piano compositions echoed down the Palácio Hotel's first-floor hallway until late into the night. His sister was his only audience. She sat barely visible in the green velvet arm-chair in the corner, mostly dozing, tipsy, purring rather than snoring. Her face was white, her nose red; she resembled a sleeping clown.

The hall of the Grand Casino Estoril is an intimate space, exactly the kind of room in which Chopin liked to play. At the appointed hour on Thursday, 7 October 1940, there was not an empty seat in the hall. People who had not bought their tickets in time were allowed to attend the cultural highlight of the season in return for hefty donations to the Polish cause, but it was standing room only. They stood in their evening attire against the wall, trying not to block the view. The evening was not cool enough to justify so many fur stoles, and yet not warm enough to justify the presence of so many bared shoulders. No one could remember ever having seen such a fabulous display of jewellery, not even at the ball given the previous year in honour of the Duke of Windsor.

The lights dimmed. The audience settled down. They spent the first few seconds looking at the piano gleaming under the stage lights. A cry from the audience broke the silence:

'Wielki Polak! Wielki pianist! Wielki czlowiek!'

And then, as if he was slowly pushed out from the dark recesses of the stage, the artist appeared and stood in front of the audience. The applause was deafening. That he had not expected.

Ignacy Paderewski, once famous for his thrilling perform- ances and charisma, stood in the middle of the stage slightly stooped, blinking under the glare of the lights. Who knows how long it had been since he had had so many eyes fixed on him. Visibly thinner than when his tuxedo had been made for him, his bird-like neck peered out of the starched collar that was now too big for him. His face was drawn, his mous- tache snow-white. His brow, in a frame of long, almost trans- lucent hair, shone when he bowed. The applause thundered fortissimo.

They knew why they were giving him such a rapturous welcome. The man was a legend. Almost twenty years earlier he had played in front of twenty thousand people at New York's Madison Square Garden. He had not performed publicly since the death of his wife more than ten years ago. And so the audience felt privileged, especially as everybody was seized with that sad if momentary feeling that this might be his last concert, and if so it would make history.

In the expectant silence, the quality of the acoustics could be judged by the sound of the pianist adjusting his stool. He announced:

'Frédéric Chopin, Piano Sonata No. 2, opus 35, dedicated to my Fatherland.'

'The Funeral March' sounded more funereal than ever. From one bar to the next, it became increasingly clear that the pianist had seen better days. His playing was like the late Romantics – old-fashioned, a bit imprecise, somewhat disjointed. But how else could an old man play? The piano only enhanced this overall impression; it was a good English piano but in places it was out of tune by a fraction of a tone, as if it too had aged. There were shouts from the audience of *'Bravo! Bravo maestro!' 'Vive la Pologne!' 'Long Live Poland!'* The pianist had no choice but to stand up.

The ovations were unusually protracted, especially considering that this was already the second bow he had taken and the concert had barely begun. The old man did not mind; he bowed, and the audience kept applauding until he turned around and, waving, walked off the stage. He reappeared a few seconds later, walked over to the piano, sat down and said:

'In conclusion, I'd like to play for you something truly special: the "Revolutionary Etude".'

Encouraged by his rapturous reception, the old man's playing became more confident, more heartfelt, and the audience could feel it. Nobody was bothered by the unintended variations in tempo, or the barely noticeable fact that his right hand and left were not always quite in sync. Born out of indignation and revolt, in support of the Polish rebels against the Russian occupation, the piece conveyed its message without a single word being said. It was not a matter of *if*, but *when* Poland would again rise from the ashes as it had done so many times before.

He concluded the piece as abruptly and forcefully as he had begun it. When the old man lifted his hands from the keyboard and the last strains faded from the room, there was a moment of complete silence. Then, like a summer storm, the audience burst into renewed applause. They were on their feet, clapping and clapping and he was bowing and bowing. It looked as if it would never end but at last the clearly exhausted musician made his way off the stage. You could read his lips saying:

'*Merci. Merci.* Thank you! *Obrigado! Au revoir. Vive la Pologne libre!*'

*Au revoir?* Is that it? It's over? It really did look like the end, but except for the pianist, nobody moved. They were not yet ready for it to be over. They had had only about ten minutes of live performance and, counting the three interruptions of bowing and applause, it had been less than twenty minutes since the concert began. The tickets were extremely expensive and the programme had promised nine pieces. They had heard only two. The audience whispered and muttered in disbelief but stayed seated. Nobody knew what was happening.

Superintendent Cardoso had been hiding in the crowd from the very beginning. It was his job to pre-empt any undesirable situations or, if that proved impossible, to resolve them as painlessly as he could. An experienced professional, he was able to sense trouble before it occurred. The first time the pianist stepped off the stage, he noticed that he was waving, as if saying farewell to the audience. His suspicions were reinforced when he heard the musician announce the second part by saying 'and in conclusion'. Although he wasn't sure he had understood it properly, as soon as the 'Revolutionary Etude' finished he took the precautionary measure of slipping out of his hiding place and, using channels inaccessible to ordinary mortals, making his way backstage.

'Superintendent Cardoso from the Police for Foreigners,' he said, introducing himself to the Prime Minister's Polish helpers.

They shared his concern. They too thought that the old man believed he had performed his entire programme. Joining them, the Prime Minister soon confirmed their fears.

'I don't remember ever having been so happy and so tired. It was a unique experience but, thank God, that too is now behind us,' he said, looking drained.

Before the concert Cardoso had had all sorts of ideas about what might happen. He was afraid that somebody in the audience might shout out anti-Hitler and anti-Reich slogans, which would have been unfortunate and hard to control. He combed through the list of invitees to see if he could identify potential provocateurs. Through various channels he passed the word to foreign guests that the police would not tolerate any political demonstrations. He threatened deportation. But it was Paderewski himself he feared the most. The man could use the opportunity to make a political speech or, say, play the Polish national anthem and provoke an incident. Once little things like that leaked into the press they could become extremely unpleasant, especially for him because the entire circus was taking place within his territorial jurisdiction.

His fears had included all sorts of scenarios, but the last thing he had expected was that the old fart would cause him this sort of trouble. Now what?

The policeman took immediate action. First he tried persuading the pianist that it would be good if he could play just a little more. The exhausted Prime Minister paid him no heed; instead, with his sister on his arm, he retired to the cloakroom. That did not surprise Cardoso. His late mother-in-law had suffered from progressive dementia for years and he knew from experience that any attempt to explain to the elderly and forgetful what was happening was almost certainly useless. He knew that he could not count on the evening's star attraction.

The next burning issue was the audience. He issued orders asking for patience, without giving any explanation or making any promises. Then he turned to the Poles.

'Sirs, is there perhaps a pianist among you? Somebody who could continue the concert … ? No … ?'

As there was no answer, the policeman quickly issued another order:

'Find me the Bulgarian, that violinist from the hotel band. I saw him in the concert hall just now. He was standing by the wall on the left.'

The musician was located and brought to the agent of law and order. Cardoso briefly explained what was expected of him and finished by saying:

'I would be most grateful if you could accommodate us.'

The terrified Bulgarian merely said:

'I don't have my violin with me …'

52

If he had hoped that this would save him he was wrong. A fleet-footed young man was sent to the Palácio to fetch the instrument. While his collar, shirt cuffs and tie were hurriedly being adjusted, the musician stood there as rigid as a matador being readied to enter the bullring.

The young man appeared on the stage next to the piano, holding his violin. He was wearing a borrowed tuxedo whose sleeves were slightly too short. He bowed quickly, introduced himself with a long Slavic name, said he was a pupil of Mr Paderewski's, raised his violin to his shoulder and proceeded to play. The young man had done exactly what Cardoso had told him to do. As he was neither a Pole nor a pianist he could hardly have been a pupil of the demented maestro.

He started with Monti's *czárdás*; the audience was slightly confused but loved it. The Bulgarian played well but, as he had warned Cardoso, he was no soloist. Luckily, he soon had the backing of four string players from his band whom the superintendent had mobilized and sent onto the stage. And so, the five of them continued with the programme, giving it their best, though their playing was more suited for a ballroom than a concert of classical music. They finished their more than hour-long performance with a rousing rendition of some Balkan folk dance that had the whole audience stamping their feet to the music. The musicians, whose names were never recorded, were seen off with such applause that it almost matched the reception received by the Prime Minister.

To everybody's great surprise, the encore saw Mr Paderewski come out on stage again; in the meantime, somebody had persuaded him to play at least once more for the audience. He chose Chopin's 'Etude Tristesse', a piece he had played more often than any other in his life. But this time he played it so that the audience mourned not the sad fate of Poland, but the inevitability of old age and the genius whose last trace would soon forever disappear; nothing could stop or revert the process. It received the most honest and heart-warming applause of the evening. For his lifetime's work.

In the end, everybody was happy, both the performers and the audience, because they had all experienced something they would be able to tell their grandchildren about.

But it was not yet time for Cardoso to relax. While the concert was still in progress, he issued instructions that he wanted all the journalists present to go quietly to the office of the casino's managing director as soon as the concert was over.

'Gentlemen, we shall not talk this evening about freedom of the press but rather about elementary decency. Surely that's clear to everybody?' he said to the group of three reporters and two photographers.

It wasn't clear, but Cardoso ploughed ahead mournfully:

'You all saw it for yourselves ...'

Nobody said a word. No one in his right mind would start arguing with the police.

Using this brief pause to add weight to what he was about to say next, Cardoso tried to catch a glimpse of what the young woman journalist was writing in her notebook. She turned the page just in time to prevent him from seeing what she had jotted down. Otherwise, her notes would have convinced him that he had been right to take such unusual, repressive action. The young woman had compressed her impression of the concert into one short but clear line: *Great man. Noble idea. Poor performance.*

Choosing his words and adjusting his tone to an audience of journalists from the world of the arts and culture, Cardoso continued with his speech:

'You are educated people, civilized, you know better than I do that this is a great musician and admirable statesman from a friendly, Catholic country, which is currently facing enormous, unimaginable problems. It is amazing that a man of his age can manage, despite ill health, to find such inner strength. It is admirable. What we witnessed this evening is an interesting, even inspiring and instructive story, but personally I think the event risks being ridiculed and that is something we don't want, do we? It would be unkind to laugh at old age and make fun of our honoured guest,' the superintendent said to the assembled members of the press. They remained silent and so he continued:

'I hope you now understand my reasons for kindly asking you not to write about this. You listened to, saw and enjoyed the concert, but please, this time keep your impressions to yourself... Agreed?'

As they were leaving, he placed a friendly hand on the shoulder of an American correspondent, the only foreign reporter at the concert.

'Do you like Portugal?'

The American was surprised by the friendliness.

'It's all fine,' he replied honestly.

'Good… I'm glad to hear it. Just so you know, if, God forbid, you should ever have any trouble with the bureaucracy over your visa, I'm here to help.'

Late that evening, when he finally got to bed, Cardoso couldn't help speaking his mind.

'I think the old man is pretending. He's not like your late mother. There's intelligence in his eyes.'

'Never mind. That's all water under the bridge now,' his wife said.

As for the interview at the beginning of this story, the one Mr Paderewski gave to *Diário de Notícias*, it was never published. It failed to pass the censors.

STRICTLY CONFIDENTIAL

Surveillance and State Defence Police
Central Service
Lisbon
26 November 1940

## REPORT

I have the honour of informing you that your order of 5 October this year has been successfully implemented, to which I can personally attest, having been in the field and overseen the assignment. Mr Paderewski's stay in the country was without incident, and of no interest to the press.

Of frail but stable health, he left the territory of our country for New York on the evening of 25 November 1940, travelling on the *Excambion* passenger ship.

For the Well-being of the Nation!
Superintendent

(signature illegible)

# THE TALE OF THE
# DESERT FOX

*An homage to the pilot*

If it happened the way he later described it, that day Big Man fell asleep on the sand miles away from the nearest town. He felt alone, more isolated than a shipwrecked sailor on a raft in the middle of the ocean. He had not even noticed that he had dozed off. You can imagine his amazement, at sunset, when he was awakened by an odd litle voice. It said:

'If you please, would you catch me a puppy?'

Big Man opened one eye. To the boy he looked like a bear waking up from his winter sleep.

'What?' He didn't understand what the boy wanted.

'Please… Catch me a puppy…' the boy said.

Big Man was lying stretched out on the sand. He was two metres tall, a giant. He had a huge round head and rubbed his huge round eyes with his huge paws. At first he thought he was still dreaming. For a moment he even thought that he was dazed by the sun, but he immediately realized that this could not be the case. It was late autumn. He stood up. He took a second look at a most extraordinary small person, who stood there examining him with great seriousness.

'Please do that for me!' the strange little boy said.

The boy was ten years old and Big Man thought, 'This child looks like a miniature grown-up.' Now, he stared at this sudden apparition with his eyes fairly starting out of his head with astonishment. The boy did not mind. He knew that people could be envious of those who are different. When you are strange, you get used to surprising people from a young age and it stops bothering you. Anyway, Big Man was just as strange to him. With his big head and bulging eyes, he reminded the boy of a giant Mickey Mouse.

When at last he was able to speak, Big Man asked the boy:

'Excuse me, son, but what are you doing here?'

They were alone, the two of them, if you don't count the stray dogs and handful of seagulls prancing in the shallow water, leaving a sinuous trail behind them. It was not an odd question because adults usually care for children, especially when they come across someone who is alone and unprotected. And yet, as he would later write, this little man seemed neither to be straying uncertainly among the sands, nor to be fainting from fatigue or hunger or thirst or fear. Nothing about him gave any suggestion of a child lost on a deserted, secluded beach very far from any habitation; there was not even a dirt road nearby. The man asked the boy what he was doing there, and in answer the boy repeated, very slowly, as if he were speaking of a matter of great consequence:

'What am I doing? I'm asking you for a favour. For you to catch me a puppy.'

'What do you want with a puppy? Why don't you leave them alone and let them play?' Big Man seemed a bit grumpy.

But the child pressed on.

'I need it for company. So that I always have someone to play with. Come on, be kind enough to catch me one of those puppies, please… Please…'

'Why don't you go and catch one yourself?'

'Please. You're three times bigger than I am,' the boy replied.

Big Man set off to hunt one down even though it all seemed silly to him. He did not know that it was anything but easy to catch a wild puppy on a beach. However hard he tried to get close, the four-legged creatures outran him because Big Man, heavy and long-limbed as he was, sank into the sand, slipping as he climbed up and down the dunes. After several attempts and hilarious falls, the ungainly giant grabbed a grey, scrawny little puppy and brought it to the boy. The child looked at it carefully and said:

'No, that's not it! It should be a girl. They are smaller when they grow up and will take up less space. And they are sweeter.'

So Big Man went and caught another puppy, motley-coloured this time, but it too was rejected.

'It's cute but it is not a girl. I can see its willy.'

Having lost all patience, Big Man grabbed a little yellow girl puppy with pointed ears and a round stomach, wrapped it up in his jacket with only its little nose peering out, and brought it to the boy.

'Your puppy is here inside.'

He was very surprised to see a light break over the face of his young judge.

'That's exactly the one I wanted!' and he took it into his arms. 'Do you think it will need a lot to eat?'

'Why?'

'Because I'll have to share some of my lunch with it. At the hotel, they give me children's portions, you know.'

'She doesn't need a lot to eat. Look at how small she is,' said Big Man.

The strange boy leaned over the bundle.

'She's not really that small. She's got big ears… Look! She's fallen asleep…' He thought a bit and then said: 'We have to give her a name. Any ideas?'

'She reminds me of a desert fox. You know the small ones with the big ears? The Bedouins call them fennec foxes. You can call her Fennec,' suggested Big Man.

'Perfect. Her name will be Fennec. And what's your name?'

'Antoine. Tonio. And yours?'

'I'm Gavriel. Gaby. Thank you, Tonio.'

'Don't mention it. But take good care of Fennec. Promise?'

'Promise.'

And they headed for town, walking along the sea. The sand shifted under their feet.

'It's hard when you don't look like everybody else, isn't it?' said Big Man. It was both a question and a statement.

'Yes, it is,' agreed the boy. 'How do you know?'

'How? Look at how much taller I am than everybody else.'

'It's the suit,' the boy said, 'and the sideburns.'

'Do you know, in 1909 a Turkish astronomer saw a new asteroid through his telescope. He officially introduced his discovery at the International Astronomical Congress but nobody believed him. You know why? Because of how he was dressed. He was wearing wide trousers, like a skirt, a narrow sleeveless embroidered jacket and a strange cap, like an upside-down flowerpot, only red. People are suspicious of the unknown, they are like that. Later, a Turkish dictator made a law that his subjects, under pain of death, should change to European costume. So in 1920 the astronomer gave his demonstration all over again, dressed with impressive style and elegance. And this time everybody accepted his report.'

'Are you saying that I should start dressing differently too?'

'No, of course not. You wear what you want. You just have to know that it is not always easy.'

Their walk in the sand was taking time.

'Have you ever had a dog?' the boy asked.

'Yes, several, but a long time ago, when I was a boy. In the meantime, I had a fox as well, but only for a short while,' Big Man replied.

'Really? A real fox?'

'A real, honest to God fennec. A small desert fox. She weighed less than two kilos, like a fat chicken, if that much.'

'Where was that?'

'In the desert.'

'You were in the desert?' the boy asked surprised.

'Yep. For over a year I lived in Mauritania where the Sahara meets the ocean. I was a pilot.'

'You flew over the desert?'

'Yes. I carried the mail.'

'When was that?'

'A long time ago. When I was young.'

'How old were you when you were young?'

'Twenty-eight.'

'Did you like it there?'

'I never liked home as much as I did there. I had a little house, actually a wood cabin smaller than your room. I had a board and straw mattress to sleep on, but my bed was short so I added a crate to extend it.'

'The crate was for your feet or your head?' asked the boy.

'It served as my pillow, of course,' Big Man said, laughing. 'I made a table out of two barrels and a wooden door. That's where I did my writing. I had a jug of water, a tin wash-basin, a typewriter, a bookshelf, a wind-up gramophone and a deck of cards.'

'Were you all alone there?' asked the boy.

'There was a fortress nearby; Spanish soldiers slept there but they were afraid to go out so we didn't run into them often. All of it together was a thousand kilometres from the nearest bar. But I wasn't exactly alone in the camp. A human being can't be alone like a piece of wood. With me were four other Frenchmen, mechanics, and a dozen Moors. We weren't friends but we all worked for the same company… If you think of yourself as being alone because you haven't got any friends nearby, then yes, I was alone. But I was seldom lonely or sad.'

'Of course it's nicer when you've got somebody next to you. Even just a friend. Or a dog.'

'Pilot friends would sometimes visit. But there were days and nights when I was completely alone. I wasn't sad, except sometimes, at night. But I had more pets than ever before. We had a dog, a little monkey, his name was Kiki, a fat cat, twice the size of Fennec, and a hyena, she was completely tame but she stank...'

'You had a hyena?' the boy asked, intrigued.

'Yes. If I had taken her away with me she would probably still be alive. She was still a cub, and they live a long time.'

'How long?'

'Up to twenty years.'

'How old are you?'

'Forty.'

'And what happened to the fox?' the boy remembered to ask.

'I tried to tame her. I wanted to give her to my sister, but it didn't work out.'

'What does that mean exactly – to tame?'

'To establish ties... become friends... Something like that.'

'So you didn't establish ties with her?'

'Not really... She was hurt when I found her and while I was nursing her wounds she was with me in the cabin and ate whatever I gave her. But as soon as she was back on her feet she ran away because she didn't want to have anything to do with me. Not anything. It made no difference that I gave her food and water, that there was nothing in the desert; she ran away. She preferred to be free.'

After a brief silence the boy revealed his thoughts.

'It must be fantastic in the desert,' he pronounced.

'It is wonderful,' confirmed the pilot. 'And I have lived in South America as well. In Patagonia.'

'Patagonia? What were you doing there?'

'I flew my plane from Chile, over the Andes. Again, carrying the post.'

'Tell me about it,' the boy asked.

'It's a long story. I can't talk about it now. I'll tell you tomorrow. You're staying here at the Palácio? Have you got any obligations? How about having lunch together, what do you say, eh?'

'Okay.'

They continued walking in the sand along the shoreline.

'You know, I've heard that sometimes people appear here on this beach dressed in suits and toting suitcases.'

'Really?'

'Yes. They say that they're spies dropped off by German submarines.'

The boy didn't like stories about German spies, so he changed the subject.

'And do you know that the imperial boa swallows its prey whole? It doesn't chew it.'

'Really?'

'Really. I read it in a book called *True Stories from Nature*. When it swallows something big, the boa constrictor is not able to move and lies there like that for the six months it needs to digest it all.'

They walked on, listening to the lapping of the waves.

'Do you collect butterflies?' the boy asked out of the blue.

And that is how Big Man made the acquaintance of the strange boy. Later he even did a drawing of the boy with his blond, dishevelled hair, but he made his suit more extravagant and of a different colour, because he didn't like the one he was wearing too much. Anyway, his drawing, as he was the first to admit, was certainly very much less charming than its model.

# IVAN

'I'm terribly sorry, Sir, but at the moment the hotel has no vacancies, unless you have already booked a room,' the receptionist said apologetically, letting Ivan know that he had come in vain.

'Are you quite sure…? Couldn't you do something?' asked Ivan, two or three greenbacks peering out of the wallet he placed on the reception desk in support of his argument.

The moustachioed concierge immediately realized that the man either had not understood him or, which was more likely, did not believe him, and so he would have to explain it all over again and apologize. He was sorry about the money that was within reach of his fingers but there was no way that he could take it. Therefore, he said regretfully:

'As I said, Sir, I'm truly sorry, but if we have no vacancies, I'm afraid that's it…' From the tone of his voice and expression on his face you could tell how painful it was for him to say these words. 'Right now, I'm afraid we are one hundred per cent full.'

The man nodded in agreement, as if he completely understood, but showed no signs of leaving. The receptionist, well versed in the ways of capricious clients, was about to embark again on his explanation, if in different words, when the phone rang.

'Excuse me for just a moment, Sir,' he said, reaching for the receiver. 'Hotel Palácio, how may I help you…? Yes… Yes… Don't worry, Sir, no problem at all. Thank you for calling. Goodbye, Sir…'

As soon as he hung up, the receptionist turned back to the man, but this time his tone had completely changed.

'You are in luck, Sir,' he said, his white-gloved hand reaching for Ivan's passport. 'Somebody has just cancelled. We do have a waiting list, and the rules say… But since you're already here…'

'I can't thank you enough,' Ivan said, accepting the offer.

'Think nothing of it,' the receptionist replied, now looking honestly pleased. Inside the passport he discovered five twenty escudo notes; a hundred escudos was a lot of money, especially when it came out of the blue like that. Now convinced that he had before him a likeable, generous guest deserving of his full attention, he went on to explain:

'Believe me, if there hadn't been that cancellation I wouldn't have been able to do anything for you. What can I say when we couldn't even help out the Duke of Windsor?' he said in a hushed voice, as if this information was for the man's ears only.

'You don't say? There was no room even for the Duke of Windsor?' the surprised guest said even more quietly.

'Absolutely true,' the concierge replied, nodding. 'Not even for him… There was no way. The Duke was on a private, unannounced visit. We weren't given enough time… But that doesn't matter now, what matters is that there are just a few little bureaucratic formalities to complete and then you can go up to your room.'

Ivan filled out the requisite forms while his luggage was being taken to his room. As soon as that was done, he was offered a glass of port as a welcome. Ivan accepted, though he did not want to sit down. He wanted to walk around the hotel 'to see if everything people say about the Palácio is true,' as he told the receptionist.

Before giving him the tour, the receptionist introduced himself properly:

'I am Lino, your concierge. I've got twenty-two years of service and have been with this hotel since it opened, five years already.'

As they strolled through the hotel, the experienced concierge told Ivan some facts he considered pertinent. He dwelled on the hotel's short but exciting history, and in the process mentioned other interesting details: which colonies the different marbles in the floor intarsia came from, where the fine wood for the furniture was imported from, the period of the Chinese porcelain and the abandoned palace that the table for the tea room originally belonged to… Had he not had a moustache, his build and manners would have been reminiscent of a eunuch. He was so smooth and honey-tongued that if you did not know better you could be excused for thinking that he was trying to sell the hotel.

Ivan barely paid any attention to his talk. He took advantage of the tour to scout the escape methods that had been explained to him during his training in Rome. Admiring the gold embroidery on the ground-floor curtains, he looked to see where, if need be, he could quickly jump out. He asked them to open the windows looking out on the garden not so that he could inhale the scent of the flowers but to see what kind of locks they had and whether they were actually used. While strolling in the hotel garden and marvelling at the ripe oranges hanging from the trees, he managed to identify all the visible exits from the building and the courtyard, evacuation routes and where the surrounding security points could be penetrated. Standing in front of the door to his room he engaged the receptionist in conversation about nearby sites worth visiting and trains to Lisbon, all the while registering the layout of the floor, the corridors and the stairs. Before parting, the guest inquired about the quickest escape route in the event of a fire, but his host, dazed by so many questions and so much attention from the charming, striking foreigner, was not at all suspicious: he walked his guest along the corridor, down the auxiliary staircase to the side service entrance and back.

* * *

On his way here, Ivan had spent a few days in Rome undergoing a short intensive course with the Abwehr. They told him everything an intelligence agent needed to know about the hotel where he would be staying.

Although much talked about of late, the activities of international intelligence agencies were not in evidence at the Palácio. On the other hand, it was widely believed that a fair number of the hotel's guests and staff were agents and informants of the many intelligence and counter-intelligence services of the Allied and Axis powers and even of neutral countries; indeed not a small number were thought to be on the payroll of more than one employer. The Palácio was believed to be the centre of British espionage, though the manager was a national of the United States, a neutral country, while the Germans were believed to be operating from the nearby Hotel Atlântico, whose seaside location was more convenient for observing the movements of ships. The Atlântico was run by a German woman who often flew the flag of the Third Reich at the front of the building. All this information was to be taken with a grain of salt, of course, because in the world of espionage nothing was as it seemed and nobody could swear to knowing the whole truth. The local police probably knew more than anybody; they were everywhere, though given the category of the hotel and the calibre of its guests, they were discreet in their observations.

Ivan had been told that for security reasons the reservation would not be in his name, but that the matter would be resolved in due course. His job was to show his original valid passport with its valid visa and not to use forgeries unless otherwise instructed. Ivan completed the form for the police in sparse but truthful words – occupation: businessman; purpose of visit: transit/England.

Everything was going according to plan.

\* \* \*

Ivan's room was well placed, on the first floor. It had its own balcony, too high for anybody to reach from the courtyard without a tall ladder. Should the need arise, he could safely use the drainpipe or knot together some sheets to drop down to the ground.

By the time he had finished his cigarette Ivan had already identified two potential escape routes. One led from the ground floor, alongside the building, through the grove of evergreen trees, to a wall which he could easily jump over into the side street. That was the daytime exit, longer but better concealed. The other, shorter route took him through the middle of the courtyard and across a clearing. From there he would be visible and vulnerable from virtually all sides, so it would be better for nocturnal operations.

He did not know if the room had been aired or he had simply become used to the scent, but he no longer smelled the rosewater. Carefully he drew the curtains; the rule was that at night the curtains had to be closed so that nobody could see in. He did not disconnect the phone, there was no need; nothing that was said in the room would compromise anybody, and the mere fact that a guest had been fiddling with the phone could raise suspicion.

On the night table by the bed's headrest was a lamp: a strapping woman in bronze was holding up the light bulb. Beside it was a black telephone without a dial, and beside that a book. The gold lettering on the black leather cover said: BÍBLIA SAGRADA.

The small print on the thin, almost transparent paper of the Holy Bible smelled as if it was fresh off the press. Ivan began carefully leafing through it. It did not take him long to find what he was looking for. In the Gospel according to Matthew he quickly found a passage marked with a barely visible pencil line:

> Matthew 2:2: 'Where is he that is born king of the Jews? For we have seen his star in the east, and are come to worship him.'

He transcribed it into his notebook as best he could. In the next gospel, a bit further on, he found the second sign. He tried to read and understand it.

> Mark 8:18: 'Having eyes, see ye not? and having ears, hear ye not? and do ye not remember?'

He stopped there. He already knew what he needed to know. He just had to erase the faint pencil marks marring the Bible and place the seemingly untouched book back on the night table.

He was supposed to take a night-time stroll around the hotel and the courtyard, check the topography, see the layout of the streets, whether there was a shortcut, and which direction was the quickest and safest to take. That is what he was supposed to do, but he didn't. He did not have the energy. After a day spent in a noisy plane from Rome to Barcelona, and then on to Lisbon, fatigue hit him early. When he switched off the light and laid his head on the pillow he still had that noise roaring in his ears. Rain started drumming on the windowpane. Somewhere shutters were banging in the wind. The cotton sheets had been dried in the sun and smelled of fresh air; snuggling down, the pillows and covers carried the distant scent of lavender and camomile.

\* \* \*

The next morning, he took the train to Lisbon. He found Rossio Square easily. From there he located the public phones: four glass booths on the corner, opposite the theatre, where people were queuing up. This was the busiest phone booth in town, the last an experienced agent would think to phone from, but for Ivan, with his unknown face and the guidebook and map in his hand, it was an ideal spot in which he could go unnoticed. From here he was supposed to make his first contact with the service.

Standing in the confined space of the glass booth, Ivan called up from memory the biblical quotes: Matthew 2:2 and Mark 8:18.

'Lisbon 22-818,' he said to the operator.

A few seconds later a man's voice answered:

'Schmidt.'

'Good afternoon, Herr Schmidt, this is Thomas Schneider,' Ivan said introducing himself. 'I arrived in Lisbon recently and I have a few little things for you from your cousins in Stuttgart.'

Herr Schmidt was pleased to hear from Ivan and invited him to come to the embassy the very next day. He even offered to send an official car for him. But Ivan, in keeping with his instructions, politely declined.

'There's no need. I have the address and will find my way there. What time would suit you?'

'How about tomorrow afternoon, at three?'

'Agreed. Three o'clock, tomorrow, at the embassy,' Ivan repeated.

So far everything was still going according to plan. By introducing himself as Schneider, a friend of Schmidt's cousins, the Germans knew that it was Ivan calling and nobody else. They confirmed by inviting him to come to the embassy, though the invitation was not to be taken seriously. He absolutely was not to go near the German embassy. It was right across the way from the British embassy, and were he to go to either delegation, the Portuguese authorities would quickly hear about it from the informants swarming the area, and by the next day, through similar channels, so would London and Berlin.

Agents were trained to think that somebody was always listening in on whatever they spoke about on the phone. Everybody knew it – those doing the talking, those doing the listening and those doing the wiretapping. That was why telephone conversations were often used to dupe the enemy. Everybody knew that too. This was not to say, however, that it was impossible to conduct an expedient but safe phone conversation. It simply required that the persons on either end of the phone had agreed on a key for decoding the conversation. These skills were crucial to the work of an agent, and Ivan had been properly trained in Rome.

Believe it or not, the meeting was arranged during the conversation we were in a position to overhear. The method for working out the date was simple: you just had to subtract one day from the date mentioned. So, Friday meant Thursday, the eighteenth meant the seventeenth, and when they said tomorrow, as was the case here, it meant today. The only exception to the rule would be if, for some reason, he said 'come today'. That would mean 'come yesterday', which obviously meant that he should stop all activities and have no contact with the service until further notice. The code was equally simple when it came to the time: they would meet two hours earlier than the time arranged on the phone. Schmidt had said three o'clock, so they would be meeting at one o'clock in the afternoon.

They did not, however, discuss their meeting place on the phone. Ivan had been briefed on that back in Rome. He was shown the locations on the map and in photographs. Both places were in the centre of Lisbon and easy to find, even for somebody new to the city. He was told that if, for some reason, he had trouble finding them, he could simply ask, without worrying about drawing attention to himself because these were busy tourist venues and foreigners were a common sight. The first meeting place was under the magnificent Rua Augusta Arch, where it leads to the Terreiro do Paço. Should, for any reason, the rendezvous not take place, contact would be made half an hour later at the alternative location: the pavement in front of the second column on the left of the huge National Theatre colonnade. In both cases, he was to wait for a woman in a blue dress to make eye contact, after which he was simply to follow her. If no contact was made even then, he was to withdraw and call the same number the next day to schedule a new time.

In short, if they had understood each other well, the arrangement was: 'Today, at one in the afternoon, under the Arch at the

Terreiro do Paço. If not there, then at half past one in front of the Theatre.'

They had understood each other. A few minutes after Ivan had taken up his position under the arch, a girl, a real beauty, made unambiguous eye contact with him. That's to say, she winked at him. Following his instructions, he let her move away and then followed her. His eyes were fixed on the rise and fall of her round buttocks under her blue dress, though he made sure to maintain his distance so as not to get too close lest he be noticed, yet not too far away to lose sight of her. Suddenly, the girl surprised him: she stopped, looked over her shoulder at the heel of her shoe as if checking to see that it was intact, while making sure that he was still behind her. Seeing that he was there, she continued on her way. When the blue dress turned the corner into narrower streets where it was easier to lose her, Ivan lengthened his stride to reduce the distance between them. In the third cross-street, a black Opel was parked by the pavement. Looking as if she was going to walk past it, the girl suddenly jumped into the car, leaving the door open behind her. Ivan slipped in and closed the door.

Shortly afterwards, the car was making its way through the intricate labyrinth of streets that were so narrow it was almost impossible to follow it without being seen. Even if they were being followed, this manoeuvre would have shaken them off. Ivan and the girl in blue sat side by side. She was turned towards the window, her eyes downcast like a widow's, looking even more beautiful in the shadow of her hat than when he had seen her in the square. She gave him no chance to strike up a conversation because as soon as the car stopped to let a yellow tram pass by, she quickly opened the door, saying to Ivan: 'Please stay where you are,' and then stepped out, disappearing into the dark passageway between the buildings.

The tram passed by and the car went on its way, left and right, up and down hills until it finally came to a straight, smooth road. They drove westwards, along the riverbank, towards the ocean, and then along the beach, through the calming beauty of the subtropical landscape and the small coastal towns strung along the road. Approximately half an hour later, the driver suddenly addressed his passenger in German:

'Crouch down, please,' he said in the manner of somebody who brooks no objection. 'The facility we are going to is probably under surveillance. Do not sit up until I tell you to.'

With his cheek resting on the leather seat, Ivan could see that they had left the highway for a narrower road and were now driving through a wooded area. A few minutes later the car stopped, there was the creaking sound of a gate, and the car was moving again. The crunch of the wheels told him they were driving over gravel. A moment later, and he knew from the darkness and smell of petrol that they had entered a garage. The engine fell silent. The driver got out and opened the back door.

'You can step out, *mein Herr*.'

# IT'S JUST A WORD
# OF WARNING

High walls surrounded the inner courtyard where Ivan was standing, as if the villa were in the Maghreb. Waiting for Ivan at the garden table, by the pseudo-Moorish fountain, where they could be seen only from the house or the sky, was a slim man in his thirties, accompanied by a stunning young blonde woman. Two dachshunds were lying under the table and on the armchair a tame little monkey was wrestling with a pillow and doing somersaults.

'*Willkommen. Ich bin Ludwig von Karstoff,*' said his host, smiling warmly.

'Pleased to meet you, Sir. I'm Ivan.'

'There's no need to be so formal, Ivan. Feel free to call me Ludwig, or, if it's easier, Ludovico.' They both knew that the one's name was not Ludwig, or Ludovico or von Karstoff, and the other's was not Ivan. All Ivan knew about Ludovico was that he was his handler. And Ludwig knew only what was in Ivan's file, which was not much.

The German was a good-looking, smooth-talking man.

Although the 'von' may have been just a pretentious embellishment to his pseudonym, he was a person of aristocratic demeanour and good taste. The woman, whose clothes and manner also matched her surroundings, was introduced as 'Elizabeth Leichner, my secretary'. Ivan was introduced to the dogs as well: 'What an odd coincidence: that's Ivan I and that's Ivan II.' Only the monkey was left out of the introductions, which Ivan used as an excuse to start off the conversation.

'Does the monkey have a name?' he asked.

The question seemed to startle von Karstoff. There was something about it that he obviously did not like, though his reaction was cool and composed.

'Ivan, when we talk *I* ask the questions, not you. Trust me, the less you know about me, the better,' he said.

'When I said monkey, I was asking about *him*,' Ivan explained, scratching the little animal on the back.

The German apparently found this hilarious. He couldn't stop laughing. And laughter is therapeutic. When it subsided he was much more relaxed than before.

'Since you've been so amusing, I'll tell you, but if you tell anybody, I'll have you liquidated,' said his handler with a smile. 'His name is Benito.'

Now both of them laughed, even though the threat of being liquidated did not sound like a joke. The strange accent, which Ivan immediately recognized as some kind of Austrian dialect, along with the monkey's name and how Ludovico pronounced it, told him that his handler might be an Italian-Austrian.

'Do you speak Italian? My German is a bit rusty,' Ivan said.

'Drop the false modesty, Ivan, your German is excellent. It's all the same to me. We can speak in Italian if you prefer.'

The first few sentences in Italian confirmed his suspicions. The man was from Trieste. Ivan was pleased with his detective skills, but was not sure who might be interested in such information. He was even more pleased to see that the initial tension was fading. With the change of language came a change in von Karstoff's tone. He even started using the familiar form of speech with Ivan.

'I have very specific orders concerning you. They told me to take care of you and to help you as best I can. Now that I've met you, I think it will be a pleasure. I have to tell you that they have very ambitious plans and high hopes for you.'

The two young men, alike in age, manners, style and taste, liked each other instinctively. However, this did not stop them from getting down to serious work as soon as they sat down in von Karstoff's office. Going through every detail, topic by topic, Ludwig prepared his new colleague for his mission. He had to be taught certain skills and tricks essential to the operation, especially regarding communication.

'*Toter Briefkasten*, or dead drops, are secret, pre-arranged places where it is safe to leave and retrieve messages without the individuals involved ever meeting,' explained his handler. 'The location and alert signals are arranged in advance. For the time being, the water tank in your bathroom will serve for the dead drops, and a raised toilet seat will be the signal. It's all very simple: when you come into the room and notice the toilet seat raised, it means you've got mail in the toilet tank. So, take care not to leave the seat raised.'

He then gave Ivan a glass ampoule containing crystals.

'This is invisible ink, you dissolve a piece the size of a matchhead in half a glass of water. If you need to report something to us before or from London, use the invisible ink to write the message on the back of a private letter that you will send to one of two safe addresses in Lisbon.' He gave Ivan a piece of paper with two addresses written on it. 'Learn them by heart.'

That afternoon Ivan also learned how to shake off a tail, how to decode written messages, how to pick a lock without leaving a trace, how to check if his room had been searched or luggage opened.

When Elizabeth came by she found them smoking some foul-smelling cigarettes and laughing like boys as they thought up numbers for their phone conversations. But she kept her distance. She would come to bring them coffee, to relay a message to her boss, to bring wine glasses for them to dissolve the crystals because they had agreed that it was silly to do it with water, and to pass an iron over the paper to bring out the invisible text. Since she knew about the nature of their meeting and the secrets of their trade, she and Ludovico could be said to be close colleagues, but judging by their body language and exchange of small intimate gestures, Ivan realized that she was more than just his secretary.

Elizabeth was much more reserved with Ivan than her boyfriend was. They spoke, but formally, and not a word more than absolutely necessary; basically they talked only while she was training him on how to use a soundless camera to copy documents.

Ivan was equally formal with her: polite but reserved. He

knew that if by any chance he got too close to her, it would make his handler jealous, and these days less than that was enough to land a person in a concentration camp or be simply swallowed up by the dark.

Before leaving, Ivan was given a silent Leica camera to take with him, the last word in technology, along with four hundred pounds sterling in cash and a questionnaire that was supposed to provide the framework for his mission to Britain. As he read the mostly general questions – How are the British coping with the bombing? What is daily life like? What is the morale of the people on the island? Are there any shortages? What are prices like? – Ivan thought something wasn't right. Either the Germans were putting him to the test or they really had no idea of what was going on in Britain.

'Read and memorize the questions.'

The reason he planned to give the British border authorities for his visit to their island sounded credible. Both von Karstoff and Elizabeth thought there was no reason why the English would not believe him. He really did have talks scheduled, and he was carrying the papers to prove it. He would introduce himself as the official representative of an industrial cartel from a neutral country, interested in buying off a German merchant ship which was unable to sail out of the port of Trieste, due to the British naval blocade of the Adriatic. As for the viability of his alibi and finding travel tickets, there he could only count on his own resourcefulness and contacts, which should not be a problem, at least so Ivan claimed. The only issue was the relatively modest amount of money he was being given for almost two weeks in a country where he might have to bribe the authorities and grease the palms of collaborators. Ludwig thought about it for a moment and then handed him another four hundred pounds.

'For two weeks, this is a king's ransom,' Ludwig said, more in jest than in anger. 'For our part, that's all you'll get. Take nothing with you that could compromise you. If you get caught, don't count on us. Not even if there is an attempted exchange. Keep your head and may God be with you. If you are on the island when the invasion takes place, stay where you are and report as soon as you can to our nearest troop command; mention my name and you will be given instructions that you must follow.'

As they said their goodbyes in the garage, the slightly tipsy Ludovico again spoke to him like a friend, in Italian, which made him sound more amicable.

'Ivan, according to my information the Gestapo shows no mercy towards defectors and sooner or later all traitors get found out… Don't think this is a threat… It's just a word of warning.'

'There is something cold, something cruel about his eyes,' Elizabeth said to Ludovico, after Ivan lay down on the back seat of the black Opel.

★ ★ ★

After he had turned off the bed lamp on his second night at the Palácio, Ivan was suddenly seized with a feeling he had forgotten he could still experience. Sinking into the darkness as if it were liquid tar, a shudder ran through his body. It was not until he started shivering that he thought he might have been too sure of himself and for the first time he felt that he had accepted this adventure without giving it enough thought; that this could be a deadly game for him. For the first time, he wondered why he needed any of this. And these thoughts only increased the fear until it started to consume him. He turned onto his other side and adjusted his pillow.

'Oh, who gives a shit, anyway…' he said loud enough to hear himself, and went straight to sleep.

# MOVIE ACTOR

The elegantly dressed man in polished shoes stepped out of the even more elegant, even shinier Bavarian-made white sports car. The gravel crunched under his feet as he walked across the park. He was heading for the hotel when he noticed a little dog frolicking in the grass. He bent down, whistled, tapped his hand on his knee a few times and called out in some strange language:

'Here, doggy, doggy, come here…!'

Fennec, known to be an undiscriminating puppy who liked everybody, came running, lay down at his feet, turned on its back and, wagging its tail, waited to have its tummy scratched. Stroking its ears as if they were the finest of gloves, the man, minding his manners, turned to the boy to whom the puppy obviously belonged.

'Hello!' he said to the boy.

'Hello!' the boy replied politely.

'What's her name?'

'Fennec,' said the boy.

'Like the desert fox!' the man said, pleased. 'It looks like one, too!'

The boy observed the man and after a moment said:

'You've got a nice car. Except it doesn't have a roof.'

'It is not a nice car, young man, it's a BMW. And it does have a roof, only I took it off because it's sunny today. I put it on when it rains,' the man explained.

'Your suit is nice too… Are you a movie actor?' the boy asked.

'An actor?! Really!' the man laughed, but he was clearly pleased.

'What are you then?'

'It doesn't matter what or who I am. I'm Duško. And who are you?'

'I'm Gaby.'

'Pleased to meet you, Gaby,' said Duško, wanting to return the compliment. But he couldn't say anything nice about the boy's suit because he didn't really like it, so instead he said:

'You have nice hair. Like wheat… Anyway, how are you?'

'So-so…' Gaby didn't seem to be a particularly cheerful boy.

'Trouble?'

'Not really… I'm just not in an especially good mood. Nothing terrible. I'll get over it.'

'Shall I take you for an ice cream? That may improve your mood,' the man said.

'No, thank you. I have no appetite,' Gaby said very politely but quietly, because he wasn't sure if he was using the word appetite correctly.

'A big boy like you and you have no appetite?! How old are you?'

'I'm ten years and four months old. In two weeks, I will be ten years and five months old.'

'You're growing. You have to eat. When I was your age I ate everything in sight. My old man used to say about me and my brothers: "They eat anything, like little goats."'

The boy found that funny and he seemed to cheer up a little.

'And how old are you?'

'Me? I'm twenty-eight. And a half… Approximately. I turn twenty-nine next July…'

'And how many brothers have you got?'

'Two. How about you?'

'None yet.'

'Who are you with here?' Duško asked.

'Fennec,' replied the boy, pointing to the puppy.

The man thought the boy hadn't understood him.

'I don't mean here in the park, I mean in Portugal.'

'I just told you. Fennec.'

'No adults? You know, mum, dad, somebody like that?' Now it was the man asking the questions.

'No. Not counting Fennec, I'm here on my own.'

'There's nobody to take care of you?'

'Everybody takes care of me. I can't complain. The only time I'm alone is when I go to my room to sleep. Otherwise I've got all the company I want.

'I see… And where are your parents?'

'In France… They'll be coming very soon. I expect them any day…'

'And who exactly are all these people taking care of you until your parents come?'

'Mr Black, he comes when I'm having dinner and asks me how I'm doing. And Papagaio, he's my best friend. And Lourdes, his mother, she does the cooking. And Bruno, he drives me to school.' The boy was tired of all these questions. 'And who are you with here?'

'Me? Nobody.'

'So why does it surprise you that I'm on my own?'

'I'm not surprised anymore.' Duško wanted to change the subject. 'So, where are you from?'

'From Antwerp,' the boy replied. 'And you?'

'From Belgrade. And you go to school?'

'I've started at the French lycée.' The boy was proud of his school. 'Sixth grade.'

'Do you have any friends?'

'A few, but they live far away…'

'Hmmm… And you're not in a very good mood today, you say… Let's see what we can do about that… You don't drink beer yet, do you?'

'No.'

'Of course not. That's what I thought… You're still too young. And you're not into chicks?' Duško had his own style of communication.

'Excuse me?' The boy hadn't understood him.

'Nothing, nothing… Hmmm… Well then, I really don't know. Maybe you know how I can help you not be sad?' Duško said, trying to raise the boy's spirits.

'Why? Sometimes a person needs to be sad. Sadness, like happiness, is a part of life. Aren't you ever sad?' the boy wanted to know.

'Never. They say I'm too shallow to be sad,' the elegant man confessed.

They both laughed.

'Do you want to play with me?' Gaby asked.

'Me play?' Duško was surprised. 'I'm too old for that.'

'True,' the boy admitted. 'Grown-ups don't play.'

'They do play, but in a different way... You know what the problem is with us spending time together? We can't really spend time together unless we've become friends. And we haven't really.'

'Ah. Sorry,' Gaby said more or less automatically, but after giving it some thought, he added: 'When you say "become friends", that's like when you "connect", right?' The boy was looking for confirmation.

'Something like that.'

'You know, I don't exactly know what it means to become friends, to connect and all that...'

'Look, a person has a family. That's the luck of the draw, it is what it is. But when you find somebody you like and get along with, somebody you have fun with, well, then you "become friends". Later, when you say goodbye, you miss one another. Friends are like a family you've chosen yourself. It's especially nice to have friends if your family is far away, like yours and mine now. You understand?' That was the best explanation the elegant man could manage.

'I think I understand,' Gaby said. 'Like Papagaio and me. I think he and I have become friends... And Tonio has become my friend. And Bruno. But I don't know if that counts because they're grown-ups, and I won't be a grown-up until at least my bar mitzvah—'

'That's irrelevant,' Duško broke in. 'It doesn't matter how old your friends are if you get along well.'

'And is it hard to get along with people?'

'If you don't find fault with people and accept them as they are, it's easy to find friends. And when you've got friends, life is more joyful. Less complicated.'

'Is your life complicated?' That was already a difficult question.

'Yes and no. It depends.'

'What do you do in life?' The boy tried again to get an answer to his question.

'What kind of question is that?' Duško objected. 'Imagine if I questioned you about what they were teaching you in history and Latin class in school. You think that would be okay?'

'No. I don't have Latin in school. I've got geography, history, arithmetic and grammar.'

'That doesn't matter. What matters is that you stop asking me such tiresome questions. What do you care what I do?'

The boy either did not know what to say or did not want to answer.

'What do you say, let's become friends. Why not?' Duško finally suggested, and without waiting for a reply put his arm around the boy. 'Let's go down to the beach while the sun is still out. You can have an ice cream and I'll grab a beer. You can bring along the puppy… Fennec… Or would you like to go in my car? It's fucking good fun.'

'You just said a bad word,' the boy smiled.

'You mean "fucking"? Fucking isn't a bad word. Quite the opposite. It's a very good word, like life or fun. You'll see one day. Other words are bad. Poverty, war, death, those are bad words.'

# TRICYCLE

Until recently, the neglected four-storey house in Rua da Emenda no. 17, with its mildew and damp from the river, looked no different from the other buildings in the steep street. It was not until the passport section of the British embassy moved in that people started gathering in front of the door, the same way they did all over Lisbon, wherever there was the slightest chance of acquiring any sort of exit permit. A handful of British bureaucrats from the Foreign Ministry were there to handle the crowds of desperate people who gathered in front of the building every day. Judging by the number of travel documents they issued, their job was to approve and not reject applications for entry into Britain and its colonies. Lurking in the crowds of people were local and foreign opportunists. Some made money by tricking the refugees, others sold information to interested services, and others still did both, and who knew what else.

People thronged the building's corridors, except on the top floor. Visitors to the consular section did not go up there; there was nobody waiting in its hallways, nobody tugging at the sleeves of clerks. This was not to say that the boys working on the fourth floor had nothing to do, it was just that their work was different, it did not entail dealing with the public. These people worked for the Ministry of War, they were responsible for protecting British national security, in short, they were secret intelligence agents. The fact that MI6's Lisbon station was located on the fourth floor of no. 17 was known only to those whose work required them to know where the spies were. The Abwehr and PVDE, for instance.

The open file on the desk of Captain Jarvis of the intelligence service was waiting to be updated with notes for a meeting that was just about to take place. He did not personally know the prospective candidate. He would recognize him from the photograph and physical description in the file.

Hair combed back, parted on the right, receding hairline giving the face a heart-shaped look. Eyes green. Olive skin. Wide nostrils. Tip of nose bulbous. Ears small, well shaped. A mole on the left beneath his lips. Broad, open smile. White, straight teeth. Lips fleshy, sensual, somewhat flabby. Facial characteristics and high cheekbones, Slav-Mongolian. Shaven, scented, manicured hands. Athletic build, broad-shouldered. His walk can best be described as 'the exact opposite of a soldier's'. He dresses expensively but casually. His trouser legs always look slightly too long. Usually wears white, silk shirts and eye-catching ties. Speaks loudly. Gesticulates when he talks. His face is not unpleasant but cannot be considered handsome.

A knock at the door interrupted the captain's reading.

'Come in,' said Jarvis.

He recognized the heart-shaped face from the photograph.

'Good afternoon,' said the visitor, clearly unsure if he was in the right place.

'Please. Come in.'

He stepped into the room. His trouser legs were slightly too long, his tie colourful, his face Slav-Mongolian, with a mole on the left beneath his lips.

'Where can I find Miss Moneypenny?' the visitor said using the password.

Jarvis gave the corresponding response:

'I'm sorry, she's on maternity leave.'

They shook hands.

'I'm Jarvis.'

'Agent Scoot.'

'Let me tell you right away. You have a new codename: Tricycle.'

'Has somebody uncovered the old one?'

'Why do you say that?'

'Why else would they change my name out of the blue like that?'

'Because they thought that Tricycle suited you better.'

'Why?' The agent still wasn't convinced.

'Look, you haven't met the boys from Room 39 yet. They're a very witty bunch.'

'Yes, so?' the agent persisted.

'Well, how shall I put it? They heard that you like three-ways in bed,' Jarvis said deadpan.

The two of them burst into laughter. The ice had been broken.

'Now, the sooner we get down to work the better. What can I do for you, Tricycle?' said Jarvis.

'I was told that I could expect you to give me an entry visa and plane ticket,' he said with a broad, open smile.

'You were told correctly. But first I'd like to ask you a few questions. All right? So, how would you describe your mission in Britain?'

Tricycle was somewhat startled by the question. Suddenly he wasn't sure if he was in the right place.

'Please don't get me wrong, but I was told that somebody familiar with the case would help me out.'

'I am familiar with the case, don't worry, but all the same I would like to hear your version. It's common practice, just to avoid any misunderstanding...'

'All right. So, you want to know how I would describe my work in Britain?'

'Only in the briefest of terms, if it's not a problem,' Jarvis confirmed.

'In the briefest of terms? Well, let's say that the Abwehr recruited me to infiltrate high society in London, collect as much information as I could and give them the names of as many potential collaborators as possible in the event of an invasion.'

Jarvis listened attentively, nodding his head.

'Go on, please. I'm interested in how this was envisaged in operational terms.'

'With your colleagues, I agreed to do my own work in London and, before going back, they would tell me what I was later to tell the Germans... Nobody knows about this except for me, you and a few of your colleagues in the service. That's pretty much it.'

'I'm afraid that would be a rather simplified view of your assignment. You will not be given information, you will undergo training, intensive training. I hope that's not a problem?'

'As you wish...' Clearly, Tricycle was not easily upset.

'You've already met with the Abwehr?' was Jarvis's next question.

Tricycle nodded.

'And your impression?'

'My impression is that they lack sufficient troops for an invasion and serious intelligence agents in Britain. They heard that Churchill told the Americans that, in the event of an invasion, his government would retreat to Canada. In other words, they know you're scared. They are hoping that I will discover a fifth column in England that they could then count on after the occupation. Sort of like in Norway and France.'

'Do you think it exists?' Jarvis asked.

'What?'

'A fifth column.'

'It's all the same to me. It's as you call it.'

Jarvis continued with his questions.

'What's your motive for getting involved in what is a highly risky job? What do you expect from us in return?'

Jarvis's colleagues had asked Tricycle this question so many times before going to Portugal that he could not believe he would have to go through it all over again. But he would.

'Well, the Germans pay me a salary and expenses. To be fair, they are very generous. From you I don't expect money, at least not for the time being, but I do expect proper accommodation in London.'

'Would you like to explain what you mean by proper accommodation?'

'I usually stay at the Savoy in the Strand. I also need the necessary papers for making certain trade deals. Permits from your government. Do I need to go into details about the kind of deals I'm talking about? They're quite complicated and anyway you probably have it written down somewhere.'

'No need... So, your motive, you say, is only money.'

'It sounds ugly when you put it that way. Not the money so much as a comfortable life, and that has quite a lot to do with money, though not entirely. I prefer democracy over dictatorship, which helps make your side more appealing, but without the money I wouldn't risk my neck for anybody.'

'Is that all? Is there anything else you would like to tell me?' Jarvis wanted to wind up the meeting quickly now. Officially, Tricycle had simply come to submit his papers for a visa and that shouldn't take too long.

'There's a fat Czech staying at my hotel, he works at the

American embassy. I have the impression that he's in touch with the Krauts.'

'How do you know?'

'I don't have the time to tell you now, but you'd do well to check him out.'

'Anything else?'

'Nothing that comes to mind. The important thing is that nobody learns about this meeting. Especially not the Germans,' the agent added.

'As far as that's concerned, you can put your mind at rest. We try to keep everything we can from them. You can pick up your plane ticket at BOAC tomorrow. You have a seat booked for 20 December. Somebody from the service will meet you at the airport in Bristol and take you through passport control. You'll be working with excellent people… They'll take you where they think you should go and show you what they think you should pass on to the enemy. Some of it will be true, some of it far from that, but you won't know. Your assignment is to accept everything as fact and to pass it on as faithfully as possible.'

'So, is that about it?' Tricycle rose to his feet, holding out his hand.

'Yes, that's about it.' Captain Jarvis stood up, holding out his own.

'Lastly, it is my duty to tell you that if you get caught we won't be able to jump in and help. If they doubt your loyalty, you'll be tried and the punishment is usually death. At least that's how we do it. I'm sure the Germans have the same policy, except they don't waste time with phony trials. You know that if you get into trouble and get caught, either by them or by us, you're sure to be executed. So, whatever you do, you do at your own risk, and it's not a small one,' Jarvis said, walking him to the door. 'I hope you realize that.'

'No, *you* realize it,' Tricycle winked on his way out.

Alone again, Jarvis looked at the notes he had been taking during their talk, and now added:

I do not feel competent to judge Tricycle's honesty, although I did not notice anything inconsistent or illogical in what he said. His information that a certain minor clerk at the US embassy is working for the Abwehr will be checked immediately. I shall inform you of that in a separate report.

Tricycle's plan is to conclude a trade deal in Britain (a transaction concerning ships, the details of which are given on pages 14 to 17 of this case file). For that he needs permits from us. He maintains that such favours mean more to him than a salary and therefore does not expect us to pay him. He does not seem to be interested in politics. The motives he gives are credible, sound and consistent, especially with regard to money and a luxurious lifestyle, to which I would add my own personal impression that he is also driven by a desire for adventure and a taste for living dangerously.

Despite all this, one should not lose sight of the possibility that he has been planted as an agent to muddle things up. It is my impression that this is not to be ruled out, but even if true, that he is not aware of it.

# I'D LIKE TO BE A TRAVELLER

*An homage to the Captain of the Birds*

The boy in the strange hat and the little yellow dog were playing among the flowerbeds in the rose garden. Big Man came back from somewhere scowling. He looked as if he was silently arguing with himself. He was carrying a tattered notebook under his arm. He did not even notice the two of them until Fennec started running between his legs, barking. Big Man recognized the dog and was pleased to see her. He looked around, scanning the area.

'Here I am!' Gaby said, running over.

Big Man was suddenly extremely happy. He swiped the hat off the boy's head and plonked it on his own big pate. Then he took the dog into his arms.

'It just about covers your bald spot,' the boy laughed. 'I looked for you today. You weren't here all day.'

'I was in Lisbon, I went to see the exhibition on the Portuguese Empire. Have you been there yet?'

'I'm going with my school.'

'You mustn't miss it. It's marvellous. I'd go again except I don't think I'll be able to. It looks as if I'm going on a trip.'

'Really? Where?'

'To America. New York.'

The boy was used to everybody leaving the place sooner or later, but you could see that he was saddened by the news.

'Pity. We had just made friends… Why do you have to go so far away? Do you have work there?'

'Not really. But I can't stand it here anymore. I simply have to get out of Europe. It's become unbearable.'

The boy did not like the answer because it was not logical.

'You're exaggerating. What's so unbearable about it? This is a nice place.'

'It's a wonderful place. But right now it looks like a sacred, sad paradise. I have a sinking feeling when I look at the people around me. Not contempt, or irony, just a slight sinking feeling. Like being at the zoo and looking at the last surviving examples of a soon-to-be extinct animal. I watch them pretending that nothing unusual is happening. Gambling away enormous amounts of money just to feel alive. Like a puppet show, but a sad one.'

'You're leaving because of them?'

'Of course not. I'm leaving because of myself. I feel imprisoned by this unhealthy beauty, like a mosquito captured in amber…' Big Man seemed to be trying to convince himself.

'What if you don't like America?'

'I don't know how I will feel there, but I don't expect much. I just don't want to be a refugee anymore. Or an émigré. I want to be a traveller, that's all.'

'Have you got anybody over there? Somebody who could be your friend?' the boy asked.

'I do. A publisher.'

'Who is it?'

'A man who isn't exactly a real friend, but makes money with my books, and so he will take care of me,' Big Man explained. He was dispirited.

'It's no use being sad now. Why don't you come with us for a little walk? Fennec and I were just about to go and watch the sunset.'

They set off hoping to find solace somewhere. Slowly they walked along the shore, listening to the waves. Antoine began talking.

'Did you know that people occupy very little space on Earth? If the two billion inhabitants of the planet were to squeeze in together at some meeting, say, they could fit into a square that was fifty kilometres long and fifty kilometres wide. You understand? You could squeeze the whole of humankind onto a small Pacific island.'

'No, I didn't know that,' the boy confessed and then remembered something interesting himself. 'And did you know that the baobab is the biggest tree in the world and grows from a seed no bigger than a hazelnut?'

'First I've heard of it,' Big Man confessed.

'And did you know that the baobab lives for a thousand years?'

'I did hear something about that.'

Most of the time they walked in silence, barefoot, holding their shoes in their hands, while the yellow puppy gambolled around their legs. Behind them, the sky above the land had already turned dark. Ahead of them, the copper sun was slowly sinking into the sea. Big Man was almost delirious with inexplicable sadness. The boy kept on walking, his eyes on the sand.

'I love the sunset... You know... when somebody is sad he loves sunsets, when somebody is so sad...'

'And you are sad?' Big Man asked the boy with some surprise because the child looked happy and pleased.

'Not all the time... Only when I miss my parents. I haven't seen them for a long time.'

Again they fell silent.

'Do you think of them?' Big Man asked.

'Yes. I think of them when I say my prayers. But most of all I think of them at night, in bed. Until I fall asleep. They keep appearing in my dreams but I can't see their faces... I'm not even sure if I remember them anymore.'

Big Man suddenly felt tired. He sat down on the sand. The boy silently lay down next to him and looked up at the starry firmament.

'The stars are beautiful. And there are so many of them,' the boy observed.

The moon now appeared; it was not a full moon but enough to light their way back.

'Did you know that scientists have established that there are more stars in the sky than there are grains of sand on the whole of Earth?' he asked Big Man.

'Than on all beaches put together?'

'I'm telling you, than on the entire planet of Earth. Not just on the beaches but even if you counted all the grains of sand at the bottom of the sea and in the deserts.'

The boy said nothing but just looked at the stars. It was no use counting them.

'This place reminds me of the desert,' Big Man went on.

At the mention of the desert, the boy reverted to his favourite pastime: asking questions.

'Is the desert beautiful?'

'What makes the desert beautiful is that somewhere it hides a well.'

'Have you discovered a well?'

'I've flown over some. I've seen them from the air.'

'Where were you flying to?'

'I was carrying mail between Europe and Africa. The Moors called me Captain of the Birds.'

'And what did you do when you weren't flying?'

'I spent most of my time writing. I was going through a phase of scribomania.'

'Is scribomania some kind of disease?'

Big Man seemed unable to answer. Gaby did not insist. He proceeded to ask about something that interested him much more.

'Tell me something about the desert.'

'You know, there in the Sahara, the horizon is everything. A ship would sometimes appear where the sea is, and nomads' tents would sometimes appear where the desert is. I would often lie in the dunes, like you and me now, and watch the twinkling lights in the darkness… If you try hard and look patiently into the dark, you can see it here too. There it is… Look over there! See it?'

Silence.

'I see it,' said the boy after a minute.

They continued watching the stars.

'Will you come back here?'

'I don't know. I don't think so…'

'It's sad when you forget your friends,' Gaby said.

'That's not going to happen if we correspond with each other. Will you write to me?'

'What would I write to you about?'

'About all and sundry. What's happening to you. What you're thinking about. The people you meet. What you'd tell me if we met,' Big Man explained.

'I will write. But you have to write to me too.'

'I will. I intended to anyway.'

They listened to the silence again.

'You have a nice way of talking. Come on, tell me more about the desert, will you?'

'Over there, in the Sahara… everything is different. Even the silence is different. And it's never the same. There is a silence of peace, when the tribes are reconciled, when the evening once more brings its coolness, and it seems as if one had furled the sails and taken up moorings in a quiet harbour. There is a silence of the noon, when the sun suspends all thought and movement. There is a false silence when the north wind has dropped, and the appearance of insects, drawn away like pollen from their inner oasis, announces the eastern storm, carrier of sand. There is a silence of intrigue, when one knows that a distant tribe is brooding. There is a silence of mystery, when the Arabs join up in their intricate cabals. There is a tense silence when the messenger is slow to return. A sharp silence when, at night, you hold your breath to listen. A melancholic silence when you remember those you love…'

Big Man looked at the boy and saw that his chest was rising and falling, and his quiet breathing merged with the rhythmic pounding of the waves.

He picked the boy up in his arms and headed back to Estoril. The boy did not wake up. He was a skinny little thing and was easy to carry. The huge man thought that nothing on Earth could be more fragile. He did not have to worry about the pup. Fennec had already learned how to trot behind them.

When they reached the hotel, the doorman offered to take the boy and carry him up to his room.

'No, I'll carry him there. Just show me the way,' Big Man whispered, not wanting to wake his sleeping friend.

The boy's room was small, one of the smallest in the hotel. Big Man laid him down on the bed. He took off his shoes, but not his suit. It was too big for him anyway and did not constrain him. He covered the child.

'You take care of him,' he said to Fennec before walking out.

Down in the lobby, the doorman opened his soul.

'Poor child. He's got nobody. My colleagues and I keep an eye on him as best we can. When I'm on duty I look in on him when he's asleep. He often cries himself to sleep… All the money in the world isn't worth a thing when you're so unhappy… and he's a good child. Honestly, I've never seen anything like him. He makes his own bed, he doesn't leave it for the maids to do. He studies on his own; he doesn't need any reminding. He does everything himself… Poor boy.'

# DEUS EX MACHINA

I t is no coincidence that foreign correspondents jokingly call Portugal *Neutralia*. Every day planes take off from the grassy runway in Sintra for Bristol, Madrid, Barcelona, Rome, Marseille, Siam, Stuttgart, Berlin, Tangiers and, via the Azores and Bermuda, for New York. These days Lisbon airport is the only place in the world where you can fly on a regular passenger airliner to both England and Germany on the same day. The German Lufthansa JU52 passenger plane stands quietly on the airstrip, wing to wing, with the Dutch Royal Airlines DC-3 planes, the ones that last year took off to find refuge on English soil. Ever since, KLM's planes have been flying twice a week under the British flag, maintaining BOAC's pre-war Bristol–Lisbon–Bristol route.

One can fly direct to Berlin without any problem, as if there was no war on, whereas the flight to England, which is geographically closer, takes almost as long as flying to America – the plane follows an unusual westward or even south-west trajectory, and then turns north over the open sea, not far from the Azores, approaching its destination from the Irish coast. That allows it to avoid the peacetime route, which, while considerably shorter, runs almost entirely through corridors within range of German fighter planes and anti-aircraft artillery dotting the length of occupied France's Atlantic. Flying through wartime corridors takes longer, although some people consider such precautionary measures to be excessive because, in truth, nothing unpleasant has happened yet nor is any side expected to target a civilian aeroplane flying back on its regular route from a neutral country. Such a precedent would not be to anyone's advantage.

On the second day of 1941, a young man in an expensively tailored suit from Jermyn Street disembarked from a silver plane onto the airstrip in Sintra, and headed confidently for the terminal building. He did not stop until he reached passport control, where an official, dressed in a brass-buttoned dark blue suit with shiny epaulettes on the shoulders, took his passport, opened it, and spent an unusually long time flicking through it with his white, gloved fingers. The passport said:

Краљевина Југославија/*Royaume de Yougoslavie*

The official, a younger man who had obviously not had occasion to see such a passport before, punctiliously went through the passenger's details:

име/nom: Душан Попов/Dušan Popov
место рођења/lieu de naissance: Тител/Titel
датум рођења/date de naissance: 10-07-1912

пасош број/numéro de passeport: 4822
издат/delivré: Београд/Belgrade
дне/en: 16-11-1940

Then, even more carefully, he started checking the photograph against the person in front of him, and when he could find nothing amiss even there, he went back to examining the entry visa as if looking for a reason not to let the newcomer onto Portuguese soil.

From the very outset of the war, the state's official instructions were clear. In its circular letter number 14, the Ministry of Foreign Affairs stipulated that '*entry to the country not be permitted to foreigners of undetermined nationality, stateless persons, bearers of Nansen refugee passports issued by the League of Nations, primarily to Jews driven out of their countries, Czechoslovaks, Poles and Russians* (and, judging by his name and the strange alphabet used in the passport, the present person could be a Russian or something similar), *as well as to anyone at all suspected of being unable to return to his country*' – a criterion that, at this particular moment in history, could be more or less applied to anybody. Anyway, according to the rules, anybody not in possession of a valid entry permit was to be denied entry to the country whose uniform the passport officer was wearing. Caution dictated that the official take a strict approach.

'Your visa is not in order,' he finally said in poor French.

'Really?' the young man said in a tone making it sound that he could not care less whether he entered Portugal or not.

'This is a transit visa,' the official said, explaining the official stance he was taking. 'It is valid for only one entry, and you already used it last November. See, it's here on this stamp.'

'Oh? I'm truly sorry about that,' the young man said politely, if unconvincingly. He did not dignify the stamp by looking at it.

'So?' asked the conscientious official who was both irritated and disarmed by the traveller's evident lack of deference.

'So what now?' the traveller asked just as coldly. He looked utterly bored by the whole thing.

As soon as the question was asked, the traveller's problem became the problem of the border guard and he did not know how to resolve it. Indeed, what now? He had in front of him a man who had no permission to be here and should not be allowed into the country. On the other hand, he did not know what to do with him. He could not deport him because the plane returning to England the next day and all other planes were completely full for the foreseeable future. He could not arrest him, because it would incur an added expense for the state, and because such drastic measures were taken only *in extremis*, and it appeared that here the unwanted visitor was not some good-for-nothing, but a gentleman. After briefly giving the matter some thought, the border guard asked the traveller to wait and took himself off somewhere, taking the man's passport with him.

A few minutes later, he returned with a slightly older colleague in a similar uniform and, judging by the luxuriant moustache, rounded stomach, shiny buttons and braiding across his chest, of a higher rank. Using the same arguments in even shakier French if with more authority, the official introduced as *Senhor Chefe* now vainly tried to explain to the visitor that unfortunately he was not welcome on Portuguese territory.

'I'm terribly sorry but you do not have the proper permit to enter the country,' he finished by saying as rigidly as an Appeal Court judge issuing a verdict.

Neither this unpleasant fact nor the manner in which it had been presented to him seemed of any concern to the traveller. He still looked as if he could not understand why these two men had turned so serious.

'I don't understand it. How could the English let you onto the plane without a valid visa?' asked the older official. Shrugging his shoulders the traveller said:

'Believe me, I am wondering the same thing myself.'

So, we have got three people facing a seemingly insoluble problem: a traveller without a visa and two official figures without either the will or the grounds for letting him into the country, and without a way to send him back to where he came from, or anywhere else for that matter.

In ancient Greek drama, when the protagonists found themselves in such a hopeless situation, the dramatist usually had some kind of god lowered onto the stage by means of a crane, a *deus ex machina*, who then untangled the mess by heavenly decree. Life, as we know, can imitate art. This was the right time for the 'god from the machine' to descend onto the stage.

Out of the blue, a man who was considerably taller, bigger, more moustachioed, older and of higher rank than any of them approached the three preoccupied men. With a uniform setting off his strapping physique, collar and sleeve cuffs generously embroidered in gold, chest punctuated with big shiny buttons and a single large, obviously important medal, he overshadowed them in both appearance and manner. Completely ignoring the two uniformed men, he spoke to the young civilian in a language the others did not understand.

'Dušan, is it you?!'

'Mr Ambassador!' Duško's face lit up, not as if he had just recognized his saviour but rather like somebody sincerely happy to see a friend.

'Are you having a problem here, *mon ami*?' the ambassador asked, stressing *mon ami*, just so that the pen-pushers would realize they were close.

'Not particularly. The two of them are letting off some steam,' said Duško smiling.

'Is it a bother, *mon ami*?'

Duško simply nodded his head.

'We mustn't allow that,' said the diplomat turning to the two dumbstruck uniformed men. During the ensuing brief but dramatic pause, he stood there like a royal peacock facing two country roosters whose size, lustre and plumage were no match for his. Following the decrees of protocol, he turned to the one who seemed of higher rank, behaving as if the other man, who had been holding the disputed passport all this time, did not exist.

'*Bonjour, messieurs. Je suis l'ambassadeur extraordinaire et plénipotentiaire de la Royaume de Yougoslavie résident à Madrid, Monsieur Jovan Dutchich.* I am also accredited as the non-resident ambassador plenipotentiary in Lisbon.' He paused briefly to give them time to digest this information, and then resumed the pompous tone that went so well with his character and even more with his dress.

'Since this gentleman is a subject of the kingdom I represent here, a close friend and a great humanist,' he said, slowly and carefully placing his hand on his protégé's shoulder, 'please tell me in a few words what the problem is.'

'Your Excellency, the gentleman's visa... It's not...' the officer stammered, trying to show him some stamps in the passport. However, the diplomat seemed uninterested in such details.

'Gentlemen, I would like to ask you a big favour. I am exhausted from my trip and I don't think I'm capable right now of understanding what the problem is. May I perhaps suggest a way out of this situation? If I take responsibility, both personally and in my capacity as a minister of the kingdom I represent here, would you be kind enough, on behalf of Portugal, to grant Dr Popov hospitality, if only temporarily, and then submit to me a short report, briefly outlining the problem that has arisen and that I am certain can be easily resolved? You can do it right now, we'll wait in the sitting area. I will study your report and inform the President of the Council of Ministers, Dr Oliveira Salazar, first thing at tomorrow's meeting. If it transpires that my friend's presence in any way brings law and order in Portugal into question, I shall personally see to it that he leaves your country as soon as possible.'

This torrent of words was unnecessary. The little arrogance that the border guards still had left evaporated at the mere mention of writing an official report, however short, that the Prime Minister would personally read the very next day. The passport was quickly stamped, with a flurry of bows and apologies, and handed over to the diplomat. In appreciation, a twenty escudo bill was slipped into the pocket of the higher-rank officer.

'There you are, Dušan. A multi-entry-exit visa,' said Dučić, handing the passport to Popov. 'It's better this way. Just in case. You may need it again tomorrow. One never knows. These are dangerous times.'

'I can't thank you enough, Mr Dučić. I am at your service,' Popov said.

'Don't mention it. It is my duty to serve the interests of our country and our citizens. Now, let us go. Our chargé d'affaires should have a limousine waiting for me outside already. Where are you staying?'

'In Estoril. At the Palácio.'

'What a coincidence!' the ambassador laughed. 'So am I. Can we give you a lift?'

'I accept your kind offer,' Popov smiled back, 'and allow me to take this opportunity to say what a pleasure it is.'

They continued their casual conversation on their way out.

'And what brings *you* to these parts, young man?' the ambassador asked.

'Work,' he replied briefly.

'Aha!' the ambassador said, as if he had not noticed that the other man was bored by such conversations. 'I wonder how the English let you into the country when they aren't letting anybody in right now. What kind of work, if I may ask?'

'Legal work. A German merchant ship is trapped in the port of Trieste whilst British ships patrol the Adriatic. We're trying to buy it, as a neutral country. The prices are dirt cheap because the bureaucracy is terrible. But if we manage to pull it off, I'll be rich.'

'You, Dušan, were born rich.'

'Yes and no, Your Excellency. It's one thing to inherit, another to earn something on your own.'

'Perhaps so, you may be right. That's something that I'll never know.'

'And you, Mr Dučić? How are you?' Duško asked.

'How am I? Old, that's how.'

'If that's so, Ambassador, then you are holding up very well.'

'That's not my doing. It's hereditary. Some people age like cathedrals, others like slippers, but age is not easy for either… Work is becoming a problem in my old age. I find it harder and harder to do what I'm doing.'

'And what brings you here?' Popov asked with interest.

'What can I tell you, my friend? My job is to fight against history, and for those to whom it has always been cruel. Our unfortunate country is exhausted from all the historical events it has experienced. It lies between two warring sides and is trying to stay neutral. It is high time for us, at least this once, to get by without any bloodshed. We need every friend we can get. That's what I'm working on in both Madrid and here, to see what kind of support we can expect from Portugal and Spain.'

'And?'

'Waste of time, my friend. They're afraid of their own shadow, and of us.'

'That bad?'

'They are poorer than we are. Half their military is armed with German weapons and their aviation is obsolete. They're not used to war. As for Prime Minister Salazar, he's a clever, literate peasant, like our own Prime Minister Cvetković, only more personable and with better manners, which makes him that much slimier. He's tight-fisted and conservative, and he runs the country single-handed, like a shopkeeper runs his store. He knows everything and is asked about everything. He's shrewd and it's hard to get anything out of him. Even if it weren't, how could he help us anyway?'

'Who'd have thought it?' Popov said in surprise. 'How are things in Spain? What's Franco like?'

'That's a completely different story. He's cocky, the way short people can be. He's not that bright, either. He's much more sinister than Salazar but easier to work with. Either way, both are looking out only for themselves,' said the ambassador. And he would have gone on in this vein had a gleaming limousine flying the tricoloured flag not pulled up in front of them. The liveried chauffeur jumped out of the car, greeted the gentlemen in their language and opened the car door for them with a bow. As the chauffeur was putting away their luggage, the ambassador whispered to Popov:

'Be careful what you say, Duško. Every word uttered in front of him, or another witness, is bound to wind up in a report somewhere. You can be sure of it. So, be careful,' he said, sounding very serious.

They did not resume their conversation until the car was driving through a light forest of eucalyptus trees towards the sea.

'What were we talking about, Popov?' the ambassador asked.

'You were talking about your job, Your Excellency.'

'Oh yes. We were saying how time passes but things remain the same…' and there he stopped. Then he asked Popov:

'Young man, do you know the story of our Prince Miloš who sent Archpriest Mateja Nenadović to Istanbul on one of his first diplomatic missions?'

'No, I don't, Your Excellency.'

'That's unforgivable, Popov! All patriots have to know what is an instructive tale from our national history. Well, it wasn't that long ago, some one hundred odd years past, when Serbia was still a principality and the Serbs had a big worry, something important had to be asked of the High Porte and important issues negotiated with the Turks; so, the prince decided to send a delegation to Istanbul,' Dučić started slowly, portentously, the way epic tales were passed on from generation to generation in his native mountains. 'The prince summoned Archpriest Mateja Nenadović of Valjevo, because he had already been to Russia on state business, and had been to Austria to buy weapons and ammunition, and there was not a wiser nor more experienced "diplomat" to be found in Serbia. On the eve of his departure, he was summoned by the prince who wanted to give him his instructions, as we would say today, to brief him and tell him how he should behave and…' and here the ambassador stopped, as if his mind had drifted.

'And?' Popov asked.

'And says the prince to the archpriest: "Do you know how powerful they are?" And the archpriest replies: "I do, my Lord."

Then the prince says: "And do you know how weak we are?" And the archpriest again says: "I do, my Lord."' The prince then says: "Do you know that it will not be easy with the Turks?" And again the archpriest says: "I do, my Lord." Then the prince says: "Do you know what the vizier likes the most? … You don't?"' And here he pauses for dramatic effect before continuing: "The vizier, my dear archpriest, likes money and a good piece of ass the most… And in Serbia we don't have money!"'

They laughed, of course, even the chauffeur smiled under his moustache, but the ambassador quickly turned serious and went on in a conciliatory voice.

'And it's the same today, young man. They are still powerful, we are still weak and we still have no money. If that's how things are for me, I wonder how they are for Ambassador Andrić in Berlin?'

Outside it was the second day of January. A sunny day. If it is true that a good beginning makes for a good ending, then 1941 was off to a promising start.

# HIS EYES HAVE SOMETHING COLD AND CRUEL ABOUT THEM

M ost hospitality establishments can count on peak attendance on Fridays and Saturdays, especially at the start
of the month, when people still have most of their salaries
left. In that respect, the Grand Casino Estoril was an estab-
lishment unto itself. There was no way of even imagining how
many people would be in the casino on any given night, what
the atmosphere would be like, how high the stakes would
be, or whether they would play into the early hours of the
morning. Whether tomorrow was Tuesday or Sunday, or when
their salary was due was of no concern to its clientele. Last
Wednesday, for instance, the first day of the new year, when
people were expected to be recuperating from the revelry of
the previous night, the casino had a record number of guests,
whereas today, 3 January, a Friday, attendance was poor, the
stakes low, and time passed so slowly that both the customers
and the croupiers were twiddling their thumbs in boredom.
Outside it was drizzling.

Ivan would not have come if he had not had to. A message

waiting for him at the reception desk after lunch said that Mademoiselle Maristela had phoned, and that meant that he was to appear at the casino that very same evening, at the appointed time. It was not yet ten o'clock but he had already taken up a strategic position at the bar and was waiting. Punctuality was important to the Germans.

He did not know how he could have missed her when she came in, but there was Elizabeth, bare-shouldered, standing by the roulette table. She was just looking, not playing. With glass in hand, Ivan began meandering around the room, looking at what was happening at the first table, then the baccarat table, until finally he joined the onlookers at the roulette table, right opposite Elizabeth. He did nothing to attract attention, he was languid and casual, like everybody else there. For a second their eyes met, and then she decided to play. She placed a chip on red – so, the Lisbon road – and lost. She let a round go by and then placed a chip on the number 4 – tomorrow, 4 January. Again she lost. Finally she played number 9. In other words, nine in the morning. She lost again. Having lost three rounds, the blonde beauty withdrew, a faint look of disgust on her face.

Ivan had received the message: the car that would secretly take him to his meeting would be waiting for him at the usual place on the Lisbon road the next morning at nine.

★ ★ ★

At nine o'clock, plus the few minutes claimed by the circular route taken to the handler's house, Ivan stood face to face with

Ludovico von Karstoff and Fraulein Leichner, who back home would have been described as fair rather than blonde.

Everything was the same as before, only a bit different. The first time they had done the talking; now it was his turn. He was impatient to share his impressions of the trip, his 'baptism by fire' as von Karstoff put it, though the only fire had been from the German bombing. Over a cup of coffee, he talked at random, informally, about who he had met and been with, the way a close friend would do after returning from his distant travels. Ludwig was amiably cordial. Elizabeth had softened slightly, helped by the box of chocolates he had brought her, a small gesture but a great luxury in wartime.

'London is half-empty. They've sent the elderly and children away into the countryside. The only people who have remained in the city are those who have to, and many of them are sleeping in the tunnels of the underground. Quite a lot of buildings have been destroyed, but they clear away the rubble very quickly. Traffic is almost normal. There are ration cards for food, so they've dug up the lawns to plant potatoes and onions. There are no newspapers because there is no paper. People listen to the radio: a bit of light music, a bit of comedy...'

'Are people panicking?' Ludwig asked. You could see he was hoping for an affirmative answer.

'The only sign of nervousness I noticed was that they have taken down the signposts. To make it difficult for anybody who lands to find his way. Other than that, nothing. They behave as if nothing is happening. The English are a strange bunch, very strange. One morning the warning siren sounded but I didn't manage to get out of bed. Suddenly, a bomb fell close to the hotel and the whole room shook. I looked out the window and saw an overturned red bus in the street. I ran out to see what had happened… There was a large crater in the little park behind the hotel, water gushing out of the ruptured pipes, trees uprooted, the iron fence deformed as if it had been melted down, broken windows, open roofs, disfigured façades. I looked around; not a soul in sight, no fire brigade, just a few terrified quacking ducks. Suddenly, an old lady emerged from the cloud of dust. She was dressed up, replete with her hat, going out. I said: "Madam, the danger isn't over yet!" And she said: "I couldn't care less!" and off she went.'

'Be careful now not to let your imagination run away with you,' the German warned Ivan as they came to the official part of the visit. 'Don't tell us what you wished had happened, tell us how it really was. You're not a writer, so don't invent. Understand?'

The roles were now clear: von Karstoff stopped asking questions and listened, taking notes; his guest stopped chatting and concentrated on what he was saying; the German's secretary stopped smiling and pedantically transcribed every word, like in court, occasionally interrupting the men to remind them that it was time to take a break or to eat.

Von Karstoff knew how to ask questions without making it sound like an interrogation. Under his guiding hand, Ivan gave a chronological account of his stay, from the moment he stepped off the plane in Bristol to the moment his plane landed back in Lisbon.

He slowly recounted every event he could remember: how he travelled, what the customs officers asked him, what he saw through the train window, what he said at the reception desk, whom he met work-wise and whom he met privately. He described the places he had stayed at, where he had travelled, whom he had spoken to and about what, how he had spent Christmas Eve and Christmas Day, whom he had flirted with, who had confided in him, what he had noticed. Von Karstoff was interested in every little detail, he went over every event several times. He seemed to believe Ivan and yet he kept tripping him up with follow-up questions, as if trying to catch him in a lie.

When asked, Ivan spoke openly about his love life in London. He had had three security-irrelevant encounters with a young lady in need of financial help (the first night she visited him in his hotel room, and the other two times she brought along her 'sister'), and brief flings with two high society ladies: the daughter of a high-level naval officer who needed consolation after her fiancé was mobilized, and the obviously neglected wife of an often-absent aristocrat close to the party in power. Under different circumstances Ivan would not have talked about such things in front of Elizabeth.

'Were you ever told anything of interest on these occasions?' von Karstoff asked.

'No… Not that I remember… We did more gymnastics than talking…'

Von Karstoff gave a conspiratorial laugh. The cold expression on Elizabeth's face did not change.

That is how spies are debriefed; every story, every incident, anecdote and event has to be recounted several times and if a new detail should emerge in the process or one version diverge from another, they would have to stop and again go through the report with a fine-tooth comb until every piece of the story fell into place. That was the handler's skill: it was his job to question, to doubt. And it was the agent's job to remember.

Being with von Karstoff was like being in a cage with a tamed panther. An elegant, seductive creature, but one wrong move in his presence could cost you your life. Ivan could not for a minute relax. Anything illogical about his report, any inconsistency about the names, places, times, circumstances, the smallest detail, could automatically trigger suspicion, and if such suspicion were proved to be justified, then, however much the handler might like his agent, the Gestapo would step in, and, as Ivan knew even if he had not been warned, they could make a stone talk.

He had learned little from his contacts at the Yugoslav embassy. If they knew anything, which was unlikely, they were in no mood to tell him. The little he had managed to glean was rather general information about the British fleet, the distribution of its ships and naval forces. But von Karstoff was not particularly interested. He listened simply in order to check these facts against other reports he had received; once he had established that they all matched up, he moved on to another subject.

They had spent virtually the whole tiring day going over his stay in England, and for a moment Ivan thought that his debriefing was finished, but it turned out that this had only been round one. Ludwig had a new trick up his sleeve. This time he opted for an innovative method – to repeat the entire marathon exercise in another language.

'Our conversation in German has tired me out. Please, repeat it all for me again, but this time in Italian.'

And so, Ivan started again from the beginning.

'*Sono arrivato a Bristol ...*'

Again, he talked about the Savoy hotel, the blackout, the fact that there was hot water, that there were power outages, where the nearest bomb had fallen, what people were complaining about. He described the city traffic and the damage he had seen from the bombing. He was particularly careful when talking about his conversations at the club he had frequented, where he had met a variety of London gentlemen. Von Karstoff listened closely and was so assiduous in checking the facts that he even questioned the spelling.

'I've got a trick question for you. Is it spelled *Whitchurch* or *Whitechurch*?' he asked Ivan. 'You wrote *Whit* but here I've got *White*.'

'I wrote it correctly. *Whitchurch*. You can check it on the map. The airport is just south of Bristol.'

'You're right,' the German confirmed after checking. 'This Dutchman got it wrong. And he's been there any number of times. The dope.'

'Dope?'

'Forget it.' Ludovico was not inclined to take the subject any further, but he clearly liked his Dutch informant far less than he did Ivan. He embarked on a fresh topic. 'Tell us exactly what you heard about that new plane.'

'I've told you five times already. I heard nothing reliable. Just rumours, and even then, just fragments. Allegedly there is a new fighter plane, an upgraded version of the *Beaufighter*. It was a Norwegian diplomat who first alluded to it, but he didn't tell me where he got his information. Later, at the Naval and Military Club in St James's Square, the In & Out, I was talking one evening to an officer and a clerk from the War Ministry. We were already in our cups when they boasted that they had this new deadly plane. Even they didn't know much about it, but they thought that its mass production would mark a turning-point in the war,' said Ivan. 'My impression is that their expectations are too high. I didn't manage to learn where the plane was being made, I just heard that it was in underground tunnels and that the first few planes would be flying soon. You probably know more about it than I do.'

'I heard that they were being built somewhere in Scotland,' the sceptical German said. 'Maybe they don't even exist, maybe it's all propaganda. What do you think? Maybe it's to raise people's morale or to make us believe that they're more powerful than they actually are.'

'My friend, nothing would surprise me from such liars and cheats.' Coming out of Ivan's mouth, it sounded like a compliment.

'And finally, one last question: what's the London underground like?'

'What do you mean?'

'How do the English feel about sleeping down there? What are the living conditions there like? What about their personal hygiene? That's the sort of thing that interests me.'

Ivan had no answer.

'I'm sorry, but did you instruct me to go down into that hole? It wouldn't occur to me on my own ...'

The handler changed the subject.

'All that remains is for you to study this questionnaire.'

They spent the next half an hour in silence. Von Karstoff read the notes from the meeting and Ivan went through the nine single-spaced typed pages of the questionnaire, with its more than fifty questions and follow-up questions, mostly about things that Ivan had no clue about, especially the distribution of British land and air forces.

'Is that it?' he asked when he finished reading it. 'I don't suppose you want me to find out what Churchill has for dinner as well?'

Von Karstoff was in no mood for jokes this time.

'That's it. When do you plan to leave for London?' he asked seriously.

'It's hard to find a plane ticket, and I don't want to attract too much attention. I figure I'll make it there in two to three weeks at most.'

'Meanwhile, memorize the questions. Don't take any notes with you, but if you do have to write something down, make sure you're the only one who can understand what you wrote. Don't contact me unless it's absolutely necessary or you are specifically instructed to.'

They spoke no more about work. Ivan left just before midnight.

'His eyes have something cold and cruel about them,' Elizabeth said when he was gone.

'You said the same thing last time,' Ludovico observed.

'So what? So what if I did?' she snapped, walking back into the house.

# THE GENIE FROM
# THE LAMP

'A fine evening, isn't it?' Jarvis said to the man at the next urinal. Of course, an intelligence officer would never have acted so openly had he not first checked that all the booths were empty and that it was only the two of them in the men's toilet.

During his trips to Lisbon, agent Tricycle had not really been on assignment and so had been in touch with the service only sporadically, in short encounters with Jarvis, almost always sudden, at the Englishman's initiative, often in unusual places. Just like now, late at night, in the men's toilet of the Grand Casino Estoril. Actually, except for once or twice in the park, Jarvis almost always waylaid him in toilets, which for some reason Tricycle found extremely annoying.

'It's almost morning,' said Tricycle, still staring at the ceramic tiles on the wall in front of him. 'You're like the genie from the lamp. I take hold of my dick and you appear out of nowhere.'

'Anything new?' Jarvis asked, as if talking to the wall.

'It looks as if somebody is singing to them,' Tricycle said, speaking to the same wall.

'Name?'

'I don't have one. Some Dutchman. Somebody maybe from KLM.'

'Anything else?' Jarvis asked.

Tricycle did not answer right away. He was concentrating on peeing; most men found it hard to do so when being questioned. In the end, he was successful.

Inspired by Tricycle's tinkle, Jarvis started peeing himself, which did not stop him from asking:

'Did you learn anything about the Argentinian?'

'He's not Argentinian, he's Italian. A good guy. Plays an excellent hand of bridge. Doesn't seem to have much money. He's with a kid, she looks twenty but is actually sixteen. Twenty-six years younger than he is.'

'And would you happen to have any relevant information about him?' Jarvis knew when an informer was throwing dust in his eyes.

'Aha, so you're interested in the relevant? Why didn't you say so to begin with? He often phones Rome and Vichy. I don't know whom.' He stopped talking and peeing at the same time.

'That's all?'

'Considering how much you're paying me, even that is too much,' Tricycle said, tapping his last drops of pee into the urinal.

'You're right,' the Englishman said, buttoning up his trousers.

It was only when they were at the sink that their eyes met in the mirror.

'And you? Know anything I should know?'

'Not really,' the Englishman lied. Because there was a lot that he knew; for instance, that news had reached Berlin that agent Ivan was back in Lisbon, but he could not say that because then Tricycle would know that London was listening in on Berlin, from which he could deduce that the English had managed to decrypt the Germans' secret Enigma code. As much as he trusted Tricycle, which admittedly was not a lot, he could not share that kind of information with him.

As if washing his hands reminded him of something, Tricycle added:

'Oh yes… I wouldn't be surprised if they were planning to infect the underground with some contagious disease.'

'London's underground?'

'No, Moscow's,' Tricycle winked in the mirror, just to make sure that his colleague knew he was being ironic.

'Where did you hear that?'

'They're asking too many questions about hygiene down there.'

Jarvis changed the subject.

'The girl you've been going out with these last few evenings, she's just an expensive call girl. A professional. You realize that, I hope?'

'Ah, my friend. She's not a professional, she's way more than that. And you should see her girlfriend! Top class! Trust me,' Tricycle laughed as he walked out of the marble toilet, past its soft towels, to join his tipsy pals lost in the smoky haze of the casino.

That was all that was said during their brief meeting and all that entered the official note sent by diplomatic pouch to London.

# A STRANGE CHILD

In a remote corner of the card room, removed from sight and away from the bustle, two elegant men sat drinking their morning *café mélange*. The older, moustachioed man in his forties was sitting in a high-backed armchair perusing the *Diário de Lisboa*. It might lead you to believe that he was Portuguese, though he looked like a foreigner. And so he was. He was not actually reading the Portuguese newspaper, he was amusing himself by trying to guess what it said. And he was not bad at it. It helped that he was proficient in several languages. It also helped that the articles were about football, not metaphysics. It was an entertaining way to kill time.

The other man could not have been more than thirty-five. He was rather short, had a big nose and jet-black hair slicked back with brilliantine. He could have passed for a Portuguese had he not been wearing the uniform of an air force major of who knows which army. He was browsing through a days-old London *Times*; the foreign press arrived with a few days' delay. He seemed to have come upon something interesting, and informed his friend.

'Here it is.'

'What?'

'Associated Press reports: *Romania's ex-King Carol and his mistress flee to Portugal.*' He raised his eyes. 'Shall I read on?'

It took the civilian a few seconds to think about it before saying:

'Well… all right, go ahead.'

*'Bucharest, 5 March. Romania's ex-King Carol and his long-standing mistress, the redhead Elena, better known as Magda Lupescu, have fled Spain for Portugal, carrying Polish diplomatic papers. Until yesterday the controversial couple had been in Andalusia under police surveillance following Romania's extradition request on charges of having embezzled state funds and illegally appropriated state goods. Carol abdicated last September in favour of his son Michael, and together with his mistress he travelled across Europe until he reached Spain where he was detained by the authorities and unsuccessfully fought for permission to continue his journey, most probably to the United States. They took flight last Monday while on their daily drive in the countryside, when their powerful American motorcar raced away from their police escort near Seville and headed for the Portuguese border. The automobile was later found abandoned in the woods. The couple was alone in the car and it is believed that they carried no luggage except for their personal effects and the crown jewels. They left nothing of value behind other than a pack of dogs and three automobiles, including the said Buick abandoned in the woods. All their valuable luggage, including Madame Lupescu's furs and an invaluable collection of more than forty works of art, had been secretly transferred abroad a few days earlier. When the police searched their hotel rooms in Seville*

*they did not even find the manuscript of the memoirs the king is believed to be writing… Continued on the next page…* Wait until I find it. Here it is… Aha… *It has been learned in Lisbon that Carol has arrived in the country and is in a safe place, in a friend's villa in the coastal town of Estoril. It has also been learned that the king, an experienced rally driver, drove all the way from Seville himself.'*

The man with the moustache sighed.

'Does it all have to be like this?'

'What exactly do you mean?' the major asked, pretending not to understand.

'Well, this bit about the driving. And what on earth is this about the memoirs?'

'Well, we need something to keep it interesting.'

'If you say so. I guess you understand these things…' The man sighed as placidly as before. 'Anything else interesting there?'

'Most of the world news is from these parts. Things over there are heating up,' said the major, looking at the other man askance as if not knowing whether he should continue reading. He was encouraged by what he saw and so he read on.

'All right: *Belgrade, 5 March. AP. High-level diplomatic sources in the Yugoslav capital claim that Ion Antonescu, the Prime Minister of Romania, left for Vienna today for urgent consultations with Reichsmarschall Göring on the Soviet demand that Romania cede its Black Sea ports to Russia without delay. The same circles claim that the Russian demand is in the nature of an ultimatum and that…'*

'Wait. Stop there!' The man with the moustache did not want to listen to any more. 'How about in the future you spare me such news? You're upsetting me for no reason… I don't want to hear anything about that man.'

The officer simply nodded and the civilian returned to perusing the sports page. An awkward silence ensued, the kind that usually follows such emotional outbursts. Suddenly he felt he had been too hard on his friend, and so he pretended that he wanted to know what else was new, just to ease the tension.

'Is there anything that isn't to do with Antonescu?' he asked the man with the moustache.

'Yes.'

'What?'

'That all the neighbouring countries have mobilized their armies. Us, the Yugoslavs, the Bulgarians. And that tomorrow Prince Paul of Yugoslavia is going to Ribbentrop to see what he can do. That's more or less it…'

'I feel sorry for them. Especially for my dear Prince Paul. They're trying to avoid getting any blood on their sleeves… I don't know if anybody can avoid war now. This war is like a pandemic, don't you think? If war breaks out in the Balkans as well, then all that's missing is Spain and Portugal… Is it possible to pull through without devastation and bloodshed? I don't know if I'd be able to do it if I were in power…' the gentleman with the moustache said, contemplating his friend. And he would have continued had somebody or something cavorting around his trouser legs not stopped him in mid-sentence.

★ ★ ★

It was Sunday and there was no school. Until a little while ago, Gaby had been practising piano scales; they were so boring you would think they had been invented just to torture children. After that he had roamed aimlessly around the hotel with Fennec. He set off for the front door to keep Manuel company, as they had agreed the day before. Outside, it was as sunny as a summer's day.

The doorman was not at his post, not inside or outside the front door. Now what? Should he and Fennec wait for him? Or should they go to the kitchen? While he was making up his mind, Fennec made the decision for them. She ran off to the card room. Gaby went after her and found himself standing face to face with a gentleman he did not know.

This gentleman was wearing a light suit. His moustache was so pompous that it looked fake, and his slightly red nose was the kind often found on people who like to drink. True, Gaby was used to being looked at like a ghost, but this man eyed him differently. He appeared interested rather than surprised. The man gave him such a friendly look that the boy thought he must have recognized him from somewhere. The gentleman smiled at him, saying:

'*Sunteti roman?*'

'*S'il vous plait, monsieur?*' the boy said, not understanding.

'I am Carol,' the gentleman introduced himself.

'I am Gavriel; Gaby,' the boy replied politely.

'Pleased to meet you, Gaby.'

'Pleased to meet you too, Sir.'

'May I know where you're from?' the gentleman with the moustache asked.

'I'm from Belgium. And you, Sir?'

'I am from Romania.'

'We haven't met before?'

'No. We haven't met before.'

'May I ask you something, Mr Carol, without you getting offended?'

'Go right ahead.'

'Why are you talking to me when you've never seen me before?'

'From the way you dress I thought you might be Romanian, like me. I only asked you if you were Romanian.'

'My ancestors moved to Belgium from Romania,' said the boy.

'Interesting,' Mr Carol said, pleased. 'I'll tell you something. Now that you have removed your hat there is something about you that reminds me of my son when he was a child. He is fair like you. In any case, I'm sorry if I disturbed you.'

'You didn't disturb me. Are you new here?'

'I've just arrived,' Carol explained. 'And you?'

'I've been here since last spring,' replied the boy.

'How old are you?'

'Almost eleven.'

'Do you go to school?'

'Yes, of course.'

'Are you a good student?'

'Yes… More or less… And what work do you do?'

'It's complicated,' the gentleman replied. 'The closest to the truth is that I don't work.'

'I thought all grown-ups work, just as all children go to school.'

'I used to work. I don't work now because I'm retired,' Carol confessed. 'Sit down, let's talk properly. Ernest, order a juice for my new friend here.'

The boy sat down, but he kept on with his questions.

'Who would guess that you're a pensioner? You're not old … What did you do before you became a pensioner?'

'What did I do?' Here the gentleman stopped to think for a minute, as if that was a really difficult question. Finally, he said:

'I was a monarch.'

'A monarch? A king or an emperor?'

'A king. The King of Romania.'

'And now you're not the King of Romania anymore?'

'Now I'm not the king of anything anymore.'

'Does Romania have a king now?'

'It does. My son is the king now.'

'The son I look like?'

'The very one.'

'Nice! Are you sorry that you're not the king anymore?'

'No!' the king replied like a shot, then stopped to ponder whether he was being honest, and decided he was. 'No, I'm not the least sorry. But I'm not sorry that I was what I was, either.'

'How many subjects did you have?'

'According to the 1930 census, over eighteen million.'

'And now that you're not the king anymore, do you still have subjects?'

'Of course not,' the king laughed.

'Your son didn't let you keep even one?'

Now the king roared with laughter.

'I don't really have subjects. It hasn't occurred to anybody yet to leave me some subjects. Even I haven't thought of it,' Carol said laughing, as if he had discovered something very funny and new. But now that I think about it, I do have some left over. A very small number, mind you ... Let's see ...' and his lips moved as he started counting to himself, until he finally declared:

'I have exactly eleven subjects. They are people who have decided, in the name of our friendship, not to accept my abdication.'

'That's very nice of them. Why did they decide that?'

'Some out of friendship, some to take advantage of it, some out of pity and some because they had no choice. Isn't that right, Ernest? Have I forgotten anything?'

That startled the officer, who had been leafing through the papers, pretending not to be listening to their conversation. He took his time before answering.

'I don't think so, Your Majesty.'

The boy wanted to know more.

'Is it enough to have eleven subjects?'

'It depends on what you want to achieve. If you are actually a ruler, then whether they like it or not, people are born as your subjects. If you are an ex-king, as in my case, then, judging from today's conversation, the only subjects I have left are those who decide of their own free will to be so. They are fewer in number, but made of better stuff.'

'What does *free will* mean?'

'It means that you do what you want, are with whom you want and are where you want to be. What would you do if you could?'

'I wish I could be with my mother and father, regardless of where they are.'

'And where are your parents?'

'They are on their way… I am waiting for them here.' The boy did not want to dwell on the subject.

'You came on your own?'

'Yes. I came on my own, but I'm not alone. I've got friends. And I've got a dog.' He pointed to the little dog running around.

The boy suddenly felt sad and decided to ask the king for something.

'Your Majesty, I wish my mother and father could be here as quickly as possible… Being a king, could you help me somehow?'

The king, who seemed to have discovered a new talent as a teacher, proceeded to explain:

'Well, my young friend, one of the most important skills a good ruler must have is not to make promises he cannot keep. Imagine if I were to order my people to look for your parents. Where would they start? Where would they look for them? I don't think it's feasible right now because your parents are probably hiding from the war and hardly anybody knows where they are. If I were to send somebody out to look for them, Ernest for example, and if that somebody were to fail, whose fault would it be?'

Gaby replied without a second's hesitation:

'Yours.'

'That's right,' said the king. 'All we can expect of somebody is what that person can do at the given moment. But I promise to do everything in my power to help you as soon as the time is right.'

'I understand. And when do you think that might be?' Gaby wanted to know.

'The soonest is if there is a truce, the latest is when the war is over,' said the king.

'Is it hard being a king?'

'Well… it is not easy,' replied the king.

'I think it must be much easier to be a king than to be a doorman,' the boy declared.

'Yes and no. Kings, I cannot deny, have many privileges, but being a doorman has its advantages as well.'

'For example?'

'For example, when a doorman wants to marry, he can choose from lots of girls and fall in love with anyone he wants. But when I wanted to marry, I could only choose from among princesses. There were only three suitable girls at the time and I was simply unable to fall in love with any of them.'

'And what if a doorman wants to marry a princess?'

'You have a point there, I must admit.'

'I won't be able to fall in love with just any girl either. She'll have to be of my faith. And my parents will have to like her.'

'There you go. Like me.'

The king looked at his watch. As he started to stand up the fleet Ernest was on his feet ready to come to his assistance.

'I see that this conversation can go on and on, and we have things to do… What do you think about coming to see me tomorrow and giving me some information about your parents? Does that sound like a reasonable proposition?'

'Perfectly reasonable,' Gaby was glad that the king had not forgotten his promise.

'As of today, we won't be staying at the Palácio anymore. The major will pick you up in the car. He likes to drive. He was a rally racer in his youth. Isn't that so, Ernest?'

'At your service, Your Majesty,' said Ernest saluting. Urdăreanu took advantage of any opportunity to salute.

'Agreed?' the king asked his young friend.

'Agreed. We'll see each other tomorrow,' Gaby said as he was leaving.

'A nice boy,' said Carol to his most loyal subject. 'It's as if he's from another planet.'

Major Urdăreanu laughed. He always laughed at all of the king's jokes, even when they were not funny, but this one made him really laugh. His royal friend's sincere liking for this unusual boy surprised him, especially as the king had two sons of his own, one born out of wedlock and the other in marriage, but he took no interest in either of them.

# THE IRON CROWN

The two friends met one spring day on the terrace of a villa with a view of the pale sky and the steel grey ocean.

'Good afternoon, Your Majesty!' Gaby said bowing; apparently somebody had taught him in the interim how to address a king.

As usual, the boy was wearing his only black suit. With his starched, white shirt, and trying to make sure to follow protocol, he looked like a functionary from a funeral parlour who has come to express condolences and measure the deceased for his coffin. Except he was a child.

Fennec immediately inserted herself among the pedigree dogs. They sniffed under each other's tails until Fennec was fully integrated into the royal pack. Violating royal protocol, the king rose from his rattan throne, a masterpiece of workmanship, to shake the boy's hand.

'Welcome, my young friend, to our humble temporary home!' the king said, and introduced him to the redheaded lady in a light dress sitting next to him.

'Elena, this is my friend Gavriel. Gaby, this is Elena.'

'Pleased to meet you, young man. Carol often mentions you, and in a good way too,' said the lady.

'Really?' You could tell from the boy's expression that he was pleased.

'Only the best,' affirmed the lady.

Gaby did not know how to address her, so he asked very politely:

'Are you the queen?'

'No, I'm not,' she replied in a tone that immediately made it clear she did not like the question. Gaby was somewhat wrong-footed. He had apparently tripped up somehow. After a moment's silence Elena said:

'The first strawberries of the season have arrived. Let's go and see how they taste!' she said briskly, walking into the house as if she was going to serve the fruit herself.

'I missed an excellent opportunity to keep quiet,' the boy said.

Carol did not appear to be particularly upset.

'Don't worry. Just don't mention queens and everything will be all right.'

'I'm sorry, I didn't know it would upset her.'

'How could you know?'

'But what's the problem?'

'It's hard to explain even to an adult.'

Gaby shrugged his shoulders.

'All right, whatever you say. But I don't see what can be so complicated that I wouldn't be able to understand it.'

'You're right,' the king said, and since Elena was not coming back he had time to try to explain their complicated relationship to his young friend.

'The two of us are not, so to speak, quite married ... We have been living together for years and we love each other, but we haven't yet had it officially recorded ...'

'You can't get married?'

'We could now but that would not make Elena queen. Since I'm no longer king, she could, at best, be a princess. Anything you don't understand?'

'I think I understood everything. She is your mistress. Like Madame de Pompadour? Right?'

'Something like that,' laughed the king. 'Let's not talk about it anymore.'

'Certainly. Again, I'm sorry. I really don't want to bother you. I'd like to give this to you and then I can go straight home,' said the slightly embarrassed boy, holding out a scrap of paper with names written out in a child's handwriting.

'Goodness, son, you're not bothering me at all! Quite the opposite,' Carol said, putting on his reading glasses to check that everything was in order. 'I can't pronounce their names properly but it all looks legible. I'll put it all down in my official diary later.'

'I have their pictures as well ...' The boy pulled three photographs out of the inside pocket of his jacket. 'This is my mother, this is my father and this is the three of us.'

The first photo was of a roundish woman in a simple dark dress, wearing a scarf over her hair. The second was of a man in a dark suit and white shirt, with a strange hat and long sideburns hanging on either side of his face. The third was of the two adults and a boy, a small version of his father, dressed identically. That was probably Gaby a few years earlier.

The king looked at the pictures and asked a few questions, but out of decency he did not inquire any further and gave the photos back to Gaby. The boy received the pictures as reverently as if they were religious relics and slipped them back into his jacket pocket.

'Your Majesty, do you have any photographs of your family that I could see?'

One look from the king was enough for Ernest, who had been standing silently nearby, to bring over a thick photo album. Imprinted in gold on the leather binding were the initials CII and a royal crown. The king placed the album on the table so that the boy could look through it. The first photo was of a bearded older man. He had so many medals on his chest that at first Gaby thought it was some kind of armour.

'That is my great-uncle, Carol I,' said Carol II.

'He looks angry,' the boy observed.

'He's not angry. He was constantly worried. He wasn't a bad man, but before becoming king he was a Prussian officer and he took his job too seriously. His wife, the queen, used to tease him that he slept with the crown on his head,' the king laughed. 'This is her, Queen Elizabeth, with their daughter. The child died when she was three and so the king named his nephew, my father, the heir presumptive. The queen never recovered from the loss of their daughter. You can't imagine what a dear woman my great-aunt was. She was nice, she painted, she wrote poetry and, you won't believe it, she was a republican,' Carol said.

Turning the page, they came to a photo of three men: one a bearded older man, the other a young officer with a moustache and the third a golden-haired young boy, all three in the same kind of uniform, their swords hanging from their belts.

'This is the three of us, my great-uncle, my father when he was the crown prince and me. I was as old then as you are now,' Carol said, moving on to a picture of a bearded gentleman with a crown on his head, taken in profile, as if for a postage stamp. 'That's my late father when he was king. He had his photograph taken wearing a crown but he never ruled. My mother ruled. She was English, a grand-daughter of Queen Victoria, and she looked down on everybody.'

'Is there a picture of you wearing a crown?'

'No. I'm not particularly fond of crowns. I was so busy with more urgent matters that I never even got around to organizing a proper coronation.'

'Is this crown old?'

'Not that old for a crown. Why?'

'It doesn't look very shiny.'

'It's made of iron.'

The boy stopped to think for a moment.

'I thought crowns were made of gold ...' he confessed.

'Who says? The kings of colonial powers have gold crowns embedded with jewels, but I wound up being the king of a poor country. And I didn't do so badly either,' he laughed. 'In Africa, some kings have crowns made of plumes and leopard skin. Ours was forged from a cannon captured from the Turks during the liberation wars and is a symbol not of wealth but of courage.'

'I see. And I think that was very considerate of you. It wouldn't be logical to ask the people to get gold and jewels for a crown if they lacked more basic things.'

The next photograph was of a middle-aged woman with an oversized coronet.

'Is this your mother?'

'Yes, it is. She died two years ago.'

'She was pretty. Did the two of you get along well?'

'Not really. I told you, she liked to boss people around.'

Feeling that he may have touched upon an awkward subject the boy moved on to the next photograph. It was of a younger, slimmer Carol and a blond young man, both in hunting outfits.

'This is your son?'

'Yes. Michael when he was younger. The one you remind me of.'

The next picture was of father and son; the boy was already older and in naval uniform, standing on the deck of a big ship.

'That was in '38, when I took him to England to see relatives in London.'

'Where is he now?'

'Where a ruler should be. With his people.'

'How old is he?' the boy asked.

'He's grown up now. Nineteen.'

'Do you write to each other?'

'I haven't received a single letter so far.'

'Do you talk on the telephone?' The boy continued to pepper him with questions.

'He doesn't call. He's mad at me…'

'Why don't you call him? You're older and wiser,' the boy suggested.

'I did actually think of calling him,' the king admitted, 'but I'm afraid he won't speak to me.'

'All the same, he'll be happy to know that his father is thinking of him.'

The next photo was again of Carol and Michael when he was ten. Dressed in civilian clothes, they were sitting on a wall, laughing.

'He looks like you here. Do you miss him?' asked the boy.

'I miss him. Do you miss your parents?'

'All the time… But I can't write to them because I don't know where they are,' explained the boy.

'Wherever they are… at least you know that they love you,' the king said, awkwardly hugging the boy. Kings don't do a lot of hugging.

'Have you got enough money for your needs?' he asked.

'I've got something. I brought it in the bag.'

'Enough?'

'Yes.'

'In what currency?'

'I've got dollars, Swiss francs, pounds and some escudos. My father always says: "Don't put all your eggs in one basket"… And I've also got diamonds.'

'Excellent…' The king was satisfied with the boy's understanding of the subject. 'I trust that's enough for a period of time.'

'It is. Considering the current price of diamonds, which is pretty low, and all the cash, and considering the price of the hotel, I think I'm covered for the next 388, maybe 389 years,' the boy said.

'Oh, excellent!' said the king, pleased. 'I don't have to worry then.'

★

After dinner Carol told him a few more stories about his life. The best one was when he was king in 1930 and all on his own chose the national football team for the World Cup in Uruguay, paying for their trip, accommodation and equipment. He even had to wrangle with the players' employers to give them their jobs back when they returned home from the championship.

The king's stories were interesting but Gaby, who had got up early for school that day, started at one point to yawn. The king chuckled.

'Do you know that it's rude to yawn in a public place?'

'I do. I apologize,' the boy giggled. 'I couldn't help it.'

'Never mind. It's nice. I haven't seen anybody yawn for years,' the king laughed. 'You must be tired. Take yourself home and to bed. Do you want to go with Ernest and me to Lisbon the day after tomorrow and watch a game? Benfica are playing.'

★ ★ ★

When he returned to the hotel Gaby had just enough time to play a game of chess with Bruno. He and Fennec slept well that night in their hotel room by the sea. But the king, in his villa on the hill, did not sleep a wink.

'What's the matter with you this evening, my love?' asked Elena, who could not sleep from all his tossing and turning. 'Shall I ring the bell and have them bring you a soothing cup of camomile…?'

'Nothing's the matter, I'm just thinking about that child. His parents are probably dead and he probably knows it. You and I have only each other. True, I have two sons, but I never saw them grow up and have no relationship with either of them. And I'm forty-seven already.'

The tick-tocking of the wall clock punctuated the silence.

'He is such a good, dear, clever boy,' the king went on.

Carol thought that Elena would come to his aid, that she would understand before he said anything; he even hoped that she shared his secret wish, would tell him so now and make it easier for him to decide. But Elena said nothing. And the wall clock tick-tocked.

'What do you think, darling?' said Carol. 'Shall we take the child to America with us and take care of him as if he were ours? There's something special about him. He's like the son I never had…'

'And if his parents turn up?' she asked, the voice of reason.

'We'll inform the hotel where we'll be. If they turn up, all the better. If they don't, he can be ours, forever. What do you think?'

'It's for you to decide. But how can we adopt a child, my darling, if we're not married…? I don't know. Whatever you decide, you know I will always support you.'

# REVIEWED BY THE NATIONAL
# COMMISSION FOR CENSORSHIP

The news of the day is: *A Thrilling Football Duel*. Then comes the headline, splashed in bold letters across the whole page:

SPAIN BEATS PORTUGAL 5–1

and the subtitle:

Spanish team better. Portugal not up to expectations.

Apart from that, there is not a single other news item on the front page of today's 16 March 1941 edition of the weekly *Diário de Lisboa*. All four columns are devoted to the friendly game played in Bilbao the day before.

Another seven pages in the newspaper offer a wide choice of articles. The *Sports* column has news about cycling, boxing, basketball, volleyball, equestrianism; *City Life* carries announcements ranging from the birthdays of prominent ladies, dances, and evenings of fado to the viva voce of a doctoral dissertation on *The Idealization of Love in Portuguese Romanticism*. There is also a big paid advertisement announcing scheduling changes in Radio London's services in Portuguese, French and Spanish, and the results of the current week's lotto draw.

The third page is devoted to entertainment and culture. The theatre, revues, musicals, operettas and parodies. The most popular films are the Hollywood melodrama *I Take This Woman* with Hedy Lamarr and *Flash Gordon Conquers the Universe*.

The middle pages are full of news about the war, divided into two equal sections. It is clear from what is written and what is left unsaid, that the war is going badly for the Allies, both militarily and politically. Then there is a geopolitical analysis that draws no conclusions and is devoid of bias. Its dry style and absence of emotion makes it read more like a formal historical record than last week's war report.

In Portugal, it's business as usual: a forger arrested, a local feast held, a new shipping route to America opened, an attempted murder with an axe, the property of a bankrupt company auctioned off, numerous offspring left to mourn the death of an eighty-eight-year-old widower.

Next comes news from parts of the world that are not at war: in Seville an explosion at a fireworks shop, in the US a snowstorm, in Sweden military manoeuvres, in China riots at a football game. Then sales and advertisements for coffee, the lotto, clothes, watches, Bayer aspirin, cures for addiction to gambling and itching and ageing, raincoats, original Italian razors and brilliantine. There is room left only for one line: *This edition was reviewed by the Commission for Censorship.*

ANO 20.º       DOMINGO, 16 DE MARÇO DE 1941       N. 6577

# Diario de Lisbôa

Numero avulso: 40 CENTAVOS
Editor—JOÃO CHRYSOSTOMO DE SÁ
ADMINISTRAÇÃO—Rua da Rosa, 51, 1.º
Enderoço telegráfico: DISOA

**DIRECTOR**
**JOAQUIM MANSO**

Propriedade da RENASCENÇA GRAFICA
Redacção, composição e impressão
RUA LUZ SORIANO, 44
TELEFONES—2 3575, 2 6775 e 2 2272

## Um desafio de futebol emocionante
# A selecção de Espanha venceu a de Portugal por 5 a 1
### A équipe espanhola foi superior á portuguesa
### que jogou abaixo do que se esperava da sua formação

***

Shortly after ten in the evening, a gleaming limousine pulled up on the white sand in front of the entrance to the Grand Casino Estoril. Liveried young men ran up to help the guests step onto the red carpet where the manager welcomed them with a bow and led them inside.

'*Votre majesté…*'

They were taken along the outer rim of the room to their carefully chosen table; the plan had been to draw as little attention as possible. But, as soon as they appeared, the crowded room was buzzing, couples rose to their feet and bowed. Management's efforts had been in vain; secrets get out.

Carol and Elena were virtually the sole topic of conversation at the casino that evening.

'Twenty years ago, when they were living in Paris, she was one of my clients. I must say she's gained quite a bit of weight since then,' whispered Madame Rabinovitch, who until recently had owned a fashion boutique in Paris.

'An affair?' Miss Lang, an artist from London's West End, wondered aloud. 'Affairs subside once you've been to bed a few times. This, my dear, is love.'

'If they had wanted to reign, he and England's King Edward, they would have held onto their crowns, but they are too fond of the Germans. They use women just as an excuse,' said Dr Walbaum, a former member of the Austrian Medical Society.

'He's a major stockholder in Deutsche Bank and AEG. What problems can he have?' the doctor's son, a liberal economist, asked rhetorically.

'If he weren't taking her with him, the English would grant him a visa. But not like this. What do the English need an ousted monarch and his mistress for? No, they'll have to go across the ocean. Anything goes over there,' was all that a Spanish diplomat with an aristocratic name too long to pronounce had to say on the subject of Lupescu.

Elena was already at the roulette table. She took no risks; she was a cautious player. When she lost, she could not hide her disappointment; when she won, you could see she was happy, though discreetly so.

Carol did not feel like gambling that evening. He sat down at the dining table with its starched tablecloth, his bow tie tucked under his chin and a glass of red wine in his hand. Beside him was the ever-loyal Urdăreanu. People said that until recently the triumvirate he formed with Elena and the king had shaped the fate of Romania. They also said that he had acquired power not because of any particular skills or knowledge he possessed, but solely because he had the trust of Carol and Elena. Especially Elena. None of them were doing anything special at the moment. Urdăreanu concerned himself with Carol. Such were the circumstances that His Majesty could not be left alone or unprotected for even a second. So many people had read about the playboy king, about even the most intimate details of his life, that they felt they knew him personally and that is how they approached and spoke to him.

'Your Majesty. Brinkman, radio engineer from Toronto, Canada… My wife, my daughter… We're on our way home after three years in Rome,' said the tall plain man in the company of two equally plain women. 'We wish you the best for your return to freedom.'

'Your Majesty. Dr Carneiro,' a portly man from Porto presented himself. 'I keep your country, your people and you in my prayers.'

'Your Majesty. Superintendent Cardoso from the Surveillance and State Defence Police,' a small, bald man introduced himself. 'I'm a great admirer of yours. I have the good fortune and honour to have been placed in charge of your security while you are in Estoril.'

Time passed; different faces came and went as they introduced themselves to Carol: a loud Greek ship-owner, a haughty Italian diplomat, the pretentious widow of a Danish industrialist, a pacifist professor and a deserter from the German army... Carol was well versed in the secrets of being a monarch, which was not an easy job. He had been trained for it since childhood. Be pleasant to everyone who speaks to you but as soon as you feel like it, make it clear that the audience is drawing to a close. The only exception was if somebody started talking about politics. That young American journalist, for instance.

As soon as the young man had introduced himself as a freelance reporter, the king slightly recoiled, and when he asked him some stupid question about whether it was true that he had brought into exile with him the crown jewels, paintings by Rembrandt and Rubens, and even the crown itself, Urdăreanu stepped in and asked the inquisitive young man to step away. He also ignored the question about why an international warrant had been issued for him.

\* \* \*

No one was being let into the hotel anymore without a reservation.

'I'm sorry, really sorry. There's too big a crowd in there, believe me, you'd be crushed,' everybody was told.

But sometimes, like now, a mere smile sufficed.

'*Bienvenue, Monsieur Popoff*,' the doorman said with a welcoming smile to the unannounced guest.

Popov walked up to Carol's table with wide-open arms, as if expecting to be embraced. He cried out:

'*Votre Majesté!* Ernest!'

Unusually for a monarch, Carol responded in kind.

'Duško!? *Mon ami*. What brings you to this part of the world?'

'Work, Your Majesty,' Popov said with a shrug. 'This is my third time here in the past year. And I like the place. I'd love to stay but every few months I have to go back to London. I may even have to nip over to America …'

'It's better if I don't know what kind of work you're involved in, my dear Duško,' laughed the king, and then asked, 'How do you spend your time?'

'How? People here live like there's no tomorrow,' replied Duško. 'What about you? The last I heard, you were being held prisoner in Spain.'

'And we were, until not so long ago when we managed to get away. But let's drop that now. Pity we didn't run into each other sooner. We're leaving in a few days.'

'Where to, if I may ask?'

'We don't know ourselves. As far away from Europe as possible… You probably know what's been happening to me of late?' But as Popov just listened to him attentively, giving no indication what he knew, the king continued. 'Had our common friend Prince Paul not come to my aid, the rebels would have executed me… They fired at the train when I was crossing the border!'

'Dreadful! And?'

'And nothing. Listen, let's not dwell on such sorry matters now,' he said, adopting a more cheerful tone. 'You know, Duško, I often remember our time together in Belgrade. If this damn war ever ends, I'll go back there…'

'You'll always be welcome,' Popov promised.

'I remember it fondly. Truly,' the king said wistfully.

'And they remember you fondly too. You remember my two lady friends, with whom you had such nice conversations?' Popov asked.

The king nodded. 'How could I forget them?'

'Well, they, for instance, mention you often. They've got fond memories of you.'

The two men had to end their conversation when a plump lady with fiery red hair and a red lace dress walked over to them. Her oval, snow white face was like a porcelain plate, graced with bright green eyes, a small nose and full lips, highlighted by dark red lipstick. Clasped on the décolleté over her enormous breasts was the best piece of the evening's display of jewellery: a brooch with a huge Burmese ruby the colour of pigeon blood, encircled by a wreath of half-carat diamonds. And yet she was not exactly how we imagine a princess. Even with the brooch she looked like a piano teacher or the wife of a provincial doctor dressed up for a wedding. She stepped up to the table and, pleased with herself, showed Carol a purse full of chips.

'That's it for this evening,' Elena said; she had what she wanted and was now ready to take the money home.

The gentlemen, whom one could not fault for manners, rose to their feet.

'*Madame*,' Popov bowed, kissing her hand.

'My friend, Duško Popov,' Carol introduced him. 'We spent time together when I was in Belgrade visiting my sister, the queen.'

'Such a small world!' Elena pretended to be pleased.

But Carol's laugh was genuine as he patted his friend on the back. Although curious, Elena was unable to discover more because two stunningly beautiful girls walked up to them. They had probably come with Popov. One was a green-eyed platinum blonde and the other a grey-eyed brunette. They held out their empty hands.

'We lost everything…' they giggled, the blonde saying, 'Unlucky with dice, lucky in love.'

'This is…' Popov proudly introduced the two young women to his exalted company, pronouncing two unusual two-syllable nicknames that nobody either heard properly or remembered afterwards.

The young women curtsied, uttering some polite, heavily accented phrases in French. They tittered, every so often bursting into ringing laughter, as if they were in an operetta. Popov laughed too, putting his arms around them as if to console them for their losses at the roulette table.

The two sisters' beauty captivated everybody at the casino.

They impressed even the royal couple, though each differently. Elena whispered to Carol in Romanian, so that they wouldn't understand:

'Who on earth is this pimp?'

'He is a very dear friend of mine. Relax, you'll like him. Everybody likes him.'

One thing was for sure: Carol liked women. When he was younger, the talk in Bucharest was that he liked them a little too much. The rumours came from all sides: at court the servant girls would say 'it's useless to try to fend off the crown prince'; in high society boudoirs, he was described as a 'sexual giant'; in brothels and theatre dressing rooms the word was that 'the Crown Prince prefers devouring women to eating bread'. The court doctor had told his late father King Ferdinand that he thought the son was suffering from satyriasis, male hyper-sexuality. He prescribed bromide, which is given to soldiers to stop them from chasing women. Carol drank the bromide for months, but it was no use. If the stories are to be believed, he only changed his lifestyle when he found a mistress equal to his lust: Elena.

Carol may have liked women, but he did not really under-stand them. Elena would not have been so upset otherwise.

'Forgive me, Carol, but this is unseemly,' she whispered, again in Romanian.

'What is, darling?'

'Do you think we should be in the company of an adventurer and these two girls?'

If anybody knew Carol well it was Elena. He was a good man, he did truly love her, otherwise he would not twice have given up the crown for her, but he could easily get carried away, become insatiable, forget himself and misbehave in company. It never lasted for long. This would not be the first time that he had found some sort of rogue with whom to carouse. Elena had had more than enough opportunity these last ten years to develop a special tactic for sabotaging such situations.

'I'm a little tired, *mon amour*. Let's go to bed and get some sleep. We'll be travelling in a few days,' she whispered lovingly in his ear.

'You go ahead, *mon amour*,' said the king, full of under-standing.

Most often it was enough for Elena to plead a headache or heartburn for both of them to retire from a party. Actually, Carol liked it when she pretended to be frail; it made him feel protective. But this evening seemed to be one of those times when he was fixated and it was best to leave him be. Her best bet was to stop focusing on him and work on neutralizing the competition.

And so she struck up a casual conversation with the girls, asking them about themselves, where they came from and where they were going. They said they were from Budapest and had arrived in Estoril a few months earlier with their father, an officer, and their mother, a highly gifted, prematurely retired opera singer who had sacrificed her career for her family. There were three sisters. The brunette was a year older than the blonde, and the youngest was already married and waiting for them in America. You could see that they had been well brought up, taught to move in high circles, but this evening, probably because she had drunk too much champagne, the younger sister suddenly started babbling away. She boasted about how wealthy her parents had been; what they had once enjoyed and what they had lost in the political upheavals of the last few years. She talked about their aristocratic roots, her mother's voice and perfect pitch, something all three daughters had inherited, and about how she had won the Miss Hungary contest in 1936. She talked on and on, as liars often do, even though nobody was asking her any questions.

Elena saw through it right away. The parents had realized that their greatest capital was their good-looking daughters and they knew that no time was to be lost, not because of the war (Hungary was not at war, at least not yet) but because suitable husbands had to be found for the girls while they were still young and beautiful.

While Elena was chatting with the girls and buying time, the king suddenly remembered that he and Popov had drifted apart and that in the future they should spend more time together.

'You know what, Duško, the next time I go to Belgrade I won't stay at court with my sister. She won't mind; anyway she thinks I'm a bad influence on my nephews. I'll come incognito and stay in a hotel.'

'If you want to travel incognito, then you would do better to stay with a friend. I still have that apartment behind the theatre. You can always stay with me.'

'Thank you. If you don't have a room for me I can always sleep on the sofa,' the king laughed.

'I don't think you'll have to sleep on the sofa, but who knows?' Popov smiled.

It amused Popov that when men of a certain age realized they were no longer young they wanted to prove to themselves, whatever the cost, that if not exactly in the flush of youth neither were they senile. At least not yet.

The king laughed and laughed, not even knowing what he found so amusing; then suddenly, well into his cups, he said out of the blue:

'Let's all go to our place!'

Had anybody else made a proposal like that, it would have been something to consider, and nothing more. However, when it was a king making the suggestion, one word was enough for everybody to jump up and get going.

Urdăreanu was quick to act. He ordered a car. Everybody was happy with the idea, except for the hostess. She gave Carol a sad, pleading look that said: 'Why are you doing this to me?', hoping that he would take pity on her. He did not notice when she sighed:

'But I'm exhausted.'

It was useless. Nobody was paying any attention to her. She knew that the more she carped and nagged, the more she would be ignored and treated like a servant instead of a wife. She had to appear level-headed and calm.

* * *

Above them was the starry sky, around them a wooded glade that on one side opened out to the sea, before them a villa with a huge tiled roof. The chauffeur opened the car door. The king stepped out first, followed by Elena who took his arm;

then Popov, a jacket over his shoulders, with the two pretty girls, one on each arm. All that was missing was a bottle of brandy. Behind was Urdăreanu, tanned, in a white suit, like an elegant gypsy musician. All that was missing was a fiddle. The moon, which was full only two days ago, had started to wane. Whether because of the cold moonlight or the silence broken only by the distant echo of the sea, everybody suddenly went quiet, as if they were hiding from some unseen presence. No lights were on in the house; it looked deserted.

'Where are the staff?' a nervous Elena asked Carol.

'They were told we did not want to be disturbed,' came the answer not from Carol but from Urdăreanu.

They entered the house in a different formation. Carol was still in front, but now he was locked arm in arm with Duško, his special guest; behind them was Elena, walking between the two girls. Only now could you see that she was old enough to be their mother. As soon as she stepped on her own turf, her walk became more assured, as if she wanted the heels of her shoes to ring on the marble floor.

The king politely invited them to sit down. He placed Popov in an armchair next to his own, and the three women across the way. Urdăreanu was running in all directions; on rare occasions like this, when the servants were not around, there was nobody else to serve the drinks.

'Tell me, how's London? I haven't been since '38,' Carol asked, placing the needle on the gramophone record.

'How's London? How it's got to be. You can always find entertainment if you look for it.' Their conversation picked up where they had left off at the casino – with women.

With a prohibition-age jazz standard playing in the background, the two men seemed to find everything funny. The women could not hear them because of the music, and the court minister pouring their drinks did not inhibit them. He was serving champagne. The very best.

One of the girls seemed to have already succumbed to the alcohol; as soon as she sat down she dozed off. The blonde, younger sister was not sleepy. Used to being the centre of attention, she was now bored. Unable to sit still, she started walking around the room. She strolled in the half-light, studying the wall panels of blue ceramic tiles. On the one in front of her, a horseman wearing a tricorn hat, his sword drawn, was riding through an unusual tropical landscape, the work of an artist who knew about exotic places only from stories. The girl did not mind the dilettantism of the picture. What she minded was that the horseman was looking straight at her.

Two pairs of eyes on the other panel were trained on her as well – two Jesuits staring fixedly at her rather than at the river in front of them where a white man, also a priest, was standing waist-deep in the water, baptizing two natives. That was when she had an idea:

'Does this place have a swimming pool?'

No reply. So the blonde girl crept out into the courtyard. She would have gone unnoticed had there not been the sound of a big splash a few minutes later.

The people in the sitting room looked at each other and saw who was missing. Everybody leapt to their feet, even the sister who had been startled awake. Everybody except Carol. He remained seated. He had no intention of moving; instead he grabbed Popov by the arm and pulled him back into his chair.

'Let them go. They'll solve it on their own.'

Nobody tried to stop the three who ran outside. First you could hear them calling out in several languages, then another splash.

'That's Ernest,' the king said, turning up the volume on the gramophone.

He was right. Urdăreanu had jumped into the cold water. He couldn't let the young girl drown; it would be all over the press the next day.

The girl and her rescuer were in the pool. She was splashing around, grabbing hold of him one minute, pushing him away the next. Standing at the edge of the pool was the brunette in her evening gown, holding out her hands and calling to her sister: 'Zsa, Zsa! Zsa, Zsa! Sári!' Ernest somehow managed to get the girl to the side of the pool and her sister tried to pull her out, but it was no use, even with Ernest's help. Elena, who had been giving advice from the sidelines, realized that the matter would never be resolved unless she took over. The important thing was to prioritize and then put out each fire one by one. She went to the pool, leaned over the edge, her bottom up and head down, and with both hands grabbed the drowning girl by her arms and pulled her out of the pool, like an Eskimo pulling a seal onto the ice with a hook. Elena was small but she was strong.

Urdăreanu came out of the water but before he even managed to take off his waterlogged shoes Elena was marching back into the sitting room to give Carol and that Yugoslav crook an earful.

This was the last straw! It was high time to break up this band of debauched bingers. Somebody could get killed. Anyway, this wasn't the sort of thing a decent house should have to put up with. Why aren't we in bed? It's almost daybreak.

But she said none of this. She stood next to the king, her hands on her hips, but he looked at her, smiled and before she could embark on her tirade he turned back to Popov and said:

'Go on, Duško.'

If that's how it was, if he wasn't prepared to listen, then she had better bite her tongue and keep quiet. If she started shouting, she risked Carol sending her away, as he once did at the beginning of their relationship, before she knew how far she could push him. That time, Carol had kissed her with a smile and ordered the staff to take her off to bed and, when she protested, he offered to get her a hotel room until she calmed down and got some sleep. Now, with much more experience, she knew how to contain her anger. Suppressing her emotions and making her voice as sweet as possible, she spoke with feigned concern.

'Carol, I think it might not be a bad idea to call the servants to help the poor girl… She'll freeze like this.'

'Leave her be…' said the king.

For a few seconds Elena still held out hope that he would have a change of heart and that she would wake up from this nightmare but when she saw that it was useless, reluctantly she went back outside, looking dishevelled and disgruntled.

She encountered Ernest as he was carrying the soaking wet girl back into the house. Nobody would have held it against her had Elena retired to her bedroom at that moment but, being the kind of woman she was, she could not desert the battlefield. Who knew what turn this could still take unless there was somebody sensible there to keep an eye on things?

'Well, Elena, my girl, you've come far!' she muttered as she walked over to help them.

Meanwhile, the king and Popov were still listening to music in the sitting room.

'Just listen to this, Duško,' said the king, putting on another record. A woman's nasal voice started singing a Romanian folk song.

He raised his head only to find himself looking not at Popov but at a girl. A naked girl. We will never know how she managed to slip away from the other two, but there was the blonde, standing between the two men, facing Carol with her back to Popov.

'I took a dip in the pool,' she announced as if revealing a big secret.

Who knows what kind of reaction her inebriated brain expected, but she was clearly disappointed by the king's. His eyes at half-mast, he continued to listen to the crackling music on the record player as if she were not there.

'I'm wet,' the naked girl said. And indeed she was wet, her skin goosepimply, her nipples pert, a hand awkwardly placed over her Venus mound.

The king deigned to cast her a brief look, raising his finger to his lips for her not to talk, while to Popov he said:

'This is a song from Banat, not far from where you were born.'

Unlike Carol, Popov was more interested in the sight in front of him, but was unable to enjoy it for long.

The search party came rushing onto the scene. They had obviously been looking for the fugitive in the other rooms but they arrived too late to lay their hands on her. As soon as she spotted them she let out a scream and ran. They tried to catch her but her wet body slipped out of their hands and she escaped on drunken, teetering legs to the next room, hurled herself onto the bed, buried her head in the pillows and started sobbing in Hungarian.

A furious Elena and a worried Urdăreanu tried everything they could think of. They covered her with a sheet, she kicked it off; they tried to dress her, she pushed them away; they tried to comfort her, she screamed. She knew to what depths she had sunk and was angry at herself.

'You're too old to behave like this, kid,' Elena muttered through her teeth in a futile attempt to wrap her peignoir around the girl.

Meanwhile, back in the sitting room, Carol and Popov were listening to an American orchestra playing more lively music. The commotion in the background gradually died down. Now and then there was the odd whimper until silence finally prevailed.

Nobody knows how the blonde girl managed to creep out of her bed. It did not take long to find her. She was discovered in the bathroom hugging the toilet. She had not made it in time. In the middle of the room was a repulsive, spreading puddle of alcohol and gastric acids, floating with chunks of meat, masticated cucumbers and crêpes. The rescue team had limited manoeuvring space. Ernest slid along the wall, left of the vomit. Elena trod a little more carefully on the opposite side, looking disgusted. They had not got far when the brunette burst into the bathroom and, as if spellbound, went to her sister's aid. But after taking just two steps, she slipped, fell, kept trying to get up several times but failed, as if the revolting puke had her glued to the floor. Every time she tried to stand up she slipped and fell flat on her back again, until she was covered with spew.

Urdăreanu again had to take charge. He took a deep breath and stepped forward. Effortlessly, he picked up the brunette and handed her over to Elena. Then he pulled the naked blonde off the toilet.

Soon there were two naked young bodies in the big tub and a middle-aged woman rinsing them off with a shower hose, not gently the way a mother or lover might do it, but like somebody hosing down a dirty trough.

'Girls, girls, you should be ashamed of yourselves! You, too, you old pervert!' said Elena, yelling at the girls and at Ernest, who was helping her soap down the girls' firm breasts and buttocks.

Everything eventually settled down. Carol rose from his chair, holding his glass in his hand and the champagne bottle under his arm, and beckoned to Popov to follow him.

The two friends sat down on the stoop of the side door to the villa, like two laggards in front of a church. Everything seemed more agreeable outside in the fresh air and silence.

'Would you like a cigar? A Cuban cigar?' the host asked his guest.

'Wait, Your Majesty. I think I may have something you

might like. I got hold of some green tobacco. First class; fishermen smuggle it in from Mauritania. It relaxes you. I'll roll us each a cigarette,' Popov offered, taking a case of tobacco and cigarette paper out of his pocket. When he finished rolling the cigarettes, each lit up for himself.

'I am a lonely man,' the king said, blowing blue smoke from his nose.

The two tuxedoed men sat on the stoop in silence. Maybe for a minute, maybe for an eternity. They gazed out at the sea, into the night, as the sky slowly, imperceptibly, changed colour, as if somebody behind them was adding milk to the darkness, drop by drop. Popov broke the silence.

'Your Majesty… Carol… I'd love to sit here with you longer but it's time to get some sleep… I have to go.'

The king choked on the smoke.

'This is superb tobacco you've got here, Dušan.'

They fell silent again. The only sound came from the soft rustling of awakening nature, the wind and the birds chirping. And then a cry ripped through the air. An unpleasant, inhuman screech. The two men looked in the same direction. A bird was prancing in the clearing in front of the hedges. Its neck thrust forward, it trailed a long tail, the way a king drags his long mantle in picture books.

In the half-dark, the peacock was simply a silhouette, its beauty invisible, its dance merely disturbing the air. But with the first rays of the still pale sun, the bird, mesmerized by the attention, strutted like a cock waiting for a fight: it spread wide its tail on the ground and when each of its golden eyes was in place it slowly lifted the entire display and calmed down.

As colour infused the monochrome dawn the light slowly changed. The royal blue of the peacock's breast, the colourful fan of its gold-studded tail, and its royal crown began to blaze. Hidden in the semi-darkness between two burning cigarettes were two pairs of eyes that had never seen anything so beautiful. The king took a deep drag on his cigarette, waited for a second, and then exhaled it through his nose before speaking.

'Popov, what do you think?' He hesitated before finishing his question. 'Do you eat those?'

'What do you mean "those"?' Popov did not understand.

'Those,' pointed the king.

'The peacock ... ? Hmm ... It must be gamey?'

'That's what I thought. You'd have to marinate it first ...' the king decided.

# TODAY IS TOMORROW'S YESTERDAY

The warring sides are issuing assurances that ships sailing under the flags of neutral countries are not in danger. In town, especially in refugee circles, rumours keep circulating about new forms of transport. Basque fishermen are reportedly taking people to French Morocco at a more reasonable price, but nobody knows where or how to go on from Casablanca, or if they can stay there. South American ships, which until now have sailed to Rio, Buenos Aires and Havana, will reportedly start sailing to New York and Boston because trips to North America are more profitable now: the travel time is shorter, the tickets more expensive – the cheapest is three hundred and fifty dollars – and, most important of all, the ships have started coming back full of passengers. It is becoming increasingly clear that the United States will enter the war on the side of the Allies, and so German citizens are expected to start returning to Europe, via Lisbon of course.

The Portuguese ship *Mouzinho de Albuquerque* is expected to sail to New York again. It has a capacity of 620 beds, perhaps more in the current circumstances, but nobody yet knows when it is departing or where the tickets can be bought. If, as they say, the Spanish freighter *Navemar*, which has been quickly converted into a passenger ship, joins the *Mouzinho*, Lisbon would be suddenly relieved of 1,200, mostly third class souls. Forged tickets for the two ships have been showing up on the black market, but the public has been warned and the fraudsters, two foreign nationals, have been arrested and taken to court.

The only thing we can say with certainty is that the *Excambion*, a big, blue-hulled ship sailing under the American flag, sets sail today. The *Excambion* is moored at the pier where it was often berthed even before the war, when, as one of the famous '4 Aces' ships, it took Americans on tours of the Mediterranean. Since there is no tourism now, the cruise liner has been engaged to transport refugees, with up to 200 first class beds.

Relevant to our story is the fact that among the passengers sailing on the *Excambion* is a controversial couple: ex-King Carol II and Elena Lupescu. They are travelling incognito.

* * *

Ex-King Carol II of Romania had arrived in Portugal a few weeks earlier with a clear plan to get out of Europe as quickly as possible.

Immediately upon arrival, during the first round of visits that Carol's Court Minister Urdăreanu made to the Allied powers' embassies, it had been made clear that soon they would not be able to count on obtaining entry visas for Great Britain, or even its colonies. He had a similar impression about the United States. The king reacted by changing his instructions.

'Forget the big powers, Ernest. Find me somebody who won't mind a loser like me and who doesn't mind whose money it is.'

This did not mean that Carol was now apathetic, just that he had had enough. After the unpleasantness of being held virtually hostage in Spain, Estoril felt like a spa. He was treated with the utmost respect here, but without too much pomp or ceremony, as if he were a real king on an unofficial visit to a friendly country. But it gave him no illusion of momentary power or value on the political market. He knew that his political and family history disqualified him from any such consideration. Still, he was aware, and with reason, that the social status he had by virtue of birth and wealth required that he be treated with a certain level of dignity.

The question of dignity had been tested on his relative, the Duke of Windsor, whose situation, similar to Carol's in many ways, had been resolved in this same place only a few months before. The fate prescribed for Edward sent out a clear message to everyone: if you violate the code of conduct defined by your social status, the fact that you are a direct descendant of Queen Victoria and a Russian tsar and closely related to all the rulers of Europe will not help you.

The similarity between the two cases stemmed from the fact that both men had renounced their crown and were left without any actual power. Edward's behaviour was the more arrogant. As soon as he was degraded to Duke of Windsor, which he experienced as a personal slight, he moved to France and married his mistress, the fatal Mrs Wallis Simpson. So it was that a commoner, an American, a woman twice divorced with both husbands still living, became sister-in-law to the King and Queen of England, and aunt to the princesses who were next in line to the throne. That same year, in 1937, Edward and Wallis paid a private visit to Germany where they were welcomed with great ceremony. They met Adolf Hitler and visited an SS division. The family dispute culminated last spring as France was falling. Disregarding the German advance from the northern front, Edward stayed in the South of France until London ordered him to return home. He placed himself at the disposal of the crown, offering to actively join in the fighting as captain of a ship, provided that his younger brother granted him a brief audience, no more than twenty minutes, and that he could bring along his wife. Not only did London refuse this blackmail, it did everything it could to make his stay in Portugal one long humiliation, from his first day to his last. The British embassy completely ignored its former sovereign, his family did not answer his letters, and Churchill communicated with him mostly by telegram, using the imperative, as if he were no different from any other conscript. Nobody was prepared to mention the Duchess, not even as Mrs Simpson.

Carol had heard the story from a witness to the entire drama, a Portuguese banker who had hosted the Windsors during their stay in Portugal. Even taking into account the prejudice of the sleazy banker, Ricardo something, who was a great supporter of the Nazis, it was quite a story.

'In the end, they simply informed him that he had been appointed Governor of the Bahamas.' Edward took his appointment to a third-rate colony as an insult.

Carol hoped to fare better. He figured that being a small monarchical fish would make it easier for him. He also knew that he had not done anything that would call for such severe punishment or for making an example out of him. True, Europe's aristocracy was rather offended when he replaced his Greek princess with a commoner of dubious morals, but that was ancient history and had happened in better families too. On the other hand, he did not seek a place for Elena in the self-important tribe of European monarchs. As for Germany, Carol had himself met with Hitler, but only in a desperate attempt to save his country from war.

Carol swallowed his pride, making it clear that he did not want to provoke anybody. He had no special wishes and he set no conditions. He did not pull strings. He did not exert pressure. He just wanted to be allowed to leave Portugal, that was all. He instructed Ernest to make it known that the former king wished to get as far away from Europe as possible and that he had enough money to guarantee that he would not be a burden to anybody. While they waited for an answer, he forgot his worries and enjoyed the Estoril Riviera with Elena.

The first country to offer him its hospitality was Cuba. He expressed great delight upon receiving the invitation. The Americans, who until then had been silent, kindly issued him a transit visa.

★ ★ ★

A crowd of reporters and photographers was waiting for them at the dock, in front of the *Excambion*. The king was surprised because he had asked the Portuguese authorities to make sure that there would be no unnecessary publicity. True, the local press was not there; the crowd consisted mostly of foreign correspondents over whom the Portuguese censors had no jurisdiction.

Stepping out of the limousine in dark glasses and simple summer dress, Carol and Elena walked to the ship's ramp as if the crowd had nothing to do with them. As soon as the reporters spotted them, they rushed over. The attending policemen made sure that there was no contact, using their bodies and weapons to shield the couple from curious intruders, but they could not stop the photographers from snapping photographs or the reporters from taking notes:

The ex-King of Romania and his concubine arrived at the dock in their shiny limousine and pulled up right next to the ship's ramp. Paying no attention to representatives of the press, they were taken to their cabins on the top floor of the ship, to what is known as the royal suite. The *Excambion* is both a passenger and a freight ship, which is the best solution for royal passengers. According to sources in the port of Lisbon, Carol and Elena are taking with them approximately two wagon-loads of trunks and a whole mountain of hand luggage, boxes and suitcases clearly marked with the gold royal crest and stickers saying 'His Royal Highness King Carol II of Romania, to Cuba via New York'. They are also taking several servants and members of their entourage, along with the 'royal pack' of seven dogs. Carol's former Court Minister Ernest Urdăreanu made a statement to the press, saying that His Highness had wanted to embark on this trip without any fuss, but it was not to be. Thanking Portugal for its hospitality in the king's and his own name, he explained that they were going to Cuba rather than some other country because of its neutrality and pleasant climate. 'The king is still in need of some rest,' Urdăreanu said. 'Quite clearly, His Highness will not engage in politics while he is outside of his country,' he confirmed. He did not mention Mrs Lupescu.

* * *

The royal couple was personally welcomed on board in the royal suite by the ship's captain. Standing next to him were Gaby and Popov. When the king saw them his face broke into a smile.

'How wonderful that you are here, my friends. It would be sad if you were not here to see me off…'

They all sat down to drink to a *bon voyage*. Even Elena, holding her third glass of gin and tonic since the morning, smiled; and her smile was sincere, almost. They had not been chatting for long when a white-clad sailor appeared at the door.

'Half an hour until departure. All visitors on board are kindly asked to slowly disembark.'

Clearly moved by this moment of parting and by the attention his young friends had paid him, the king said:

'Before you leave, let me say that I hope to see you again. Duško, if not sooner then in Belgrade, to celebrate the end of the war.'

'That's a deal,' said Duško, holding out what looked like a wooden box. 'This is for you. That green tobacco, from Morocco. It will make your voyage pass more quickly. And as long as it lasts, it will make you think of me every day.'

'You, Duško, are a true friend. I too have something for you to remember me by,' he said, putting his gold cigarette case in the palm of Popov's hand.

Duško did not know that he would be using that cigarette case until his dying day. He died of lung cancer at the age of seventy.

'As for you, Gavriel, let me again invite you to come with me. I asked Duško to bring your passport. You've got a visa, like us. Be smart; reconsider.'

The boy looked downcast and stared at the floor.

'You know that I can't. My father told me to wait for them here.'

Carol now looked dispirited himself. Visitors should have already disembarked from the ship, but they could not leave the king looking so sad. And so Gaby turned to Carol and implored:

'Please, Your Highness, give me an order that is reasonable.'

Since the king did not answer, Gaby hesitated for a few seconds, heaved a sigh and turned to leave.

'Wait!' Carol said. 'Since you won't listen to me, I'm changing my orders. I order you to stay in Europe, but in my service. As an ambassador. Is that a duty you can accept?'

'But I don't know how to do an ambassador's job,' confessed the boy.

'Duško will explain it all to you, won't you, Duško? He's a past master at these things.'

'Don't worry, Your Highness,' Popov promised.

'Well then, Gavriel, I appoint you my ambassador to the Old World,' said the ex-king. 'I take this opportunity to congratulate Your Excellency on your new appointment!'

As befitted his new title, the boy bowed rather more ceremoniously than before.

'I will keep you informed of our movements,' Carol said, using the formal mode of address, in accordance with Gaby's new status. 'You can join my court whenever you wish, because by virtue of your appointment you are now officially a part of it. In any event, you can count on my help. That I hope is clear. And write. I will write to you as well. Don't worry that I may have forgotten your request; I will do everything in my power when the time comes... As soon as the circumstances are right.'

The sailor in white knocked at the door again.

'Sirs, I'm sorry, but this is the last call for visitors to disembark.'

There was only enough time left for them to shake hands. Once they were alone again, the king went back out onto the private deck in front of their sitting room. Elena was there, lounging on a deck chair in the shade. They had a splendid view of the city, and across the calm waters of the river they could see the thin mist-shrouded strip of the Tejo's shoreline. Even when he closed his eyes, the wind, the salt smell of the air, the screeching of the seagulls above, would not let Carol forget that he was on a ship.

The dogs padded around, sniffing at the corners of their new territory. Urdăreanu had disappeared somewhere. Everything had settled down; only the occasional servant passed by. Carol rolled himself a cigarette and sat down to read the newspaper.

He supposed that this was the last time he would see his two young friends. What he could not even imagine was that only a few years later he would return to this city, married to Elena, that he would live here in Estoril until the end of his life, and be buried in the family tomb of distant relatives, who came from here and whose own dynasty had also been overthrown.

\* \* \*

'He must be very fond of you for him to have made all this fuss about you,' Duško said to the boy.

'The king is a lonely man,' the child said.

They walked to the car, lost in thought.

'Today is tomorrow's yesterday, isn't it?' the boy asked out of the blue.

Popov stopped for a second, as if he needed time to solve the riddle.

'Something like that ... I suppose.'

# DULCE ET DECORUM EST
## PRO PATRIA MORI

They phoned Ivan early in the morning, waking him up. Mademoiselle Maristela wished to speak to him. By the time the call was transferred the person had already hung up. That was a signal from the Abwehr that it was urgent. At two in the afternoon he was sitting at the roulette table, across from Elizabeth. He arrived at von Karstoff's villa just after four.

He found a politely reserved von Karstoff, which made him even more nervous and suspicious.

'As you probably already know,' the German started their meeting by saying, 'since our last encounter the geopolitical situation has changed. The Kingdom of Yugoslavia has capitulated.'

Ivan nodded, impatient to hear what was coming.

'I have a question for you in that regard… It may be awkward…'

'Go ahead. Ask. I've taken some excellent medicine. A double dose. Nothing is awkward to me anymore. Just tell me what's happening.' Ivan was afraid the news was bad.

'What nationality are you?'

'Me?'

'You.'

'As if you don't know what I am. I'm a Yugoslav.'

'You see, that's no longer an option. Berlin wants to know if you are a Serb or a Croat,' von Karstoff explained.

Ivan responded in Italian:

'*Scusi, ma che cazzo vuoi?*' he snapped, gesticulating accordingly. 'What the fuck is your problem?'

Von Karstoff continued speaking in German:

'Just answer me, please, it's not funny.'

'Why does it matter to you when it doesn't matter to me?' the Yugoslav continued, speaking in Italian.

'It doesn't matter to you?' said the German now switching to Italian.

'Not in the least. It's all the same.'

'Berlin says it isn't all the same and is urgently asking for an answer. Why don't you just say what you are?'

'I'm telling you, it's all the same shit. A great Croatian writer once said: "the two nations are one and the same pad of cow dung that the wheel of history accidentally cut in half".'

'It's not the same. One side is with us, the others are against us,' von Karstoff said, replicating Berlin's message to the letter.

Ivan thought for a minute. He could not deny that he was a Serb, in other words one of those who were supposedly against the Germans. That could easily be checked. And the Gestapo did not tolerate liars.

'I don't know. It's a complex question. All right, let me

explain it to you and maybe you can be of help. So, like you, I was born in Austria-Hungary. When I was seven the empire disappeared and I became a citizen of Yugoslavia just as you became a citizen of Italy. I was christened in the Serbian church, but I'm not a believer. I lived in Dubrovnik, among Croats. I speak both dialects fluently. I have only a Yugoslav passport but there is no Yugoslavia anymore, just as there is no Austria-Hungary. As things currently stand I could try to get one from the Hungarians, based on my property in Baczka, or from the Germans, because Banat, where I was born, has now been annexed directly to the Reich. I could also try in Serbia, I studied in Belgrade; and in Germany, why not? That's where I got my doctorate, and also I work for you. You tell me, what should I choose?'

'Ivan, I want to keep players like you in the team, believe me. It's in my interest to find an answer acceptable to Berlin. So, help me out here and tell me: which is closer to the truth – Serb or Croat? I will write down whatever you say.'

'Neither. If I'm allowed to choose then write that I'm a Ragusino.'

'Just explain to me what the hell that is,' the German said.

'That means I'm from Dubrovnik. Say that and you won't be lying. I grew up in Dubrovnik and if I weren't here right now I'd probably be there. As far as I know my family is there. You can also say that for hundreds of years Dubrovnik was an independent republic, Ragusa. That they call us the *sette bandiere* because we're fickle and submissive to power. You can add that I am a Christian. That I am not a Jew. They're bound to like that.'

Von Karstoff looked up from his notes. When he caught his eye, Ivan said:

'Do you realize how cruel you're being?'

Now it was von Karstoff's turn not to understand. Ivan lit a cigarette and gave himself a few seconds, as if rethinking everything.

'Since war broke out back home, and it's now into its eleventh day, I haven't been able to sleep or eat or think about anything else. When you phoned, I was afraid you had news about my family. Good or bad. The last thing I expected was that you would harass me with stupid questions like this.'

'I'm sorry...' von Karstoff muttered.

Ivan fingered his face as if removing an invisible spider's web.

'Remind Berlin that I am satisfied with our co-operation and would like to keep it that way. Especially now when I need your help...' The words came out of his mouth in a cloud of smoke. 'I hear that it's chaos over there in Yugoslavia. People are dying. I don't know where my family is. They're not in Dubrovnik and they're not in Belgrade. It would be an understatement to say that I'm worried. Please do what you can to make sure that nothing happens to them. Protect them somehow, if you can. Protect their lives. The property's not a problem. I'm begging you. Tell them to have Johnny do something to protect them, he has all the addresses. Please: be a friend.'

'As far as that goes you can count on me, and I'm sure on the entire service,' von Karstoff said.

The report sent to Berlin on the meeting included the following:

Ivan is bitter about the politics in his homeland and refuses to identify with either the Serbs or the Croats, whom he calls dung. He claims he is a citizen of the Republic of Dubrovnik, a statelet that ceased to exist after the Napoleonic wars. ( … ) Ivan is under enormous stress, he does not know what has happened to his closest relatives in the war zone. He openly asked us for help. In my opinion, everything should be done to locate his immediate family and bring them to Belgrade. And to make their lives as comfortable as possible. Please contact the Viking, he knows all the details and can be of great help. Our supervision of their safety is a huge argument in our favour, if Ivan were ever to think of betraying us.

The report was intercepted by the English service. They never mentioned it to Popov. They couldn't, because of Enigma.

# EVERYBODY COMES
# TO BLACK'S

Superintendent Cardoso no longer has either the energy or the health to slave away like this from dawn to dusk. And he has been doing it without a break for more than a year. He is sick and tired of everything and not a day goes by that he doesn't pine for the pre-war days when Estoril was a seaside resort for gamblers and the rich. Even in peak season there was never as much work as there is now. And the inspector is already fifty-three years old.

He consoles himself by thinking of his colleagues who have been assigned to working class suburbs to watch the poor, with people whose minds have been poisoned by unlawful ideas. Cardoso has been lucky that way. He does not have to interrogate or slap anybody around. A very special class of people, not easily troubled, comes to the Estoril Riviera. They just have to be kept as far away as possible from the locals to prevent the spread of any harmful influences alien to the Portuguese mentality. It is not just about indecent swimsuits and women who smoke and go alone to cafés. It is about much bigger issues.

A professional of Cardoso's calibre knows that the secret to success in this job is to have a good grasp of the situation in the field. And that he has. In principle, he can tell you at any moment who is who in Estoril and what they do. If somebody in particular catches his eye, he is capable of finding out by the next day whatever there is to know about the person: his health, finances, the neighbours' impressions, down to the smallest details about his family, social, business and sex life. If there is anything to know, Cardoso will find out. How? Only he knows how.

Cardoso knows, but he keeps it mostly to himself. He doesn't create problems where there are none. For instance, there is no way he would not know that the musicians in the Palácio band are foreign nationals working at the hotel for black money. He knows but will not do anything unless somebody complains about them. He feels that it is never too late to arrest or deport someone, and even when he is forced to intervene, he always tries to be as discreet as possible. Cardoso is also aware that numerous intelligence activities are taking place right here under his nose. Generally speaking, he also knows who the agents are and who they are working for, but again he does not meddle in the affairs of people who know the meaning of moderation and good taste; in other words who do not draw attention to themselves or interfere in the affairs of Portugal.

Cardoso has the ease of manner and speech of a priest. His polished ways and tact set him apart from his colleagues, who are themselves mostly educated men (it is hard to enter the service if you haven't finished ninth grade). The inspector comes from good stock. He is the youngest son of an appellate court judge. He started Law School in Coimbra but for reasons unknown dropped out close to graduation. He got married and did not go back to university. Because of his knowledge of foreign languages, he hardly had to pull any strings to get into the PVDE. He found work in the section for foreigners. His daughter was born a few months later. He has been head of the Department for Estoril for more than ten years now. Everybody in the service envies him but nobody questions his ability.

Dinner is coming to a close at the Palácio and the music programme is about to start. As usual at this hour, we find Cardoso sitting in his regular place at the bar of the hotel restaurant, carefully scanning the room as if it were a stage: the actors in their tuxedos, the actresses in their evening gowns. The hustle and bustle drowns out the dialogue. It does not matter, the speeches are just meaningless polite words of flattery. Nothing important is likely to be said here this evening, and if it is, it will reach his ears in time, through the usual channels.

There is Bruno arriving. He has finished work for the day. But he is still in his uniform, just in case. He has taken off his cap. Unless prevented by work, he too comes here around this time almost every day, sometimes a bit before, sometimes a little later than Cardoso. The civilian in uniform and the policeman in civvies sit together at the tail end of the bar, where they have a good view of the room and can make a quick exit. They usually each have a drink, just one because neither employer allows alcohol on the job. They say what they have to say before eleven, when the music starts. Then they listen to a few numbers and quietly slip away, each to their own home.

Bruno is considerably younger than Cardoso. He is Portuguese too, but of a different kind. He was born in a village, in a semi-desert region south of the river. His father was a day labourer, working as a harvester of cork; his mother was a housewife, had children, grew vegetables in the garden and fed the poultry and one pig a year. She gave birth to a large number of children; a few survived. Like most poor people with an intelligent child of fragile health, when Bruno finished the fourth grade his parents sent him to a seminary in Lisbon. The city impressed him more than the school. He did not want to be a priest, but a waiter; he liked the elegant way they dressed. His wish came true when he ran away from the boarding school. He was sixteen years old. Adroit, literate, nice-looking and polite, he found a job on a cruise liner that happened to have sailed into port. He worked as a barman on the ship for quite a while, sailing around the world several times.

Bruno arrived at the Palácio shortly after it opened. Black himself brought him in. That was all Cardoso knew about him. He never learned where the two met, but they seemed to get on very well, as if they had known each other all their lives, so he decided that they must have worked together before somewhere. But after asking questions and comparing their two files he was none the wiser as to when and where that might have been.

When Bruno joined the hotel staff, the Crown Prince of Japan and his wife were holidaying there. Cardoso's very first contact with Bruno was in connection with the royal couple.

Bruno proved to be of great help because he knew about unusual Japanese customs and was even able to say a few words in Japanese. From the very outset the inspector realized that the new manager's driver could be very useful, and he tried to get closer to him, hoping to recruit him for the service. But Bruno refused even to discuss the subject. Still, the two men continued to see each other at the bar almost every evening. Over the past several years, they seemed to have developed a relationship that might almost be called a friendship.

\* \* \*

'Bruno,' Cardoso almost whispered, 'you wouldn't happen to know who these officers are, would you?'

Six German officers of different ages and ranks were sitting at a large table in front of the hotel band.

'They were here last night, too, but you missed them. They came after you left and stayed until closing time. It seems they're not real military, they're artists serving in the army. The talk in the hotel is that in private life they are singers, probably opera singers.'

'Ah yes, I heard that.' Cardoso pretended to be just checking his facts. 'They're off to North Africa to entertain the troops at the front, right? Are they celebrating something?' the inspector continued in a confidential tone.

'I think they're celebrating the birth of a baby...'

'You're right!' said Cardoso as if just remembering. 'One of them got a telegram today. So many things pass through my hands it's no wonder that I forget half of them.'

The evening seemed to be going quite well, as it usually did at the Palácio, and around eleven-thirty Cardoso went home for a well-earned rest. He had to go to work early the next day.

Meanwhile, the Germans behaved as if they were at a concert. They listened to the music more than they talked. Except for the modest if sincere applause, they were very unassuming, and yet they caught everybody's eye. In those uniforms they could hardly do otherwise. But wonders last only so long: yesterday they were an eyesore, today everybody seemed used to them, and by tomorrow nobody would even notice them anymore.

That evening the band's playing was more spirited than usual. They sensed that fellow musicians were in the audience or people who loved and knew about music. They were buoyed by the attention and the accolades. Yet, a certain nervousness could be detected among the musicians. A fair number were Jewish and the Germans' odious military dress understandably struck fear in their hearts. Meanwhile, the German officers at the table were already on to their third or fourth bottle of champagne.

'*Für meine Tochter, Maria!* To my daughter Maria!' they said and raised their glasses in a toast, confirming that Bruno's information was correct.

After more toasts, urged on by his colleagues, the child's father, the shyest in the group, went over to the bandleader and whispered something in his ear. The bandleader sent for the manager. After a brief conversation with the young soldier, Mr Black gestured for him to step onto the stage. As he did so, the German whispered something to the bandleader, stood in front of the microphone, squared his shoulders and clasped his hands halfway across his chest, as if fingering worry beads. The room fell silent.

'*Pour ma fille Marie!*' he repeated, in French this time, just to make sure that everybody understood him.

After the first notes on the piano, played *lento assai*, the fair-haired, boyish-looking man, already father to a child he had yet to meet, stood in front of the restaurant audience. Looking up as if he was turning to heaven, he sang exactly the way Schubert had written on the score: *sempre marcato, dolce, molto espressivo*.

'*Ave Maria, Maria gratia plena, Maria gratia plena, ave, ave Dominus, Dominus tecum…*'

Then one by one his colleagues rose from the table and walked over to join him in singing the prayer, very softly, as Schubert had instructed – *gli accompagnamenti sempre dolcis*.

'*Benedicta tu in mulieribus et benedictus, benedictus fructus ventris tui, ventris tui, Jesus…*' he sang, *sempre redolcendo*.

'*Ave Maria, Mater Dei,*' came the words in Latin, the language of all and none.

There was no end to the applause. The soloist bowed humbly, his hand on his chest. His colleagues joined in the applause. It was not the repeated calls for an encore that made them want to sing another song; it was that musicians, even in uniform, understand what the audience is saying when it applauds like that. On the other hand, they did not forget that they had invited themselves onto the stage. They looked at each other as if unsure whether it was appropriate for them to sing some more and if so what they should choose. Just then somebody cried out in English-accented French:

'"Lili Marleen", s'il vous plait!'

The officers exchanged looks. They did not seem inclined to sing this very beautiful, but very German song. Without warning, the bandleader acted on the idea. The trumpet sounded a few notes, like the brass call to reveille. Then the band came in, followed a second later by the warm baritone of a man bearing a lieutenant's insignia on his shoulders, singing the nostalgic song about a girl waiting under the streetlamp.

'Vor der Kaserne, Vor dem grossen Tor ...'

The song, in a melancholy alto version, was broadcast every evening on *Soldatensender Belgrad*, the German military radio station in occupied Belgrade. Soldiers on both sides listened to it. The song could even be heard at balls in Estoril, but just in its instrumental arrangement, because that was the only way the bandleader might agree to play it. Then he did not have to think about uniforms.

They had barely begun the song when they were interrupted by some commotion at one of the tables. Carried away by a drunken sense of patriotism, the correspondent of an English newspaper rose to his shaky feet and pushed his way to the stage, knocking over a chair on the way.

'Stop! Stop that rubbish!' he shouted.

The bandleader froze. The music stopped. The musicians looked disheartened; these refugees did not want any trouble. But the reporter kept shouting:

'Play "Hitler Has Only Got One Ball"! What are you waiting for?! Play it!'

Since the bandleader did not react, the Englishman took matters into his own hands and started shouting at the top of his lungs:

*'Hitler has only got one ball.'*

It turned out that there were several Englishmen in the room, probably officers in civvies.

*'Himmler has something sim'lar.'*

And suddenly the whole room burst into song. That is what happens when people not particularly keen on going to the front pick up on an idea and are given an opportunity to show, without repercussions, whose side they are on. They sing as one, at the top of their lungs, carried away by a spirit of patriotism and anti-fascism; they feel they have to support the just efforts of those waging battle in their name and for their sake, in whatever way they can.

*'But poor old Goebbels has no balls at all!'*

At the first sign of trouble the German singers stopped singing and hurriedly evacuated the room, leaving behind the victorious international choir, a dissonant but as democratic a group as you might find, formed spontaneously by all those who had something against Nazism, and they were many. They sang their hearts out.

*'Hitler has only got one ball,*
*Goering has two but very small*
*Himmler has something sim'lar*
*But poor old Goebbels has no balls at all!'*

The situation resolved itself when Mr Black stepped into the middle of the room and addressed the guests in his usual, calm voice.

'I'm sorry for the trouble, ladies and gentlemen. It's all over now. Everything is all right. Enjoy yourselves. Have fun!'

The pianist played a light American tune, the theme song of a new American film that the censors in Portugal had banned. Slavcho the Bulgarian from the band took over the microphone and started singing:

*You must remember this.*
*A kiss is just a kiss, a sigh is just a sigh.*
*The fundamental things apply.*
*As time goes by …'*

★ ★ ★

By the time Inspector Cardoso arrived half an hour later, having been informed of what was going on, the band was playing to a half-empty room. The happy, tipsy crowd had withdrawn, some retiring to bed, others choosing to move on to the casino, bars and brothels.

The inspector took his regular seat at the bar. He did not want to talk to anyone until he had had at least one more glass of Scotch on the house. Then, when the evening programme was over, he asked Mr Black and the bandleader to come to the card room.

He started off in a self-pitying voice:

'Tell me, gentlemen, what did we need all this for?'

Like schoolboys, the two men looked down at the floor. Even Mr Black did not have the courage to meet Cardoso's eye. As a result, the policeman had no other choice than to continue.

'You should be ashamed of yourselves, making me work at this hour of night. It's not right, gentlemen, it's really not… You got me out of bed, for God's sake…' He heaved a sigh. 'You're in charge, Mr Black, so tell me, how did you allow such a public disturbance to happen?'

'I didn't think they would take the song so personally… But no need to worry. Everything is under control now.'

The inspector turned to the bandleader.

'And who ordered the controversial song to even go on the programme?'

The bandleader was so terrified that he immediately went on the defensive.

'It's not a controversial song. It's a love song like any other. Except it's German… It wasn't on the list of banned songs… How was I to know…?'

'Never mind, it doesn't matter now. That's all water under the bridge. Let's see, what conclusion can we draw? There would not have been an incident if you had not forgotten a very important detail, and that is: where you happen to be.'

Here the inspector paused for dramatic effect, looked at the one and then at the other, before addressing himself mostly to Mr Black, even though he knew that none of this was news to him.

'You forgot that this is Portugal. It is not Germany, or England, or France, gentlemen. I don't want to have to keep repeating it like a parrot, so never forget that this, for better and for worse, is P-O-R-T-U-G-A-L… Portugal is the land of the Portuguese and we may have our faults but one thing is for certain: we don't like war and we don't like trouble. Some people think war is normal, but we, you see, give ourselves the right not to share that opinion. Some people even say that we are cowards. So what, even if we are?! Better a live coward than a dead hero. Right?'

The two men nodded and the inspector continued with his speech.

'Because of that, because of our love of law and order, we do everything we can to make sure that we have law and order here. And we intend to continue that good tradition. I don't know if I have made myself clear but there will be no fighting here! Full stop! Who is fighting abroad is of no concern to us *at all*. AT ALL. What is of concern to us is our PEACE and our EQUIDISTANT NEUTRALITY.'

The policeman spoke with such conviction in the truth of his own words that you had to believe him. But he was not satisfied with the dejected nods of his audience so he went on.

'It's true that we are a hospitable people, but only as long as our guests behave decently. We do not support the excessive, we avoid the extreme. Everything can be done nicely, decently, through compromise. And if we can do it, so can foreigners in our country. The moment somebody goes over the top, we say *Adeus.*'

The poor bandleader, a refugee himself, a Slovak or maybe a Slovene, suddenly thought that he and his colleagues were being threatened with expulsion, and he started fidgeting nervously. Cardoso adopted a more conciliatory tone now.

'Come now… Let's put that in the past. There's nothing we can do about it now. Nobody died. It's just that I have enough worries without you adding to them so I'm going to ask you for one more favour. Draw up a list of all the songs you play and give it to me by Monday, so I can send it to the censors. If they approve it, you can play all of them. If there's a problem later, nobody can hold me responsible.'

The meeting was over and Mr Black accompanied Cardoso to the door.

'These things happen,' Black again said in his defence.

'Allow me to remind you, Sir, that all your hotel guests pay a lot of money to have their peace and quiet. It's not right... It's really not...'

# WHERE THE LAND ENDS AND THE SEA BEGINS

*(Notes from exile)*

SPECIAL SPANISH RAILWAY TRAIN NO. 2002
1 MAY 1941

Our train is carrying one hundred and twenty lost souls through lands where we don't belong. Less than a month ago we were diplomats of the Kingdom of Yugoslavia serving in Italy, Albania, Germany. Now we are the banished citizens of a non-existent country protected under international conventions.

'We're on a journey with no end in sight,' said Crnjanski, a colleague from Rome and a poet.

'*A telegraph pole, a telegraph pole, a frozen field, and a view unremittingly dull, and no will to live,*' I said, quoting another poet, Cesarić.

Without too much wrangling, neutral Portugal granted us a group transit visa on condition that we 'remain no longer than necessary'. In London our government guaranteed that 'we would not, under any circumstance, be a burden to the host state' and that we would leave Portugal 'as soon as the conditions presented themselves'. And so, we headed westwards.

We arrived at the frontier on a sunny morning. The Portuguese customs officers in their dark blue uniforms and white gloves asked each and every one of us to declare how much money we were carrying. I have eight hundred dollars, that is as much as I managed to save. My older colleagues declared bigger amounts. I heard with my own ears Ambassador Hristić declare twenty-five thousand dollars! The words twenty-five thousand, twenty-five thousand, twenty-five thousand spread from mouth to mouth, compartment to compartment. That same afternoon we continued our journey westwards, across the plain.

ESTORIL
17 JUNE 1941

The strawberries were over, it was the cherry season now, and I had moved to Estoril, to the Hotel Inglaterra. It wasn't one of the top hotels but it was clean and reasonably priced. Quite by chance I ran into the writer Miloš Crnjanski and his wife

Vida. They were staying at the same hotel but because they had too much luggage for one room, they took separate rooms and visited each other.

Waiting is stressful and boring, so to kill time Miloš and I, neighbours now, take a stroll in the park and by the sea every day, and we talk. He is dejected and unhappy. The stench of the dung used to fertilize the rose beds in the park disgusts him. He complains that it's always hot here, like in Africa, and that the mosquitos are bloodthirsty like in the Amazon, that the noisy croaking of the frogs keeps him awake at night and that the birds wake him up too early with their song. He complains that only hot water comes out of the taps in his bathroom but he does not want to sleep in his wife's room because, he says, the smells wafting in from the hotel kitchen are even worse.

'I'm lucky. Downstairs in the cellar it's cool and I don't hear the birds,' I said.

ESTORIL
22 JUNE 1941

Some people say that they never bought gold and jewellery for so little; others complain that they never sold them for so little. I see that everybody around me is coping as best he can. I hear horrible stories about young girls and boys from once wealthy families selling their bodies just to survive.

We haven't received our salaries for three months now. We are living off our savings. Luckily, life here isn't expensive. The price of a meal for two with good wine in the restaurant is the same as the price of an imported toothbrush in the shop next door. For now, I can make ends meet.

Crnjanski tells me that his wife Vida is selling some of the clothes she bought in Italy. The daughter of the former President of the Republic of Spain and her husband are staying in the room opposite. They are refugees but they have money, and since the two women are the same size, she often comes over to Vida's room and buys some of her dresses, shoes and leather bags. Miloš doesn't like it, but he tells himself that maybe it is better to sell their extra clothes now than do it in a rush before they leave. The only thing we still don't know is if, when and where we will go.

ESTORIL
22 JULY 1941

Yesterday morning Crnjanski said: 'Please, my friend, come along with me to see Dučić in Lisbon. Vida is indisposed.' My ear caught the word friend. In the course of these last few wasted months in Portugal, the two of us have spent quite a bit of time together, but friends? I don't know. I don't know if he has ever even had any friends.

On the train, Crnjanski told me that Dučić was staying in the city centre, in an elegant hotel on the broad Avenida da Liberdade.

Dučić welcomed us nicely. He was happy, he said, that he could talk to someone in his language. He missed it. In fact, we were a convenient shoulder for him to cry on.

He is a man of deep feeling and he has a dramatic way of

speaking, like delivering a soliloquy on the stage. He had not a kind word to say about anybody. He railed against everybody: the English, the Russians, the king, the government, us.

He calls the embassy 'a grotesque vestige of a non-existent country'. After the embassy in Madrid closed down, he became, *de jure*, the Yugoslav royal government-in-exile's accredited ambassador to Portugal. *De facto*, the embassy is now run by people who are profiteering from the situation. There was an incident when he tried to persuade Kojić, the chargé d'affaires, to hand over the embassy's cash-box.

He admits that he was the first to raise his voice and call Kojić an ingrate, and the latter, who is certainly thirty years his junior, responded by shouting and hurling crass insults at him, calling him 'a decrepit old goat' and a 'senile old fogey', saying that he was 'a shit of a man' and that he 'shits in his ambassadorial robes'. The old man, vain as he is, grabbed an inkwell to throw at him but he was so worked up that he dropped it. Then Kojić grabbed a chair, wanting to hit the ambassador with it, but the others stopped him. Ever since, the chargé d'affaires and the downgraded ambassador have been communicating exclusively via the chauffeur. Dučić complains that, to the shock of the Portuguese and contrary to all protocol, he had to go to the Foreign Ministry himself to get his exit visa.

Lastly, some good news. He is thinking of going to America and wants to know if we would go with him. He says that a relative, a prominent man who lives there, could send us a letter of invitation. My friend and I said nothing.

When we were leaving, the ambassador embraced us

warmly and again invited us to come with him. Miloš said: 'The great republic of the United States of America has just one condition for entering the country. You have to show them that you have four thousand dollars.' To which Mr Dučić replied with surprise: 'It's a pity, Crnjanski, that you didn't manage to save at least that much … A pity.'

ESTORIL
28 JULY 1941

Crnjanski invited me to go for a walk with him last night. 'Let's go to the sea, my friend. I find the sea air recuperative.' We took off our shoes and walked along the beach when suddenly, off in the distance, we saw a man sitting in the sand. 'Look at Hristić,' said Crnjanski, 'sitting and watching the waves roll in.'

Our diplomatic colony is slowly beginning to melt away; one person after another is leaving for England. Hristić is still very much out of favour. He is dogged by rumours that he is working for Germany. But the Germans aren't asking for him and the English don't want him. Despite all that money, he's not welcome anywhere. We walked over to him. 'There's no ship and we can't swim across,' he said, his eyes glued to the horizon.

'The Turks say: *"Allah gives soup to the one and a spoon to the other"*,' said Crnjanski.

# IT'S A SPORTS CAR

t's a sports car – Bavarian make, white, roof down. It left a cloud of dust in its wake. It hurtled along the narrow roads between the stone walls of the olive groves and the cabbage fields. The young man at the rosewood wheel was racing along as if driving at a rally; too fast for this old, narrow, rutted road.

It was hard to keep up with him. The black Citroën a few bends behind on the road was trying not to lose sight of the white car, without getting too close.

The BMW slowed down; the driver was searching for a road sign. But the sign he was looking for had not been at the last crossroads and was not at this one either. Some men were standing in front of a tavern. It was Sunday, and they had come after church for a quick glass of wine and a chat while the women finished making lunch. When the car pulled up by the side of the road and the driver beckoned to them, three or four of the men ran over, saying 'Good afternoon'. The others followed to get a better look at that wonder of a car.

'Quinta dos Grilos?' the driver with the dark glasses and leather gloves asked. You could tell from the way he pronounced it that he was foreign.

The locals were happy to be of assistance. They removed their caps while talking to him. Everybody knew where the property that used to belong to the viscount was and that some foreigners were living there. They replied loudly, gesticulating, the way people do when talking to somebody who doesn't speak their language.

Following their directions, the car drove through the freshly cut fields. At the end of a dusty road it came up against a white wall with an iron gate. The gate stood wide open. They were expecting him, as he had told them he was coming. The sign said: 'Beware of the Dog'. But there was no sound of barking. Not far off a small herd of sheep was chomping at the yellowed grass under the shade of a tree.

Past the gate the car reached an archway made of palm leaves and twigs that let in barely a ray of light to dilute the darkness. A rabbit was faster than a sports car on this rough terrain and the low car had to proceed very, very slowly. Coming out of the tunnel was like emerging from a cave into a sun-drenched, stone-flagged clearing. Above him a blue sky, in front of him an elegant two-storey villa, as big as the chancellery of some impoverished kingdom, its walls painted pink and fronted by a family crest carved in white stone.

He left the car in the shade, next to the sculpture of a Roman soldier. A trickle of water as thin as the thread of sand in an hourglass poured out of the moss-covered stone well into the granite goldfish pond.

Dogs barked at the newcomer, jumping at the iron gate from inside the courtyard. A servant appeared out of nowhere, calmed down the dogs, opened the gate for the visitor and relieved him of the huge bouquet of flowers and prettily wrapped presents he had brought. Running out to welcome him was a long-legged young man, a first year student at best.

'Duško!'

'Look at you, Grada! You've grown! Fucking anything these days?'

The men embraced like old friends, as if to test how strong they each were. Two girls were waiting for them at the front door. They kissed him, each on one cheek. Gordana was older than Grada; Lila was the youngest. Duško somehow pulled free and, as good manners dictate, turned to their mother who was standing there waiting for the girls to finish. She was delighted to see them so happy and looking so pretty. Duško moved to kiss her hand, but she stopped him and embraced him instead, clutching him to her breast as if he were one of her own, kissing him on the forehead the way you do only with somebody you've known since he was a child.

Their friendship went back several generations and they were part of each other's family history. Such a display of joy would move anyone, for it was a reminder that we all have or would like to have somebody somewhere who wants to see and hug us. Such encounters are rare anywhere, let alone here in exile, under these circumstances.

They asked after each other's health. Everybody was alive and well, thank God.

'How is your family?' they asked him.

'Hopefully they are out of danger too, now,' Duško replied.

They sat down for lunch in the dappled shade of the vine arbour. The smell of home cooking and the sea air, the sound of the ever-present nearby crickets, brought back memories of family gatherings on the terrace of Duško's house in Dubrovnik.

'Help yourselves, children. Eat the pie while it's hot.'

They caught up over lunch. Duško started with his own family's war saga. For a long time, he did not know what had happened to them, he received letters from them erratically and hadn't talked about them to anybody until now. Who else but close friends would care about such things? He told the Bajlonis everything he knew, just the facts, without embellishment or drama.

In April, when the war started there, none of his family happened to be in Belgrade. He was here in Portugal; his older brother Ivo had been drafted as a doctor and was on the Albanian border. After the capitulation, rather than surrender, Ivo changed into civilian clothes and trekked across half of the Balkans to get home.

The rest of the family was in their Dubrovnik villa when the war broke out. With the division of Yugoslavia, Dubrovnik came under the Independent State of Croatia, which treated minority groups brutally, and the Popovs were Serbs and indecently rich. Luckily, their neighbours warned them in time that they were on the list to be murdered. They left to take the night train to Belgrade but were intercepted at the railway station by the Ustasha. His youngest brother, who was still a student, used his best Italian to speak to the Italian soldiers who were there as back-up. That persuaded the commander, if any more persuasion was necessary, that these people were not the sort that should be arrested. After lengthy wrangling with the Ustasha, their necks were saved but they missed their train. The Italians secretly took them to the port where a friend was waiting with a boat and took them to the island of Mljet. There they hid for almost six weeks. In the course of their escape his sister had lost her milk, but her baby survived because the grandmother fed him fish that she had chewed into mush. From Mljet they headed for Belgrade. For a whole week they were on the road, moving sometimes on foot, sometimes by truck and sometimes by ox-cart, but always following the rule that money talks. And finally, one day, they made it home. Duško had no news of them for almost two months. The letter he got from them through the Red Cross said that they were in good health and safe. Not everybody was so fortunate. Duško's uncle and cousins refused to leave Dubrovnik; it was their home. All three were strung up on a pole in front of their house. His aunt survived. She, too, was saved by the Italians.

Everybody knows that in wartime people die, but when it is someone you know, when it is someone from your own protected circle of people, when there is no rational explanation of the person's guilt and why they have become a victim, you realize that no one is immune and it makes you very afraid.

'Oh, children, we've become such animals,' Aunt Radmila said.

For them the war started early Sunday morning on 6 April, when the Luftwaffe bombed a largely defenceless Belgrade. It brought terrible devastation; more than a thousand people were killed. She mentioned several mutual friends who perished and whose houses and property were razed to the ground. One wing of the palace was destroyed and the State Mortgage Bank on Theatre Square was badly damaged; the National Library went up in flames and a bomb fell on the Church of the Ascension, killing people as they said their prayers, people who had sought safety in the house of God.

'There is no military justification for destroying Belgrade so ruthlessly,' Duško said shaking his head. 'Nobody in his right mind would waste so many bombs on us. But our people pretended to be a big power, and Hitler wanted to remind us how little we are. He's a despicable lunatic. And we, pardon my French, like giving the finger.'

The young ones at the table giggled, and Radmila shrugged her shoulders, because she didn't like swearing but she could not think of anything better. She went back to telling them about what they had gone through, about the deserted streets as columns of German soldiers entered Belgrade. She talked about how civil war had immediately broken out in the mountains, where people of different religions turned against each other, some taking the side of the occupying forces, others, call them patriots, divided between the monarchists and communists, and a war of all against all.

'Peasants killing each other with axes, slaughtering each other,' Radmila said.

The Gestapo moved into the Officers' Club, right across the way from Sava, their family bank, where Gordana worked. The club was turned into a prison and all day long you could hear screams from the basement. One day, at the start of summer, two prisoners garrotted the guard and escaped. In the bank they saw the young men running through their premises; they did not help them but they did not stop them either. That same day the Gestapo took all the bank employees and lined them up out in the street. The law stipulated that for every German soldier killed, one hundred people were to be executed. Fortunately, the guard they had killed was a Serbian policeman so the rule was not applied, but the staff were terrified. Gordana, as she herself admitted, resorted to her feminine charms. She kept looking the German in the eye until he relented and spared all their lives; he released the women and sent the men to a camp. The German, an officer, finally came to their house to apologize and was invited to stay for tea. It was when he found himself in their family circle, and especially when he saw their late father's diploma on his office wall showing that he had a doctorate from Berlin, that his apologies started to sound sincere. The German was particularly attentive to Gordana. He called on them several times, always bearing presents. He complained that he had too much work because so many people were denouncing each other that the Gestapo lacked the manpower to check them all out. It had reached the point where they had been obliged to put up a bilingual sign on the door of the occupying forces' central administration office in Belgrade warning that it was a crime to report on a fellow citizen without credible grounds for suspicion.

'When I heard that I realized that the world had gone mad and that it was time for us to get out,' Aunt Radmila said. 'You, my boy, have studied history more recently than me so you know that every generation of ours goes through a war. It's like part of our lives. We're not surprised when war breaks out.

I've already got three of them under my belt. I wouldn't be able to bear a fourth.'

They left the properties in the care of friends and family, and put their most valuable paintings in a safe. She talked about the people who had helped them, some out of pity, others for money; about how they had greased palms to obtain visas and passes; about how, encountering all sorts of problems along the way, it took them over two months to get here.

They took the family icon with them when they left, in case anyone thought they were Jewish. They wired whatever money they had in Switzerland to Lisbon. They smuggled in the jewellery.

'I hid the gold coins in the biscuits I had baked. I made a basketful. The longer you keep them the better they are, so they are perfect for long journeys. I placed the ordinary biscuits on top and the ones with the coins on the bottom. Whenever we were searched Lila would offer the soldiers biscuits. That's how we got through.'

Radmila mentioned the part about the money only in passing, so that Duško would not worry. She did not dwell on it because, being the daughter of one millionaire and the widow of another, she had no sense of money and anyway thought it was impolite to talk about it.

'Have you been thinking about where to go from here? And what to do?' Duško asked.

'We wanted to move on, but they won't let us. Nobody seems to want us,' Radmila said sadly.

When they moved on to practical matters, it was Gordana they turned to.

'We have submitted all the necessary papers for entry visas to England and America, but again they won't have us. I think it's because of my late father. He was friends with former Prime Minister Cvetković who was supposedly close to Hitler. I met with Jovanović, the Prime Minister of the government-in-exile, when he was passing through Lisbon. I asked him to press our case with the English and he promised he would do everything he could. And that was it.'

'I have the impression that you can kill time and stay here a little longer without worrying about it,' said Popov.

'We certainly won't sit here twiddling our thumbs. We'll work,' Gordana said.

There was something Duško seemed not to understand.

'Who will work?'

'We will. That's to say I will,' Gordana clarified.

'You? And what exactly will you do?'

Gordana did not hesitate.

'We are renting the property from an older woman, a viscountess. We pay her by the month. We'll see how long that will last. We're in no hurry, it's quiet, we have our own springs of water and over twenty hectares of arable land. We won't go hungry even if the country is occupied. And it costs us only a little more than room and board at the hotel.'

All this was of little interest to Lila, who was only eighteen. She wanted to know more about Duško. They had heard he was in Portugal from Mr Dučić, the ambassador, whom they had run into on the street in Lisbon.

'What about you? You haven't told us anything about yourself. How did you get here and what are your plans?'

'Don't make me talk about work right now,' Duško beseeched her.

'Mr Dučić couldn't tell us anything about you except that you are a great success when it comes to matters of love. He says you're twice as good as anybody else,' said Gordana.

Popov could not but smile. It was no small thing when an old lascivious smooth-talker like Dučić spoke to young girls about romantic affairs, which was as close as he would ever get to love.

'I don't know what Dučić told you but I do know that one should never trust writers; they are liars by trade. As for the rest, do you know that I have had a law firm since even before the war? Do you know that?'

They nodded.

'Well, last summer I came up with an idea for a big project with the English. That's why I am going to London and in a week or two I am off to America to see if I can do something there.'

But most of their conversation was about what refugees really like to talk about: what they had left behind. With old friends one can talk about it for hours. They asked each other about common friends and acquaintances, recalling the past; they did not have to explain anything to each other.

They took their visitor on a tour of the property. The shed with the cows, the dairy farm, the cellar where the cheese was left on the shelves to age, the chicken coops, the beehives, the granary. The dogs followed them as they walked through the parkland on that summer's day. They sat in the shade by the lake, eating cake made with fruit they had grown. It was like a

Russian novel; the only difference was that they did not drink tea, but Turkish coffee.

Duško did not leave until late in the afternoon. Before going, Radmila put her hands on his shoulders and looked him up and down.

'How old are you now?'

'Twenty-nine,' Duško said.

'I remember when you were knee high. You were so lively. But so cute.'

★ ★ ★

Duško enjoyed seeing them enormously. It was different from all his other recent encounters. He was glad to have somebody nearby who could testify to the existence of such a life. He was happy to have a door he could knock on at any hour and find somebody here, away from home, who was like a close relative. Suddenly he felt an odd pressure in his chest. He was overcome with a strange wistfulness. He did not feel like going back to his hotel room. He looked at his watch. It was too early for the casino, and he was still too full from lunch to go out to dinner. He stopped at an intersection where two signs pointed in opposite directions, one to the right and Cascais, and the other to the left and Lisbon. He stopped for a moment, thought about it and decided to drive towards Lisbon and the onset of nightfall.

Duško found his way around town easily. He drove to the old quarter and its little, dimly lit streets. He parked in front of a building he would have been hard put to find had he not been there before. He climbed up to the first floor and knocked at a door that had no name plate on it. The bolt moved, an eye peered out at the visitor, and the door immediately opened.

A middle-aged lady, once a striking beauty, dressed in a long piece of dark blue silk, greeted him. Her eyebrows were like raised thin arches, her cheeks powdered and she wore eye shadow and lipstick. Strings of pearls hung down her neck and breasts, and big pearl earrings were suspended from her earlobes.

She was happy to see him. She called him by his name, speaking in a slow, soft, husky voice. She led him down the narrow hallway to the sitting room. The visitor opened the curtains just enough to peek out of the window. It was dark; under the flickering streetlights the white marble cobblestones glistened like fish scales. He could not see the black Citroën but he assumed it was there somewhere. He stretched out on the brocade divan. The etchings on the blood-red velvet wallpaper were such as you would not find in a family home. Gold-framed mirrors hung in places where no decent house would have them. The big ceiling mirror reflected the same thing, only upside-down: Japanese screens, Indian drapery, Asian furniture, bouquets of peacock feathers, illustrations of couples in the throes of love, lampshades softening the light, tassels the colour of old gold, and the metallic sheen of silk. A thin, bleating voice coming from the gramophone horn was singing a pre-war Argentinian hit song. A bottle of champagne on ice arrived by his side.

'I won't drink tonight,' Duško said, signalling to the woman not to remove the champagne. 'No, Madame. Leave it. The girls will need it.'

'It's early. The girls aren't ready yet ... You tell me which one you want and I'll hurry her up ...'

'No need to hurry. Any of them who feel like company can come when they're ready. As for me, bring me a hookah and some good hash. I feel like some company,' he said with a wink. 'I haven't come here today for gymnastics. I'm feeling wistful. I just need company.'

# THE GRAND CASINO ESTORIL

THE SCENT and smoke and sweat of a casino are nauseating at three in the morning. Then the soul-erosion produced by high gambling – a compost of greed and fear and nervous tension – becomes unbearable and the senses awake and revolt from it.

Ian Fleming, *Casino Royale*

He opened his eyes to darkness. He was lying on his back among the crumpled sheets and crushed scattered pillows. He did not know whether it was the church bells that woke him up or the blackbird singing in the laurel bush under his window. He did not even know what time of day it was; he was still too dazed to count the bells, and since there was no light he could not see the dial on his wristwatch. Judging by the sound of the voices in the hallway, of the distant murmuring and doors opening and closing, he guessed the day was well under way.

He moved carefully to get out of bed, the way you do when you get up in the dead of night; he sat on the edge of the bed for a few seconds, his feet planted on the floor, and tried to pull himself together. Afraid that if he put it off for much longer he might have a change of heart and go back to bed, he mustered all his strength and stood up. He teetered the few steps to the window and pulled back the curtains. The little light that managed to seep through the cracks of the closed shutters sufficed for him to look at his watch. There was no need to hurry; he had slept through breakfast and it was still too early for lunch. He opened wide the wooden slats of the shutters.

Blinding sunlight poured in and the rhythmic chirping of crickets seemed to pulsate through the air. Wisps of a breeze wafted into the room, replacing the stale air, diluting the bad breath of the man who had sobered up in his sleep, alleviating the stench of tobacco smoke that permeated his clothes and hair after a heavy night. Vestiges of the recognizable smell of recent love-making and traces of perfume disappeared in an instant. Slowly, unsteadily, he made his way to the bathroom. Sometimes you find that in the morning the room tends to sway a little.


Not half an hour later, Duško was sitting in the half-shade of the hotel garden's pergola, freshly shaven, perfumed, immaculately dressed, a flower in his lapel and, most importantly, smiling. The waiter wished him a good morning.

The tinge of empathy in the waiter's smile only showed that there were no secrets at the Palácio. His smile proved that the waiter had sensitive information about this guest. Colleagues from the night shift had told him that Popov had again been observed in the early hours of the morning, returning from the casino in the company of not one but two ladies, and it was not until dawn that they emerged from his room. There was that genuine respect that men naturally feel when they recognize a great military leader, hunter or charmer.

Popov was a regular guest. Without even ordering he was served a black coffee, *à la turque*, to clear his head, and a glass of water to quench his thirst from the night before. The waiter tried to leave a bread roll on the table as well, but the guest waved it away as if the very sight of it made him sick. The waiter then discreetly suggested that while waiting for lunch the gentleman might at least have a little snack. Fruit perhaps. The offer was met with a smile and polite shake of the head, and the waiter, seeing that his efforts were in vain, bowed and withdrew. He did not even offer to bring the guest the newspapers; he knew there was nothing in the news that would amuse him.

You know that feeling when you think that somebody is looking at you? Sitting in that same translucent shade, just a few tables away, was another guest: a tall, lanky man, around Popov's age, maybe a year or two older. He was wearing a superbly tailored navy blue suit that was too warm for the weather, and reading an issue of the London *Times* that was several days old. He appeared to be taking a keen interest in Popov; he kept peering from behind his newspaper. Although sitting sideways, Popov could feel the man's eyes on him.

Popov paid little attention to men, but he could hardly be unaware of the long-legged Englishman. On the second day, the new guest followed him wherever he went. Popov's demeanour and attitude had always attracted attention; he was used to being an object of curiosity and it did not bother him. But having somebody's eyes obsessively trained on him like that had only happened to him a few times before, always with women, and he knew how to handle women, even obsessive ones. Whether the Englishman was crazy or simply did not realize that he appeared aggressive, the point was that he kept looking around and glancing at Popov. For want of a better solution, Popov pretended not to notice.

\* \* \*

On that first day of August 1941, Duško Popov was lunching with one of the ladies he had recently been seeing in the privacy of his room. She was an American, the young wife of a financial magnate, on her way home to New York from Switzerland. Even though she occupied all his attention, and from their laughter you could tell that they were clearly enjoying each other's company, Duško could not relax, unable to ignore the Englishman. The man had somehow managed to get a table next to theirs in the restaurant and he spent his lunch eavesdropping on their conversation, which, to be honest, was just lighthearted nonsense of no interest to anyone but the flirting couple.

After they finished their coffee, Duško escorted the young woman to her hotel, where her husband was waiting for her; he was too concerned with his business to worry about the company his wife was keeping. Instead of going to the promenade, as he usually did, Popov decided to return to the Palácio. The fatigue of the previous night had caught up with him. Lino was, of course, waiting for him at the front door.

'Monsieur Popov, I asked around,' the concierge said in a conspiratorial voice. 'He is indeed English, his name is Fleming. Ian Fleming. He is registered as working for the Ministry of Agriculture. He is staying in the room right opposite yours. He's probably a secret agent.'

Popov said nothing, he merely smiled his thanks and slipped a tip into Lino's pocket as he always did.

'How do you learn all these things?'

The concierge did not answer. He stopped the conversation in order to help an old lady who was lost.

'Come on, at least tell me how you know he is a secret agent,' Popov persisted.

'How do I know?' It was next to impossible to get an answer out of the moustachioed Lino. But he was prompted by another note slipped unobtrusively into his pocket. 'I remember him from before. He was here not long ago, but under a different name.'

'Maybe he's just on the run. Lots of people like that use false names.'

'People on the run don't come back. And this man has huge telephone bills. That's a sure sign that he's reporting something to somebody.'

'I'll take you on faith, but then give me one good reason why anyone would be following me? Of what interest would I be, and to whom?'

'Don't sell yourself short, Sir,' Lino laughed before dropping his voice, as if telling a joke. 'Here everybody is following some-body else. They are following you as well. He's probably not the only one, it's just that the others are more discreet about it … But one thing is for sure: he is following you today. Please come over here for a moment.'

They stepped to the side, so as not to be visible from the front door. And a minute later, there was Fleming, they could see him through the glass picture window, heading their way. His long strides brought him rapidly to the front door. Manuel opened it with a 'Good afternoon'. The Englishman returned the greeting as relaxed as relaxed could be and then spotted the grinning Popov waiting to ambush him. As if caught in the act, the Englishman looked away, turned red in the face and left more quickly than he had arrived.

'Maybe the guy has a little crush on Monsieur?' laughed the concierge.

\* \* \*

The room was cool and in semi-darkness. Duško walked in but did not carry out his routine inspection. He had stopped doing that a long time ago; there was no point. Whenever he checked his room he invariably found signs that it had been searched, but that never bothered him particularly because he knew there was nothing compromising to be found.

He sat down on the chair and looked at himself in the mirror. The day had left him slightly sunburned. He slowly undid his tie and took off his shoes. He headed for the bath-room and standing barefoot on the cold stone floor he noticed something: the toilet seat was up. That pleased him but first he finished what he had come to do, flushed the toilet and only then climbed onto the toilet bowl, rolled up his sleeve and reached down into the water tank above. The packet was unusually big this time. He opened the tin box, unwrapped the waterproof cloth and found what he was expecting. The envelope said: $38,000. As agreed a few days earlier, the Abwehr had sent him the money he needed for America. He crumpled the thin tin of the box into an unrecognizable little ball, slightly bigger than a marble, then he tore up the cloth, set fire to it and held it over the sink to burn. He threw the remains into the toilet, flushed the water again, leaving not a trace of the packet, except, of course, for the money. He put it in the drawer of the night table next to his bed, without counting it. Germans were not prone to lie, and even if he had discovered a mistake, he was unlikely to be compensated.

\* \* \*

'Bonsoir, Monsieur Popoff. Bonne chance. Good luck,' the liveried security man wished him, bowing as he opened the door to the casino.

It was a warm night. The casino was full. Popov had noticed that his English shadow had abandoned him, which made him very happy, but as soon as he entered the casino he spotted him again, sitting at the roulette table with some German officers, placing his paltry bets, one chip at a time. And losing each time. He was so focused on squandering his money that he did not immediately notice Popov, but once he did he looked him up and down, from head to toe. He noticed the elegant bow tie, the amber cufflinks, the white dickey, the polished shoes and bulge under the silk lapel of his tuxedo. He presumed Popov was carrying a gun.

Popov was in no hurry. He sat down at the bar, ordered a drink, looked around and casually started up a conversation with a Frenchwoman who had a very pale complexion and copper-red hair. By the second glass she was telling him her life story. She was travelling, she herself did not know where to go. She had been stuck here for months because her mother was ill. Although Duško had heard too many stories like this before, he listened to her attentively, all the while gazing into her eyes as if he understood her suffering, and for the first time in a long while she felt that somebody really cared about her. At the right moment, when he sensed that she had overcome her fear of strangers, he invited her to join him at the card table and play a little baccarat just for fun. She surprised herself by saying yes.

\* \* \*

The baccarat table was quiet. A very short Lithuanian of unprepossessing appearance was holding the bank. He probably was not as rich as he wished to appear, and having nothing else to offer, he opted for a bombastic display of confidence. Popov had seen him before, strutting around the casino. Instead of stating the ceiling when holding the bank, as was the norm, he had the strange habit of high-handedly announcing '*Banque ouverte*', which meant that there was no ceiling. This is considered improper among serious gamblers because it would mean accepting all bets, giving an unlimited advantage to people with money to risk.

'*Banque ouverte,*' he said again.

Again the croupier did not warn him about breaking the established rules; instead, without giving it a second thought, he invited the players to place their bets.

Perfect! Popov had hit upon a sure bet of his own. And he would have a large audience for it. The Englishman had made a mistake; Popov did not have a gun in his tuxedo pocket, it was a big wad of money, thirty-eight thousand dollars to be exact. Popov had meant to put it in the hotel safe but he was side-tracked and forgot about the money in his pocket. It came in handy now.

So the arrogant Lithuanian now handed our Duško the trump card he was waiting for. Popov first let everybody at the table place their bets and then took the wad of money from his pocket and tossed it onto the green velvet table as casually as if he was tossing a penny into a fountain for good luck.

'Thirty-eight thousand US dollars,' he announced. Nobody was likely to match that amount of money.

Everybody at the table was probably rich in some way, but few of them had had the opportunity of seeing so much cash piled up in one place. Let alone of seeing somebody toss it onto the table like a pack of cigarettes. The bundle of greenbacks was so thick that Popov could have said it was two hundred thousand dollars and they would have believed him. The table suddenly fell silent; everybody was waiting with bated breath to see what would happen. The unassuming Frenchwoman, who had no idea what was going on, went quite still. But it was the Lithuanian who was the most upset by the situation; he had no way of beating Popov – no one in his right mind carried around that much money. No one matched Popov's bet. The Lithuanian was in trouble and he quietly folded. Silence. According to the rules of the game, Popov had only one option left: to collect everything on the table. He had won big, but as he rose to his feet he started grumbling about the casino's irresponsible management. He was right too. The allure of gambling is something other than raking in the money. Walking back to the bar, arm in arm with the redhead, he caught a glint of admiration in the ever-present Fleming's eye.

\* \* \*

That evening the casino was full until late into the night. Here in the south-west of the Continent, the sun rises later in the summer, and so what we call the small hours of the morning came later as well. But right now it was past three in the morning, which was late by any standard, and the gamblers had started drifting away. After all that drinking, Popov had to go to the toilet. Standing at the urinal, staring at the ceiling, he waited for that moment of relaxation that was so essential to passing water. Just then, out of the corner of his eye, he saw that the Englishman was standing right next to him. He had to be Jarvis's man, they obviously came from the same school, they liked to combine meetings with pissing. They were alone in the lavatory, he and his tail, standing in front of their urinals, each holding his dick, trying to pee. Popov pretended not to notice anything, but the quick glances the other man kept darting at him disturbed his concentration and he was unable to pass water. He would not have reacted had the Englishman not spoken first.

'Tricycle?'

Popov was startled, as if he did not understand why the man was addressing him like that. He could not pretend that he thought the words were meant for somebody else, because there was no one else in the lavatory.

'Pardon?' Whether Popov was pretending or really was perplexed we shall never know.

'Tricycle,' the Englishman repeated, a little less confidently.

'Мрш, бре, олошу, мамицу ти…'

Popov zipped up his trousers and walked out, without even washing his hands.

The meek girl and the seducer Popov spent the rest of the night chatting away in the sitting room of the casino. They whispered into each other's ear while they danced, he self-assured, she shy and purring, all of it under Fleming's vigilant eye. The dancing lasted until dawn at the casino but the couple retired earlier. We do not know where they went and for decency's sake shall not follow them. We do not know if Fleming followed them, peeked through the keyhole or eavesdropped. It would not surprise us if he did.

# QUID PRO QUO

A gent Tricycle appeared unannounced at the fourth-floor office of his superior officer in Rua da Emenda no. 17.

'Hello, Jarvis!' he said cheerfully.

'Hello, hello, hello… To what do we owe the pleasure of this unexpected visit? It's been less than a week since you were here.'

The relationship between Tricycle and Jarvis in Lisbon had evolved into something like a forbidden love affair. They saw each other secretly, and always only briefly. The opportunities for speaking at length were rare, like this moment in Jarvis's office, when Tricycle would come under the pretext of visiting the consular section.

With intelligence operations, especially in wartime, you could never be certain whether somebody was a double or even a triple agent, but Jarvis was more and more convinced after every meeting that Tricycle was, mostly, a loyal agent. All the same, he wrote in every report that it was very hard for him to assess the man because he failed to understand how, despite all the risks he took, Tricycle still managed to survive and remain operative for so long. The careers of most of his colleagues usually lasted only a few months.

Jarvis was primarily concerned with security matters.

'You were here a week ago. Maybe you shouldn't come so often. You know that they are following your every step and movement.'

'They know that I am asking for a transit visa for the Bahamas. The only thing they might find suspicious is that my request is going so smoothly when for others it takes months.'

'All right then. Do you have something important to tell me or is this merely a courtesy visit?'

'I have something important to tell you. But first I have a question. You don't happen to know who the idiot who approached me in the casino lavatory last Thursday night is, do you?'

'Why do you think I might know that?'

'He called me Tricycle, and he did it while I was pissing, so I thought he might be one of your guys. That's what you call me, and you like that sort of meeting.'

Despite this pretty strong argument, Jarvis went on shaking his head as if he did not know what Tricycle was talking about.

The trouble with spies is that nobody has unlimited confidence in them the way they often do in, say, regular soldiers. Everybody always doubts the loyalty of spies, following and checking up on them. And they are right to do so.

On the other hand, agents are aware of this distrust, and fear that their employers are in possession of information that for one reason or another they will not or cannot share with them, even though it might be of vital importance.

In an attempt to clear up a potentially dangerous situation, Tricycle offered some more details.

'The fellow is English. His name is Fleming. Ian Fleming.'

'Ah, Fleming!' said Jarvis, as if recalling the name only now.

'You know him?'

'More or less,' Jarvis admitted.

'And? What can you tell me about him?'

'Nothing. What would I have to tell?'

What troubled Tricycle was Jarvis denying that he had any connection with the incident, even though Fleming was obviously his man. That had never happened before. In the past, if Tricycle noticed that he was being followed and reported it to Jarvis, Jarvis would admit everything. This time, he was playing dumb. Tricycle had been taught to react to any irregular behaviour. Those were the rules of the game. That is how he had been trained.

'Why don't you tell me what this is all about?' he persisted.

Jarvis kept dodging the question.

'It's got nothing to do with you, trust me. It's completely irrelevant.'

'Never mind then. I won't tell you why I came. And I'm warning you it has to do with exclusive information that I think you will find very useful.'

Jarvis knew when somebody was telling the truth.

'It's unimportant, but go ahead, ask! What exactly interests you?'

'On whose orders was he following me?'

'As far as I know, nobody's.'

'What did he want from me, anyway? What was so important that he had to speak to me in the lavatory? We could have been overheard.'

'Wait, weren't you alone?'

'Yes, we were alone, but how would he know if we were alone or not when he was as drunk as a skunk?'

'I'm sorry, I simply don't know the answer to that question.'

'I have the feeling that you're keeping something from me. That troubles me and affects my trust in you,' said Tricycle.

Jarvis immediately changed his tone.

'All right, all joking aside. He's from central office and is only passing through. I don't know why he followed you. He was not on duty. I guess he wanted to be useful. As for you and the lavatory – that's the first time I've heard of it. He did not mention it in his report.'

'He probably doesn't remember it himself.'

'I think, and this is just between us, that he can get a bit excited and that's why he keeps creating problems. When he joined the service he thought he was going to be a secret agent, whereas in fact his is a desk job. He's been sitting in the office doing paperwork since the beginning of the war. The first time they sent him into the field he made a mess of it. In Tangiers he provoked an incident with the Spanish.'

'What kind of incident?'

'Some nonsense. He got a young diplomat to help him draw a big V for Victory on the runway at the airport.'

'Why?'

'Why? Because they were sloshed.'

'All right. And then?'

'And then, when he sobered up, he supposedly feared for his life and instead of flying back by regular transport, he hired a private plane. For around a hundred pounds.'

'And?'

'And nothing. He was in trouble with the Admiralty.'

'So why did they let him travel on his own again when they know he's an idiot?'

'They didn't let him go on his own, he travelled with his boss and they thought he would be reasonable. He didn't do anything stupid until the evening you saw him. His boss went to bed earlier and Fleming stayed behind at the casino. He had another drink or two and then he was on a high again. The worst thing wasn't that he followed you, it was that he gambled all the money he had and lost. We had to lend him the money for the trip home. I understand that he won't be budging from his desk anymore.'

Tricycle still felt that the Englishman was throwing dust in his eyes with these anecdotes.

'Are you sure that's all it was?'

'I'm sure. Are you satisfied now?'

'Yes... I suppose so.'

'Now will you tell me what you have to say?' the Englishman asked, genuinely curious.

'I've got big news for you. I don't know if London knows, if you've heard anything, but the Germans have developed a system. *Mikropunkt.*'

Jarvis now became deadly serious.

'What is it?'

'To quote von Karstoff: *a new revolutionary system for sending messages.* Invisible ink is used to transform them into these microdots.'

'What exactly is it supposed to be?'

'It's not supposed to be, it already exists. It sounds quite simple: a letter is written on a typewriter and photographed, then the photograph is reduced to the size of a dot that is glued onto the end of a sentence in the letter and sent in the mail. You hold the letter up to the light and the microdot appears. They read it with a microscope. He showed me. You can see it perfectly.'

'Have you got a sample?'

'No, I saw it just for a second; it wasn't for me. He'll communicate with me like that only when I get to America.'

Jarvis stopped to think for a moment.

'Nothing then. When you get it, report it to our people over there. I'll check with London and let you know what they think – whether you should share it with the Americans or not. They'll probably say yes, but I don't want to be the one to take the decision.' Jarvis started jotting something down in his notebook. 'What do you say it's called, micro?'

'Microdot. *Mikropunkt.*'

'All right… Is that it for today?' At the end of every meeting, after they had gone through all the items on the agenda, Jarvis would pour each of them a glass of Scotch, but it was not time for that yet.

'No. There's one more thing,' said Tricycle.

'What now?' He never knew what to expect from this agent. Anything was possible. He had already said he needed some special equipment that was crucial for his assignment. It might be champagne or caviar, a Cambridge University tie or ring, box tickets for the opera.

'Listen… I know it sounds crazy… but… I've got a feeling the Japanese are planning to attack America.'

Jarvis was pretty dubious.

'When you say America, you mean the United States?'

'Exactly. The United States. To be precise, Hawaii.'

It sounded to Jarvis like another one of Tricycle's jokes. A very stupid joke.

'Who told you that?'

'Nobody. They just told me that while I'm in America I'll probably have to go to Hawaii.'

'Maybe your imagination is working overtime? Or you're gullible?'

'I don't think so. They mentioned Hawaii and the American fleet several times.'

'That still doesn't prove anything. And where did you get the idea that it's the Japanese?'

Intuition is extremely important in intelligence work, but even so, big decisions cannot be made on the basis of intuition, and all Tricycle had to offer was: *I've got a feeling something incredible is going to happen.*

'Take my word for it.' That was the best he could do.

The source, though nobody was supposed to know, was credible. It was an Abwehr agent, an old school friend, a German who had brought him into the whole business in the first place. If you ever wanted to know how Tricycle wound up in this predicament, perhaps now is the time to tell you.

The British agent Tricycle, the German agent Ivan, or Duško Popov when he was just a Belgrade playboy, once went to study in Freiburg. The choice fell on the German university because by 1935 his father, who had sent his sons to English and French boarding schools, had already developed strong business ties with the Third Reich. His factories were delivering fabric to the Hugo Boss clothing company near Stuttgart, which supplied the German army with uniforms. It was a huge, steadily expanding operation, and Mr Popov felt that it would be smart to send his lawyer son to Germany for graduate study because it would allow him to improve his language skills and develop useful contacts. Duško was naturally sociable and resourceful and in Freiburg he soon found kindred company. He became inseparable from his classmate Johann 'Johnny' Jebsen. If Duško was a rich spoiled brat, then Johnny was that times ten. For almost two years, the two of them went on wild drinking sprees, drove fast cars and bedded women, until one day the Gestapo arrested Duško. He found a logical reason for his arrest: he had allegedly run afoul of a German officer over a girl. But that did not sound entirely credible because he would not have been kept in solitude for six days just because of a woman. His release required the intervention of the then Yugoslav Prime Minister and the head of Hugo Boss. Duško was deported from Germany.

Johnny and Duško met again in Belgrade at the end of 1939, when the British and Germans were already at war and Yugoslavia was still maintaining its neutrality. Johnny told his friend that he had been drafted but that thanks to his father's connections he had not been sent to the front; he had been assigned instead to military intelligence, to the Abwehr. Johnny invited Duško to work for the Germans, saying it was *an easy job for big money*. The idea was that Duško, being a citizen of a neutral country, would go to England and collect information for the Abwehr.

Of all the citizens of all the neutral countries in the world, why Duško? There were two reasons. First, because Johnny remembered that at the beginning of their friendship Duško had told him how he had been sailing with the Duke of Kent and had bedded the wives of some eminent aristocrats in London. Duško had indeed once been on the Duke of Kent's yacht in Dubrovnik, where they had shaken hands and exchanged a few words. The bit about sleeping with women of the aristocracy was much closer to the truth. He had exaggerated somewhat when telling Jebsen about it, and Jebsen had embellished the story still further when passing it on to his bosses in military intelligence, which immediately grabbed their interest. Second, the Germans had few agents in Britain at the time. They had sent several dozen that year, some in rubber boats, others dropped by parachute, but they were all quickly captured. So the German spymasters liked the idea of having a well-connected man in England who could enter the country through regular channels and move around freely.

Popov accepted the offer in principle but spent that night thinking about it. The next day he reported to the consular section of the British embassy in Belgrade, told the local intelligence officer everything and offered his services as a counter-intelligence agent. Jarvis knew all this because it was written in black and white in the file he had received from London.

It is not clear if Jebsen, codenamed Artist in the reports, knew about Popov's double role, but even if he did, Popov never told anybody. Jarvis, on the other hand, knew from intercepted communications that Artist was watching Tricycle's back at the Abwehr, but he did not know why. What MI6 did not know, and it explains why Tricycle protected his source so staunchly, was that the two men met often. Even the Germans did not know about all their meetings. The last time had been just a few days earlier when Jebsen had secretly come to Duško's hotel room in the dead of night. No one will never know why and how he got there, but the fact is they sat for hours in the bathroom talking, letting the water run in the sink to muffle the sound in case anyone was listening. Although both the British and the Germans kept an eye on each other, neither could have dreamed of such an encounter taking place.

It was during that secret meeting between the two old friends that Artist, maybe deliberately or perhaps under the influence of alcohol and Moroccan tobacco, told him that the Japanese had asked the Germans to send somebody to Hawaii because they were probably going to bomb the US fleet in Pearl Harbor and it would attract too much attention if they sent over a Japanese person. Von Karstoff implicitly confirmed this information by instructing him to go to Hawaii. His loyalty to Jebsen did not allow Duško to name him as his source. Jebsen was not just his best friend and protector at work, he was also crucial to the survival of his family in occupied Belgrade. When the war broke out he had helped them get out of Croatia, had made sure they had whatever they needed under the occupation and that nobody touched them. For all these reasons, when they asked him who his source was, Tricycle could only say:

'Take my word for it.'

'Sorry, my friend, but that sounds too much like speculation. There's no room here for "I think" or "I feel". What we need is

"I read" or "I saw" or "so and so told me". We're talking about something big here,' said his handler.

'All right. I heard it from a highly reliable source,' Tricycle conceded.

'And what reliable source is that?'

'Sorry,' Tricycle shook his head. Pushing him was obviously pointless.

Jarvis stopped to think for a minute.

'I doubt that anybody will take you seriously just because you say so. Still, you go and tell the Yanks about it and I'll brief London, even though I don't think our people will be very interested.'

'You don't?'

'What can I say? First of all, it doesn't seem credible, and even if true...' and here Jarvis stopped.

Popov waited a few seconds before finishing Jarvis's sentence for him:

'... it would force Roosevelt to hurry up and take sides.'

Nobody heard this conversation. No minutes were taken. Nobody saw Popov enter or leave. In other words, the meeting never took place. Two or three days later, Tricycle was on a seaplane, flying via the Azores and the Bahamas to New York.

# LIKE A JEWEL LOST
# IN THE DARK

*An homage to the poet*

When you are in a foreign country, where it is hard to find somebody to share your troubles with, friendships are forged quickly and easily. Refugees, the dispirited, the subservient, fraternize and make friends with anybody who comes up to talk to them.

Miloš Crnjanski and his wife Vida, née Ružić, had been here for more than three months now. They lived from day to day, had withdrawn into themselves and were in constant fear of never being able to return home. So as not to forget, Miloš wrote in his diary:

> The majority of people in Estoril are Jews fleeing from the Germans and looking to leave Europe. They are rich, but difficult and sickly. When they hear me speaking German they come over and we sit on a bench and talk. They tell me how they were robbed on their travels, and console themselves with the thought that if the Germans enter Spain,

the British fleet will come to rescue us. The mixed couples among them are touching; they never leave each other's side. Often the husband is Jewish and the wife Christian, or the other way round. These couples walk in the park with a tired, heavy tread or sit in the hotel in silence.

We have become particularly friendly with a couple from Vienna. They are clearly very wealthy but they haven't smiled once. The man is tall, well proportioned, elegant; the woman is tired, with wrinkles on her face and the vestiges of great beauty in her bearing.

The man, who was younger, more talkative and less preoccupied with their fate than she, had joined Miloš for a swim in the sea. While the husbands were in the water the wives sat at the top of the beach; Vida was reading and the Viennese woman was reclining in the deck chair, her green eyes silently staring straight ahead from under her big straw hat.

Far out in the distance, the white-crested waves were travelling towards them across the grey, impenetrable sea. They slid into the cove in an array of thin, curved arches. The closer a wave got to the shore, the higher it rose until, just within reach of the shore where the shallows begin, it reared up into a translucent, straight wall of green and then, as the sun copper-coated the surface of the rising water, it came crashing down on itself and dissolved into a thick milky foam. Attenuated, bubbling, it would not stop here. It continued to crawl towards the beach, evermore slowly, as far as it could go, until it lost its last ounce of strength, gave up, and began to retreat to where it came from, pulling with it the pebbles that rustled like drizzle on a tin roof. Little white stones rolled back and forth, back and forth in the sand, following the rhythm of the waves that come and go, come and go…

Standing at the line of the tide, where the sand was dry on this particular day, were the two friends who had just come out of the sea: the Austrian, lanky and fair, his movements smooth, and Crnjanski, forever restless, on the short side, wiry and sunburned. They were drying off in the late afternoon sun.

'The water is freezing, but invigorating. Makes you feel regenerated, liberated,' said Miloš, stamping his feet. The Austrian merely nodded.

'Do you know when you'll be leaving this place? And for where?' Miloš knew that this was what was on his friend's mind right now.

'We don't know yet. I'm trying to persuade her to come to Africa. I even bought tickets for the ship. The climate there is mild, good for one's health, and you can live well, comfortably. We could grow old in Mozambique. We wouldn't be alone. There's a colony of Europeans there, they must have somebody there who is at least a little like us. We'd probably develop a circle of friends,' said the Austrian.

'And?'

'She doesn't want to go… She says we've done enough traipsing around; we've been in Dubrovnik, in Italy, in France, in Spain, and now, after six months in Portugal, she's had enough. She doesn't want to move again. She says she doesn't have the strength.'

'What does she think would be the best thing to do?'

'She always used to know what she wanted, and I just

followed. Now all she knows is what she doesn't want. She won't listen to me…'

'Does she have any solution to offer?'

'No… Well, that's not true, she does… She suggests that we commit suicide.'

'Ah, women. They're like actresses; they always want a sentimental death…'

The mention of death left them thinking and shut them up for a moment. The Viennese was the first to break the silence.

'She's aged a lot and life with her isn't fun anymore… She cries every morning, I almost think she enjoys her grief. That's why I walk by her side without smiling, but without sadness either.'

Miloš was quiet. What was there to say? He looked at the gulls. They were flying over the water and floating in the sun's reflection on the endlessly flat sea.

'If I didn't leave her before, I'm not about to do so now,' the Viennese went on, as if in self-justification.

'If it's any consolation, we don't know what fate has in store for us either, nor do I plan to leave my Vida,' said Miloš, trying to lighten the conversation at least a little.

'In all honesty… My biggest regret is for myself,' the Austrian said.

Again, Miloš could find nothing to say. Such hard, honest confessions were always draining, and left one with a heavy heart.

Gusts of wind swirled grains of sand across the shore, bringing in little clouds of sea foam, and carrying away some of their words, as if they were tiny boats. They had to strain to both talk and listen. Tired, drunk on the sea air, they fell silent. Miloš gazed at the beach.

Sitting on the sand not far from each other were two families. One was German: husband, wife, nanny and three small children. The parents were basking in the sun and the children, like children everywhere, were rolling half-naked in the sand. Away from the water, the eldest was busily building sandcastles and digging deep trenches. His structures would be short-lived. They would disappear in the course of the night, when the tide came in and flooded the beach. When the sun rose over Estoril the following day, instead of their sandcastles and the human footprints and the three-toed traces of seagulls that punctuated the beach, there would be a pink surface unmarked by a single crease, like a tightly made army cot.

Sitting a few steps away was a blond, pretty child; he looked as if he would never grow up. You could tell from his clothes that he was Jewish. Barefoot but in a suit with rolled-up trouser legs, he both walked and talked softly. He was not alone; he was playing with a little yellow dog that looked like a fox.

It was as if neither group noticed the other. They avoided any contact with each other, including the children. Even the dog, an irrational creature that enjoyed attention no matter where it came from, did not leave the boy's side and had eyes only for him.

Across from them, a bit further on, close to the waves, was a group of Englishwomen. They had come to this way station from all over Europe and Asia, hoping to be sent home. Whoever won this war, and its end was nowhere in sight, it was not going to be them. These women were already defeated. Some of them had lost their home and family, most of them had lost sleep and their peace of mind. Some would tell whoever was willing to listen to them how they had seen the Japanese rape, stab and kill. They made do with living in a foreign country with the modest help they received from their embassy. They wandered around, waiting, never knowing how long this agony would last, with no one to call their own. Among them were children, mostly the sons and daughters of officers of the British colonial army travelling from overseas territories to their homeland, which few remembered and where many of them had never set foot. Most of the children did not know where their families were, or even if they were still alive, if they were safe, if their fathers were at the front, or if their mothers were interned in camps in some malaria-infested tropical country.

One of them, a woman he knew from the beach, came up to Crnjanski to say hello before stepping into the water. She was young, an officer's daughter, homeless, inconsolable. She did not cry, the English do not shed tears easily, but she so pined for her family that her eyes were full of suppressed sorrow. Yet now here she was, regenerated by the sea, jumping in the waves, shrieking with the cold, calling out to her friends, urging them to come into the water with her. Happy and smiling, she could forget, if only for a moment, that she did not know if she was all alone in the world or not.

Miloš spoke first, half-talking to his Viennese companion, half-putting his own thoughts in order.

'You know, I think all these people around us are no longer living beings, they are shadows of themselves... helpless, weak... sad...'

The man from Vienna looked at him askance. Miloš proceeded to explain.

'I was talking to a German colonel yesterday, you must have noticed him, a big man with the bearing of a gentleman, he is attached to their military mission here… He is from Hamburg; before the war he was a professor of literature at the university and spent his summers in Abbazia, so he knows a few words of our language. We strolled along the beach. I came across the broken wing of a seagull in the sand. He asked me how I was. I said: "What can I say? Nobody likes living like a refugee. I'd like to go home, but I've got nowhere to go." He asked me how my people were. I told him: "My people are all groans and graves," but that was not enough for him. I told him with a heavy heart what people fleeing the war had told me about what was happening in my country: about the destroyed capital city, the deaths, the crimes against civilians, the reprisals, the gangs of men slaughtering people, the bloody fratricidal war… As I was talking, he kept waving his hand dismissively and mumbling: "*Nein, nein, nein,*" then switching to our language and saying "*Ne, ne*". He refused to believe it and did his best to show that he was not to blame, that if anyone was to blame it had to be somebody else, maybe life itself, but not him; he was not an animal. He asked me to join him for a cup of tea, but I couldn't accept his invitation. I was afraid that if the English saw me with him they might withhold my entrance visa. Otherwise, I would have accepted.'

Waiting for them at the top of the beach were their wives, just as they had left them. Vida was reading, the Viennese woman was gazing silently out at the sea. Shortly after their husbands came back, Vida said she would like to take a stroll along the beach. The Austrian offered to accompany her, promising to bring back some ice cream. They left Miloš and the Viennese woman lying next to one another in their canvas deck chairs, mesmerized by the ocean in front of them.

'Your German is good,' she said without turning to look at him.

'My father was an Austro-Hungarian civil servant. I went to German schools and served in the Austrian army,' Crnjanski briefly explained, but in order to break the silence that followed, he went on. 'You've never spoken to us about your pre-war life in Vienna. What did the two of you do?'

'He was an officer. He served during the Hitler time as well,' the lady replied, staring off into the distance.

'Really?' said Miloš surprised. 'Forgive me for being indiscreet but I thought that the two of you had fled because you were being persecuted as Jews?'

'He has Jewish blood, through a distant relation. I am Jewish on both my mother's and my father's side,' she replied. Again silence. Then suddenly she turned to him and said: 'Tell me something about yourself.' For the first time that day she looked at him. There was a darkness to her eyes.

'Until recently I lived in Rome, near the Vatican, across the way from an impoverished suburb called Borgo. In the summer it stinks of urine and in the winter it is freezing cold. I am a diplomat of the Kingdom of Yugoslavia. I was the press attaché first in Berlin and then in Rome. That's how I earned my living and would still be doing it if the country I was representing hadn't disappeared. I don't know how much longer we'll be able to live like this. I'm also a poet, but you can't live off that.'

'Do you want to go back home?'

'The April bombing of Belgrade destroyed the house I once lived in and everything in it, including my manuscripts. Let's not talk about it. Tell me something about yourself. You?'

'I,' she said, still without smiling, 'I am an only child, the heiress of unnecessarily great wealth. In the last few years I have lost the vast majority of my property. We live off the remaining crumbs. But it's not so bad; we can go on like this for a long time as long as we can endure life. I'm a psychologist. I don't know if one can live on that; I haven't tried.'

'What is the first thing you ask your patients?' Miloš asked.

'I ask them what they dream about… What do you dream about?'

'You're asking me?'

'Yes, I'm asking you.'

'What do I dream about…? Hmm… Since coming here I have been dreaming about all sorts of things. I am quiet, sleepless, dying, cold. Volcanic islands in the polar north visit me in my dreams, my beloved homeland, Paris, my dead friends, cherries in China. Night after night I dream about Belgrade, more beautiful and splendid than it really is. In my dreams I see images of my youth, of the village, the occasional butterfly, field poppies, wheat. Sometimes I hear footsteps; I look only to discover that it is not her, because her voice is full of laughter, it's not like this. What I hear is some kind of inarticulate screeching. Instead of her I see a bird with wild, black wings.'

She said nothing, waiting for him to continue.

'And I sleep a lot. I have never spent so much time sleeping since I was a boy. Ill-humour makes me want to dream because it is a better world in dreams, my wishes and plans come true. Nothing troubles me when I fall asleep. I manage to guide my dream rather than let it guide me, to turn it into something real. Then I dream about lovely things. I dream about Belgrade and its sleeping rivers. About the young Venetian women of my youth. About my beloved plains. When I start dreaming about Lisbon and this trip of ours it upsets me and I wake up. Sometimes I'm not sure what is real: the Lisbon of my waking hours or the Belgrade of my dreams. Does that tell you something about me?'

'It tells me that you are fonder of your dreams than of reality… That you are despondent. That you suffer from nostalgia. But don't worry. It will pass… May I ask you a slightly harder question now?'

'Go ahead. I hope I will be able to answer it.'

'What is your highest ideal?'

'Freedom,' said the poet without hesitation.

'Do you think you will ever achieve complete freedom?'

'I don't know. I hope so but I doubt it… Your turn now. What is your highest ideal?'

'Love.'

'Do you have it?'

Her answer was silence.

Like a dentist whose drill accidentally touches the soft pulp of a tooth, the poet inadvertently penetrated the sad woman's inner soul, causing her pain. Again they both stared blankly into the endless distance, their eyes arrested only by the clear blue sky. They stayed like that for a long time. Suddenly Miloš remembered what Dučić had said, and Dučić was a man who

understood women: 'A woman never discusses love with somebody she wouldn't be able to love or desire...'

She broke the awkward silence. She had decided to tell him
a love story.

'We married for love. And there was love, some kind of love
for sure; I could feel it. Now I feel that he would be happier if I
weren't around anymore.'

'After everything the two of you have been through together,
such thoughts still plague you? Do you still love him?'

'Yes. Of course I love him. I love him so much that I'm
thinking of giving him my own suicide for his fiftieth birthday.'

'But he has stayed by your side. He didn't leave you even
when things were at their worst.'

'That's true. He didn't leave me. Do you want to know why?'

Miloš said nothing, so she continued.

'He didn't leave me because I am the one with the money.
Even now, after having been robbed, I am the one with the
jewellery that can allow us to live decently. I am the source of
his security and the pillar of his dignity, and he loves himself
above all else. His self-love is greater than any other love he
might feel, and certainly greater than any love he ever felt for
me. It's always been like that, I've known that from the very
first day... And it didn't bother me because he did love me in
his way. Now I think that he feels nothing but self-love.'

'That can't be true,' Crnjanski protested.

'Still, it's a good thing that I have him,' she picked up where
she had left off. 'Imagine if I didn't: a woman alone, without
protection, in a foreign country... If he weren't with me, who
knows, somebody might kill me for the jewellery...'

'I honestly don't understand you. You have love. It is in your veins. Love is usually one great act of imagination, because we imagine all the virtues of the person we love, we tell ourselves that all kinds of happiness are possible and that all obstacles are small and insignificant...'

'I'll tell you something, poet,' she continued. 'There is no such thing on this planet as real, true, ever-lasting love. There isn't,' she said waving her hand dismissively and crossing her lovely legs. 'Fortunately, we don't have children... What are you writing there?' she asked, seeing that Miloš was penning something in his notebook.

'I write all sorts of things that I don't like remembering,' he replied.

Off in the distance, the sun sank into the sea, leaving the peach-toned sand dunes to the haze of darkness and the scattered, fluffy clouds reflecting the dying red of the day.

\* \* \*

A few days later, the woman with the big, sad eyes started going out with a cane. Walking was becoming more and more difficult for her. The two couples continued to see each other every day; sometimes they were friendlier, sometimes more reserved, depending on her mood, which was erratic.

Around this time, when they had lost almost all hope, Crnjanski finally received good news. They had been granted visas for London so that Miloš could be at the disposal of the royal Yugoslav government-in-exile.

The night before their departure, his insomnia returned.

He lay in the darkness of his hotel room, his eyes wide open, amazed. His wife, with whom he was sharing the room that night, was asleep on his arm, her head resting on his chest. He spent the whole night listening to the wind, the intermittent barking of the dogs and the distant roar of the sea. Shortly after the first roosters announced the dawn, he saw through half-closed eyes the thin light of daybreak. It was time for them to go.

When Miloš and Vida got into the car to go to the pier, the woman with the cane came out of the hotel to see them off. They parted without a smile and without a tear, and she followed them with her eyes for a long time as they drove away.

'Now I see that after pity there is nothing,' Miloš whispered to Vida, looking back at the figure of the sad, rich, homeless woman.

When they boarded the craft, the poet, lest he forgot, wrote the following in his notebook:

The transoceanic seaplane rocked in the waters of the Tejo like a small hypermodern aluminium ship.

They go through our luggage and take away the cameras, and on the seaplane we are told not to open the curtains. Soon the craft, which had just arrived with passengers from America, is speeding across the water and I can feel it lifting up into the air. The engines are so loud that we can't hear each other.

Suddenly, an hour later, I can feel that we are descending and landing. A steward comes onto the plane and tells us that we are back in Lisbon but will be taking off again in half an hour.

Half an hour later we are again lifting off the water. I peek through the curtain and see that Lisbon is down there behind us, like a jewel lost in the dark. Its lights glitter. The chairs on the craft are wide and everybody prepares to catch some sleep. Only the children are playing.

# SILK STOCKINGS, THREE PAIRS

Lisbon lies on the slopes of at least seven hills. The Avenida da Liberdade, its central traffic artery, runs from the point of convergence of two major hillsides down to the plain along the river and its Downtown. The avenue is bordered on both sides by rows of trees and the kind of buildings you see only in imperial capitals. The last rays of the autumn sun were reflected off the high west-facing windows stretching above the plane and palm trees.

The hour was between day and night. In the few seconds of incomplete darkness before the streetlights went on, a brief sequence of small, seemingly insignificant events occurred on the tree-lined avenue. First a car with no lights stopped at the corner, as if to let a pedestrian cross the road. Then, a spark flew out of the darkness of the park, and before it hit the cobblestones it was followed by the silhouette of a man. He stamped out the cigarette butt with one foot and entered the waiting car with the other.

The automobile turned on its headlights and headed uphill,

along the lateral road on the eastern side of the avenue. It was too dark for Ivan to see the driver's face or the direction they took after pulling out of the roundabout. He had not been to Lisbon in a long time but he had a strong feeling that he had never seen these streets before.

The fact that they were on the territory of a neutral country meant nothing to Ivan other than a false sense of security. Terrible stories were circulating in Lisbon, and they were too similar to be taken lightly: people, in particular foreigners, were disappearing. The Gestapo, it was rumoured, was kidnapping enemies of the Third Reich, sedating and tying them up, putting them in trunks and car boots and smuggling them across the border. Needless to say, there were no witnesses to confirm any of these stories. This was a country where news of such incidents was never made public, even if they were the subject of police reports. The host country's official stance was that peace and security were guaranteed to everyone, including foreigners. The famous case of Austria's Habsburg archdukes, whose extradition Berlin had sought numerous times but to no avail, was cited in support of the claims. It was also an open secret that in 1940 the Germans had planned to kidnap the Duke and Duchess of Windsor and move them secretly to Berlin, but it all fell through. This was little consolation for Ivan, however. Kings and emperors were big fish, too big for even the Gestapo. Those rules did not apply to ordinary people. But if nobody touched the Portuguese, if the job was done cleanly, swiftly and professionally, without disturbing law and order, and if nobody reported it, then the Portuguese authorities would not react. In other words, little could save him from a concentration camp if the Germans discovered anything they did not like about him and he fell into their trap.

Ivan finally caught the driver's eye in the rear-view mirror. His first impression had been right; he did not know the man and could not read anything in his eyes.

'Excuse me, where are we going?' Ivan asked in German. He did not sound worried, just curious.

'To a new address,' said the young man at the wheel.

The information given was too spare to satisfy a double agent who suspected he was being kidnapped. The dilemma remained, however: stay in the car or jump out in the dark as soon as the vehicle stopped or slowed down? If he escaped, the game was over. He would have to go into hiding until the end of the war. They would probably take it out on his family. If he stayed in the vehicle and the worst came to the worst, could the pistol chafing him under his left arm be of any help? Was it smart to rely on the half-dozen bullets in his charger? If push came to shove, there was always the honourable death offered by the cross he wore on the chain around his neck. Concealed behind the oval crystal glass was something that could instantly spare him any agony: cyanide. All he had to do was kiss the crucifix – it was unlikely that anybody would try to stop him – then bite down on the ampoule embedded in the gold and it would all be over.

He did not jump out of the car. He did what he was told and lay down on the back seat. When ordered to step out of the car into the semi-darkness of the garage he did so.

The 'new address' was in an elegant part of town, near the Praça de Espanha. He was taken through a side entrance to an apartment on the second floor. He took the fact that they did not put a sack over his head as a sign that he would at least be given a chance to explain himself.

The first to come running out when the door opened were the dachshunds. They were happy to see him so he spoke to them first.

'Where've you been, boys?!' he said, scratching their backs as they sniffed his legs. 'Are you happy to see me or do I smell like a female? There's a knock-out of a seductress at my hotel named Fennec.'

His attempt to worm a smile out of his hosts failed. They greeted him with unusual coldness so Ivan switched to a more serious tone.

'I'm sorry I didn't report as soon as I arrived. I met some American government employees on the seaplane and thought I'd add them to my report,' said Ivan, trying to explain why it took him more than twelve hours to report to his handler since landing. 'I spent the whole day with them; it wasn't until the evening that I managed to get away for a minute and call you from a phone box—'

'We know that,' von Karstoff broke in. 'Did you manage to at least learn something from them?'

'Nothing. Nothing specific. And I really did try my best. I entertained them the entire trip, helped them settle in, took them around… but nothing to show for it. The only thing that occurs to me is that their arrival may have something to do with the military base…'

'Where did you get that idea from?'

'Well… when we were flying over the Azores, I thought

they were looking out the window a little too intently… It's just an impression, maybe I'm wrong …' And as he had nothing more to say, he changed the subject.

'Here, I brought you a few things,' Ivan said, holding out little presents from his trip.

Elizabeth found a lipstick and three pairs of silk stockings wrapped in fine tissue paper.

'You shouldn't have,' she blushed.

But even a box of the finest Cuban cigars could not mollify Ludwig. The situation was extremely serious.

Ivan had counted on there being problems. After his previous meeting with them he had gone to America, which was still neutral at the time, on an extremely serious, ambitious assignment: to find out as much as he could about the Americans, especially about their naval fleet and Pacific port in Pearl Harbor, and, over time, to organize a network of agents in the field who would collect information for the Germans. This was the purpose of the thirty-eight thousand dollars in cash they had given him.

Returning fourteen months later, the only thing he had for them, apart from the mementos, were his debts. Huge debts. Debts he would not be able to repay even by Judgement Day. And not only had he failed to establish a network of informers, he could not even boast of a single agent. Even the radio set he used in the States occasionally to contact the Abwehr had inexplicably fallen silent. So he had spent a stack of money and gone into debt without anything to show for it. But Ivan knew all the things they could accuse him of and had a ready defence.

'Believe me, I find this very awkward,' von Karstoff began.

It did not bode well. But judging by Karstoff's demeanour and the fact that he was avoiding looking him in the eye, Ivan figured that Ludwig was simply the bearer of bad news. He felt no personal animosity.

'Berlin is disappointed with your results in America. Its official assessment is: "Excellent in England, good in America until his trip to Rio de Janeiro, mediocre for the next three months, and lately beneath criticism",' he said reading from his notes.

Ivan listened as if none of it had anything to do with him.

'Now at least you know what they think of you in the service,' Ludwig finished and then stopped, as if wondering whether he should say what was on his mind. He decided to continue: 'If you are interested in my own opinion, I am personally very sorry to have to read such a report about one of my best agents, somebody in whom I placed great hope.' He sounded as if nothing would make him happier than to hear a persuasive explanation for Ivan's inactivity.

Which he was about to get. A few days before leaving New York, Ivan had worked on his explanation with two English experts on fabricating stories. And he had ready answers for every disputed issue his German handlers might be able to raise. He began, as agreed, by accepting the criticism levelled at him.

'If you are interested in my opinion, I consider that assessment, if anything, too mild. My results were, from beginning to end, a big fat zero. Beneath criticism, as you say.' As predicted, this admission rather surprised his handler.

'Some people think that you've changed sides,' Ludwig said somewhat reluctantly.

That gave him his cue to go on the offensive.

'I would think the same thing if I were in your shoes. But let's remember one thing. Why am I doing all this?'

Ludwig did not reply, but Ivan pressed him.

'Tell me, what is my motive again?'

'Money?'

'Exactly. And not just any money, but *my fee*. And I'm not talking here about the actual fee but about simply covering my costs. I didn't have enough even for that. You sent me on too expensive an assignment with too little money. The longer I was there the less I was able to do… In a nutshell: you need dollars to get things done. Full stop… Frankly, considering the hard time I had it's amazing that they didn't turn me.'

Ludwig decided that rather than argue he would say what he had been told to say.

'Berlin thinks that you had enough money but that you squandered it. They really didn't like seeing your photograph with various Hollywood stars in the tabloids.'

The German took from the folder on his desk a dozen newspaper clippings of Ivan in the company of a gorgeous woman: the two of them on the beach, the two of them skiing in Aspen, the two of them in evening dress at a banquet and in white shirts on a yacht, always looking happy, young and in love. In one of them they looked particularly infatuated. He in his tuxedo and she in a long white gown were posing for the camera, but it was obvious that they had eyes only for one another. The caption under the picture was: *Simone Simon, star of the latest Hollywood movie* Cat People, *with her escort at last night's opening.*

Ivan looked through the pictures as if examining important

evidentiary material. For a moment he felt wistful, which was unusual for him.

'Now you see why they think that you spent too much time in America having fun and too little working. You were given a lot of money...' Ludwig continued.

Ivan, as planned, went on the counter-offensive.

'Forgive me but what does *a lot of money* mean exactly? It was a lot if you were thinking of me moving to a small town in Alabama, living the life of an average American and briefing you on what was happening in the neighbourhood. In that case it really was a lot of money. An outrageously large amount of money. But our agreement was that my work would entail mixing with high society. That was our agreement, wasn't it? Nobody told me that the rules had changed. So let's see. What was specific to my work in London when they assessed it as excellent?'

Again Ludwig did not reply, so Ivan had to do it for him.

'In London I had enough money. And what was different in America? Especially in the last three months, when I was beneath criticism? First I didn't have much cash, and later I stacked up debts. You sent me to America like a kid with empty pockets to the market, and then you wonder why he didn't buy anything. And you're annoyed that he had a little fun along the way... That's not how it goes...'

'What do you mean by "empty pockets"?' said Ludwig, surprised.

'Right off, I spent almost everything I brought with me on getting a decent flat, radio set, furniture and car,' Ivan said, counting off these basic expenses on his fingers.

'Do you really not know how much money you took with you or are you shitting me?' Ludwig suddenly looked astonished.

'And do you know how much a flat in Manhattan costs? A limo? How many presents I had to dole out? How do you think I got invited to receptions and cocktail parties? How did I meet important people? How, for instance, did I get to J. Edgar Hoover, the director of the FBI? How else could I have found out and told you that he's a queer and that he's screwing his deputy? Things work differently in America, my friend. In England it's about status and who you know. In America the only way you can get to the top is with millions in your pocket or a film star on your arm. You think that's cheap? I had *only* thirty-eight thousand to make my way with millionaires. And I was lucky that Simone fell in love with me and gave me a free pass into society. She is at the peak of her fame.' He had to show off a little but quickly returned to the plan. 'And it would have all paid off if you hadn't screwed up just when I was getting somewhere.'

Von Karstoff was feeling more and more uncomfortable.

'If only you had at least recruited somebody… then I would have easily explained it to them,' he tried to justify himself.

'What do you mean "if I had recruited somebody"? Didn't I recruit? In the days when I had money, and that, I repeat, was *precisely* the period when you assessed me as good, I recruited several people, and I hadn't even really found my feet in my new surroundings yet. I wrote to you about it. I didn't…? Remember the engineer who told me about the new plane engines? And didn't I find a radio telegraphist? Both had started working for me but quickly dropped me because they hadn't received a cent. That drooly-mouthed signalman never returned the radio I bought him because I owed him money... As for agent Schatz, who works for the War Ministry, I had him in the palm of my hand. First I found him a girl. She was a real looker. He'd never seen anything like her, let alone been with somebody like that. And he fell hard for her. Everything was going smoothly, according to plan. Then he began to realize how much this little pleasure was costing him, but he didn't want to lose her, so, fuck it, he got into debt. And by the time I could have bought all sorts of information from him, I didn't have a cent to my name! How was I supposed to bribe the miserable wretch? With what?'

Nobody said anything. Ivan's histrionic monologue left him drained and he sat there hunched over, his elbows on his knees, his arms hanging. Elizabeth, who until then had been sitting there looking as quiet and blank as a stuffed pheasant on a wall, glanced over at Ludovico as if asking him to say a kind word to his friend. And when he did finally speak, his tone was different.

'I understand you. I didn't know the details but I could have guessed... As I said, personally I see your situation in a much better light than Berlin... I know you and your methods well... I'll put down in my report everything you said. I'm sure the mistake is on our side, at least in part, and I'll try to explain that to them... I'll say that you were left without money in the middle of an expensive mission, and after that everything went downhill.' Ludovico was rehearsing aloud what he was going to say to Berlin in a form his bosses could accept.

Now that he was clearly on a roll, Popov did not want to lose his momentum. He went on complaining.

'The less money I had, the fewer the results. You think I don't know that?' Now he sounded both repentant and despairing. He stopped arguing, stopped trying to convince anybody of anything. He simply used different words to talk about his woeful American adventure, as if he were confiding in close friends. 'Meanwhile, everybody I had recruited abandoned me. What could I offer them? The promise that one day I might have some money for them? How could I expect them to risk their lives on credit…? That's not how things are done… As for me personally, I was placed in the humiliating position of having to borrow money from my girlfriend. For the last three months, while I waited in vain for you to send me dollars, she supported me… Like some gigolo… It's lucky nobody heard about it. Simone really does love me.'

Ludovico and Elizabeth had never seen him so dejected and it moved them. They never dreamed that this cheerful, positive man could sink to such depths of despair. And he convinced them not because of his slick performance, but because he truly believed that *he* was the real victim here. It was when he came to actually believe this that he forgot the plan and started to improvise. He got carried away with his role, as actors would say.

'Anyway, what's the point of me trying to explain anything?' Ivan said as if talking to himself. 'Frankly, I can't work under these conditions anymore,' he went on, quite calmly. 'You owe me; I'm drowning in debt. If I mess up, who knows what can happen – you're holding my family hostage and…' Here he stopped and changed the subject. It was too hard for him to even mention his fears for his family. 'We're friends. That's clear, I hope. You are the only one who knows the kind of work I do. I spend months in enemy territory. Do you think that just because I'm cheerful and don't complain it means that I'm not afraid? I risk my life knowingly and I carry out my assignments conscientiously. You can't say I haven't been useful up to now, and you can hardly blame me for not having been more useful... But since my work has been assessed as "beneath criticism", maybe it's time for us to part ways. What do you think?' It was only with this last question that Ivan looked up at Ludovico. He had convinced not just him, but himself as well.

Partly because of his performance, partly because of those three pairs of silk stockings, and maybe also because they had had a brief but unforgettable fling when they had met in Rio the previous November, the first to give way was Elizabeth. She, who had never been heard to express an opinion, unexpectedly took Ivan's side.

'We have fallen victim to cuts ourselves lately. That's why we moved here... even though our safety is now at risk.'

'If you want to leave, the problem will be that you know too much,' von Karstoff said. 'I'd rather you stayed and continued to work for us. I'll try to explain it to Berlin. I'm flying over there tomorrow. Tell me, what are your conditions for us to continue co-operating despite everything?'

Now this was the part that Popov had down pat, but since he was having trouble dropping the role he had just taken on, he continued to speak with the same restrained pathos:

'For you to pay me what you owe me, for me to give back

what I owe you. I'm not asking for much, just what we agreed on and you didn't honour... Being honourable people, that's what I expect of you. If there hadn't been trust I would never have got involved with you ...'

'And how much do you reckon that is?' Ludovico asked. He was prepared for a whopping big figure.

'Forty-five,' said Ivan.

'Forty-five thousand?' said a somewhat startled von Karstoff.

'Well, yes.' Ivan did not look like a man who would be thrown by such an amount. 'I owe forty, and I need five for my next trip to London. There's a chance I may be going in a couple of weeks.'

Von Karstoff looked at him in amazement for a few seconds. Then he wrote down *45,000!!!* in his notebook.

'If you manage to arrange it, just leave the money in the tank in my toilet. If not, we go our different ways. In that event, I'll have no other choice than to disappear. I'm afraid of my creditors. We'll see each other after the war, God willing.' Ivan was much more positive now. 'We've lost a lot of time. I want to finish this job properly, correctly. Here are my notes. Take them so that we can write up the report as quickly as possible. After that, what will be will be. Shall we start?'

Elizabeth sat down at the typewriter; Ludwig took some paper and a pencil and started from the beginning.

'Remind me the pretext under which you went to the States.' Von Karstoff always started with questions he knew the answers to.

'I went as a representative of the Yugoslav government-in-exile,' Popov replied smoothly.

'Can you tell me exactly what work that entailed?'

The questions went on for hours. Where? With whom? How? Why? What had happened to him in the States? He asked him everything. Even about movies. He asked him about the latest films, whether he had seen them and what were they like. No detail or event was too small for von Karstoff.

It was almost dawn by the time Ivan crept out of the second-floor apartment at Avenida de Berna no. 6. Ludwig accompanied him across the courtyard to the side entrance. Then he returned home and sat down to read his report. It was well into the day when he composed the conclusion that he would take to Berlin. It said:

> Based on the above, and considering that he is the only agent we have of this category, I suggest that he be granted the fifty thousand US dollars he is asking for in order to remain in the service, claiming that he fears for his life unless he settles the large debts he has incurred. I know that the amount he is asking for is astronomical but allow me to remind you that Ivan is one of our most valuable agents. If you deem that his life is not worth that much, then the question is whether to liquidate him or just let him 'go down the drain'.

# THE INCREDIBLE, SAD STORY OF
# THE SENSITIVE MISS TONITA AND
# HARD REALITY

Early every morning, before going on what he called his 'parish rounds', Cardoso would stop off at the office to browse through the daily press. Once this was done, he would go downstairs for his first coffee of the day. It was Monday, and yesterday's and today's issues were waiting for him. Fortunately, there was not much real news. For the past two days the *Diário de Lisboa* had been focusing on domestic themes: yesterday on some new archaeological finds in the country, and today on Portugal's traditionally good relations with Brazil. News about the war was interesting but not really earthshattering. It mostly concerned two regions: North Africa, where Australian troops had joined the British in Egypt and things were going well, and the eastern front, where the Germans were advancing, especially in the southern sector along the Black Sea, towards the symbolically key town of Stalingrad.

In the next newspaper he found a story from the said southern sector of the eastern front. The article had appeared in the new June–July issue of the bimonthly *Young Europe*, which was edited and printed in Berlin and then translated into a dozen languages and distributed worldwide. This issue had a letter written from the front by a German soldier named Georg B. to his Portuguese friend. That was all Cardoso managed to read from the title and a cursory look at the text because the print was small.

'Miss Tonita, please come over here. I mustn't tire my eyes,' the inspector said to the secretary, as he did every time, holding out the journal and pointing. 'This article here that says "Letter from a German Soldier".'

Miss Tonita was already an old hand at this and started to read aloud:

CRIMEA, 17/3/42, ARMY POST OFFICE 31.268

MY DEAR PEDRO,

As I write, the other soldiers are sitting around the table playing cards, and our guns and steel helmets are hanging above our beds, ready for use. A year ago we were setting up telephone lines on the La Manche coast and coming under attack from English hunter-planes. Today we're on the Black Sea coast in Crimea, cursing the loathsome, savage Russians who are ruthlessly attacking us in the most awful, unimaginable ways. They change into civilian clothes or into the uniforms they've taken off our dead. During a street fight, they cut off the ears of our captured men, gouged out their eyes, crushed their bones and left them to die a slow, agonizing death.

Here Miss Tonita stopped for a moment to breathe, before continuing to read:

I watched my fellow soldiers die there on the bare ground, lying next to each other. Some were only eighteen years old and they gave the Fatherland and Europe the most valuable thing they had to give. Yes, my dear Pedro, they died for their Fatherland, but for yours as well, and for your Faith.

Cardoso saw that the girl was on the verge of tears and he stopped her from reading any further.

'Stop there, Tonita.'

She blinked at him with wet eyes. She sniffled and wiped her nose with the back of her hand, smearing her tears and powder over her face.

'For heaven's sake, Miss Tonita, no tears, please. I don't like to see tears…' He gave her the hanky from his breast pocket and took back the journal.

'You see how important peace is, Miss Tonita. That's what we are working for. And you shouldn't cry, you should be proud. Off with you now. Go and freshen up. I'll finish reading on my own.'

Tonita, a homely but sensitive girl from a good family, always pleasant and cheerful, managed to wipe away the snivel from her red nose, but not her mental image of the boy whose letter she'd been reading: a handsome, blond, blue-eyed boy.

She could not fathom the kind of monsters they must be to be able to cut off people's ears and nose, and break their bones.

Miss Tonita went, or to be more precise, ran to the bathroom, while the inspector took his glasses out of his pocket, placed them on his nose and proceeded, with moving lips, to read the same article.

The battles we waged last winter were like nothing before. In the bitter cold, with temperatures below forty degrees centigrade, we had to fight off a horde of charging Russians who had a slew of weapons and armoured vehicles. We held them off, but wherever they did manage to break through our lines they surrounded our men, who had stayed in position, and liquidated them.

This was enough even for Cardoso.

He put down the journal, angry at the author of the article but even more at whoever had allowed these horrors to be published. An unnecessary letter had brought his secretary to tears and placed him in the awkward situation of having to console a woman with whom he had a strictly professional relationship. Muttering, he started arguing with who knows whom.

'That's not the way to do it, gentlemen. Not the way...'

In the end he simply sighed. It would be so much easier if he could live off rentals or dividends, just so long as he did not have to work much with people. That is what he wanted. Not this.

# ALWAYS THE SAME STORY

*I* 'm broke,' Tricycle said.

'So?' asked Jarvis.

'So I think it's time for you to loosen your purse strings a little.'

'We had a different agreement,' observed Jarvis.

'The circumstances were different then. They're not giving me as much as I need,' replied Tricycle.

'In short: you need money for your extravagant lifestyle, is that it?'

'That's exactly it.'

'Any idea as to how I should justify this?'

'Tell them that for the first time in our long and fruitful relationship agent Tricycle is asking for the money he needs to lead an extravagant life; it's his trademark.'

'So how much do you need?' asked Jarvis.

'Five.'

'Five what?'

'Five thousand.'

'So, five thousand dollars.'

'Pounds,' the agent corrected him.

'Five thousand pounds?' Jarvis repeated to be sure.

'Five thousand pounds,' confirmed the agent.

'Frankly, we expected you to ask us for money, but not for this much.'

'That's how much I need, what can I do?'

'You need a whole five thousand pounds?'

'Five thousand pounds.'

'And if they don't approve it?' Jarvis was curious to know.

'They'll approve it.'

'But suppose they don't.'

'Then I'm moving to Rio. I've been in this job too long anyway.'

'Just give me a little time to consult,' Jarvis said, locking his desk and walking out of the office. It was a while before he returned with an envelope.

'You've got two thousand in here. That's all we have in the safe. Where do you want us to leave you the rest?'

'Leave it in my water tank.'

'All right. Is there anything else I can do for the gentleman?'

'I need a visa for the Bajlonis,' replied the agent.

Jarvis shrugged his shoulders. The subject always came up each time they met, and each time he would tell Tricycle that he couldn't help him, which did not stop the agent from raising the question at every subsequent meeting, as if they had never discussed it before.

'Again?' asked Jarvis wearily.

'I owe them a lot of money. Be a pal and arrange it somehow. It would mean a lot to me.'

'Unfortunately, I can't help you there,' Jarvis said, repeating the official position, as he always did.

'Who will help me if not you?' Tricycle asked, as he always did.

'The appropriate office. Have them submit the necessary papers on the ground floor, their case will be examined and they will receive an answer,' said Jarvis, as he always did.

'You're playing dumb. You know that we've tried that already and it didn't work. Your people are digging in their heels and won't grant them a visa. Please, give it a push. It would mean a lot to me.'

'You certainly are persistent. Maybe in the Balkans it's normal to do favours for friends through connections, but we don't do that. That way of resolving problems is to us unacceptable,' said Jarvis, laying out the position of Western civilization.

'All right, if that's how it is,' said Tricycle with a shrug.

As soon as the meeting was over, Jarvis wired somebody in Room 39. Among other things the message said:

Tricycle again raised the issue of visas for the Bajloni family. It was made clear to him that such decisions are not within the purview of the persons conducting this case.

And also:

Tricycle was paid from the embassy safe 6,000 pounds sterling for debt repayment. The receipt has been given to Accounting.

★ ★ ★

Tricycle left no. 17 and started walking uphill to the square. He did not feel like going back to Estoril. He sat in the plaza and ordered a beer. He was sipping his drink, looking around aimlessly, killing time, when an unknown woman appeared in front of him.

'Don't be sad, my friend,' she said.

'I'm not sad,' he smiled. 'I was just daydreaming.'

But the stranger did not believe him. How could she when his eyes had suddenly welled up with tears and he himself did not know why. It wasn't sadness, truly it wasn't; he was probably just moved by her words.

# A BOY MEETS
# A GIRL

And what if, after almost three years, in the course of a number of highly unusual events in a very special place and time, we encounter a perfectly ordinary love story about requited love? Usually such stories are boring and, in honesty, we would not be missing much if we skipped over it. On the other hand, can and should one keep quiet about something as important and human as when your protagonist falls in love like a schoolboy?

In order for a love story to be interesting, it has to have something just a little bit special about it. Let's say that what makes this one unusual is that Duško had been staring at her for over an hour without her noticing, because she was standing under the stage lights and he was sitting in the audience in the dark. And it was not that he fell in love with her straight away. He fell in love with her, a little more than with any other potential beloved, only when she started singing the song about the rose:

*Tu és divina e graciosa*
*Estátua majestosa do amor,*
*Por Deus esculturada*
*E formada com ardor*
*Da alma…*

When she finished her performance and stepped off the stage, he was there waiting for her. He took her hand, glad to see that she was not wearing a wedding or any other ring, raised it to his lips, looked into her eyes and said:

'Popov, Duško Popov, *mademoiselle, je suis vraiment enchanté!* It's a true pleasure to meet you.'

'Maria Elera.'

'Even your name is poetic. Marry me, *mademoiselle*. Be the mother of my child.'

She giggled. And, just for a fraction of a moment, imagined the possibility.

Nobody knows what they talked about that evening, but at the time everything pointed to this being just another one of Popov's flings. That first evening he walked her to her room. They parted at the door; she did not invite him in. Never mind, such things happened, even to him.

Dušan Popov had notable success with women. He owed it, as he himself said, to being persistent. The people who followed his love affairs knew that he would fall for her, that he would work at it until he won her over. The more she resisted, the harder he would work to win her affection. He would not take no for an answer. It was a matter of days before he achieved his goal.

The next morning he confided in his best friend.

'I've fallen in love with a singer. She's beautiful, sings like an angel but is not overly intelligent. Just how I like them.'

The undivided attention he paid her made her feel wanted and special. He knew she would be his if he worked at it long enough, if he bounced back after every defeat and did not worry about the consequences. Slowly, like a tenacious worm, he made his way into her heart and into her life. Women fall in love with people they feel good with. And he did his heroic best to make sure she felt good. His approach was: *You'll be mine sooner or later so there's no point fighting it.*

Every morning he made sure she thought of him as soon as she woke up. A bouquet of red roses would arrive along with her breakfast.

At the beach, along the promenade, in the park, at the café, at the travelling circus, at the casino, at the corrida or in the ballroom, they attracted attention wherever they went, she with her beauty, he with his wanton ways, and together with their glowing love. They were happy whatever they did, taking a stroll, dining, whatever…

He would walk her to her room every evening and they would meet again the next day. He could think of nothing else but this beautiful Brazilian woman. The initial stages of love have some of the symptoms of an acute emotional disorder.

She told him about herself. When she was a little girl in Rio she had wanted to be an opera singer. When she was fourteen she started studying voice. When she was sixteen her father gave her a record player and records. She learned about jazz, the blues and the samba. When she was eighteen she went to Rome where she continued to study music and began to perform, singing both baroque and jazz. An Italian violinist accompanied her. The two of them fell in love through music and married in 1938.

He was conscripted in 1939 and sent to fight in Albania. The day after he disembarked from the ship he was killed. They sent her his bullet-riddled violin.

Devastated, she went back to Brazil. She did not sing for a whole year. She was grieving. And when she discarded her mourning clothes she went to New York to sing in the clubs. After a few months, she needed a change again. The invitation to sing at the casino in Lisbon came just at the right moment.

He was far less talkative than she was. When she asked him to tell her something about himself, he said:

'I'm in love.'

And so it went for almost two weeks. If we didn't know him we would think that Popov was a man of the old school who honoured platonic love and a girl's pre-marital chastity. But since we know the kind of libertine he was, she must have been a very special woman indeed.

Until one evening when they were dancing and she suddenly looked up.

'Let's get away from all these people,' she whispered, her lips brushing his ear, sending quivers down his back. He led her out by the hand.

Later, watching his cigarette illuminate his profile in the dark room, she whispered:

'One day I won't know if I lived this, read about it or dreamed it all up.' They fell asleep in each other's arms.

After so much sunny weather, the next day dawned grey and wet, so they stayed in bed.

'All I know about you is that your eyes are blue,' she said. They picked up where they had left off the night before.

'They're green,' he said. 'I should know; they're my eyes.'

'They're blue now', she replied. 'I can see them; you can't. And please shave. Your stubble is scratching my face.'

The next day he woke up to a clear sky, but found himself alone in bed. She was not in the bathroom either, or in the hallway or in her own room. He could not find her anywhere. She hadn't left a message. The maid told him that her luggage was still in the hotel, she had not checked out. He did not find her in the street, or under the parasols, or among the dinner guests or dancing. He got drunk but did not find her.

She found him, the next day, sitting on a bench under the lemon tree.

She kissed him and said:

'I'm fine. I just needed to get away for a bit. To be by myself and think.'

'It's a beautiful day. Come with me,' he said, taking her by the hand to the car.

They drove along the winding seaside road, through the flat, monotonous landscape. On one side, stretching far into the hinterland, were sand dunes scattered with clumps of long grass beaten down by the wind. On the other side was the grey ocean. Seen from the convertible, the sea and the land formed a flat disk that met the sky in the low-hanging, curved distance. Disturbing this horizontal view were only the rosettes of the agave, its slender, bare stems sticking out here and there like desert trees.

They left the beaten track and stopped at a vantage point overlooking the sea. The place had a terrible name: Boca do Inferno. The Mouth of Hell. Long ago, when people believed that the world had a limit, this is where they thought it ended.

Standing side by side, just a step away from the abyss, they were the sole witnesses to this magnificent void. She stepped dangerously close to the edge; had he let go of her arm she would have fallen into the sea foaming white below. He took her into his arms, kissed her hair and led her back to the car.

Sharing the cigarette he had rolled them, they leaned back in their seats and quietly gazed out at the landscape as if it were a screen projection. The sun was setting.

'What makes you happy?' she asked.

'Happy? Really, really happy? This,' he said, slapping the polished rosewood steering wheel.

'A car?'

'No, this isn't a car, it's a six cylinder, 1,970 cc, eighty horse-power BMW 328 Roadster. It hugs bends in the road like a snake.'

The car's canvas roof trembled noisily in the wind.

'It's a strange feeling when you're sad because you think you're going to lose somebody who isn't yours,' she said.

As there was no response, she went on.

'I want to tell you something, but promise that you'll at least try to understand and forgive me. Promise?'

'Promise.'

'Really?'

'Really.'

'I lied to you…'

He stared out at the ocean as if he hadn't heard her.

'I've been lying to you from the start,' she said.

'It doesn't matter; forget it.'

'Do you understand what I'm trying to say?' she said, her voice quivering as if she were on the verge of tears. 'I work for the Abwehr. You were my assignment.'

He sensed her vulnerability. He held her tight in his arms. Her sobs were barely audible.

'You are my target. I'm doing this officially. You understand? For money,' she whispered.

'Calm down, darling, don't cry… There's no need to be unhappy.' He held her to his chest.

'Please forgive me, I beg you.'

'Don't cry, darling. It will pass…'

Tricycle's MI6 file included several testimonies from various sources concerning this seemingly unimportant episode.

First there was the message the Lisbon station had sent to London by diplomatic pouch.

As stated in the report of 20/10/43, Tricycle is very happy in Lisbon and is avoiding confirming the date of his next trip to Britain. The reason is probably a Brazilian woman named Maria Elera with whom, despite our warnings, he had an affair lasting a little over two weeks until it abruptly ended. Judging by messages intercepted from the Abwehr's Lisbon office in the meantime, our suspicions were well founded. Tricycle's mistress is the German agent Monica, already known to us from Operation Cardinal in Rome. Although he ignored all our warnings, Tricycle, from everything we know, here again did not risk his own or the operation's safety. All the indications are that, like the other five cases we know of (three enemy female agents and two agents of our own), the girl failed to gather any information about him but rather, like the others, became emotionally involved and even admitted to him that she was an agent. Tricycle refuses to talk about her since he does not see why he would share details about his private life with us.

Enclosed with Jarvis's report was an English translation of the deciphered German intercept. It read:

Regarding Ivan, he was checked but with no result. Agent Monica, an extremely attractive woman experienced in such matters, was assigned to cover him. The Italians, for whom she had successfully worked under the codename Inferno, recommended her. It took approx. two weeks after their first meeting for her to get close to him. After spending forty-eight hours in her room, on 13 October, having taken every precautionary measure, she appeared at our headquarters.

She stated that the relationship between the two of them had got off to a good start, in fact too good, but that he avoided talking about himself and she had only managed to glean a few irrelevant details; they were proved to be correct, which suggests that Monica had done whatever she could. She informed us, however, that she had broken off the relationship the night before. She said she had done so because of 'his warped proclivities'. During her time with Ivan she had not noticed anything unusual to indicate that he was involved in any kind of intelligence work. At the end of the meeting, Monica was instructed to make one more attempt to get close to him, to make up with him so that she could continue working on him.

They met the next day, 14/10/43, in the hotel garden and he drove her to a remote cliff overlooking the ocean. Our field agents followed from a distance and witnessed her simulated attempt to commit suicide, which he prevented, moving her away from the dangerous site. They spent another night together but the next morning, 15/10/42, he broke off all contact with her, except for two occasions (21/10/42 and 26/10/42) when he came to her room drunk, once on his own and once with a local prostitute. He did not stay the night on either occasion. Several days later, on 30/10/42, agent Monica checked out of the hotel and flew to Rome.

Enclosed in the same file was an envelope addressed to Popov that Maria Elera had left at the Palácio's reception desk before leaving.

It contained a photograph of her standing on the steps of the plane. She was wearing a white summer suit and plumed hat. On the back of the picture was a handwritten note in Italian.

MY BELOVED DUDU,

I can't live like this. I feel as if the door is saying 'Push' and I'm pulling. I shall never forget how safe I felt with your arms around me. You are the biggest shit of all the shits I have loved.

Your M.

Added neatly underneath in English, in blue ink, was the following:

Abwehr Agent 3, Monica, photographed at Lisbon's newly opened Portela airport. No traces of invisible ink, microdots or any other valuable intelligence material were detected on either the photograph or the envelope.

# AT LUNCHTIME

The church standing at the site where St Anthony was born looks more like a hospital for sinners and the wretched than a museum of saints. Its doors are wide open to worshippers from before morning mass until after evening service. And it has many visitors because St Anthony is well-known as an able and helpful miracle-worker, and there are always people who want a miracle in life, even a small one.

It was one of those November days when you did not leave the house unless you had to. The sky was leaden, the air turbid, drizzling and saturated.

On Tuesday, at around one o'clock in the afternoon, when everybody who had food to eat was sitting down to lunch, a man in a trench coat walked into Lisbon's empty Church of Santo António. He left his furled umbrella in the narthex, removed his hat, shook the water off his coat and made for the altar. His steps echoed on the stone floor. He sat in the front row pew, facing the large figure of the saint, and deathly silence resumed. Had an experienced priest been present he would have approached the lost soul to offer help. But there was no priest. Other than the stranger and the saint, there was nobody in the church. If it was a troubled soul that had brought the stranger here, there was no one to make him feel he had to control himself; he could even have cried if he felt like it.

However, the visitor did nothing so dramatic. He rose to his feet and went to the confessional. He carefully drew the curtain, knelt in the small booth and, facing the wooden lattice that conceals the face but not the voice of the priest, whispered:

'*Ave Maria.*'

'*Dominus tecum,*' a man's voice whispered back from the other side of the latticed screen.

'Go ahead, tell me what you have to say,' the worshipper said to the priest in English.

'Through the good services of Mr Black—' the priest said.

'No names, please,' the Englishman cut in sternly.

'Through the good services of the manager,' the voice on the other side of the screen said.

The Englishman did not like these opening words either.

'Listen, we don't have much time. Just tell me briefly on whose behalf you are speaking and what you propose.'

'I am here on behalf of MUNAF, the anti-fascist movement of Portugal. I have with me an offer for co-operation,' said the priest.

'What is your position in the organisation?' the Englishman asked.

'We are all comrades. I'm a worker, but I have full authority to negotiate with you,' the priest replied.

'On what basis?'

'On the basis of the decision taken by the leadership. And are you authorized to speak with me?'

'Yes, I am authorized,' responded the Englishman.

'And what is your position in the organisation?' the priest retorted.

'I am simply in the service of His Majesty King George. We don't have much time. Tell me what you have to say.'

Judging by the way the priest spoke, he was a Portuguese who lived in America and he was probably anything but a priest. He went on speaking.

'The situation in Portugal is intolerable. The price of food has gone up because it is being exported at a higher price than the Portuguese worker can afford. Farmers are having the fruits of their labour seized and sold for gold, which goes into the coffers of the state and the pockets of the rich. The confiscated food is sent to the front, while our workers are going hungry; our bread is feeding the aggressor's troops. Our tungsten is killing our brother proletarians. Meanwhile, the authoritarian regime is using the war as an excuse to tighten political oppression and to further exhaust, impoverish and disenfranchise the proletariat.'

The Portuguese man was highly inclined to detail his country's social ills and his class's misfortunes, but the Englishman was not inclined to listen.

'You're communists?'

'No, we're not… That's to say, I am, but the movement I represent is not. It is an anti-fascist movement assembling virtually the entire opposition to the regime: democrats, socialists, Catholic intellectuals, Freemasons. The Communist Party is the linchpin because we are the most threatened of all resistance groups and have nothing to lose but our chains.

And we're the best organized. We're prepared to operate in the field,' said the Portuguese. He used the ready empty phrases that are expected of a seasoned propagandist.

'What sort of operations are you talking about?' the Englishman wanted to know.

'We are ready and able to carry out acts of sabotage, organize strikes and obstruct railways if necessary.'

The Englishman said nothing. Although he was glad to hear that there were people prepared to engage in sabotage on somebody else's behalf, he was not interested in such drastic measures. His interlocutor continued:

'You probably know that, though illegal, the Communist Party is the only political force in the country that has supported the Allies since the very beginning of the war.'

'Yes, I know,' the Englishman said, accepting the man's arguments because they were true, especially since the USSR had entered the war. 'But, we do not consider the destabilization of Portugal to be in our interest. We are only interested in information.'

'There is a wide network of comrades in the field,' the invisible communist explained.

'Have you got anybody in the Azores?'

'Yes, we have our people there, in the harbour and at the airport.'

'What about the railway? Are you in a position to find out, at least roughly, what is being exported, how much and where? We're particularly interested in food and tungsten ore.'

'What we don't know we can find out,' said the Portuguese.

The Englishman then logically asked:

'And what do you expect from us in return? What do you think we can do for you right now? How much money are you asking for?'

'We're not asking for money. We expect you to help us achieve a fairer society. We are calling for freedom of political organisation, parliamentary democracy, the abolition of censorship and of the political police, the release of political prisoners, the closure of penal colonies. We want free elections. We want a country where every citizen will have bread on the table, where every child will go to school, everybody will know how to read and write, every sick person will have a doctor to treat them.'

'And how do you think we could help with that?' asked the Englishman.

'By pressuring Salazar and the forces around him. By pressing for a provisional democratic government of national salvation, where all anti-fascist forces will be represented. That government's first task would be to stop the present authorities' shameful collaboration with the Nazis. It would also be charged with calling free general elections for the National Assembly within a reasonable period of time.'

'According to the instructions I have been given, I can, in principle, accept your offer to help us with information. But I can hardly offer you anything in return. However just we consider your demands, there will be no political pressure exerted until the war is over. If you think it pays for you to work on credit, you can contact us through our common friend, your boss.'

'Agreed.'

'Agreed.'

# HAVE YOU EVER TRIED TO
# SELL A STONE?

It was a warm winter's day and the two friends sat down on the park bench in the sun. They watched the sand-coloured dog run around the gravel, scattering the pigeons. They did not talk; each seemed lost in his own thoughts.

'You are really, really upset today, aren't you, Duško?' Gaby asked.

'Not upset. Beside myself.'

They say it is good for children to be curious, but Gaby could take that too far.

'A woman?'

'Are you nuts?' Duško smiled in spite of himself. 'A woman?!'

'Your car broke down?'

'Do you really think I'd let a pile of metal screw with me?'

'What then?'

'Just drop it, please!' Duško really did not feel like talking.

'Tell me. What is it?' The boy was known for being as tiresome as a tick.

'What do you care…? Mind your own business while you still can, kid.'

'Tell me. I always tell you everything you ask me.'

Gaby would not give up. He never gave up. Anybody who spent time with him knew that, and also knew it was useless to resist.

'Oh, it's nothing terrible. I'm a bit short of cash…' said Duško. He seemed to be ashamed of himself for just uttering the words, even though it was to a friend.

At first the boy said nothing.

'You know, Duško, don't be mad at me for saying this but I've told you a hundred times that you're too much of a spend-thrift. Happiness is a balance between what you need and what you have. A modest person is a happier person because he needs less and has fewer worries.'

'And that's why I didn't want to tell you. All I need are your lectures,' said Duško. He did not sound angry; he seemed to have reconciled himself to his fate.

'Last night you ordered lobster and a bottle of champagne, and you know that I don't eat lobster and that I don't drink. You always order the most expensive things on the menu and then throw half of it away. You throw away foie gras.'

'That's for health reasons. Liver is good for your blood count, and you're still growing. If you ate as you should, I wouldn't be throwing anything away.'

'You're just making excuses,' diagnosed the boy.

'I'm making excuses… What can I say? It's how I am. I simply can't control myself,' Popov confessed.

'That's a bummer,' the boy decided. 'How much money do you need?'

'You know, Gaby, it's not polite to ask questions like that.'
Now it was Duško's turn to lecture.

'I want to lend it to you. If you want?'

'You have it?' Popov perked up.

'No.'

'No!? Weren't you bragging that you have enough cash to last half the millennium?'

'I wasn't bragging. You asked me and I told you. And I did have it, but I invested it and I have no cash left. But I can get it if you'll help me.'

\* \* \*

Above the shop window and door, stylized gold letters interlaced with floral motifs, as was the fashion at the turn of the century, read:

Ourivesaria Rossio Lda
Jewellery – Filigree – Silver

Before pushing open the door, Duško asked the boy once again:

'Are you sure you know what you're doing?'

'I'm sure,' the boy said decisively. 'Just follow the plan and everything will be fine. You start, then I run in, and you just stay quiet and watch until I toss the ball back to you. All right?'

'All right, all right…'

They strode confidently into the shop, as if intending to buy something. Duško briefly flirted with the salesgirl and was told that, in view of the nature of his visit, it might be better if he spoke to the owner. Mr Popov agreed. He took his young friend along without asking or explaining, as if it should be obvious to everyone that the two of them were partners. They were taken past glass cases full of precious jewellery to a smallish office lined with mirrors. Everything was going according to plan.

The two of them sat down on the same side of the desk. Soon an elderly gentleman wearing a bow tie appeared. He had a proud, obliging air about him, like a butler. He welcomed the customers, sat down opposite them and very politely inquired of Popov how he could be of service. Popov asked to see what loose diamonds they had. He said he had heard that the shop had the finest stones in town and he was interested in the best that they had.

The jeweller nodded and disappeared. A few minutes later he was back, carrying a silver tray with four black cloth pouches. As if handling relics, he emptied them carefully one by one, and four large gems dropped onto the black-velvet-lined tray.

'These pieces are of the highest quality. They are approximately two carats each.'

Popov simply gave a nod of his head. He picked up the diamonds one by one, so that they would not scratch each other, and held them with his thumb and index finger, turning them to and away from the light, checking their purity, colour, transparency, gleam, first with his naked eye and then with a loupe. Then he gave the boy all four gems, one by one. The boy looked at the diamonds against the light, away from the light, against the black and then against the white background, with and without the loupe. One minute he looked like a serious expert, the next like a child who had been given a magnifying glass to play jeweller with.

Suddenly the boy spoke up:

'Sir, I'll be honest with you,' he said speaking as if he were the one negotiating here and not his adult friend. 'These pieces are good, they're valuable, but we have something to show you that I am sure you will find of interest.' The boy took a thin velvet pouch out of his pocket and untied it.

At that moment the shop-owner lost all trace of servility and took on a supercilious, offended air. Had they told him from the start that they had come to sell, not to buy, he would not have wasted his time with them. But he was slow to react. The boy had already dropped his stone onto the tray. Now a stone of about a carat was mixed up with the four that were already on the tray's black velvet.

This made the jeweller sit up. He had already heard about buyers trying to cheat and replace precious stones with their own. But even a cursory glance sufficed for him to see that there was not the slightest chance of confusing the diamonds. Next to the boy's, the first four stones, the stars of the jeweller's collection, looked dull, like mere pieces of glass. The boy's stone, which was half the size of the others, blazed with light.

The jeweller's arrogance vanished as quickly as it had appeared. He looked surprised, perplexed, one might even say slightly disturbed. Duško seemed to have a better hold on himself, although it was perfectly clear that neither of them had ever seen a gem of such beauty and brilliance before.

'May I take a closer look?' asked the jeweller.

He picked up the loupe and examined the stone with the attention of someone doubtful of its authenticity.

'Something like this…' he muttered to himself in Portuguese, switching to French for his visitors. 'This is the first time I've seen anything like this… Whose work is it?'

'My father's,' replied the boy.

A glance at Popov and the jeweller realized that he could not be the boy's father.

'And why didn't your father come with you?'

'He's not here.'

'Do you know the secret of this stone?'

That was the question Gaby was waiting for.

'The secret is not in the stone, it's in the light.'

'What do you mean?'

'My father is an engineer. He figured out how to cut the diamond so it gets this kind of brilliance.'

The jeweller kept looking for a flaw from different angles and against the light. He found none in either the polish or the crystal. They let him play for a few more minutes before the boy asked him for the stone back. While the child was putting it back in its pouch, Popov asked:

'Could I have a sheet of paper and an envelope, please?'

When they arrived, he took a fountain pen from his pocket.

'See, a silver Parker pen. Simone gave it to me.' Her film *Cat People*, scored at the box office almost double what *Casablanca* took in. He took the opportunity to boast a little bit to his friend. Then he wrote down a figure on the piece of paper, folded it in half and placed it in the envelope.

'This is our minimum price. You now know everything about our offer. If you are interested, we will be at the Chave d'Ouro for the next half an hour, and as of tomorrow you can find me at the Palácio in Estoril. My name is Popov,' he said, sliding the envelope across the table before walking out.

\* \* \*

A distinguished author once wrote: *Lisbon. A restless town on volcanic soil. Nowhere in the world are people calmer and more polite when you speak to them individually, but all those quiet and polite people make such a noise when together that you can't sleep.*

Lisbon was very noisy. Cars raced through town, often honking their horns. The most clamorous area was Rossio Square, in the city centre, traditionally considered to be the best place for mass demonstrations. In the past, public executions used to be staged here. Another great writer once wrote: *The inhabitants of Lisbon emerge from their homes and pour into the city's streets and squares, crowds descend from the upper quarters of the city and gather in the Rossio to watch Jews and lapsed converts, heretics and sorcerers being tortured, along with criminals, who are less easily classified, such as those found guilty of sodomy, blasphemy, rape and prostitution, and various other misdeeds that warrant exile or the stake.* But the square has also always been a popular place for other sorts of spontaneous gatherings, from pogroms to demonstrations in support of the leaders of the country and those who chase the ball in its name.

Vehicles, trams and pedestrians all converged on Rossio Square. This was where flowers, newspapers, tobacco and fruit were sold, lottery and raffle tickets. Black cabs lined up in front of the theatre, and across the way, long lines of people stood waiting in front of the phone booths. The only traffic light in the city was to be found here, and people would gather to watch the light change. Sometimes one could see ox-carts laden with greens and vegetables, and fishwives bearing baskets of fish on their heads would come this far into town. Although it was against the law to walk barefoot in the city, they were such tourist attractions that the authorities turned a blind eye.

The old, neglected buildings lining the square had few residents. But the catering establishments on the ground floors were buzzing with activity. In the promenades most of the visitors were still foreigners. Times had changed. Nobody was shocked anymore to see a woman sitting on her own in a café, lighting a cigarette; everybody knew that she was not Portuguese. People get used to all sorts of things.

The waiter immediately identified the two friends as foreigners, not merely because of their dress and style, but because no Portuguese in his right mind would sit in a café with such a young child. And so the waiter addressed them in some sort of French. Suddenly, it was the boy who replied, as if he were the adult here.

'Give us two glasses of champagne.'

'Wait a minute, you're getting ahead of yourself. We haven't struck a deal yet and you already want to celebrate,' the gentleman interceded.

'We have struck a deal,' said the boy, trying to placate him.

'All right, if you say so. You're the boss … Still, I'd just like to make sure I've understood everything. You showed him a kind of diamond that he had never seen before? Is that right?' Duško asked.

'Exactly.'

'Did we offer it to him for a lot of money?'

'It's not cheap. But it's not that expensive either; they're just spoiled, they're used to buying from desperate people for peanuts.'

'Is that the only one of its kind you've got?' asked Duško.

'Not at all. This one is the poorest of the lot, I just didn't want to show him the others. This way he'll think he's buying something nobody else has.'

'I take my hat off to you, young man,' said Duško. 'Now tell me something, if it's not a secret. What did you invest all that money in?'

'You don't know? I didn't tell you?' said the boy, surprised. 'I invested it in Gordana's factory.'

'Oh, okay, I've got nothing to worry about then. You're a clever one. That woman turns one penny into three. The two of you should stick together; you'll go far.'

Just then a young man appeared in front of them. He wished them a good day and said that the jeweller would like to speak with them.

'Tell your boss that we will drop by before lunch,' said Popov.

The young man disappeared and they stayed, sipping their champagne in the sunshine.

'How old are you again?' Duško asked the boy.

'Twelve and a half.'

'Isn't it about time for your bar mitzvah?'

'Yes, but I'd like to read in temple when my mother and father come…' said the boy. He stopped, thought for a moment, then turned to Duško and asked him out of the blue: 'Do you think they will come?'

'I don't know,' his friend replied honestly.

'I don't know either anymore…'

Saddened, the two of them dropped the subject. They looked straight ahead, in case either should shed a tear.

Duško pointed to the monument of King Pedro looking out over the city from his tall column.

'Look up there! At the column! At the male pigeon jumping on the female on top of the fellow's head,' he laughed. 'Look at that maniac, for heaven's sake.'

Estoril, 27 March 1944

Tonio, my friend, how are you?

Thanks very much for the book. I've read it twice, and
some parts even more than that. What I liked most were all
the sunsets on the little planet and the pictures of the boa
constrictor with the elephant in his stomach. What I liked
least was the ending. It would have been much better if the
prince had returned to his planet and if he had a mother and
father there so that he was not so alone. There you are. You
asked for my honest opinion so don't now hold it against me.

I'm fine. I had my bar mitzvah. It was a few months late
but the rabbi said it didn't matter. I stumbled only two or
three times reading, but hardly anybody noticed.

After the synagogue we all went to my friends', the
Bajlonis, place. Lunch was my present from their mother.
Grada Bajloni wants to be a pilot like you. He can drive and

he went to aviation school. He was thrilled when I told him you and I are friends. He says he's read your books and you're his idol. He sends you his best.

My friends from the hotel came too – Duško, Papagaio, Bruno, Mr Black and Lourdes. Manuel and Lino couldn't come, they couldn't get the day off from work.

I got lots of presents. Grada gave me an Argentinian pencil, the kind RAF pilots have; it writes with ink but you don't have to fill it. Gordana and Lila gave me a new prayer shawl and a see-through ball with a little house inside; it snows when you shake it. I don't remember if I ever saw snow. Lourdes and Papagaio gave me a shirt, Mr Black a magazine about cars and Bruno a book in English, *Moby Dick*. Duško brought the musicians from the hotel as his present. They played for us all day, and Duško tucked money into their instruments.

Aunt Radmila kept shoving food at me during lunch. Later we played football. But Duško got uppity and wouldn't play. Bruno was in defence. I kicked two goals and Mr Black kicked the ball into the lake. Papagaio fell and hurt his knee and after that he couldn't play anymore. Even Gordana played a bit with us men. Afterwards we had cake, and then I went for a walk with Papagaio. It's a very interesting place and there's so much to explore. We went to a spot that looks like the prehistoric forest we saw at the Natural History Museum, remember? The palms are like gigantic ferns and underneath it's all dark. All that's missing are those huge dragonflies. There's also a big round rock pool with goldfish. (They're called goldfish but actually they're red.) Papagaio told me that while we were playing football he saw Duško and Lila kissing by the pool. He said they were kissing like in the movies and that he was touching her breasts but couldn't do much because she kept moving his hands away.

When we went home, I sat in the car with Duško. Slavcho, the musician, came with us. It was funny because Duško's car has only two seats so we put him in the trunk. Duško said that Gypsies are a noble people, they don't need much to be happy. While we were driving back, Duško kept shouting, 'Come on, Slavcho, play!' Then Slavcho would play something from the closed trunk. Like a radio. I don't know why Slavcho is so fond of him when Duško gives him such a hard time.

Duško sends his best. He already has forty hours of flying time with an instructor, but he still can't fly on his own. He needs another twenty hours, but is too busy to fit it in.

I go to the Bajlonis often. I invested money in the tinned food factory they opened on their property. We are reinvesting the excellent dividends. I was very lucky to find a partner like Gordana. Duško's business isn't going well, for instance. I can see that he's trying, he goes to London, he's been to the US, but nothing's happening.

The hotel is much less crowded than when you were here. The other day Fennec got into a scrap with a female dog called Sisi. Fennec is much smaller, but, like David and Goliath, she got the better of her. We barely managed to pull them apart. Then the boy who owns Sisi called me a Jewish pig. I didn't get mad, but Duško heard him and said something to him. I'm too embarrassed to repeat it. Later he said something even worse to the boy's father. The father is a German officer and he took offence. He challenged Duško to a duel. Duško told him to eat shit and that if it was killing he liked he should kill himself. Later Duško even reported the man to Inspector Cardoso. He said he had threatened to shoot him dead.

I play chess with whoever is around, mostly with Bruno. I've been the top chess player at the hotel for the past few months. I can't play with children anymore. I win straight off.

There's no news from my parents.

I can't write anymore, I have to do my geometry homework. I've got French to do too, but that's easy.

I drew the mythical cow above for you.

PS: Did you know that in India cows are considered to be sacred?

PPS: Can you tell me what you meant when you said 'It is only with the heart that one can see rightly; what is essential is invisible to the eye'? I'm not sure I quite understood it.

# THERE ARE DEAD BODIES INSIDE!

'It's not the walls or the furniture that are the key, it's the service,' Mr Black maintained. 'You can't have a good hotel without good staff.'

That is why here at the Palácio, every employee must meet several basic criteria; they must speak at least two or three languages and be amiable, which is not one but a cocktail of qualities, such as patience, forbearance, politeness, diplomacy, being good-natured, cheerful, even physically attractive. All of that is important because the hotel's guests are demanding and capricious; they give themselves liberties that others would never even dream of. One really does have to be amiable to deal with them.

Bruno was recruited from a cruise ship where he had been working, and he was hired solely because Mr Black felt he fitted the required profile. The fact that it later transpired that the two of them shared similar interests was pure luck. They both like to discuss abstract subjects, especially politics, and they are not merely each other's ideal but rather only possible partner for this kind of entertainment, because it is not a popular sport in these parts; often it is not even legal.

Fortunately, the Portuguese are not particularly fond of politics, that most dangerous of all topics. They are a gentle, dutiful people, as everybody agrees, but whereas the majority believe that this is because of their God-given, kind nature, Bruno thinks their submissiveness comes from long years of oppression stretching from the Inquisition to Salazarism. 'Here, anybody who doesn't keep his mouth shut is considered an extremist,' said Bruno; it was not an accusation, merely an observation. 'If you come out with any, especially political opinion, people move away from you lest anybody think that they are complicit. Then you can shout your head off.'

Needless to say, he would only express such extreme views in front of Mr Black. And even then, only when they were alone.

Every morning and afternoon, the two of them read the newspapers. Mr Black read the stale English and American press, and Bruno read those papers and the fresh but censored Portuguese papers. They listened to the news on Radio London whenever they had a chance.

Later, when they had an opportunity to talk, which was when Bruno was driving the manager somewhere, they exchanged views on current affairs and on the future. Sometimes they agreed, sometimes they didn't. Sometimes their predictions came true, sometimes they didn't. With time, it started to look like a game.

The other person Bruno talked to was Gaby. Every day except Sunday he drove him to Lisbon and back, sometimes to the French lycée, at other times to the synagogue. Thus, every day the two of them spent more than an hour in the car talking. If it happened that they were both free at the same time, they enjoyed playing a game of chess. Papagaio was like a brother, but Bruno, while not exactly like Gaby's father, though he was old enough to be, was more like his best adult friend.

There is a lot that can be said in an hour. Gaby usually talked about what they had learned at school that day. Then Bruno, who had left school after learning how to read, write and count and therefore had little to say on the subject, would tell Gaby something about his own experience in reference to the topic at hand. For instance, when Gaby explained to Bruno the connection between the tilt of the Earth, the changing seasons and the planet's climate zones, the former sailor told Gaby that when you sailed from Tierra del Fuego to Greenland you passed through all these zones and all four seasons of the year. Or, for instance, when Gaby was learning ancient history, Bruno, who had been to the Mediterranean ports hundreds of times, described to him the size of the Colosseum in Rome, the pyramids in Egypt and what Constantinople and the Parthenon looked like today. Bruno kept telling Gaby to study because knowledge was power. He told him how happy he was that Gaby was clever and had money for his education because most people lacked either the brains or the money, usually both, to become learned. This was already the fourth year that Gaby had been growing up in Bruno's car; the boy was precocious, the driver curious, and they got along well.

\*

It was a spring day. Bruno dropped Gaby off at school, then quickly finished his chores in Lisbon, taking some packages to the post office and papers to the notary. On his way back he stopped off at a hardware store on the outskirts of town and bought two shovels and a pair of secateurs to prune the hedges. It was around nine-thirty in the morning when he finished and headed back for Estoril; he would be returning along the same road at five in the afternoon to pick up the boy from school.

He was driving, lost in thought, when suddenly he heard a loud whirring, buzzing noise coming from the direction of the sea. A two-engined plane was flying low towards him on his left, trailing smoke. It looked as if the pilot was attempting an emergency landing but had lost control. The plane was rapidly losing altitude and rocking right and left, like when the pilot at an air show greets the public by tipping the wings of his plane. It was flying so low that Bruno thought it would hit him. But it didn't. It came down a bit further on, into a field. There was a tremendous crash and the roar of the engine fell silent. The wreckage lay there in the field, just a few hundred metres away from Bruno.

By the time Bruno had found a way to get to the crash scene with his car, a number of peasants and children had already reached the spot. The children were probably shepherd boys because they were not in school. They crept up to the site of the crash, trod on the deep ruts left by the plane, but did not approach the smoking aircraft. They were afraid it might explode. A woman could be heard wailing:

'There are dead bodies inside! Oh, my goodness, they are dead!'

Bruno immediately dispatched one of the boys to fetch the police and tell them what had happened and where. Then he ran over to the plane. The blades of the propeller were mangled. Behind the pilot cabin's shattered, blood-splattered windshield were two men wearing pilot caps. One of them was hanging his head in a strange way, as if he had broken his neck. The other looked as if he had lost his face. The door was stuck so Bruno ripped it off. The engine was not on fire, but the plane's metal body was broken and bent and everything in its belly was strewn all over the ground. The bodies of two uniformed soldiers were in the fuselage crushed between heavy boxes and mangled metal. One of them, a young officer, showed signs of life. He was groaning.

It is hard to say whether it was humanity that got the better of fear or if it was sheer curiosity, but suddenly the peasants ran over to the plane. Together, they tried to pull at least the surviving soldier out of the wreckage but they couldn't because the slightest movement made him scream in pain. They reorganized themselves, dragged away the boxes of ammunition, knapsacks and armaments, and freed his crushed legs. He was still stuck. Then Bruno remembered that he had a big pair of secateurs in the boot of the car. He retrieved them, quickly cut through the wires and metal and managed to free the injured man. As the six of them were pulling him out of the fuselage, the German kept moaning and groaning through clenched teeth. Both his legs were limp. His left thighbone, very white, was sticking out of his trouser leg. Meanwhile, on Bruno's instructions, somebody had already brought a plank of wood from a nearby truck and they used it as a stretcher for the poor man. It was only when they moved him onto the plank that they realized how badly he was bleeding. Bruno tied his belt around the man's leg, above the open wound, to stop any more loss of blood.

As there was no sign of either the police or fire-fighters, they lifted the wounded man on the plank into the truck and drove for the hospital.

It was at the hospital that Bruno realized he looked as if he had been in a bullfight: his uniform, shirt, hands and face were smeared with the injured man's blood. Luckily, he always had a fresh change of clothes in the car. He washed and changed his clothes; then he noticed the police. They led him to the side, checked his papers and took his statement. Everything that Bruno had been through that day – the blood, the death, the open fractures, the screaming and the pain – had been hard, but hardest of all was being interrogated by the police.

'Do you know that, unless on official duty, citizens are strictly forbidden from approaching an aircraft that has landed in Portugal irregularly until the authorities arrive on the scene?' they asked him.

'Just as well I didn't know. If we hadn't run over right away the man would have bled to death,' Bruno replied.

'Where did you learn how to administer first aid?' they asked him.

'I worked on a ship. We had training.'

'And why didn't you first notify the authorities?' they wanted to know.

'I did. I sent a boy on his motorbike to tell you, but you needed time,' Bruno answered.

'How do you know how to dress a wound?'

'I told you, I had a first aid course in America.'

'Where did you get the secateurs?'

'They were in the car.'

'Who put them there?'

'I did. I was supposed to take them to the hotel. They're for pruning the hedges,' Bruno said.

Their job was to look for the guilty, to question suspects, but in the absence of any criminal they questioned him. As if they suspected that he might somehow be responsible for the plane crash, they kept asking him the same questions, hoping they might eventually extract something from him. They let him go only when Cardoso and some uniformed Germans arrived and brought them to their senses.

The wounded man was undergoing surgery in the operating theatre. Bruno was in a hurry; at the hotel they had probably already noticed that he was missing, they were maybe even worried, and anyway he had to pick Gaby up from school. But even though the police had finally let him go, Bruno still could not just leave. He felt it would be inhumane to leave while the poor man was fighting for his life. He asked if he could phone the hotel to tell them that he would not be able to drive and that they should send somebody else to pick up the boy. But before he managed to make the call, a man in a blood-stained white coat walked out into the corridor.

'Gentlemen, the officer has unfortunately died,' said the surgeon.

Everybody cast down their eyes.

'He died in pain,' said Bruno.

But there was no time to mourn; he left the hospital just in time to pick up Gaby from school.

\* \* \*

Gaby was chatty that day. As soon as he got into the car he asked the driver:

'Do you know how long it takes for honey to go bad?'

'I know it can become sugary, but I've never heard of it going bad.'

'But do you know how many years it takes for it to go bad so that it's inedible?'

Bruno thought for a minute and then confessed that he did not know.

'No end of years,' said the boy proudly, revealing the secret. 'Because honey can't go bad.'

'Where did you learn that?'

'They found honey in the pyramids of Egypt. They opened the jars and the honey was still edible. After five thousand years!'

'If I'd died today, I'd have died without knowing that,' said the amazed driver.

# IT IS ONLY WITH THE HEART
# THAT ONE CAN SEE RIGHTLY

On the other side of the glass pane it was spring. It had stopped raining and the sun was shining. Ivan looked out at the surrounding buildings, their wet façades shining like polished scenery. He was startled out of his reverie by a voice, almost a whisper. It came from behind.

'Don't move.'

It was von Karstoff. Ivan had not heard him come in. He obeyed. He did not move.

'Now turn around slowly… Very slowly. No sudden moves,' his handler said softly.

From Ivan's point of view, the situation was more than worrying: a Nazi officer had a gun aimed at his back.

Realistically speaking, there was no chance of escape: behind him was a man with a firearm, in front the option of jumping through a closed second-floor window. He was unlikely to survive either. In such a situation a practised agent does what he is told. Slowly, calmly, Ivan started turning around as instructed, aware that even the smallest sign of nervousness could be fatal.

He did not raise his hands, nor, in honesty, had he been told to do so. Instead, slowly, inch by inch, he moved his right hand towards his belt and pistol. Midway, as if in slow motion, he caught sight of von Karstoff's reflection in the mirror and breathed a sigh of relief.

False alarm. Ludovico was not armed. He was standing in the middle of the room, looking somewhat grandfatherly, dressed in a silk dressing gown and slippers. His hands were raised, as if in surrender, and his head slightly sunken between his shoulders. He was looking not at Ivan but at the little animal perched on his left shoulder. It was a small, reddish monkey, like the ones organ grinders use to collect money from the public. All the little creature needed was a red fez and a vest. Ivan stopped reaching for his pistol and completed his slow-motion pirouette. It seems that we will not see a single bullet fired in our wartime novel.

'Benito?' Ivan asked, though he knew it wasn't Benito. Benito was darker and considerably bigger.

'Ssssh! Quiet!' von Karstoff beseeched him. 'I brought her just for you to see her. You wait here until I put her back in her cage.'

Holding his body and neck stiffly to one side, he shuffled across the parquet to the next room.

'It's a female. Her name is Josefina. Benito died while you were in the States. He came down with pneumonia and was gone in a matter of days. He was old. I got this one the other day from a colleague in Africa.'

'Why did you tell me not to move?'

'She's young and is easily unnerved. And when that happens

she likes to pull your hair. They need time to get used to people. When he was a baby the late Benito bit me straight through my fingernail,' he said, showing the scar on the tip of his index finger.

Ludovico was more than satisfied with what Ivan brought back from Britain: sketches, notes, maps and photographs, slightly overexposed but usable all the same. Then he began asking the questions on his list:

'Did you see any unusual convoys of vehicles?'

'No,' replied the agent.

'Do you know where Eisenhower's headquarters is?'

'I heard various versions. I think it's on Grosvenor Square, but south London and Kent are also being mentioned.'

'Did you see any equipment for a naval landing?' asked the handler.

'Just once I saw four trucks with something that looked like boats, but made of wood and tarpaulin. I don't know if that's what they were.'

'What do you know about their underwater mine fields?'

'You've got some photographed maps there,' replied the agent, pointing to the documents the Englishman had given him.

This was followed by a question asked of all agents at the time.

'Have you got any idea of the most likely site for the Allied landing?'

'Nobody knows that yet. But there will be one,' said the agent.

'What do you think?'

'I think it will be Pas de Calais or even Brittany. Rumour has it that it might be Norway. Or Greece. Some say that Dalmatia and Montenegro are out of the game, others that they are ideal because the local population is ready to fight on the side of the Allies,' said the agent.

'Normandy?' asked the handler.

'Anything is possible. That option has also been mentioned, but less often. The officers I talked to don't know, but most of them think that there would be too many casualties because of the terrain there.' Ivan's answer was as confused as the reports of all the other German agents in Britain. And that was no accident. Every last one of them had been turned; their dispatches said what the British told them to say, the aim being to confuse the enemy.

'When are you going back to London?' asked the handler, pouring drinks.

'As soon as I find a ticket,' replied the agent.

'Make it soon and come back quickly,' said von Karstoff. 'The boss, Admiral Canaris, will be coming to Lisbon soon. I'm sorry to tell you but in his opinion you are not worth the money they are paying you. I hope this report will change his mind. I think the best thing would be for the two of you to meet each other in person and talk. And one more thing: try not to stay in central London. Our side has a new weapon and is planning to use it soon.'

'What do you think about it?' Duško wanted to know.

'Honestly?'

'Honestly.'

'I'm getting more and more afraid. We're fucked when they

win anyway, but if we destroy London, no German will escape alive.'

★ ★ ★

That same afternoon, Duško said to Gaby:

'Let me take you out to dinner. A proper, elegant dinner. Put on something nice.'

The irony of the request did not escape the boy who had only one suit to his name, but he pretended wide-eyed innocence.

'Why? Are we celebrating something?'

'We are.'

'What?'

'Whatever. Why not celebrate?'

★ ★ ★

Gaby had now started to have a drink on special occasions. At the age of thirteen he began having a glass of wine with lunch, because the hotel staff said it was good for his growth. More recently, he would also have a glass of champagne with Duško. Raising their glasses, Popov confessed to his friend:

'I'd like to discuss something of vital importance with you but you must promise not to say a word about it to anybody. Promise?'

The boy nodded his head. But that was not enough for Duško.

'Listen, I'm confiding in you because you are my best friend; if you tell anybody I could get into a lot of trouble. You understand?'

'I understand, I understand! I won't tell a soul,' the boy promised.

'What do you think, my wise man of the East, what should a person do if he's afraid?'

'Afraid of what?'

'Not *of* what, *for* what. I'm afraid for my life,' said Duško.

'How afraid?'

'So afraid that I've even started being afraid of my own friends. Today I wanted to kill a man who is my friend, because I thought my life was at stake.'

'That's weird. I don't know what to tell you. Maybe you should get out of here until you're over it,' said Gaby after giving it some thought.

'I think so too!' Duško agreed.

'Get going, then.'

'Thanks for your support. You're a true friend. But I can't. I don't have any money. Could you lend me some?'

'Again?'

'I know you said you wouldn't give me any more. I wouldn't be asking if the situation weren't so serious.'

The boy sat there, thinking. His older friend pressed on:

'Come on, I'm just asking you to lend me money, and you look as if I want to take out your kidney. My life is in danger. It's no joke. Who's going to help me if not you?'

The boy said nothing. Duško had not expected him to be so unwilling.

'Why are you being so tight-fisted? It's not money you earned working in a coal mine, for heaven's sake. You're my best friend. Who else would you give it to if not me?'

The boy finally made up his mind. Objectively speaking, it was true: after Papagaio, Duško was his best friend.

'All right. I'll lend you enough to keep you going for a while. After that you're on your own. You're a grown-up man. How much do you need?'

'Ten thousand will do it.'

'I'm sorry. I only lend as much as I am prepared to write off. I'll give you five thousand,' the boy said.

'Are you nuts? You don't have to write it off. You know me! I'll repay it.'

'I said five, and five you'll get. Five thousand is a lot of money. Take it or leave it.'

It was obviously Gaby's final offer.

'All right, all right. Give me the money now, before you change your mind.'

'No. You'll squander it. It's better if I give it to you when you leave. All right?'

'You don't trust me?' Duško said, trying to manipulate him.

'No, I don't,' said the boy.

There was no room for further negotiation. The boy switched to a completely different subject.

'Let me ask you something. How did you interpret the sentence: *It is only with the heart that one can see rightly; what is essential is invisible to the eye*?'

'Where did you get that from?' asked Duško, perplexed.

'From Tonio's book, the one I lent you. So you didn't read it, after all?'

'Yes, I did,' Duško lied. 'It's just that I've become somewhat forgetful lately.'

'So, what do you think?' the boy wanted to know.

'I'm rather shallow and Tonio is a philosopher,' Duško replied. 'You'd better ask him.'

'I asked him in a letter, but he hasn't answered it yet. Anyway, I want to know what you think. What did he really mean to say?'

'What did it say exactly again?'

'*It is only with the heart that one can see rightly; what is essential is invisible to the eye,*' repeated the boy.

'Aha, *It is only with the heart that one can see rightly; what is essential is invisible to the eye…* I would say, offhand, that he meant we men are not particularly clever. We just care what a woman looks like, if she has a pretty face, a good body… Understand? But actually, what is essential is invisible to the eye. She can be the best-looking girl in the world but if you don't understand each other, forget it.'

'All right,' the boy said, his voice flat. He did not find the explanation persuasive. In the final analysis, how can you ask someone to explain literature to you if he doesn't read?

# THINGS HAVE BECOME
# A LITTLE COMPLICATED

Mademoiselle Maristela got in touch with Popov early that evening for no particular reason. The message was: *Tomorrow morning at ten.* In other words, they were to meet at the casino at ten o'clock that evening, which was less than two hours away.

He arrived at the casino fifteen minutes early. He found Elizabeth at the bar. She did not usually come early. He was even more surprised when she caught his eye. That was strictly forbidden and had never happened before in a public place. Duško had an undefined, uncomfortable premonition. They quickly took their places at the roulette table.

Elizabeth placed her first chip on the zero. This was a secret signal activating a so-called reserve code. It meant the situation was urgent. That was news in itself. Duško had been trained for this procedure but he had never seen it in practice. He placed his bet on black, signalling that he understood. She started her dictation by placing her chip on the number 12. That was the letter L. Then, after skipping a round, she went for the following:

22-5-18-8-1-6-20-5-20. So, 12-space-22-5-18-8-1-6-20-5-20. That meant L VERHAFTET. L ARRESTED. L? Ludwig!? So somebody had arrested Ludwig.

It was a balmy evening. On his way back from the casino, he sat down on a bench to smoke a cigarette and think about the possible repercussions of Ludwig's arrest. He smoked three cigarettes. He could not come up with anything intelligent.

He returned to the hotel relatively early, considerably before midnight. Manuel greeted him at the door, Renato smiled at him as he passed Reception, and a vodka vermouth was waiting for him at the bar. The music was loud. It was an evening like any other at the Palácio. And then Black walked up to him. He was acting strangely, as if they had not seen each other for days. Embracing Duško warmly, Black whispered something into his ear.

A few drinks later, Duško announced that he was going to bed early. Taking the lift to the third floor, he joked with the lift boy ('Fucking anything these days, kid?'), teetered out and unsteadily made his way down the long corridor to his room. The hotel bellboy who was following him that evening put his ear to the door but heard nothing, so he went on his way.

Duško expected to find Jarvis waiting for him in the room. That is what the hotel manager had whispered in his ear when he'd embraced him. But he was wrong. Jarvis was waiting for him in the bathroom. They said not a word, shook hands, closed the door, turned on all the taps so that the sound of the running water bounced off the ceramic tiles, and sat on the edge of the bathtub.

'Johnny Jebsen has disappeared. He was last seen the night

before last entering an apartment near the German embassy. They think the Gestapo drugged him and took him across the border in the boot of a car.'

Jarvis stopped there. Jebsen was a good friend of Popov's, maybe his best friend, and he would need a moment to digest such bad news.

'Johnny has been caught?'

'Yes. And he wasn't alone. They've arrested von Karstoff too. He left urgently for Berlin the day before yesterday. The Gestapo arrested him at the airport.'

'Is the source reliable?' Duško asked.

'Yes,' said the Englishman. 'Luckily, none of it seems to be connected to you. The information I have is that they were arrested because of some financial misappropriation. Were you involved in anything?'

'I don't know what you mean exactly, but probably not.'

'Even better. All the same, the service feels it would be best to remove you as soon as possible. They'll interrogate the two of them. Torture them. Your name may crop up. You know too much. We can't let the Germans get their hands on you.'

'What exactly do you mean when you say it would be best to remove me? You're not planning to get rid of me, are you?'

'As far as I know – no. They just want to transfer you to London. Do you have a Portuguese entry-exit visa in your passport?'

'Yes.'

'Then try using that passport to leave the country. This is a British passport in your name.' He handed a new document to Popov. 'With a visa. Use it only in a crunch. It's better if nobody knows that you've got two passports. In the event that they won't let you out of the country even with British papers, our consul, who will be discreetly on the scene, will intervene. Here is a ticket for tomorrow. And eight hundred pounds. That will be enough until you find your feet.'

'And my family in Belgrade?' Popov asked. 'They can be caught and sent to a concentration camp at any moment.'

'We've thought of that as well. Tomorrow, as late as possible before you leave, you will send Elizabeth a letter. Best do it from the airport. Tell her that a ticket suddenly came up for the same day, that you're leaving and will contact her from London. Then all we have to do is convince Berlin that you were arrested in London and sentenced for espionage. The Germans will see your family as a guarantee that you won't talk while in prison. Soon they'll forget all about you. They have more important things to do than take their revenge on you.'

Only one question remained:

'I must remind you that the Bajlonis have still not been issued visas,' said Duško.

The playboy envisaged Jarvis telling him that visas were not within his jurisdiction and that he should try going to the right office. He started by saying:

'Listen …'

But the agent stopped him.

'You listen to me for once. Listen to me and think good and hard whether it is wise, in this case, to be so rigid. I'm afraid we may jeopardize the security of the operation.'

'Why?' The mere mention of security being jeopardized upset Jarvis.

'Lila knows too much,' said Duško.

'What's "too much"?'

'Enough for you to listen to me so that we don't have another Pearl Harbor.'

'Are you bluffing?' Jarvis asked.

'Look, you're the boss, you have the final say, but I want the record to show that I think it would be better for everybody if she was on your territory and not here. Especially now, with this situation. It's as if we're saying to the Germans "be my guest".'

'You're bluffing,' Jarvis insisted.

'No. I'm warning,' the agent replied.

The very next day, a dispatch marked *State Secret* and addressed to Room 39 flew by diplomatic pouch to England. What follows are the most interesting parts of the document:

1) Upon the subject's arrival immediately stage his arrest at the hotel.

2) Provide Tricycle with discreet accommodation and a false identity until the war is over. (Under no circumstances can he be allowed to leave Britain. Keep him under observation as he is prone to be wilful and cause incidents.)

3) Using the usual diplomatic channels, officially request the Yugoslav embassy in Lisbon to compile a report on Tricycle's possible business activities in Portugal.

4) Using the usual diplomatic channels, officially request

that the Portuguese judiciary ask for Tricycle's bank statements from Banca Nacional Ultramarino, starting from 1939 to the present day.

5) Two months later, in at least two relevant newspapers, publish the news that foreign national D.P. (32) has been sentenced to fifteen years in prison for fraud.

6) Before leaving, Tricycle said he was afraid that Miss Lila Bajloni could pose a threat to the security of our operations, because she allegedly knows too much about his activities. It is possible that he is bluffing. On the other hand, for some time now Tricycle has been paying considerable attention to the said girl, they have been spending quite a lot of time together and there is a good chance that she knows something. So far, our department has found no indication that either she, or anyone in her family, is collaborating or has collaborated with the enemy. Therefore, given the circumstances, and for the sake of our higher goal, I strongly suggest that the relevant department be asked to issue entry visas urgently for the four-member Bajloni family.

7) Tricycle has been paid a thousand pounds out of the cash box.

★ ★ ★

Just before noon the next day, Mr Gradimir Bajloni asked at Reception for Bruno. As instructed by Popov the previous evening, Bruno brought the white BMW from the garage to the hotel and handed it over to Gradimir. The young man was thrilled at the chance to drive such a machine. Before leaving, Bruno warned him that there were fragile objects in the boot of the car and it would be wise to drive slowly. The boy promised to take care.

'Well then, off you go, or you'll be late,' said Bruno, slapping the back of the car the way you do a good horse.

Grada drove straight to his estate, but he did not stay there for long. Just an hour later, he was back on the road with the same car, its roof now up. He headed north, as if going to Porto, but turned off the road and made for the airport.

In front of the main terminal, the driver stepped out of the car and took the suitcases out of the boot. Meanwhile, a younger man wearing a hat and sunglasses rose from the seat next to the driver's.

The friends kissed each other goodbye on the cheek, like brothers.

'Can I ask you something?' Grada had the temerity to say.

'Go ahead, ask.'

'What do you really do?'

'Grada, my friend, what I do is like a septic tank. Most of those who fall in drown, and the few who survive reek of shit.'

The porter had already taken the luggage into the terminal. Grada watched from a distance as Duško smiled and chatted with the border police officer. A minute later, he was already in no man's land.

\* \* \*

That same evening, after dinner, Gaby was told that Mr Black wanted to see him. The hotel manager came straight to the point.

'Gaby, I just want to pass on a message to you. Duško has left.'

'For where?'

'For London. He had to leave urgently,' said the manager. 'He asked me to give you this letter.'

The envelope was open. Inside, the folded sheet of hotel writing paper said:

Sorry, kid. Things have become complicated.

I'll give you back the money as soon as I can.

Don't worry, I'll find you.

Your friend D.

After the boy had read the letter, the hotel manager said:

'Before leaving, Mr Popov asked me to advance him some money for the trip. He said that you would give it back to me. That the two of you had an agreement to that effect. Can I count on you in that regard?'

'I promised that I would give him five thousand dollars, but in person; however, given the situation, we can do it this way too.'

'Hmmm…' said Mr Black, slightly hesitating. 'I think I foresee a small problem here. I gave him nine thousand, that's what he asked for; together with what he owes the hotel that would make it just under ten thousand… I had no reason not to believe him.'

Gaby shrugged his shoulders.

'I'm sorry. I promised him five thousand dollars. He cheated you out of the rest.'

'I like your way of thinking, young man. It's logical and fair,' agreed Mr Black. Later they went to the safe and settled their accounts.

\* \* \*

'If only I knew where that pervert disappeared to,' Cardoso said to Black on one of his regular evening visits to the hotel. 'Did he leave owing you anything?'

'Forgive me, Inspector, but I would rather not discuss it,' said the American.

'So he did. That's why the good-for-nothing fled. I always suspected he was up to something. I had my eye on him for a long time. But we didn't discover a thing. Just, partying, whoring, binging… We didn't have enough agents to cover him. Later I stopped the surveillance. It's disgraceful to make people watch such debauchery, married, serious men… Following him was no joke. You know how he drives? Peçanha skidded off the road twice chasing him. They say you were the last person to see him?'

'You heard wrong. The last person to see him was the lift boy.'

# RODRIGUEZ

'It says in our press that we are slowly changing sides,' said the driver, looking at the hotel manager in the rear-view mirror.

'I would say myself that the war is coming to an end, but I'm not quite sure where it says that.'

'It's in our papers, though not exactly in those words. I'm telling you, it's all there, you just have to know how to read,' Bruno laughed.

'What exactly does it say?' Black did not read the national press.

'The government has stopped exporting tungsten under pressure from the British. Didn't I tell you? The big boss first gave the Allies the Azores, and now he's depriving the Germans of tungsten.'

'He didn't concede the Azores voluntarily. If he hadn't handed them over, the Americans would have taken them by force,' said Black. 'But the tungsten is certainly a sign that he's giving way.'

'Not only that. They've started talking about the historical alliance with the English. They've remembered that the fourteenth-century Anglo-Portuguese Alliance is still in force.

Why didn't they write about that in '39 or '41, when things were going so well for Hitler? No, our Prime Minister is trying, cunningly, while there's still time, to approach the victor. But not in an unseemly way; he's doing it slowly, concession by concession. He's smart, the old man is,' said Bruno, giving his interpretation of the day's press. 'It's all interconnected,' he decided.

Bruno's claim that everything was connected was to be confirmed a few days later, when Superintendent Cardoso paid an afternoon visit to the manager of the Palácio.

He knocked at the door unannounced, without waiting for a reply. He walked into the office looking morose, muttered 'Good afternoon' through clenched teeth, sat down opposite the somewhat surprised American and waited for him to ask:

'What brings you here, Inspector?'

The inspector spoke with immense pathos:

'I knew it all along, Black…' He stretched out the words, pausing after each. 'I knew about you and your activities from the very start, and you, I am sure, knew that I knew. Am I right?'

The American looked the inspector straight in the eye but said nothing. His face was expressionless, as if the man hadn't asked him anything.

'So,' the policeman continued, 'I knew but I tolerated it. In any case, I could have had you kicked out, but I didn't. That's because I respect you as a fair, hard-working man.'

Black still said nothing. His eyes were focused somewhere on the middle of the inspector's face.

'I came to ask you, Mr Black, how, after all that, you had the cheek to do to me what you did…? I'd like to know, please.'

'Believe me, I have no idea what you're talking about.' And, indeed, he honestly looked as if he did not have a clue what all the fuss was about.

'You knew all along about his secret activities but you didn't tell me,' Cardoso said.

'What secret activities are you talking about, Inspector? And can you tell me exactly who "he" is?' said Black, pretending not to understand.

'I was naïve. I thought I knew everything about everybody, but I didn't. I didn't know crucial things about those who were the closest… I didn't know about him.'

'About whom? What?'

'About Bruno. He's a member of the Communist Party,' said the policeman. He made the word communist sound like a swearword.

Black's reaction was, for him, quite vigorous.

'Are you certain? What's your basis for such a conclusion? I am in touch with him every day, so I would know. Or at least sense it.'

'There's no doubt about it.'

'Well, Inspector, I didn't know, but even if I had known, I'm not sure I would have told you.'

A prolonged silence ensued.

'And what happens now?' asked the American.

Silence.

'Who reported him?' the American asked.

334

'The English. The whole organisation was penetrated – we arrested around thirty of them ...' Cardoso replied.

They sat there in silence for a few minutes, each like an eternity, as if waiting for something. Black did not dare to ask any questions. The silence was broken by a knock at the door.

'Come in,' Black called out.

Bruno came in, looking slightly puzzled. The door closed, and Cardoso took over, as if this was his office, not Black's.

'Sit down,' he said to Bruno, indicating a chair.

When Bruno sat down, everybody fell silent until Cardoso suddenly asked:

'They call you Rodriguez?'

'Some do,' Bruno replied after a moment's hesitation.

'You see, the thing is that I've been ordered to arrest Rodriguez who, and I quote,' he proceeded to read, *"is a member of the Communist Party of Portugal and an informer for foreign intelligence services"*. Those are two major criminal offences. Are you this Rodriguez?'

Silence.

'You see, Bruno...' the inspector started, looking at a point on the floor, 'I thought that we were... friends.'

'And we are friends,' the driver suddenly spoke up, as if responding to a grave insult.

'If we're not, we were...' the policeman confirmed, continuing in the same monotone voice. 'So, why didn't you come to me as a friend and say: here's the situation. Why didn't you? If you had, I would have found a way to help you out... If you had, we wouldn't be arresting you. But no... You didn't say a word to me, your friend… Friendship is, first and foremost, a matter of trust, Bruno my man.'

What could Bruno say? Nothing. He remained silent.

'And now I can't help you… You do, of course, realize the situation you have put me in? I ask myself: what did you need this for? What was missing in your life? You had a good job, you did it well, you lived comfortably, you had friends… and of all things for it to be this…' said Cardoso coldly.

The three of them sat in silence a while longer.

'Come with me, Bruno, quietly, we don't want to create a commotion. It would be unfair to the guests,' the inspector said. 'We'll say that your mother has fallen ill and you have to go home urgently.'

'I'm sorry,' the hotel manager said to the driver as they were leaving.

Bruno did not say a word to him. He walked out and went quietly, as directed, to the car waiting for him on the other side of the railing. He did not try to run away; he knew that they had their guns aimed at him.

# HALF AN HOUR BEFORE LUNCH

'Look at this heat, my dear Isaura. It's like being in Hell, God forbid. I can hardly wait for winter when people outside will be freezing but here in the kitchen we will be nice and warm…' Lourdes was standing by the stove, fanning herself with her apron.

Isaura silently empathized. She could not herself complain because if she dared to say anything her boss would bristle and remind her that these days anybody with a job like hers should be singing with joy, not griping. That's what Lourdes would tell her, Lourdes who moaned enough for the two of them. But she didn't complain about anything, except about her body, which was not what it used to be.

'I keep feeling dizzy. When I stand, my feet swell; when I sit, my back hurts,' Lourdes said to her assistant that sweltering afternoon, while peas were simmering in the pot; on a day like this, lunch had to be light.

Lourdes' sandals shuffled when she walked. She went over to the door where there was a breeze; it was less humid there.

The heat forced Senhor Armando, too, to look for a breeze out in the courtyard. He had done the morning drive, polished the limousine and moved it out of the sun and under the eaves of the house. When he had finished everything, he sat down on the little chair in the shade by the kitchen door, where he could keep an eye on the car. He spread open the newspaper and read.

Just before noon, the cook popped her head out from behind the door.

'Good afternoon, Senhor Armando,' she said. 'My goodness, what a sweltering day we're having.'

We haven't mentioned him before, but Senhor Armando has been working at the hotel from the beginning. When Bruno suddenly left, he was on the day shift at Reception and Black thought that he would be the best person to replace him. They worked well together, but they never developed the closeness that Black had had with Bruno. Armando also took over driving Gaby to school. He got along well with him, too, but not like Bruno.

'Good afternoon, Lourdes. How are you? Please come over here, I want you to see something,' he said, opening the newspaper to show her. 'Look at this, please. Maybe your memory is better than mine. Is that the French gentleman who was here a few years ago? The one who made friends with our Gaby?'

Before even seeing the page Lourdes said:

'How should I know who's who, when I never step out of the kitchen?'

But all the same, she looked at the picture and suddenly she became serious:

'Well, if it isn't he certainly looks like him. I know the man, Gaby once brought him over to the kitchen to introduce us.

What does it say about him?' Lourdes did not read much, and if she had to she always found somebody to help her, so that she had forgotten the few letters she knew anyway.

Senhor Armando adjusted his glasses on his nose:

Rome, August 9 (AP) – Antoine de Saint-Exupéry, the forty-four-year-old pilot and writer, has been reported missing during a reconnaissance flight over France, it was officially announced at Allied headquarters in Rome today. Born into an aristocratic family, in his youth Saint-Exupéry was a pilot with the French postal service in Africa and South America. That experience inspired his novels *Night Flight, Man and His World*, etc. He fled France after the occupation. He recently returned to military duty, after having spent time in the USA. Last March, Saint-Exupéry, a veteran with over 13,000 hours of flight time, was rejected by the US army because of his age.

'Missing?' Lourdes asked just to make sure that she had understood it properly.

'That's what it says. Missing.'

They took a closer look at the photograph. He gave her his glasses for her to see better.

'He's a bit thinner in this picture, but it looks like him,' Lourdes said.

'It's him. He was a pilot too… A few days ago, the boy told me that the two of them were corresponding, and that he had received a package from him from America. It contained a letter and a picture book – for children.'

'I hope to God the worst hasn't happened,' Lourdes said, crossing herself.

They stood silently side by side, as if paying homage to him.

'Shall we tell Gaby?' Lourdes asked.

'He has enough troubles of his own,' Senhor Armando said. 'Maybe he just had to make an emergency landing and they'll find him.'

'You're right. We always expect the worst. Anyway, have you finished with the newspaper? If you have, I need it to light the fire,' Lourdes said, taking the paper out of the man's hands, putting it under her arm and returning to the kitchen. It was time to put the rice on the stove. Lunch was in half an hour.

Senhor Armando headed for the reception desk, but he took the longer, circuitous route rather than the shortcut through the kitchen; he was afraid of the smells permeating his uniform.

Later, over lunch, his colleagues asked him what was new, what had he read in the papers that day. Senhor Armando told them that the Americans were advancing towards Paris, the Russians were moving from the east and south towards Berlin, and that for the first time Churchill had stated he was expecting an end to the war. But what Armando's audience enjoyed most was a true story that had happened in Lisbon. When he told them about it everybody laughed.

It went like this: the previous day, a wedding party was waiting in front of the Anjos church for the bride to appear and just as they started losing patience, a young man came bearing a letter from the bride. It said that she did not want to get married. She wrote: '*At times like these, marriage would be an adventure.*'

# NINE MONTHS

I t takes nine months from conception to the newborn's first cry. That is indeed a long time, but when you are busy with work, it goes by in a flash. Exactly nine months after he suddenly vanished, Bruno reappeared at the Palácio. He came back as abruptly as he had left. He had nowhere else to go. This was the only home he had.

His colleagues were thrilled to see him. For some it was as if he had been away for nine days, for others it was more like nine years. They embraced him, the women even shed a tear or two, and Lourdes, when she saw him, simply clasped her hands on her breast and said in a shocked voice:

'Oh, poor Bruno, you're so thin! Did they starve you?' She crossed herself, without at all realizing how on the mark she was. 'That's what happens when a man is left to his own devices.'

The manager immediately received his driver in his office.

'Welcome home!' he said warmly. 'As far as I'm concerned, you can go back to your old job tomorrow, if you want. Anyway, Armando is always saying he wants to retire, to go back to his village. Or maybe you'd like some rest first? Maybe it's better if you get some sleep, get your strength back. There's no hurry; your room is waiting for you, you can move in and when you feel the time is right you can start work.' The manager was leaving all options open to him. He was talking too much. Bruno's answer was brief:

'I'll start work tomorrow. Thank you.'

'Don't thank me, Bruno. Please, there's no need.'

'Thank you,' Bruno repeated.

'You don't know how hard it is for me to hear you keep saying thank you,' the manager confessed.

Bruno did not say anything. Perhaps he knew, perhaps he didn't.

Anyway, they were both glad to see one another, although their conversation was rather stilted; they had become somewhat strangers, they did not know where to begin. If you see a face after nine months and barely recognize it, you wonder if nine months is long enough for someone to go to ruin like this, for his face to go dark and his hair white. There are so many things you want to ask him, but you say nothing.

'All right, I'm off then,' said Bruno, about to get up, when Black stopped him.

'I've got something for you.'

He gave him a large envelope, the kind given to a prisoner upon release, containing his watch, belt and shoelaces.

'I'm sorry. They opened it. The police open everything,' said Black.

Inside was another envelope, the size of a sheet of paper, and a small box. The envelope was white, impressed with a swastika. It was addressed, in Gothic script, to Bruno. The box was black leather, square, shallow, bearing the same impression of a hooked cross in the centre of a wreath.

Bruno opened the box first. Lying on the white silk lining that bore the gold insignia of the Reich was a medal in the shape of a cross, such as Bruno had seen, he remembered it vividly, on the plane that had crashed. Each of the four fields between the arms of the cross was studded with a small metal eagle carrying wreaths and crooked crosses in its talons. The accompanying letter was in German and consisted of only two long sentences. He did not understand what it said, but he saw at a glance that it was addressed to him, signed with the words DER FÜHRER and had a stamp with the same eagle, wreaths and swastika, but no words. He closed the box, returned the letter to the envelope and put it down on the desk, as if giving it back to his boss.

'That's yours,' Black said. 'The Order of the German Eagle third class. They give it to foreigners whose noble actions have in some way helped Germany or its people. Third class is a high order, especially if you're not a politician or a diplomat.' He did not know what else to say.

'That's not what I did it for,' said Bruno, rising to his feet. He said goodbye and left. The envelope remained on the desk.

At dinner Bruno did not talk much about his absence. And none of his colleagues asked much, either; they did not want to open old wounds. The manager had already told them what had happened and why he had had to leave so suddenly. His mother had fallen ill unexpectedly, and he had had to go and take care of her because there was nobody else to do it. If anybody doubted this story, their suspicions were dispelled when Cardoso confirmed it, saying that it was he who had informed Bruno of his mother's illness and had helped as much as he could with his transport.

At the hotel, only the manager and the inspector knew the truth, a rare instance of it not leaking out. For the past nine months Bruno had been undergoing re-education. As an agent of the Comintern, he had been thrown into prison without trial. They had tortured him so badly that he went deaf in one ear, and they kept at it until they beat that damned Rodriguez out of him. Then they beat him some more, to make sure that Rodriguez was gone forever.

Had it not been for Cardoso and Black, working closely together this time, each in his respective world, pulling whatever strings they had, Bruno would have probably wound up like many of his comrades – in the notorious island-prison of Tarrafal in the middle of the ocean. It was there that the regime sent its most dangerous enemies for long stretches of time.

At nine-thirty that evening, Bruno and Cardoso ran into each other at the bar. Like Black, the inspector was happy to see him. They sat side by side but did not talk, which had been known to happen before. But as Tonio said: there are different kinds of silence. This time the silence did not imply a deep understanding, like between two friends, it was a silence of tension. They sat it out until they finished their whiskies. Bruno was the first to get up and head for bed.

'I have to get up early tomorrow morning and drive Gaby to school,' he said.

'Go ahead. You need your rest,' the policeman said.

'And… I mustn't forget to thank you for everything you did for me.'

'You're welcome. Don't let me down. Please… I hear that you didn't take the German decoration they gave you. I would reconsider if I were you. It's not just that it's an honour… it could also be useful. Believe me, it was enormously helpful in making your absence so brief…'

'There'll be no need for it anymore,' said Bruno. 'Let the manager hold onto it. It's safer with him.'

It seems that it takes nine months for one man to turn into another.

Washing the dishes after dinner the next evening, Lourdes said to her assistant:

'See, Isaura, what happens to an old man who is left motherless? Unrecognizable. Honestly. He doesn't even read the papers anymore.'

# IN BETWEEN TWO
# HISTORIC PHOTOGRAPHS

The previous June, the Allies had landed on the beaches of Normandy, surprising the Germans. The landing had been a success. Despite steely resistance, the Allies had taken back one town after another. They were welcomed in Paris by the ringing of all the city's church bells and by an ecstatic people. They danced, they sang, they shaved the heads of women who had taken up with enemy soldiers during the occupation. Towards the end of the year the Allies advanced to the Ruhr River, where a consolidated German defence blocked their way forward. They set up camp for the winter and replenished their ranks.

When the snow melted and the roads reopened, the Soviets pushed forward from the east. The tactical maps hanging on the walls of both sides' military headquarters showed red flags moving towards Berlin from both the south and the east.

At the beginning of April, the Allies finally launched a new offensive. They broke through the front in Italy and made it to Bavaria in one fell swoop, encountering almost no resistance.

In Milan there was a ridiculous sight to behold: il Duce hanging from his feet in front of a petrol station.

On 25 April 1945, American and Russian troops came face to face on the Elbe River. For the 'formal handshake', each side chose a striking-looking officer to go to Torgau, on the west bank of the river, to cordially greet each other in combat uniform in front of the photographers, with the American and Soviet flags showing in the background. This historic moment was immortalized in an unintentionally amusing photograph that was published the world over under the caption '*Handshake of Torgau*'.

Both Stalin and Churchill were pleased by this symbolic meeting and said they were sorry that President Roosevelt, who had worked with them towards this end, had not lived to see victory. He had died two weeks earlier of natural causes. Hitler outlived him by eighteen days, during which time, crazed more than ever by the cocaine eye drops he was taking, he issued increasingly mad orders and made increasingly insane decisions. He committed suicide in his bunker on the last day of April 1945, when the Soviets were within firing range of the Reich's offices. His body was reportedly set ablaze.

But in Portugal everything rolled along as usual. The national press continued to write about the war as impartially as possible, though it made scant mention of the term *neutrality*, as if the word had in the meantime lost meaning. Editorials discreetly rejoiced at the Allied victory, issuing strong warnings about the bogeyman of communism, the biggest threat to Western civilization.

For some time now, the atmosphere at the Palácio hotel had been nowhere near as hectic as it had been. Foreigners still accounted for most of the guests, but there was no longer the tension that had existed at the start of the war. A good sign that things were slowly settling down was the increasingly noticeable absence of the police at the hotel. Cardoso did not drop by as often as before and did not stay long when he came. He had not had an official meeting with the manager for weeks. So, they were rather surprised at the Palácio when the superintendent of the PVDE appeared early on the morning of 3 May 1945 and asked to see the manager.

Cardoso walked into Black's office with a broad smile on his face. He looked pleased. He accepted the offer of coffee and lit up a cigarette along with his host, who could not for the life of him imagine what the man wanted.

'I see that you haven't yet managed to carry out the orders of the Council of Ministers,' said Cardoso.

Black did not know what he was talking about.

'What orders?'

'This morning's,' said the policeman. 'You don't know? Here, take a look!' Cardoso took a newspaper out of his pocket, searched the pages, found what he was looking for and read aloud:

> In connection with the death of German Chancellor Adolf Hitler, the government has declared three days of mourning and ordered that flags on public institutions and our naval ships fly at half-mast from this morning until noon tomorrow.

Black thought that the policeman was trying to provoke him again. He just did not know in connection with what.

'That strikes me at this moment as a rather unusual decision,' he observed.

'I, Sir, do not question orders, I carry them out. That is my job. In this particular case I don't see what is unusual about it. It is the law and custom here to declare mourning when a statesman of a friendly country dies in office. We are a neutral country. As long as Germany exists and we have diplomatic relations with it, we will act according to the law. And we are not alone. Look, it says right here in the newspaper,' he said, slapping the paper with his hand, 'all neutral countries have done it. See, it says here: Spain, Sweden, Switzerland, Ireland. Even the Vatican, so we have to do it too.'

Black stared at the desk in front of him. It did not pay to defy the unreasonable representative of an even more unreasonable regime. He took the newspaper and read it to himself. He found a legitimate argument.

'The order applies only to public institutions. This is a private hotel.'

'That's where I've got you!' the policeman laughed, perhaps a little too loudly. 'That's what I first thought this morning, but then I remembered that when I came by here a few weeks ago, after President Roosevelt died, I was surprised to see the flag at the front door flying half-mast.'

'So? What about it?'

The policeman did not want to argue over it anymore.

'I don't think it's appropriate for us to waste time discussing matters that are not for discussion, so let's just carry out that

349

order – it doesn't cost us anything – and then nobody will be able to say that we took sides,' he laughed, ushering Black outside.

'Rodolfo, please bring a ladder to the front door,' he said. The manager said nothing.

When the young man came with the ladder, Cardoso told him where to place it.

'See our flag up there? Lower it down a little. A bit more… That's it. Thanks very much, young man.'

The manager said nothing.

'There you are. That's fine. Now everything is as it should be,' Cardoso said. He was pleased and decided to explain his actions to the manager.

'You know, Mr Black, this is not a whim on my part; it is government policy. And this is an old and serious state. We preserved peace and dignity and maintained our neutrality all through the war. It wouldn't be nice if at the last moment we ran over to the winning side. You must admit, it wouldn't speak well of us, would it?'

A day or two after this incident took place in Estoril, another historic photograph was taken. It showed a Soviet soldier flying a red flag on top of the Reichstag, looking out at the destroyed, smouldering city.

# THE WAR IS OVER

In the evening, the radio announced that the Third Reich had capitulated. In the morning, it reported that the German army had unconditionally surrendered to the Allies, and by the afternoon that people were celebrating in the streets of London, New York, Paris and Moscow.

Portugal may not have taken part in the war, but fireworks went off in Lisbon and the people celebrated spontaneously. They had an honest love of peace. The loudest celebrations were in front of the embassies of the victorious powers.

Looking out from his fourth-floor office window, Jarvis, now a major, gazed at the steep Rua da Emenda, crowded with people from wall to wall, from top to bottom. Men, squeezed together like at a football game, were shouting slogans, calling out, waving American, British and Portuguese flags. There were no women; such frenzied demonstrations were no place for them, but by the afternoon they had filled the Corpo Santo church a few blocks down the hill. They were celebrating a *Te Deum*. At eight in the evening, when people left the streets to go home for dinner, Jarvis drove to the British embassy where there was a party. He did not write a report that day. It was over, there was no need for one anymore.

Although the demonstrations were essentially peaceful, the authorities were nervous. Reports were coming in to the PVDE's central office, warning of possible provocations. Words like *anarchism, liberalism, extremists, mercenaries* were being bandied around in police circles like swearwords. It was being said that 'unless the popular mood of celebration was carefully channelled things could turn ugly'. Plainclothes agents milling in the crowds did their job more zealously than ever. They took down the names of anyone inciting unrest and disobedience. The arrest lists included intellectuals, workers, artisans, some already known to the police, others not, such as a certain pub-owner in the small town of Régua, whose offence was that he had given some young men a free demijohn of wine who had then got drunk and started cursing Dr Oliveira Salazar. Unfortunately, the men were not arrested because nobody was able to identify them; they were not from Régua.

Shouts of '*Democracy!*' and '*Freedom!*', even '*Long Live the USSR!*' were heard in a number of places in the country, especially in the industrial outskirts of Lisbon, but it was impossible to recognize the voices in the crowd and the culprits remained anonymous. A red flag with a hammer and sickle was hoisted onto an elementary school in a village in Alentejo, in the semi-feudal agricultural south of the country. The incident was taken care of without any fuss and bother: the caretaker took down the flag but the police were duly informed. A travelling locksmith, a well-known agent provocateur, was one of the people arrested and beaten up.

They celebrated for two days, and who knows how much longer they would have gone on had somebody wiser not said 'Enough' and forbidden any more celebrations. Luckily, everything went smoothly and did not cause much of a commotion, for which we can thank the organs of law and order.

★ ★ ★

The situation in Estoril on Victory Day was calm. Cardoso was on full alert but there was only one isolated incident and that was when a young man, a shoemaker's apprentice, got drunk and started shouting slogans in support of Soviet Russia and Comrade Stalin. He was immediately arrested and spent the night in jail, where he was slapped around, told that the Bolsheviks eat children for breakfast, and eventually sent back to his parents to be re-educated. He was just fifteen and a half years old.

At the Palácio, the Victory Day celebrations were livelier than on any other holiday. The hotel's clientele was such that they celebrated more discreetly; they showed their feelings by opening more bottles of champagne than on New Year's Eve.

In the small kitchen, Lourdes had prepared roast lamb and potatoes for dinner, and made a cake with jam; she had not waited to be told by Mr Black. And so the staff celebrated the end of the war with a real feast and a glass or two of wine. Nobody was going to hold it against them on a day like that.

Gaby dined with the staff that evening. He was almost fifteen years old and felt important. For the first time in his life he felt he was witnessing a historic event. He listened to the radio, read the newspapers, remembered what the adults were saying. He hoped that now his parents would be able to come looking for him, or he for them. But he said nothing to anyone.

★ ★ ★

In the morning, the phone rang at Quinta dos Grilos. The maid answered:

'Hello! Hello! … Monsieur Gradimir!'

Gordana jumped up from the breakfast table to take the call.

'Grada, is that you?'

'We've won the war!' came the words out of the receiver.

'Grada, where are you calling from?' asked Gordana.

'Grada! Is it Grada, my son, my boy?' Radmila wept, grabbing the phone from her daughter.

Grada could not tell them where he was. He had simply called to say that he was alive and well and that Lila was also fine. And that the war was over.

'My babies are alive and well!' Radmila cried out, weeping with joy.

★ ★ ★

It was not until several days later, when things had calmed down and everyday life had resumed, that Superintendent Cardoso, dressed more formally than usual, appeared again at the hotel. He brought a good bottle of wine with him.

'Well, Black, the war is over. I've come to congratulate you on victory, both as an American but also personally,' he said and kept shaking his hand. 'For me, you, Sir, are personally one of the winners in this war.'

'What are you saying?' said Black, managing to retrieve his hand from Cardoso's steely grip.

'It's true. You are. For the last five years, you've been raking in the money like never before,' he laughed. 'I think that you have more reason than ever to treat me to lunch today.'

Black would have had no problem turning him down, but put that way, a fine lunch with the policeman of a neutral country in honour of the Allied victory seemed like a good idea. He informed the kitchen that he would be taking his meal outside on the terrace, and that he would be entertaining a guest.

The waiters marvelled at the sight of the two men sitting together at the table, raising their glasses in a toast.

'To victory!' said Black.

'To peace!' said Cardoso. 'Wholehearted congratulations for winning the war. But let me tell you, the real winners here are us Portuguese. We survived the war without spilling a drop of blood.'

'And wholehearted congratulations to you, too,' said the American.


All through lunch they reminisced about their various adventures during these wartime years. The policeman was more cheerful than usual, and they mentioned various happenings, each giving his own version. They recalled the refugee crisis, how long it had lasted and all the work they had had to do, and yet it had seemed to be over in a flash. They remembered the late President of Poland, the French film-maker Jean Renoir, the Duchess of Windsor. They agreed that the Spanish artist with twirled moustaches, whose name they could not remember, was seriously crazy, and that German dissidents were incredibly boring. The inspector took the opportunity to repeat his anecdote about the Spanish general who told him: 'As soon as I hear the word intellectual, I reach for my pistol.'

Their conversation led them to the incident with the diplomat who in 1942 killed himself and his wife after gambling away his own and the state's money. They could not remember if he had been Croatian or Estonian, or if his wife was Greek or Armenian, but they both vividly remembered the horrifying sight of human brains and blood splattered on the walls and mirrors of the hotel room.

Before leaving, the inspector felt it appropriate to warn Black:

'This is half-time for you. There'll be more work when the other side starts trying to escape. Your hotel is already full of Krauts, right?' said Cardoso, slapping Black on the back before making his way out.

\* \* \*

A week later, the two men, Cardoso with his wife and Mr Black with Gaby, ran into each other at Lisbon's Politeama cinema, after the national première of *Casablanca*. Made in 1942, its screening had been postponed for reasons understandable to anyone who knew the meaning of neutrality. This was not the first time that they had met at a première. And once again, they were pleased to see each other, and talked about their impressions of the movie. Everybody liked it very much.

'They flew away to Lisbon. Afterwards, I'm sure they stayed at our hotel,' said the boy.

'If there were any vacancies,' said Black.

'And if they could pay,' Cardoso agreed.

# CHESS PLAYERS

An elderly man walked into the green sitting room on the ground floor of the Palácio hotel. It was only up close that you could see, mostly from his eyes, that he was not as old as he seemed at first glance. He was in his late fifties or early sixties, but overweight, sallow of face and sluggish. You could tell from the way he walked and breathed that his body was worn down and that he had serious health issues. The enlarged capillaries on his nose indicated that he was probably inclined to drink; his thin grey hair, parted on the side, revealed his scalp; the skin on his head and his bloated, sickly face were marked with red, scaly patches of psoriasis; he had not shaved that day but there was no stubble; the shoulders of his dark overcoat were sprinkled with dandruff, like snow. Just as he was about to sit down in the nearest armchair he noticed a boy playing chess by himself at a table by the window. He walked over and stood behind him, but the boy was concentrating on a chess combination and did not notice the man. The boy had wheat-coloured hair and side-locks which immediately reminded the old man of the hat he had had as a child, made of fox fur and with ear flaps.

'*Bonjour,*' the man said, speaking with a soft Russian accent.

The boy jumped, as if startled awake from a dream.

'May I help you?' The corpulent gentleman reminded him of a prince from an opera. He smiled. He was still a polite child.

The man introduced himself: 'I am Alexander Alexandrovich.' The boy thought that the old man even sounded like a prince but all he said was:

'I am Gavriel Franklin. Gaby.'

'I see that you're playing chess by yourself, and I wanted to offer myself as a partner, if you need one. I haven't played in a while. I miss playing.'

'I always need a partner.'

The boy was pleased. Chess is always much better when it is played against a real rather than an imaginary opponent. True, the old man reeked of alcohol and did not look like a worthy opponent, but Gaby, chronically short of a chess partner, would accept anyone who offered to play. Usually it would be just one game, because Gaby would win in just a few moves, so it was pointless to ask for a rematch.

The man removed his overcoat and laid it down and the boy got up to help him take his seat on the opposite side of the table. They placed the pieces on the board.

'How long have you been playing?' the man asked.

'Since I was little. I played with my father, and here I play almost every day.'

'You have somebody to play against?'

'When I don't, I play against myself,' the boy said.

'I started playing at a young age too. My mother taught me and afterwards I played a lot, really a lot, but less and less these last few years, and in the past six months not once.'

The boy was all smiles, and the old man liked that.

'Since you're a guest here, I'll let you make the first move,' said Gaby, turning the board around so that the old man had the white pieces.

'Thank you so much. You're a very nice boy,' Alexander Alexandrovich said, appreciating the child's generosity.

There's no talking when you are playing chess. But the boy quickly realized that he had to take the old man seriously. Yes, he was a bit slow, but he played well, and Gaby had his work cut out to achieve a draw. The old man liked the way Gaby played, too.

'You have a good mind,' said the old man. 'Shall we play another game again tomorrow?'

'With the greatest of pleasure,' said the boy.

'I'm glad. Now I'm going to stretch my legs a bit; I've been sitting for too long.'

'And I have to walk the dog. Do you want to come with us to the park?'

'An excellent idea,' said the old man, finishing off his glass of cognac. 'My doctor says I should walk. But we'll have to take it slowly if we go together.'

They walked slowly, talking about chess, but also about other, mostly trivial things. The boy talked about his dog, and the man talked about his recently deceased cat. Both deliberately avoided mentioning an important detail that could have embarrassed the other. The boy did not tell the old man that he was the chess champion of the hotel. The old man did not tell the boy that he was the chess champion of the world.

# MANUFACTURE NATIONALE
# DE SÈVRES

Bowed over the black pieces on the board was a bald head; the older man was sitting quietly, moving slowly, observing the world through swollen eyelids. Hovering over the white pieces was the restless tousled head of the boy. Following the game from a discreet distance was a younger man with watery blue eyes and long, almost white eyelashes.

It was the boy's turn. He moved the white knight from B4 to C6. Nothing else in the room changed: three pairs of eyes continued to watch the new arrangement of the pieces. After a while, the older player said what they all saw:

'I think you've achieved another draw,' he said to his opponent, reaching out to shake hands.

The boy was Gaby, though it might be better to call him a young man now. When you are fifteen, every new hair on your chin and pimple on your face makes you that much less of a child. He had been to the barber two or three times already to shave the hair off his upper lip. He had grown. He was already taller than most adult men, and judging by his long legs he still had more to grow.

On the other hand, he looked less extraordinary than he had when he was a child. When he first came, he had been very striking indeed. In the meantime, his hair had lost some of the golden glow of his childhood and his clothes were different. When he outgrew his suit or scraped his knee or elbow, he needed a new outfit, which meant that in the last year or two he had had a new suit made for him every few months. Yes, the tailors were told that the new suit had to be *de la même façon* as the old one, and yes, they did their best to ensure that it was so, but tailors are artists and each one of them, sometimes without even knowing it, left their mark. The result was that each new suit looked less and less like the long lost original, and the boy came to look more and more like a person of the times. The only unusual thing about it was that, young though he might be, he always wore black, as if in mourning.

Even the wide-brimmed hat that differentiated him from everybody else no longer looked like the one he had worn when he first arrived. He had changed more hats than suits, always ordering another one in black. Once he lost his hat somewhere, another time the wind swept it off into the sea, and twice Fennec chewed it up. So, the hatters often had nothing to copy a new one from. In such situations, Gaby and Bruno would choose the block that most resembled the original. As a result, the black Hassidic hat suffered even more drastic changes than his suit; it no longer stuck out as it used to, and he had become so relaxed that he often even forgot to take it with him, especially if he was not going into town. Now only the side-locks attracted attention, and the hotel barber, the slicked-down Senhor-Silvio, tried to make sure they were not too noticeable.

Before the grandmaster's arrival, Gaby had been the hotel's reigning champion. That was not mentioned anymore; there was no point now that the world champion was present. The two of them played chess every day. The world champion swore that Gaby was a promising chess player and was improving by the day.

The inebriated grandmaster seldom stood up, and when he did it was with difficulty. Ensconced in his armchair, he straightened the blanket over his legs to keep them warm.

'Is it tomorrow that you don't have school?' he asked the boy.

'No. Tomorrow is Sunday.'

'What do you say to the two of us meeting up straight after breakfast and me showing you who's really the champion…? Eh? Instead of you constantly taking advantage of me being tipsy,' laughed the grandmaster, as if pleased that the boy was doing so well. Then he turned to the man watching them. 'Isn't that so, doctor?'

The pale man laughed.

'Do you really want me to come tomorrow morning?' the boy asked. He was fearless on the chess board.

'Come, of course come. It's agreed. Around eleven.'

The boy left, but ready to return the next day.

'Doctor, would you be so kind as to top up my drink,' the grandmaster politely asked the pale man once they were alone.

'Is that really necessary?' the man asked.

'It's best with cognac, please,' the grandmaster observed.

*

The watery-eyed doctor was Vladimir Kirilovich Potapov. The story of how he wound up here is a complicated one. He was born in Moscow of princely lineage but remembered little of Russia – he had left as a small boy. He spoke Russian fluently, with a barely noticeable French intonation. He had spent the war in Switzerland and had come to Portugal four months earlier, intending to move to Argentina and open his own surgery there. He was waiting for an immigration visa, which could take a while. He had come with his French wife and baby daughter, who had the same clear face as her father. They were planning to sail to Buenos Aires as soon as they could.

He had taken a room at the Palácio shortly after Mr Alexander Alexandrovich Alekhine; it happened to be right across from the grandmaster's but it was in the hotel restaurant that they had actually met. The old man usually ate in his room but this particular evening he was sitting alone in the restaurant. The doctor had recognized him and walked over to his table.

By addressing him in Russian, he had managed to arouse the old man's interest. There's nobody you can have a better time with than somebody who speaks your own language. Moreover, Dr Potapov was a chess fan, and the two men, both with nothing to do, spent every day together.

'The boy is special. Different,' said the doctor.

'My dear doctor, nothing is strange to me anymore. I've

met a king with republican views, a rich man who is a communist, a priest who is godless, a Jew who is anti-Semitic. I met
a tsar who was assassinated… You see that vase over there,
Vladimir Kirilovich?' The grandmaster pointed to the big vase,
eared like a jug, its pale green porcelain decorated with gilded
ornamentation.

The doctor looked at the vase standing in a corner of the
bar, partly concealed behind bottles of alcohol.

'That vase is all I have from Russia. I didn't inherit it, I earned
it. That's probably why I love it so much,' said the chess player.
He was mumbling a little, as if his tongue got in the way; it was
getting harder to understand what he was saying. 'Take a closer
look. See the coat of arms? What do you say?'

'It's the imperial coat of arms. You're not telling me that it's
an urn containing the tsar's ashes, are you?' Potapov laughed.

The idea of keeping the imperial ashes in his room amused
Alekhine too.

'It's not an urn. It's more of a vase. It has the coat of arms
because Tsar Nikolai gave it to me – personally in 1909 when I
won the all-Russian amateur tournament in St Petersburg. Not
much older than Gaby. Look at the beautiful, fine workmanship. *Manufacture nationale de Sèvres*. The finest porcelain the
West is capable of making.'

Sitting in his armchair, a glass of cognac in his hand, the
grandmaster became lost in thought. He took a sip to wet his
lips and then started to talk:

'You know, my friend, in '21, I worked as an interpreter for
the Comintern. It was considered to be a decent job at the
time in Moscow, which meant that I didn't go hungry and

didn't have to toil in a factory. I met a Swiss journalist there. I was twenty-eight and she was forty. We got married. She was a communist, a delegate attached to the Comintern, and the Bolsheviks let me leave Russia with her, though it was supposed to be just temporary. All I wanted was to get away from that God-forsaken country, our fatherland. I knew from the start that I did not want to return, at least not while they were in power. But I didn't want to attract attention. So, I packed two suitcases, as if for a long trip. The night before I left, I decided to take this vase along as well… They probably realized that I wouldn't be coming back, but they accepted my story that I was taking it as a present for my in-laws.'

The grandmaster stopped there. At such times, and they were not infrequent, when the old sot became lost in thought, his listener would have to prod him if he wanted to know the end of the story. The doctor was curious.

'And? What happened then?' he asked.

'The two of us left for Paris. In Russia, where it was bedlam, she was the only thing that looked sane, normal; I felt that she was the only person I could share my life with… But as soon as we came to the West I started noticing her faults, and we began quarrelling… The difference in age, in mentality, in everything, was simply too great. We split up that same summer… And so, the marriage, my second marriage, was over but the vase remained. I took it with me wherever I moved. When war broke out in France, I went to the front and left it behind in our country summer house, which the Germans then confiscated. Before Grace, my current so-called wife, fled the countryside for Paris she hid the vase on the property. Throughout the war, until last winter, we didn't know what had happened to my porcelain trophy. I had already reconciled myself to the fact that it had disappeared or been destroyed. As soon as we managed to get back into the house I started looking for it. The box was badly damaged, but the porcelain had miraculously survived in one piece. Grace stayed on to sell the house and I brought the vase here with me... And now?'

The old chess player sat gazing at the ornate object for a long time until he came to a decision.

'I'll give it to whoever takes my title from me... Who else?'

# OH! LIFE IS SO HARD!

The patient sat quietly while the doctor took his pulse, using his wristwatch. Then he listened to the man's chest with his cold stethoscope.

'Cough… Once more… Good. Now lie down here so that I can check your abdomen,' said the doctor.

The old man stretched out on the bed and unbuttoned his shirt, letting the doctor use both hands to feel his flabby stomach.

Dr Potapov laid his stethoscope on his lap and said:

'You seem to have just a cold, and there's no real cure for that. But that's not the worst thing. Your liver is considerably enlarged. You must stop drinking, you really must,' he said, as if pleading for a personal favour.

'I know that,' Alekhine said calmly. 'I've been told by doctors that I haven't got a liver, I've got a pâté.' But that failed to elicit a smile from the doctor. 'Moreover, your colleagues have already diagnosed cirrhosis and duodenitis and arteriosclerosis, whatever all that means.'

'That means that you are destroying yourself with every glass you take and if you don't give up your deadly habits you won't be long for this world. Believe my every word, grand-master. Your situation is alarming.'

'And if I stop drinking, how much more time will I have, doctor?'

'If you give up alcohol and live an orderly life, you could have a few more years.' Dr Potapov was an intelligent man and a dedicated medic, but he was not a prophet. He could not be more precise than that. 'The liver is a strange organ. There's always the chance that it may recover.'

Alekhine gave Potapov a pained look.

'A few more years, you say...? Well, then, dear doctor, there's really no point in me making the effort. I'd rather die of a litre than of a stroke,' said the man, gasping for breath. 'All the same, could you please give me something now so that I feel at least a little better? I just don't want to feel sick right now. When the fatal hour strikes, then I'll die.'

'You can't give up just like that, maestro,' Potapov protested. 'Let me take your temperature.'

'What do you mean "give up", doctor? I've spent my life fighting like a lion! I spent my best years between two wars, each of which destroyed my life, with one difference: I was twenty-six at the end of the First World War and had the strength and willpower that I lack now at the age of fifty-three,' Alekhine lamented, holding the thermometer under his arm. 'Frankly, I'd rather be killed by a glass of cognac than the bullet of a paid assassin, which looks as if it will be my lot.'

'Good gracious, maestro, where did you get such an idea from?' said the astonished doctor.

'Maybe it won't be a paid assassin. Maybe somebody will do it for free.'

'And who would that be, if it's not a secret?'

'The death squad,' said the chess player. 'The French resistance movement has hit lists. That's why I don't dare go back to France.'

'You think your name is on that list?'

'I don't think, doctor, I know. I still have friends and fans who tell me if my life is in danger,' said the champion in a dispirited voice.

The long strands of hair that he combed across his pate stuck to his sweaty skull. His breathing was laboured; the short hairs peering out of his nostrils trembled.

'And what do they blame you for?'

'You'd do better to ask what don't they blame me for. It was an ugly war, there was nothing noble about it; no hero on either side worthy of an epic poem. It was a war of the wretched not the heroic. And I'm only one of the many wretched people who did what they had to because they feared for their very lives. Unfortunately, I am visible from far away.'

'What could you have done that was so terrible that they are threatening to kill you?' The doctor found it hard to believe.

'What could I have done? I played chess. That's my job. And under the occupation everybody did their job. Isn't that so? Doctors were doctors under Hitler. You had to work to survive. Why would I be any different?'

'You're right, but, forgive me if I sound insensitive, don't you think you're exaggerating a little?' said the doctor. 'If that's the case, then you're not alone. Your colleagues played chess during the war as well. Then they should execute Keres and Bogolyubov and Stoltz as well.'

'They may be targeted too,' Alekhine agreed.

'Do you know if they've already killed anybody on those hit lists?' asked the doctor, checking the thermometer.

'I haven't heard anything yet. But when they start, they'll start with me. I'm always the first. Alexander Alexandrovich! A.A.!' he said, buttoning up his shirt.

'You've got a temperature. Thirty-eight degrees centigrade. I have to bring it down a little. Do you prefer it orally or with an injection?'

'However you like, it's all the same to me. I just want this temperature to go away so that I can get back to my nice cirrhosis, duodenitis and arteriosclerosis,' grumbled the chess player.

'All right then, just wait a minute. The injection will hurt a bit but it works quickly – I'll go and prepare it.' The doctor washed his hands and then took the instruments out of his bag, one by one. The glum chess player said pensively:

'You know, doctor, what Chekhov said: *And a thousand years from now man will still be sighing, "Oh! Life is so hard!" and will still, like now, be afraid of death and not want to die.'*

'So, the French planned to get rid of you?' said the doctor, trying to pick up where they had left off.

'The God's truth. And not just the French, my dear doctor. I'm even more afraid of our own people.'

'Our own people?' The doctor did not immediately understand what Alekhine meant.

'The Russians. The Bolsheviks. They are even more dangerous.'

'And how did you offend them?'

'How did I offend them, Vladimir Kirilovich? Don't you see what that country has become? Stalin won the war and now is flexing his muscles. Now he wants the Soviet Union to be first in everything. And to spoil it all, instead of having one of their Bolsheviks as chess champion, they have me, a reactionary and collaborator. They're so disgusted with me that they won't play with me. You understand? And it wasn't me who wrote those articles.' The old man was getting delirious. 'They say I'm an anti-Semite. That's why they want to get rid of me. When I die, they will organize a championship and most probably a Soviet will win.'

'What you say is interesting, but to me it sounds exaggerated. Now let me give you that injection, then you can go back to talking,' said the doctor, checking that there was no air in the needle. 'Please stand up for a moment, that's right… turn around… drop your trousers a little, that's right, a bit more… and… done! Did it hurt?'

'No, I didn't feel a thing. Thank you, doctor,' said the champion, glumly pulling up his trousers. Now he could return to his favourite place – the depths of the armchair.

'So… you say that Stalin himself wants your head,' said Potapov while Alekhine was tucking in his shirt. 'Where did you hear that? Who told you, if it's not a secret?'

'Nobody has to tell me. What more logical and likely answer could there be to my tortured life? Except for a brief break, I've been chess champion since 1927. Botvinnik challenged me recently. We're soon supposed to hear when the match will be. They're afraid I'm the better player. And very possibly I am.

Just imagine how they would see it if I defended my title – they'd see it as their own defeat. You think Stalin would let something like that happen? Go on, tell me. I am a class traitor, a defector, and he is the Soviet champion. You think they don't want me dead? Do you?'

'I don't know what to think. In any event, it's good that you're here and safe,' said the doctor.

'Didn't they assassinate Trotsky in Mexico?' the grandmaster countered.

'Mexico is different. This is a serious country,' the doctor said reassuringly.

# I'M LUCKY TO HAVE YOU CLOSE
# AT HAND, MY FRIEND

The doctor went up to the grandmaster's room for the scheduled match only to find Alekhine sitting in his armchair again, wrapped up in his Crombie coat, shivering as if he were cold.

'I'm lucky to have you close at hand, my friend Vladimir Kirilovich,' said the grandmaster, as if expecting him to perform some miracle.

There was no need to say anything to the doctor. The glazed eyes, parched lips and dark circles under his eyes were obvious signs that his patient was not well.

Alexander Alexandrovich smelled of alcohol and the unwashed, and though he was well and properly drunk and afraid of being sick, he became as obedient as a little boy. He did whatever the doctor said, and he did it without question, which, knowing him, the doctor did not expect. A large tray covered with a silver dome stood on the table in front of him.

'Would you like to eat first?'

'I don't feel like eating. You just get rid of this temperature, my good man, and there'll be no problem in me eating my dinner.'

The doctor washed his hands and took the ampoule and syringe out of his bag.

'You don't have to get up and pull down your trousers this time. I'll give you the injection in the vein,' said the doctor, helping the old man roll up his coat and shirt sleeves rather than making him strip.

'How are you feeling?' he asked after the injection.

'Better… Maybe a little better… I just feel a bit dizzy,' Alekhine replied in the slow voice of the inebriated.

'Take it easy, maestro…' said the doctor soothingly.

But Alekhine did not hear him. His head had dropped onto his chest.

The doctor stepped out onto the balcony for a cigarette.

Darkness had only just fallen and a wind was blowing in from the sea. You could hear the waves and the roar of the cars on the Marginal road down along the coast. A train pulled in from the direction of Cascais. You could hear the screech of the brakes as the clatter came to a halt. The doctor did not wait for the sound of the locomotive's departing whistle. Stubbing out his cigarette he stepped back into the room, walked over to the old man, felt his pulse and established that he was dead. He rolled down the old man's sleeve, propped him up into a comfortable sitting position, removed the dome from his dinner tray and cut a large piece of meat. Then he opened the still warm maestro's mouth and carefully pushed the piece of cold roast beef far down into his gullet, quickly closing his jaw to stop it from going rigid while still open. He placed the knife next to the plate on the table and put the fork on the floor where it would have fallen if the old man had suddenly died eating.

'Вечная памятъ, Гроссмейстер,' said Dr Vladimir Kirilovich Potapov, bidding farewell to the late world chess champion as if talking to a living being. He had become fond of the weak-willed, capricious old man.

The green Sèvres trophy cup was poking out of the doctor's bag. He had taken it with him so that, in keeping with the deceased's wishes, he could pass it on to the next champion.

# POST-MORTEM

Chief Inspector Cardoso was dictating his report to Miss Tonita, who was taking down his every word in shorthand.

'At 11 a.m. on 24 March 1946, in room number 46 of the Palácio Hotel in Estoril ...'

In short, using bureaucratic language he related how the lifeless body of Mr Alekhine had been found in his room at the Hotel Palácio that morning. The body was discovered by the hotel bellboy who was bringing his breakfast and by Dr Potapov, the deceased's friend and doctor, who arrived at the same time to look in on his patient. The doctor established his death and immediately notified the hotel management which, for its part, instantly sought assistance from the police. He roughly described the situation he found upon entering the stuffy room, which was overflowing with empty and half-empty bottles of cognac and whisky. He did not forget to mention that there was no sign of either violence or a break-in, that nothing had been established as missing and that the guest had not locked the door to his room that evening. He signed the report. The witnesses gave and signed their statements, they being the distressed doctor, the frightened bellboy and the cool-headed hotel manager.

After finishing the report, Cardoso, along with the others, looked pityingly at the overweight old man, slouched in the armchair in his heavy coat. With their silence, they seemed to be paying homage to the deceased. The late world chess champion looked like one of those inflatable dolls, but only half-inflated: his chin had dropped onto his chest, as if he were dozing, his bloated face had collapsed, his right hand was resting on his lap and his left was hanging on the side, over the fork that had fallen onto the carpet.

A few months earlier, when he had been alerted that Mr Alekhine was back, Chief Inspector Cardoso was delighted. He knew the grandmaster from his previous visits to Estoril and was looking forward to talking to him again. He was told that the old man seldom left his room and hardly ever received visitors, except for Gaby and his countryman the doctor. He heard that the grandmaster was in poor health and, not wishing to witness his deterioration, had decided not to look him up. All the same, he had been called urgently to the Palácio on this Saturday morning to investigate the scene.

'Like an oak tree felled,' said the policeman poetically. 'He was a big man, was Mr Alekhine.'

'He looks as if he's asleep,' Miss Tonita ventured to say. She was sensitive, but took it stoically and did not cry.

'May God forgive you,' said Dr Potapov.

'May God forgive you,' Black repeated, thus forever forgiving the deceased's unpaid bill of seven thousand escudos.

'What might have been the cause of death, doctor?' the inspector inquired.

'As a doctor I can tell you that he called me last night to

come urgently and take a look at him. I examined him in his room before dinner. He complained of flu-like symptoms. He had a temperature, a racing pulse and complained of a headache and aching muscles and joints. I gave him his regular injection of insulin and a Bayer aspirin. Although he was feverish he refused to go to bed, so I left and let him eat his dinner. You know how odd he was; he liked to eat alone. I noticed nothing to indicate oncoming death. At first glance, I'd say he choked on his food, but my pathologist colleagues are better placed to say what it was,' replied the Russian, clearly upset by his friend's death.

'The body will be moved today to the Forensic Laboratory in Lisbon. We still have to photograph the body for the police report, before removing him from the scene,' said the policeman.

The man holding the camera, who had been inconspicuously standing in the corner so as not to get in the way of the investigation, took the inspector's words to mean it was time for him to get down to work. With his back to the window he tried to get as good a light as possible to photograph the deceased.

'Hold it! Wait a minute,' the policeman suddenly said, raising his hand as if he had just remembered something. He took the chessboard from the dresser, laid out all the pieces and placed it on the table in front of the late grandmaster.

'There. Isn't that nicer? This way you immediately see that the man was a great chess player. Miss Tonita, you're better at placing the chess pieces on the board, would you mind...? That's it. Good... That looks much more dignified, don't you think?' The inspector was obviously very pleased with the result of his artistic touch.

It took the photographer some time to find the best angle for the picture of the dead champion and his chessboard. He repositioned the board to make the scene look grander and more impressive. He had to draw the curtains just enough to soften the light's reflection on the deceased's skull. The chiaroscuro effect gave the picture depth.

The investigation did not take long. No one likes to spend time in a room with a dead body, especially when it is close to lunchtime. And so the doctor, the policeman and the hotel manager went downstairs to the manager's office to complete all the necessary paperwork and sort out their impressions. They toasted the deceased with a glass of whisky.

'So, you think it was a natural death, death by choking.'

'As I said, at first glance that's what I would say, but…' Here the doctor stopped, as if unsure whether he should say what was on his mind or hold his tongue forever.

'Yes?' Cardoso helpfully prompted him.

'We talked a lot recently. And these last few days he often said he was afraid,' said the doctor.

'Afraid of what?' asked the policeman.

'Afraid that they want to kill him. I mean that they wanted to kill him.'

'Who wanted to kill him?' asked the policeman.

'The French resistance... They thought he was a traitor. And the Russians.'

'What Russians? You may be the only Russian around here right now!' the perplexed policeman said.

'I'm sorry, I didn't express myself properly; not the Russians, the Bolsheviks; the Soviets,' the doctor said.

'And what did he do now to offend them?' the policeman asked in utter astonishment.

'He was afraid they wanted to liquidate him so that one of the Soviets' stars could take the chess title without having to play for it. He thought they were afraid of challenging him for the title.'

'And where did he think they would kill him? Here?'

'Well, they assassinated Trotsky in Mexico,' the doctor said.

'If he was so afraid for his life, doctor, why didn't he lock the door to his room?' said the policeman, pointing to the fallacy of this logic.

'He probably would have locked it before going to bed, everybody does that, but in the meantime he choked... Or else they really did kill him.'

Black and Cardoso looked at one another, and then the Portuguese said to the Russian:

'I don't wish to offend you, doctor, but I've been a policeman for some thirty-odd years, I've seen all sorts of things and I know that anything is possible, but I also know what is not possible. And it is not possible that there are Bolshevik agents in my district and that I don't know about it. You don't know me and you don't know my work. Trust me, if there were even just a single Bolshevik around, I would know about it.'

Black nodded his agreement with this pronouncement. The policeman went on:

'I know it's hard for you, you've lost a fellow countryman and a friend, but it would be wiser to try to forget about all this; relax and enjoy your time here. This place is heaven on earth. Remember that.'

'I still think,' the doctor countered, 'you can tell when somebody has choked on his food, the person struggles, turns blue in the face… But the grandmaster…'

'Please, doctor… don't play the detective… How would it look if I tried to teach you how to treat the flu?' The policeman politely walked him to the door. 'Don't create problems where there are none. If you want to help, think about what we should do with the man's body. He's got nobody. It looks as if the funeral will have to be paid out of state funds.'

In the end, the state did not have to loosen its purse strings. A rich Portuguese chess fan donated the gravesite and paid for the funeral.

# QUINTA DOS GRILOS

The dogs' barking announced that they were coming even before they arrived. Looking out of the sitting room window Madame Radmila saw the car approaching. Perfectly coifed and nicely dressed, she could not stop herself from going out in front of the house, the way village women run out into the courtyard to happily await their guests. She hugged her children, pressed her hands against their cheeks, clasped them to her breast, kissed them on the face and head. 'Mama's little doves,' 'sunshine,' 'darling,' 'my little lamb,' 'Mama's sweetheart,' 'my angel,' she murmured. Grada looked different somehow, as if he had grown up, become a man, but Lila was as beautiful as before, slimmer than ever. Later, when they were all seated at the lunch table, their mother said:

'So, children, tell me. Tell me everything. Do you have any pictures I can see?'

Grada was the first to take a photo album out of his bag. Most of the pictures showed him in uniform, posing next to an aeroplane, first by himself, then lined up with his colleagues from the aviation unit. In the other pictures, he looked more relaxed: in one, he was sitting on the wing of a plane, clowning around while his fellow airmen stood on the runway laughing; in another, he winked at the photographer as he climbed into the cockpit.

But his mother's favourite was the one taken at the photographer's studio, with his hair slicked back, his pilot's beret at an angle, gazing into the distance. She immediately forgot all about the months, when he flew, she had spent afraid for his life, terrified if a letter arrived or the phone rang, her nights full of nightmares.

'Mama's big boy! Mama's brave young man!' she murmured, tears in her eyes as she looked at her son and then at the picture.

'It's not good for a man to be so handsome. He'll turn out to be a sissy,' said his sister Gordana.

Both his mother and his older sister kept kissing him, though. Three years is a long time not to have seen someone, and if it's a brother or son, it's far too long.

Gradimir explained that there had really been no reason for them to worry about him. He hadn't been fighting for long. First it took him some time to convince the English that he really did want to fight on their side; then he spent a few months in training, flying with Polish instructors on short flights over England, nothing too ambitious, they had to save on fuel. Immediately after the Allied landing in Normandy he started flying over the Channel and Continent. He told them how several times he had flown into liberated France and Holland, and at the end of the war, he flew over the territory of the Reich at daybreak and on one occasion found himself in danger and had to shake some German hunter-planes off his tail. He thrilled in telling them that not a stone was left standing in Germany. His mother stopped him there. She did not want to talk about unpleasant things.

But some subjects could not be avoided. Such as their own story and the miserable fate that Yugoslavia had experienced. Not much was reported in Lisbon about what was happening there, partly because it was far away and partly because of the censorship. Generally speaking, they knew that the Bolsheviks had taken over power there and that things looked bleak. People in London knew more; the king was there and the Yugoslav government-in-exile, which had spent the whole war in London and until recently had been working there, had lots of contact with people in the field. They said that things were pretty awful in Belgrade. It wasn't as badly destroyed as London, and not anywhere near as badly as Berlin and Dresden, but in the summer and autumn of 1944 the Allies had repeatedly bombed Yugoslavia, especially Belgrade. The British claimed that both the communists in the area and the government-in-exile had asked for air raids on strategic German targets in the Balkans in order to assist the local guerrillas. What they got was the carpet-bombing of Belgrade. It destroyed a wing of the maternity hospital, killing all the mothers, but the babies, who were in the other wing, survived to become orphans. The civilian toll was far higher than the military's. According to Radio Berlin, there were four thousand casualties; according to Allied sources two thousand. Whatever the number, there were too many.

When the Germans pulled out of the city in October '44, the Russians came in, and with them came the partisans. The

Russians looted and raped but they did not stay long, thank God; they continued northwards, towards Budapest and Berlin. They left power in the hands of the local communists. At first the communists established a reign of terror; then they called a plebiscite in which the vast majority of the people opted for the new government – over ninety per cent. In other words, the communists' strength and reign of terror was such that even if somebody was against them they kept as quiet as a mouse.

'Because we fled during the occupation, we have been declared traitors and the state has confiscated all our property.'

Nobody responded.

'They've taken everything away from us,' Grada repeated.

'Everything?' his mother asked.

'Everything! We've got nothing left in Yugoslavia. They've even taken away our civil rights. And the house in Knez Miloš Street. The last thing they take from you is the family home. Then all you've got left is your life.'

'Maybe with time it'll all settle down,' Madame Radmila said, thinking aloud.

'Maybe. But it won't be soon, believe me, Mama... They executed so many decent people just because they were rich. The people are afraid of them, and everything that's done is done in the name of the people.'

'In other words, we can't go back?' Gordana said.

'No, there's no going back. The only house we have for the time being is this one.'

Everyone fell silent and stared at the floor, as if they were paying tribute to the deceased with a minute of silence.

No matter how rich you are, you cannot be indifferent when you hear someone say: 'there's no going back'. Still, Lila and Grada did not take it that badly. They had gone out into the world when they were young and had quickly learned that they came from nowhere and everywhere. For them, Belgrade was merely the place where they were born and they seemed to have made their peace with the fact that they would spend the rest of their life in London or a third place. Gordana was more tied to her native land. That was where she had gone to university, where she had worked in her father's bank, where her best friends still were. And she was of a different temperament.

'Let them take the house, we'll build another,' she said. And she would. On her own. She was already doing it. In defiance of everything.

Her mother simply sighed.

'I just don't want to be buried far away from your father… But, enough of all these dark thoughts. Lila, darling, tell me, what's it like at college? Have you made friends? People you can talk to? Do you fancy anybody? Have you got a beau?'

Lila had been unusually quiet that evening; she had cuddled up to her mother and listened to her brother as if everything he said was completely new to her. She took out her own photographs to show around:

Taking a walk by the Thames; at the races with a hat; sitting on a bench with two girlfriends.

'Mother's beautiful girl. How pretty you look…'

Her favourite photograph was of her daughter in a light summer dress, sitting in a flowering garden. She took the picture to get it framed, along with the portrait of her son gazing into the distance.

It was only when they pressed her that Lila told them how when they arrived in London they had found a house at a reasonable rent on the King's Road. She enrolled at the university the following autumn and was studying fashion; that meant she had no problem getting clothes. She talked about what they got on the black market, and how they made do. She told them that she had made girlfriends, both English and from other countries.

And then three familiar faces appeared on one of the photographs. Lila in a long evening gown, wearing a glittering diamond necklace; Grada in his formal air force uniform; and a gentleman in a tuxedo, with a medal pinned to his chest.

'You look so thin in that dress, as thin as a pencil,' said her mother. It was only then that she recognized the man in the tuxedo. 'Is this, the man with the slicked-back hair, Duško?'

'Yes, it is.'

Radmila was taken aback. They had not yet said a word about Duško. His name was taboo for several reasons; mostly because when they heard of his arrest, they worried that it might harm both Grada and Lila. Also, he owed them a lot of money; reason enough to try to forget a friend like that.

'But wasn't he arrested? We heard he was arrested… It was even said that he'd been hanged as a spy!'

'He's alive and kicking!'

'Wonderful!' Radmila said, so happy that she almost cried. 'I recognized him from his mole. He's put on some weight.'

'He's thirty-four years old too, Mama,' said Gordana.

'How time flies… How is he? I wanted to ask but then I told myself, better not…'

Grada turned to his younger sister:

'Shall we tell them now?' Since she said nothing to the contrary he told Gordana and his mother:

'Please keep what I'm about to tell you in the strictest confidence… It's still not sure, and it's not a good idea to talk about it. You've got to promise me that you won't tell anybody…'

His mother and sister looked at him perplexed, but nodded their agreement with his terms.

'This, then, is strictly *entre nous*, but just so you know,' and here he stopped to take a breath before saying quietly: 'Duško was an agent all through the war… A British agent.'

Gordana laughed out loud.

'Duško was what?'

'All that time that he was travelling all over the place during the war, he was working as an agent for the British.'

'Are you sure we're talking about the same Duško?! Popov?'

'The very same, Gordana.'

'So, he's still free?' Their mother wanted to get it straight.

'Of course he is. I'm telling you, he was never arrested. First he was with us in London, for almost a year. He really helped us out…'

'And then?'

'And then, some time before the end of 1944, he left one morning on a business trip and didn't come back. We knew he was doing something for the British government. I phoned his colleagues. They told me not to worry and not to inquire about him. We didn't see each other again until recently. We were guests of honour when he received the OBE.'

Grada turned over the picture on the last page of Lila's album and asked them to read what it said:

28 Nov. 1947. OBE award ceremony, Hotel Ritz, London.

'What's an OBE?' his mother asked.

'It stands for Order of the British Empire and it's a medal. See, there it is on his chest. Duško, you know, is now an Officer of the British Empire.'

'And who gave him that decoration?' asked Gordana.

'Who represents the Empire? The king.'

'Their king? The British king?' Gordana asked her brother.

'What kind of question is that? It's certainly not the Japanese who'll give him the Order of the British Empire.'

'But if it's the British king, does he work in London at the Ritz? Is he having Buckingham Palace painted?' Gordana asked.

'They wanted it done discreetly. It was Duško who suggested the Ritz.'

'OK. OK. But what exactly did he do for Britain? It must have been very dirty if they wanted it to be so discreet,' Gordana said to her brother.

'I don't know. It's secret, but it was certainly something important. Otherwise they wouldn't have given him a decoration.'

'He says a special hello to you, Mama. He wanted me to tell you that he hasn't forgotten that he owes you.'

'Let's not talk about it now, son; it's not the time,' his mother said.

'I'm just passing on what he said. He sent a few small presents for you and our Gaby. How is Gaby? Is he here?'

'Yes, he's here. He's always asking after you. You'll see him tomorrow. He's coming to lunch.'

'Ah yes,' Gradimir said, 'speaking of greetings, while we were in touch with the court and the government-in-exile everybody kept asking about you and sending their best. Especially the Prime Minister. But we don't see them anymore. We haven't seen the king since his wedding...'

Lila remembered something.

'You know who I ran into the other day? I didn't tell even you, Grada. You remember that diplomat of ours, some poet... I can't recall his name. He and his wife were here at the start of the war. He has a slight drawl when he talks...'

'Crnjanski?' Gordana hazarded.

'Yes, Crnjanski.'

'He's not "some poet", Lila. He's probably our very best poet and you can't even remember his name.'

'Whatever. Don't nit-pick. Now let me tell you about it. I know London's a big city but I ran into his wife recently.'

'With everything that's been happening I forgot that those wonderful people even existed,' said her mother, pleased to hear that Crnjanski and his wife were alive and well. 'How are they?'

'Ever since Mr Crnjanski lost his job at the Yugoslav embassy, it hasn't been easy for them, it seems. He's afraid to return to the country; he's sure they'll put him in prison because he spoke and wrote against the communists even before the war. His wife is brave and bearing up; she's working. He's decided that the solution to his problems is to enrol at the university. He'll be a student at the age of fifty something.'

They all laughed, except for Radmila. She did not find it funny.

'Women are often braver than men,' she said. 'You've certainly heard, haven't you, children, that Mr Dučić died in America a few years ago? May God rest his soul.'

'Yes, we heard…'

Their mother, as is the custom when talking about the dead, crossed herself, sighed and then said: 'I was so excited about you coming that I woke up very early this morning and now I'm about to collapse. My head is drooping. Come and walk me to my room, Lila, child, and talk to me until I fall asleep. Then you can go back to your brother and sister. And tomorrow, God willing, we'll talk some more. Come, my darling.'

Walking across the sitting room, they stopped at the fireplace where there was an array of postcards on the mantelpiece. They were from all over the world: the Azores, the Bahamas, Cuba, New York, London, Madrid, Casablanca, Tangiers, Gibraltar, London again, Hawaii and Los Angeles. They were all addressed to the same place: *La Famille Bajloni, Quinta dos Grilos, Carnaxide, Lisbonne, Portugal*. And the message was always the same: *Love, Your D.*

'Had somebody told me…' Madame Radmila sighed, looking at the small collection, 'I would have said that he's the least discreet but, by God, the most charming young man I know.'

'Let's go to bed, Mama. We're both tired,' her daughter said. Those colourful postcards were tearing at her heart.

★ ★ ★

They were now alone in the library, each sitting in an armchair under the gold-framed portrait of the viscountess when she was young, the same woman from whom they had recently bought their property. Lately, brother and sister had been writing to each other about exporting the tins to England from Portugal.

'How are things going?' Gradimir asked his entrepreneurial sister.

'I can't complain! The farm and dairy factory are doing very well. The tins are not doing so well and are bringing in less money since the war ended. I've started making silk. I reached an agreement with the municipality where we prune their mulberry trees in the parks in return for which we can feed the worms with their leaves. Tomorrow I'll show you where we keep them… It's a lot of work.'

'Are you lonely?' her brother asked her.

'Yes, we're lonely,' she said after a pause. 'I manage but all this is much harder on Mama. Why don't you come back? You, at least; and Lila when she graduates? You'd be a welcome support for Mama. And I need your help too. It would mean a lot to us if you came back to work with me here.'

'I want to try my luck in London. And I don't want to leave Lila. She hasn't got anybody there. I'll try and help you as much as I can from there… If it doesn't work out… I can always come back.'

Silence.

'You didn't invest in shares?' he asked her.

'Just in some gold mines in South Africa, and even then

not much. I got the shares cheap. All the papers are in the safe; the combination is still the same...' She stopped, thought for a moment and then said to her brother: 'I need to sit down with you and brief you at least a little on the business. Mama knows some things but she has already started to forget. If anything should happen to me, God forbid, you need to know that the property was bought and entered in the Land Registry in Mama's name. The papers for whatever we have in the bank are in the safe. I sometimes deposit francs in Switzerland, but my turnover here is in escudos. I also bought a few paintings, small French Impressionist paintings that the Jews left behind when they fled. They're also in the safe.' She did not sound as if she had embarked on this conversation because of some presentiment about the future; it was just a natural desire to share these responsibilities with someone. 'And don't forget, I need to give you power-of-attorney for the bank accounts while you're here.'

This time it was Gordana who broke the ensuing silence.

'Now you tell me, is Lila very hurt?'

'She's better now. When I think of how she was...' her brother answered vaguely.

'When did they break up?'

'They didn't break up. At first he lived with us; then he started staying out, coming back now and then, almost as if he was duty-bound. She would sit at home waiting for him for days. And then he disappeared. And we didn't see him for over a year, until he reappeared last autumn. And when he did, he was hyperactive, euphoric, with an armful of presents. He strafed us with his story. "Hello. Here I am after all this time.

And this little girl is my wife. We got married last summer in the Alps. I'm sorry I couldn't be in touch; I'm a spy but please don't tell anybody. Will you be my guests at the presentation ceremony for the Order of the British Empire at the Ritz?"'

'And how did Lila react?'

'Very bravely. She had a smile on her face the whole time. But she retreated into herself and into the house and lost a lot of weight. She took some drops to sleep. She couldn't bear sober reality. She grieved for days but, like an actress, she put a smile on her face at the presentation ceremony. She was more than polite to that wife of his.'

'I knew that louse was going to break her heart!'

Silence.

'We all knew it… She knew it too… I'm telling you, she's over the worst of it.'

'It could have been worse, he could have persuaded you to sell the jewellery and taken your money.' That was what Gordana had secretly feared, and since her brother did not say anything, it stoked her suspicions.

'Did you sell something?'

'Nothing big,' Grada replied.

Silence.

'What's that wife of his like?'

'The French woman? She's a child, she's sixteen…'

'Sixteen?'

'Sixteen-and-a-half.'

Silence.

'Do you think Lila would stay here and live with us? She wouldn't have to work if she didn't want to.'

'I don't think so. She wants to study, and after the holidays her classes resume.'

'I still think it would be better for her to be with us. At least until the summer. She can lose a term; it's nothing terrible. She needs to gain her strength and the climate here is excellent. Look how beautiful it is,' she said, pointing at the window, which looked out onto the property's moonlit gardens sloping down to the ocean.

That year, Italy's ousted King Umberto came to their family Saint's Day celebration, attracting even more members of Portugal's upper crust than before. On the third day of St Ignatius, Grada and Lila flew back to England.

# ISAURA MARRIED!

There is no doubt about it. Food is the most rewarding of subjects for conversation. And the most democratic. Who likes to eat what and how they prefer it cooked; whether it's a veal cutlet or grilled fish, potatoes or roast peppers, you can discuss it for hours without anybody ever getting bored. Another, equally rewarding subject is football. Here again, everybody has the right to an opinion, be it the hotel manager, the doorman or Papagaio.

Today, for instance, Sporting defeated Académica 2–1, and Benfica beat Vitória 3–1. Before dinner, the men kidded around and teased each other about their respective teams, but as soon as the food was on the table, they agreed that the ball was round and tucked into their sardines and rye bread. They had to finish on time because they had work to do: as always, the hotel was full and the guests would be arriving shortly.

A quarter of an hour later and there was not a trace of the activity that had been going on in the little kitchen. Everybody had gone off to do his or her respective job. Lourdes was already soaking the dishes in the sink; she was just waiting for Gaby's plate, because he had not finished his food yet. Every so often she walked up to the table and found him staring into space, the food in his mouth uneaten.

'Eat, please. You're a growing boy and you have to eat. You've grown by half a head in just a year... And you're still growing... You'll get tuberculosis.'

Prodded, Gaby would chew the food in his mouth, but when Lourdes returned a minute later, she would find him playing with the rice on his plate with his fork.

'Come, boy... Look how Rodolfo licked his plate clean...'

Gaby was tired of her nagging and said:

'I can't eat any more.' And he got up from the table.

'Come on now, sweetie, taste that. It's a sin to leave it on the plate... There are children who have nothing to eat, don't be like that...'

But he did not listen to her. He went about his business and Lourdes cleared away what was left on his plate and returned to the sink, where she made her diagnosis:

'He's in love. For sure. That's what happens... When I think back... We women are even worse... We fall head over heels in love and lose the few brains we've got,' she said to Sara as the two of them plunged their hands into the soapy dishwater.

Just when you think that the story is coming to an end, that it's time to tie up all the loose ends, a new character appears in our novel when we least expect it. Sara. Who, now, is Sara? She is a young girl who came to replace Isaura. Isaura had handed in her notice two weeks previously because she was getting married and going to live with her husband. One had felt it coming for some time. Isaura had matured, she was already almost twenty-three. She had gained weight in the little kitchen. Grown bigger. It was time for her to get married. Last spring, she had started going out with a young man, the chauffeur of a gentleman who was a regular guest at the hotel. He had noticed her one winter evening when he had gone out to pee in the bushes and seen her at the back door of the little kitchen, taking out the rubbish. The following day, he appeared at the same place at the same time and again saw her carrying some boxes. He liked her even more this second time and so he said: 'Good evening, pretty face.' She was embarrassed and ran off. Undaunted, he continued to wait for her every evening. After a few such meetings they started talking, exchanging a few words until, bit by bit, the day came when he proposed to her. They married about ten days ago. Lourdes and two maids even went to her wedding in the village; they brought her a lovely present of embroidered bed linen. The poor girl wound up with a trousseau that was like a rich man's daughter's. Sara had come to replace her and now Lourdes talked to her all day, teaching and advising her, just as she had Isaura.

'Isaura married!' Lourdes sometimes burst out with the tail end of the thoughts in her head.

'She had a salary, a job,' said Lourdes, shelling the peas, 'but her husband says, you have to be a mother, a housewife, and she chucked it all. And she knows about Teresinha, the maid who worked here before, who got married, handed in her notice, had children and is now complaining that her husband cheats on her and beats her. Women are silly creatures… especially when they're young… When you're a girl, love is all you think about… As if you're blind and deaf to everything else. I should know… my own head was full of dreams and I fell in love with the first fool who smiled at me… But he turned out to be a good-for-nothing. He abandoned me when I was pregnant up to my eyeballs. And don't even get me started on what I went through. Who's going to hire you when you've got a kid and its birth certificate says "father unknown"? If it weren't for Mr Black, who knows how we would have survived? As for you,' she turned to Sara, 'of course you should get married, but keep your job, don't let your husband have a hold over you, don't be his slave… Never mind that he's a good man and that he loves you; it's better to be your own person.'

Sara was seventeen. She was pretty, she was good, and she was modest. As befitted her age, she had somebody she fancied and was lucky to have him always within sight. Papagaio. He was handsome and had grown into a man. Sara searched for him with her eyes. As if reading her mind, Lourdes started talking about her son.

'Don't think I'm not happy to have my Rodolfo. Goodness no, nobody is more important to me than him, but boy did I spill blood before I made a man out of him. I swear. He finished seventh grade. That's enough, he repeated only one year and he's been helping out here since he was a child. He's hard-working. He's about to turn twenty, he's never asked me for money, he can read, he can write, he can count, he's learned foreign languages…' Lourdes stopped, staring out into space, lost in thought. Then suddenly she resumed her monologue.

'And if only you knew how well he writes. His teacher swore by him. He said – not only does he have nice handwriting, he knows exactly where to place each and every word. If you dictate a letter to him, he will write it without a single mistake. He reads my sister's letters, and laughs. He says that the boy she pays to write them for her makes lots of mistakes, you can barely understand what he's written,' said Lourdes to Sara, who wondered where Papagaio had gone off to. Where had he disappeared to?

There they were, Gavriel Franklin, now seventeen and about to finish high school, and Rodolfo, who, at the age of twenty, was already ripe for marriage. The two of them were hiding under the staircase, sharing a cigarette, while Fennec sniffed around the trash can, looking for something to eat.

Gaby took from his pocket an envelope bearing the seal of the Red Cross and showed it to his friend.

'This arrived…'

'What is it?'

'A letter. I'm going back home.'

'Home where?'

'To Antwerp.'

'They found your parents?' Papagaio asked, regretting the words as soon as they were out of his mouth. If they had found his parents he wouldn't be looking so sad.

Gaby shook his head.

'The letter is from my uncle. I'm going to live with him.'

'But isn't this your home?'

'How can a hotel be a home?'

'It *is* my home. Are you going by yourself?'

'Me and Fennec. As soon as I finish the school year,' said Gaby, his cigarette glowing in the dark and the silence.

'What will you do in Antwerp? You don't remember it.'

Gaby did not answer.

'Do you really want to leave?' Papagaio asked.

'No,' Gaby confessed.

'So why are you going?'

'I'm going back to my people. That's where my place is ...'

'What? Aren't we your people?' Papagaio sounded rather sad and hurt.

'Don't make it even harder, please ...'

They sat there not speaking. It was dark all around them. The sound of the cars on the other side of the park, of the music in the sitting room, was far away. Even the noise from the kitchen, behind the closed doors where they were sitting, seemed far away. To the backdrop of all these muffled, mingling sounds, the two of them sat in silence.

'What's the hurry?' asked Papagaio.

'I've waited too long,' said Gaby. Wanting to change the subject to something less sad, he said: 'And I've also got some good news.'

'You'll come back and visit us?!' said Papagaio, more cheerfully.

'Probably. But that's not it. The news is that I've got something for you ... I want to give you a present.'

'Me? What is it?'

'Money. It's not just for you. I'll leave a little something to everybody. But the biggest amount is for you. It'll be enough for you to continue school if you want, and later, if you want to go to university; and if you don't want to, there'll be enough for you to open a restaurant where you can work.'

Papagaio embraced him and said a little bluntly:

'I'd like it better if you stayed… But I won't lie to you, I'm happy about the present. You have too much already, but nobody has ever given me money just like that. It's a really nice feeling to get money when you haven't done anything for it, isn't it? When are you going to give it to me?'

'That's a bit more complicated…' Gaby had expected the question and had prepared an answer. 'I won't give it straight to you, but it's *for* you… I don't want to put it in your hands, understand? I'll give it to Black and later he will give you some when you need it.'

'But why not straight to me? I'm not irresponsible. I've been working since the age of ten.' To Rodolfo it felt like blackmail.

'I know and forgive me for saying this but you've never had any money. And one doesn't immediately put money into the hands of somebody who has never had any. I'm afraid you'll fritter it away on stupidities… Black is trustworthy. And reasonable. I'm leaving with him the money for the others as well. I'll give him a list of who gets how much, and ask him to give them the money when they need it; it's not just for spending…'

'And what about him?' Rodolfo wanted to know.

'Who?'

'Black.'

'What about Black?'

'Are you going to leave him some money as well?'

'No. I've paid him fair and square for everything.'

'Give me another puff,' said Papagaio.

'No. You've got to get back to work,' said Gaby, stubbing out the butt.

# STOCKINGS FOR
# VARICOSE VEINS

A t the same spot where two strangers had met each other eight years previously, two friends were now saying goodbye.

Gaby was no longer a child; he had finished school now and had he not been with them from such a young age, they would have called him Senhor Gavriel. Black was the same as before, but older, more tired and yellower from all the cigarettes he smoked. He looked at his watch.

'You haven't got much time. Bruno is waiting for you downstairs with the car.'

Gaby shook his head. He did not look happy to be leaving.

'Have you packed everything?'

Gaby shrugged his shoulders.

'I don't like long goodbyes. Lots of people will probably miss you for a while. But then we'll get used to it. Write and tell us how you're doing… You know that your friends will always be here for you…' Black said. He gave him a quick hug and then stepped back and said:

'Off with you, young man. *Allez, allez! Vite!*'

When Gaby ran out and the door closed behind him, the manager poured himself a stiff glass of whisky and stood at the window. He saw the limousine waiting in front of the hotel and the young man saying goodbye to the staff. On a personal level, he felt sad. But that did not stop him from wondering, as the manager of the hotel, if anybody was left in the building or if they had all gone out to say goodbye to their favourite guest. For a second he thought that the maids might be right. He had heard that the staff thought Gaby brought the hotel good luck. Now he wondered what would happen with the boy gone...

Even if his sight had been better than it was, Black would not have been able to see what was visible from up close: how the maids cried, how warmly the doormen, receptionists and waiters embraced Gaby, how meaningfully and firmly the concierge shook his hand, how sad Papagaio was, and how Gaby grit his teeth to stop himself from crying, partly because he was sad to be leaving and partly because he was afraid of what awaited him. The only thing Black noticed was Lourdes wiping the tears from her face with her apron, but he could not hear what she was saying to the boy:

'You've got everything in here – sandwiches, meat, drumsticks, cured beef... and spring onions... and I boiled you some eggs. The beetroot is here, I know how much you like it... And the salt is here. These are almond cakes, they won't spoil, but these made with eggs will, so eat them tonight or tomorrow morning...'

After Gaby had hugged and kissed everyone goodbye, and Fennec had said her own goodbyes, they stepped into the car.

Papagaio ran after them all the way to the gate, as if wanting to stop them from going, but the car pulled away and turned onto the main road.

Walking back to the kitchen, Lourdes said to Sara:

'Look at him now. Tall, handsome… He was just a little boy when he came. Frightened. Alone, poor little thing, without anybody anywhere… A wonderful boy. Everybody loved him. And he came to love us. He didn't have anybody else. Rodolfo is like an older brother to him. I know he is, you can see he loves him. He gave him a football for Christmas. A real leather ball. And he gave me stockings for my varicose veins, so my legs won't hurt. They were expensive. He didn't have to. What am I to him that he should buy me expensive presents?'

Lisbon, November 2013 – Belgrade, June 2015

# NOTE

The hardest part of the job, the mining of information, was done by numerous historians and biographers whom I trusted and allowed to guide me as I wrote.

The exceptions were: the world chess champion, where the most complete data I found was on a Russian internet site about conspiracy theories; the ousted King of Romania and his mistress, whose life I could only follow in faded newspapers and gossip magazines; and the Hungarian-born, Hollywood proto-starlet, whose countless biographies offer everything but correct data.

I confirmed the events and settings in which they took place by reading the press of the day, daily weather reports, lists of hotel guests, calendars and ship and flight schedules.

I visited not only the Palácio Estoril Hotel and Grand Casino Estoril, but also all the other places where the events depicted took place. I also came into possession of certain items that belonged to some of the main characters of the story: Duško Popov's battered suitcase containing some of his private things, along with two underdeveloped and two unused films. The suitcase also contained medicines, parts of his radio equipment, poorly preserved instructions for radio hams in Spanish. I acquired the writing desk and lamp used by Captain Jarvis in the consular section of the British embassy in Lisbon, at 17 Rua da Emenda.

Still, what helped me most in writing this wartime novel was the art inspired by the period and the events depicted in the story.

# SELECTED BIBLIOGRAPHY

Antoine de Saint-Exupéry, *Lettre à un otage*
Antoine de Saint-Exupéry, *The Little Prince*
Miloš Crnjanski, *Embahade*
Miloš Crnjanski, *Lament nad Beogradom*
Ian Fleming, *Casino Royale*
Michael Curtiz, *Casablanca*

The careful reader of the story will find homages to writers I have translated, and above all to Saint-Exupéry.

# SOUNDTRACK

S. Rachmaninoff, *Piano Concerto No. 2, Adagio sostenuto*

F. Chopin, *Piano Sonata No. 2, Opus 35*, 'The Funeral March',
   I. Paderewski

F. Chopin, *Etudes Opus 10, No. 12 in C minor*, 'Revolutionary',
   I. Paderewski

Vittorio Monti, *Csárdás*

Folk tune, *Pašona kolo*

F. Chopin, *Etudes Opus 10, No. 3 in E major*, 'Tristesse'

F. Schubert, *Ave Maria*

Hans Leip/Nortbert Schultze, 'Lili Marleen'

F.J. Ricketts, 'Hitler has only got one ball,' to the music of
   'Colonel Bogey March'

Herman Hapfield, 'As Time Goes By'

Pixinguinha, 'Rosa', Marisa Monte

*'Pe drumul banatului'* (Romanian traditional), Maria Lataretu